D1179298

KEEP THE HOME FIRES BURNING

KEEP THE HOME FIRES BURNING

Anne Baker

KEEP THE HOME FIRES BURNING

Chapter One

Cathy Gottfried was brimming over with love; she'd never felt so happy and secure before in her whole life. Rolf, her husband of one week, was sitting so close on the crowded train that his thigh pressed against hers. He held her left hand between both of his and was slowly twisting the wedding ring on her third finger.

'The end of our honeymoon,' he whispered regretfully.

'We've had a marvellous time, haven't we?' she whispered back. 'It's been a lovely holiday, my first ever.'

Cathy's face felt tight from the sun. A spell of really hot weather had come at just the right moment, and they'd been able to spend a lot of their time on the beach.

Rolf's face, too, was lightly tanned. He looked serious as he said, 'We could have a few problems to face now.'

'We've done the right thing,' she insisted.

'It certainly feels right for me.' His brown eyes gazed into hers. 'But with the war, it could be asking a lot of you.'

Cathy shook her head. 'Whatever happens, I'm sure it'll be worth it.'

She'd been brought up in the Osborne Orphanage Home for Girls, one child in a large group. She'd had no mother and no family, nobody to single her out: no adult she could love and who would love her in return. Cathy had felt as if there was a great empty space inside her; more than anything else she longed to be part of a family. Marriage, she was quite certain, would give her everything she wanted; most of all, it would give her Rolf.

Rolf worked in his father's butcher's shop, and the newlyweds were to make their home with his parents in the rooms above it. Cathy was looking forward to being part of his family.

He smiled. 'At least we'll have had this time alone together.'

She had known that marriage was what he wanted, but she'd had to persuade him.

'Let's make a pact then,' he'd said. 'We'll get married, enjoy ourselves on honeymoon and forget the problems for a while. Face them when we come back.'

Cathy had agreed. And now the time for facing them had come, but she felt invigorated, ready to cope with anything.

Across the carriage, she could see her cobalt-blue eyes and determined chin reflected in the mottled mirror advertising the delights of a visit to Barmouth. She looked smart in her wedding outfit of blue dress and coat and a summer straw hat with forget-me-nots round the brim. Her hair was coming loose from its clips though, and tiny black curls were swinging round her face.

Rolf's trilby covered most of his dark wavy hair. He was handsome by any standard, languid and relaxed. His reflection was partly obscured by the Homburg hat of a fellow passenger opposite.

Catherine Tanner had known Rolf for years, ever since she was six. Now at twenty-two his shoulders had broadened and he looked a well set-up young man.

He murmured, 'I've saddled you with my name, Mrs Gottfried. I wish it didn't make us seem so very German. Bit of a handicap at a time like this, when we're at war.'

She said, 'The war makes things hard for everybody.'

'But especially for my family. Dad's being torn in two.'

Rolf's father had come to Merseyside from Germany many years ago and had opened a butcher's shop. He'd meant to specialise in pork and pork products, because that's what he knew best, but he'd ended up having to give his customers what they wanted. When Rolf had left school, he'd gone into the family business which had been busy and profitable until the war began. Now the shortage of meat was becoming acute and the shop wasn't making enough to support them all. Rolf's father could more than manage what business they had left without help.

'I know you want to go and fight . . .'

He shook his head. 'I don't want to fight at all, but I feel I have to.'

Cathy knew he'd been fired with patriotism when the war started and had wanted to enlist right away. Many of his friends had done so, but Rolf was an only child and his mother had pleaded with him to stay, saying his father needed him to help run the business. Now, every newspaper was carrying lists of those killed in battle, and there was talk of conscription coming in soon. She was afraid they might not have very long together.

The train was pulling into Woodside Station now, and she watched her husband wait his turn to pull their suitcases down from the luggage rack.

2

'We'll get a cab if we can,' he told her. 'Might as well finish our honeymoon in style.'

They strode out of the station together. Cathy was almost as tall as Rolf and she carried her own case. She pushed her arm through his. He felt for her hand again and squeezed it.

'I hate the thought of leaving,' he said huskily. 'It'll be even harder after having this week with you.' Cathy felt truly loved.

Before the war, motor taxis were becoming the norm, but now petrol was in short supply and the horsedrawn fly had reappeared. There was one waiting outside the station. The best horses had already been shipped to France to help fight the war, and this one looked old and tired.

'Market Street, please.' Rolf handed up their cases. 'The butcher's shop.' The driver seemed surly.

Cathy knew her father-in-law was proud to have premises in one of the main shopping areas of Birkenhead; his shop opened straight on to Market Square. One side of the square was taken up by a vast market-hall built of brick and slate, with a fine clock over the front steps.

On market days, Wednesdays and Saturdays, the square was filled with stalls selling almost everything. In peacetime it had been possible to buy ice cream in summer and hot chestnuts in winter. Nowadays, one was lucky to get enough to eat and prices were rocketing.

On Saturday nights, as the closing time of ten o'clock approached, crowds poured in to snap up the bargains in perishable food which had to be sold off, and Market Square developed something of a carnival atmosphere.

Today, there had been a thunderstorm. The square was rainswept and empty and the shops shuttered. It was late in the afternoon on Thursday, early closing day.

Rolf was sitting close enough for Cathy to feel him tense. 'My goodness!'

'What is it?'

But now she could see the mound of broken glass on the pavement in front of the butcher's shop. A boy was sweeping it up, while two workmen were replacing the plate-glass shopfront.

'What's happened?' Rolf was aghast.

The upper windows were broken too, and the premises looked as though they'd been ransacked.

'Bit of trouble here yesterday,' the driver said. 'Germans aren't too popular round here any more. Not with the war.'

'Good God! What about the owners? Have they been hurt?'

'They're Germans,' he shrugged, as if hurting them was something of which to be proud.

The shop sign had been recently painted in gold lettering on a scarlet background to make it stand out. It read Otto Gottfried & Son, Family Butchers.

'With the Germans sinking the *Lusitania*, what can you expect, sir?' The driver leered at them, his contempt for the enemy showing through his deference to a customer.

'When did this happen?'

'We heard about the sinking yesterday morning. By afternoon, the whole town was like a madhouse.'

Rolf leaped out on to the pavement. He'd been attentive to her all week, but Cathy could see he'd forgotten her now in his haste to pay off the cab and see his parents. He hammered on their door.

'They're next door,' one of the glaziers told him.

Cathy knew the Weaver family who owned the hardware shop next door. They were friends of Rolf's parents. There were only two bedrooms above the butcher's shop, and as she'd come to Birkenhead the day before her wedding, Rolf's mother had arranged for her to sleep at the Weavers' so the necessary proprieties could be observed.

Rolf rushed to ring their doorbell which was high up near the fanlight.

'Come in, lad.' Stout and grey-haired, Mrs Weaver drew him inside. 'Your mam and dad are here.' She smiled at Cathy. 'Let's have them cases inside, lass. What a homecoming for a bride.'

She led them to the living room which was behind the shop. It was small and dark, with boxes of merchandise stacked against one wall. Mildred Gottfried jumped to her feet to hug Rolf. Cathy could see how much her only son meant to her.

'Are you all right, Mam?' he asked. 'Not hurt?'

'No, I'm fine.' Mildred screwed up her round face.

Cathy could see she was upset. At almost fifty, Mildred Gottfried had the figure of a woman half her age. Her hair was short, dark and curly and her eyes seemed to miss nothing. Her movements were brisk, and there was an air of competence and efficiency about her.

'What a terrible thing to happen,' Rolf said. 'You should have sent us a telegram. We could have come home last night.'

'We didn't want to spoil things for you. Not when you're on your honeymoon.'

Cathy felt her mother-in-law's arms come round her in a hug. 'I'm glad you're both back, though it's a shame everything's in such a mess. I was going to cook a special dinner, make a bit of a fuss of you.'

'Don't worry about that. Where's Dad?'

'Upstairs in bed. He's taken it hard.'

'In bed here?'

'Yes – our place was ransacked. They peed on our beds and you should have seen what they did on our sofa. Couldn't sleep there, not last night.'

'I'll run up and see how he is.'

'No, Rolf, I looked in at him a few moments ago and he was asleep. It's better if you don't wake him.'

Cathy was full of sympathy. 'Now we're home, I'll help you clean the place up,' she offered immediately.

'Thanks, dear, but Polly and I have been at it all morning, cleaning and washing.'

'Not that we'll get the washing dry today,' Mrs Weaver commented.

'Is there more to do over there?'

'Lots – they made a right mess.'

'Then I'll—'

'No, dear, I'll just make us all a cuppa, eh?' Mrs Weaver said. 'Let you get your breath back first.'

'Did they attack Dad? Have they hurt him?' Rolf demanded.

'He got a few cuts and bruises.'

'*What?*'

'Nothing serious.' Mildred shook her head. 'But they frightened the life out of us both, waving Dad's cleavers at us. They looted all the meat we had in the place, cleaned us out. A whole forequarter of beef – hacked it up between them and took it away in bits. It was horrible. They were screaming abuse at us because your dad's German. It was the hate that got to him. Finding everyone against him.'

'You should have heard the noise,' George Weaver told them. 'Ranting and raving – it sounded bloodcurdling from in here.'

Mrs Weaver was bringing in the tea. 'But your mam told them what's what. She stood up to them.'

'I'm Liverpool born and bred, and sound like it as soon as I open my mouth. I told them straight, that we're as much against the Germans as they are. That you were joining up to fight, and Otto was naturalised British many years ago.'

'It was the sinking of the *Lusitania* that set them off,' Polly Weaver assured them.

The *Lusitania* was one of England's luxury passenger liners and had won the Blue Riband for the fastest crossing of the Atlantic.

'Yesterday, it was on the newsagent's placards that a German submarine had sunk it off Ireland. After that, crowds gathered outside your parents' shop. They were all shouting for Otto Gottfried, as though he was personally to blame.' Polly Weaver tut-tutted and shook her head.

'We read about the sinking,' Cathy said. 'It was in all the papers. It's horrible to think of twelve hundred lives lost like that.'

'Many of them local lads, too,' Mr Weaver nodded sadly. 'After all, Liverpool was her home port – they took on crew here. There were huge gangs rioting all over town. You should see the damage they did at Deletlieb's in Borough Road. The police tried to control them and stop the looting but they didn't stand a chance.'

Cathy had never seen Rolf look more serious. 'Mam, it's the name Gottfried that made the crowd turn against you. I've wanted to change it ever since the beginning of the war – I told you we should.'

'Your dad wouldn't have it.'

'Well, he will after this.'

'It was horrible, the feeling of mass hatred directed at him. As I said, that's what's upset him most. We had the doctor to him in the end; he gave him something to make him sleep.'

'He'll be better in a day or two,' Mrs Weaver said comfortingly.

'You'll have to spend the night over there, I'm afraid,' Mildred told Cathy. 'Polly's loaned us some clean bedding and we've made the bed up for you and Rolf. I hope you'll be able to sleep.'

'Thank you, we'll be fine.' Cathy felt she could sleep anywhere as long as she was with Rolf.

'I'd already springcleaned his room and got everything ready for you. The new double bed was delivered and I'd made it up with everything new. Such a shame, they spoiled it all.'

'Such a lot of work and worry for you,' Cathy sympathised.

When they'd drunk their tea, Mildred picked up Cathy's suitcase and led them next door. Despite what Cathy had been told, she wasn't prepared for the mess. The shop floor was slippery with grease and mud; bits of fat and meat had been tramped in. Splinters of glass and bone were embedded in the counter and the shelves had been torn down and left hanging askew.

There were two small rooms behind the shop. Previously Cathy had seen whole carcases of pigs and sheep hanging in the far one. The other room was used for cutting up. Not so much as an ounce of meat remained in either.

'They looted everything,' Mildred lamented. 'Took the dripping too – what they didn't smear on the floor.' Rolf struggled to right the chopping block that had been turned over.

'We started cleaning upstairs, had to get the place ready for you coming back. Come and see where you'll be sleeping, Cathy.'

Her mother-in-law believed in doing the right thing, so Cathy had not been allowed to see Rolf's bedroom before.

He said now, 'You've done a good job here, Mam. It looks fine.'

'They even broke the dressing-table mirror. I'll try and get a new one tomorrow,' Mildred promised.

'I can live for a while without a mirror,' Cathy said awkwardly.

'I wanted to make everything perfect for you. I thought I had, then this.' For a moment, Mildred looked close to tears. 'They threw that little stool at the window. I found it broken on the pavement. I'm just glad to get the glass replaced in time for your return.'

'It's fine, Mam,' Rolf said again, embracing her. 'You've done wonders.'

'Just don't walk about with bare feet, as there's glass everywhere. Oh, and Cathy – those boxes you brought . . .'

'My belongings, clothes and things?'

'Yes, there were three, weren't there? I put two in the wardrobe and they didn't find those, but that big one, I left against the wall here and it's gone. I'm so sorry.'

With a sinking heart, Cathy opened the wardrobe and looked at the two that remained. She'd packed everything she owned, all she'd accumulated in the whole of her life, into her suitcase and those three cardboard boxes.

She'd been in domestic service at Halesworth Hall, a big private house, first as a housemaid and later as a cook, and had been required to wear cotton print dresses covered by big white aprons. She'd worn her own clothes only during her time off and they'd remained in good condition. Her trousseau of new nightdresses and underwear should be here somewhere, but she was almost certain she'd packed them in the box that had gone.

'I'm sorry,' her mother-in-law said.

'It's not your fault,' Cathy choked as she slit open her remaining boxes. It was pointless looking; her new underwear wasn't here.

'Yes, they've taken my trousseau.' She'd spent months making it. 'Thank goodness I've still got my wedding presents.' There was a clock from her employer, Major Fleming, and a pair of candlesticks which the other staff had clubbed together to buy for her. In addition, the house-keeper, Mrs Bott, had bought her a fine handbag.

Rolf was watching her, sympathy in his dark eyes. 'I knew there'd be a downside to marrying me,' he tried to joke, 'but I didn't foresee this. It wouldn't have happened if the name Otto Gottfried hadn't been spelled out in gold letters over the shopfront. Tomorrow, I'll paint it out and see about changing our name.'

Cathy could feel his mother holding back and wondered why. It was surely a logical step to take.

'I'm so sorry, Cathy,' she said again. Her cheerful facade had slipped.

'I have plenty of things really, Cathy reassured her. 'I won't be short of clothes. It's just that I made new things to start my new life.'

'Of course you did.'

'You mustn't blame yourself.' Cathy felt the silence heavy between them; it dragged on. At last Mildred looked at Rolf.

'I want to get our own bedroom fixed up next, so I can bring your dad back home. Things won't seem right until I do and we're a lot of work for Polly and George. I'll get going on that.'

Left to themselves, Cathy changed out of her best clothes so she could get started. 'Your mam must have worked like a horse to get so much done,' she said. 'She's arranged to have the glass replaced in the windows and restored order in this room. I can't help but admire the way she's coping.'

Rolf smiled at her as he pulled on an old pullover. For a moment Cathy could see his resemblance to his mother.

'Mam always copes, it's her way. Really, she was doing more in the business than Dad, the accounts and the ordering and that. Dad helps with the heavy lifting and the chopping . . . Or rather, he *did*. Mam also boiled the hams and roasted the joints of beef and pork to slice and sell cold, or she did when we could get them.'

'This has made her angry,' Cathy said.

'But she's kept her head and she's doing her best to get things straight.'

'And your father? He relies on her?'

'Yes, we both do.'

Rolf opened their bedroom door and spoke to his mother. 'We'll start down in the shop, shall we?'

'If you would. Until we get that clean, we'll be tramping the mess back up here.'

Cathy began by boiling the kettle to get some hot water. With a bucketful, some soda, soap and two large scrubbing brushes, she led the way downstairs.

'This is a job and a half,' Rolf said, surveying the floors. 'It's never been like this before. Mam would never let it get into this state.'

'I was taught to scrub at the Orphanage,' Cathy shrugged, as she set to.

From the age of twelve, the girls had taken over the day-to-day running of the Home. They were being trained to work in domestic service. Cathy had laundered clothes, swept, scrubbed, polished and dusted. She'd been taught basic cooking in the kitchens, but they'd used the cheapest ingredients and she'd never cared much for the food they prepared. They'd all been forced to eat every scrap of it, though, or it would reappear on their plates for the next meal.

It took her and Rolf, using several more buckets of hot water, more than an hour to scrub the shop floors back to their normal state.

Mildred set about brushing up the broken glass from her bedroom floor. She felt exhausted; she'd hardly slept last night and every muscle in her body ached.

Every time she'd closed her eyes she'd relived that heart-stopping moment when she'd left the washing-up to go to the living-room window to see what all the commotion was about. It had been a shock to see the crowd gathering outside their shop. She'd heard the noise they were making, a real racket, but she didn't at first understand what they were shouting about.

When she caught the name *Otto Gottfried*, it sent a chill through her body. She'd skidded downstairs to him. The door between the shop and the room behind where he cut up the meat was closed, and Otto, poor love, was getting a little deaf in his old age.

He'd looked up and smiled at her. 'Lovely bit of beef, this.' He was dismembering a forequarter; it was the first meat they'd had delivered in a fortnight.

'They're coming for you!' she'd screamed. 'Lock up!'

'We're closed — the door *is* locked,' he'd frowned. 'It's the dinner-hour.'

Mildred had rushed to the shop door and shot the bolts top and bottom. She saw angry faces against the glass, inches from hers. She'd panicked and run back to drag Otto upstairs where they couldn't be seen. He'd come, still holding the cleaver he'd been using. Seconds later, there was an almighty crash as the plate-glass window shattered. Mildred nearly jumped out of her skin: one of them must have thrown a brick at it. The tinkle of falling glass seemed to go on and on. .

The shouting was louder then, as the angry horde invaded the premises and came racing up the stairs to the rooms the Gottfrieds called home. Mildred had feared for Otto's life even more than for her own.

Her hands were still shaking, hours after the event. Why hadn't she insisted on changing their name when the war started? Rolf had wanted it. If only she'd made Otto listen, this need never have happened.

She leaned the broom against the wall and went to the window. Thank goodness there was glass in it again. She must not think of what had happened. Must not dwell on it. Must not let Otto dwell on it.

She sat down on her hard bedroom chair and rested her head against the wall; she could hear the murmur of Cathy's voice on the other side. She should be glad the youngsters had not been here to witness it. She closed her eyes and tried to relax. She had to put it behind her for all their sakes.

Suddenly, everything in their lives was going wrong and she didn't know what to do for the best. The war had been a worry for some time. It was already ruining their business but having their premises ransacked would probably finish it off. It had taken them years to get on their feet, work their way up to prosperity, and now?

Mildred sighed. Retirement had come with brutal suddenness, but she and Otto had saved for their old age. He'd always been good at saving and the shop had been a little gold mine before the war. And at least he was old enough to draw his State Pension. Mildred had looked forward to having a small house somewhere quiet for themselves, and leaving the shop and its lease to Rolf. They would have been giving him a start in life. Now the lease would be a liability, all fifteen years of it. With so many food shops empty it would be hard to sell it on. They'd have to continue living in the rooms above it, but at least there was room for them all. They'd manage.

Then there was Cathy Tanner. Mildred gave herself a mental slap. Not Tanner any longer, she was a Gottfried now, one of them.

If she was honest, Mildred knew her feelings about Cathy were mixed. It hurt that Rolf loved another woman. He'd been everything to her since he'd been born and she didn't want to share him with anyone. Rolf had been her reason for living.

'Please be kind to Cathy,' he'd said the week before his wedding, as though he expected the reverse from her. 'I'd like you two to get on. She says she wants a mother, so I know she'll more than meet you halfway. She's not had an easy upbringing.'

Mildred decided she'd have to help Cathy replace the trousseau she'd lost; she mustn't give Rolf any reason to think she wasn't welcoming her. She'd thought Cathy rather a forlorn little thing at sixteen when Rolf had first brought her home. A girl from the Orphanage, not nearly good enough for her son, but Rolf had never wanted any other.

Cathy had changed. There was nothing forlorn about her now, quite the opposite. She'd blossomed in the three years since then, but that hadn't pleased Mildred either. It made her feel unaccountably resentful.

She was being pushed aside for a more comely, younger woman. In her saner moments, Mildred told herself all this was nonsense. Every young man needed a wife, and would she want her son to be any different?

She could see why Cathy attracted him. She had the colouring of a pure Celt, with those blue eyes and fair skin, while her great mane of hair was almost black. It was thick and bouncy with lots of curl. Cathy had told her she'd found her hair easy to cope with when she was young; all she'd had to do was brush it and tie it back. In her mid-teens, she was still doing just that. If Rolf had to have a girlfriend, Mildred wanted her to be someone smart, a girl who did him justice.

Cathy still looked like a child when she went out with Rolf. Mildred had had to tell her that it was usual for young ladies, especially those with an admirer, to wear their hair up and that Cathy should try to do the same.

'I have tried,' she'd laughed, 'but it makes a huge and heavy bun. I cut it to lighten the weight and reduce the bulk, but that makes it more difficult to get it up.'

'And it leaves lots of tiny corkscrew curls dangling round your face and neck,' Rolf had laughed with her.

'That looks distinctly childish,' Mildred had told her briskly. 'And unfashionable.'

Cathy had said, 'I'm all right at work because my uniform cap covers my hair, but when I want to dress up and look my best, the bun pushes all my hats forward until I can hardly see out from under them.'

Mildred had seen the solution. 'Why don't you position your bun right on top of your head rather than on the back of it? The bigger the bun, the better – it'll make you look taller.'

'I'm tall enough,' Cathy had said. 'I'm five foot seven.'

'Your bun will be on a firm base and the crown of your hats will fit over it,' Mildred persisted. 'You can wear them flat across the top of your head and tilt them if you want, in whatever is the fashionable angle.'

Everybody agreed, including Rolf, that it really suited the shape of Cathy's face and that ladies of quality wore their hair that way.

'They even collect their combings,' Mildred added, 'to make false pieces to put in their buns so they look bigger.'

Now Cathy's eyes seemed to be wider apart and were full of adoration whenever they looked at Rolf. She had a dazzling smile and perfect teeth. Mildred had found her to be sweet-natured and very willing, a good worker. She knew she had to accept Cathy into her family; she had to hide her own feelings. If she didn't, it would put Rolf off *her*, not off

Cathy. It wouldn't be easy, but she'd do her best to be friendly for Rolf's sake.

He could have done worse, but here he was, newlywed and with no means of supporting either himself or his bride. The future for the pair of them looked bleak.

Chapter Two

Cathy was tired by the time she and Rolf went back to the hardware shop for supper. His father had come downstairs in his pyjamas with a blanket round his shoulders. Both his hands were bandaged.

'Cuts,' Mildred explained, 'from his own knives and cleavers.'

'I put up my hands.' Otto demonstrated how. 'To keep them away from my body.'

'And away from me,' Mildred added. Cathy thought him much changed by what had happened.

'Come and sit up.' Mrs Weaver invited them to the table. 'It's all ready.' Rolf had to help his father to his feet.

Otto Gottfried was more than twenty-two years older than his wife; at seventy-two he seemed frail by comparison. His frame had once been strong and muscular but now his shoulders sagged.

'We're finished, lad.' He looked up at Rolf with moist eyes. 'They've cleaned us out. Taken our saws, cleavers, knives – everything we need. Can't cut up carcases without them. Our hooks, trays, everything.' His mouth turned down in misery.

'They've broken the scales too,' Rolf added.

'Even taken our aprons and straw boaters,' his mother said.

'It isn't worth opening up again,' Otto lamented. His hair was pure white – thick, strong and wavy. His complexion was pasty, and the flesh hung in heavy dewlaps on his collar. He looked exhausted.

Mildred sighed. 'It's not worth spending money to replace all those things. The shop won't earn enough to make it worthwhile.'

Food shops were closing in their hundreds all over the country. 'Until the war's over there's no point in running a business that depends on food. Can't get enough to sell,' Otto said.

'A good business ruined,' Mildred agreed. 'After you've devoted your life to it.'

'I wanted to give you something you could build on, Rolf. I tried to provide these people with good meat and look what they do, they kick me down.' A tear trickled down his lined face.

'Don't worry about it, Dad. You've said yourself, it's time you retired.'

'They seemed to think I was some sort of a spy, that it was my fault the *Lusitania* was sunk. But I've made my life here for the last thirty-five years. I think of this country as home – I couldn't go back now.'

'It's you we're worried about.' Mildred was looking at Rolf. 'You won't be able to earn a living here after this.'

Cathy shivered; she knew what that meant. She and Rolf had already talked about it. She knew he'd feel he had to join up. The very thought of that made it difficult to swallow the pork sausages Mrs Weaver had cooked for their supper.

'It releases me in a way,' Rolf said. 'There can be no excuses now for not fighting for my country, but I want to get things right for you before I go. I shall make sure the vandals won't break your windows again.'

'It wasn't just your shop.' George Weaver was handing round the bread and butter. 'And not just here. I read in today's paper that there were riots all over the country.'

Cathy saw her husband grimace. 'We've *got* to change our name, Dad. We can do it by deed poll. I've found out how it can be done. Tomorrow, I'll see a solicitor and get it sorted out. It scares me to think of violence being directed at you three. Especially when Mam and Cathy are English anyway.'

Otto roused himself. 'The Royal family are German like me, and if Saxe-Coburg-Gotha is a good enough family name for them, then Gottfried should be good enough for us.'

That took Cathy's breath away. Even Rolf seemed taken aback. He said quietly, 'But they aren't smashing the windows of Buckingham Palace and blaming the Royal family for sinking our ships, are they? We've got to face up to it, Dad. Tomorrow . . .'

'Leave it for a day or two,' his mother said, unable to look any of them in the face. 'Give us time to think.'

'What is there to think about?' Rolf was retorting hotly when Cathy gave his leg a nudge under the table. It was obvious that his parents did not want to talk about it in front of the Weavers.

'You could paint out your dad's name over the shop window tomorrow,' Mildred suggested.

'Right, I'll do that for start.' Rolf's knife and fork clattered back on his plate.

Cathy wanted Rolf to herself and suggested they have an early night. As soon as they reached their bedroom, Rolf said, 'Dad's dead against having his name changed even now, isn't he?'

'He didn't want to talk about it, and your mother wanted to shut you up, too.'

'What's so good about Gottfried? It's a terrible name – it's always been an embarrassment. I was known as "the Hun" at school. Just think of what it'll be like when I join up; every day, some bright spark will ask if I'm fighting on the right side. Can you imagine it?'

Cathy could. She'd first noticed Rolf when she was six years old. The girls from the Osborne Orphanage Home had walked in a crocodile to the local school where Rolf had been in a higher class. One day, some bigger boys at school had been bullying the Orphanage girls, and Rolf had chased them off and come to her aid. Cathy had been knocked over and he'd lifted her back on her feet.

'Are you all right?' he'd asked. 'Not hurt?'

She had been frightened more than anything else. After that, she'd admired him from afar for the next decade.

She asked now, 'What would you change your name to?'

'Godfrey – that's the nearest English equivalent – and I'd spell my name Ralph,' he frowned. 'Dad seemed agreeable when we first talked about it. Wouldn't you sooner be known as Mrs Godfrey?'

'Yes. But I'd be content with the name Gottfried, if it weren't for the war.' Once, she'd thought it set Rolf apart, made him different, but now . . . 'Yes, I'd like the English version better.'

'I won't go away until I've got it organised.'

Cathy was glad of anything that would keep Rolf with her a little longer.

The next morning, Mildred came over early and brought porridge for their breakfast. 'I was saving some ham to fry for you, but like everything else, it's gone.'

'Don't worry, Mam,' Rolf told her. 'We aren't going hungry.'

'I want to finish cleaning this place up so your dad can move back today,' she said.

'I can help with that,' Cathy offered, and as soon as breakfast was over, she set to work on the kitchen and living room, while Rolf went to borrow a step-ladder from Mr Weaver to paint out their name on the shop sign.

By mid-morning, Cathy and Mildred had every upstairs window open and the rooms above the shop were fresh and free from broken glass and dirt.

Mildred said, 'Cathy, it's time we had a break. Will you come across to the market with me? I need more crockery. I want to match these plates if I can.'

'They broke your plates?'

'Picked them off the draining board and threw them at the wall. Senseless, I call that.'

Cathy enjoyed the bustle of the market. She helped Mildred look through great baskets of dishes but they found nothing even vaguely similar. Mildred bought a few plain white plates, then led her across the market-hall to a stall that sold cloth. There she fingered a roll of pink satin.

'Do you like this, Cathy?'

'It's beautiful.'

'Then there's this lace. It would only take a few inches to trim the neckline of a nightie.'

'It would look lovely.' Cathy assumed Mildred intended it for herself.

'When I was a girl, I served my time as a dressmaker. I can soon run up a few nightgowns and some underclothes for you.'

Cathy tried to protest, but her mother-in-law insisted. 'It's only fair. You've had your things stolen from my flat before you could wear them.'

'You're very kind. Thank you.'

'And you've worked hard helping me clean up. You're a good girl.'

Mildred had fascinated Cathy from the moment they'd met. This was the first family home she'd ever set foot in and even now, the only family she knew well. She could see Mildred considered herself the linchpin; she ran the home and mostly, she made decisions for the whole family.

Cathy had never tired of watching how Mildred as a mother treated Rolf. As she'd expected, she demonstrated great devotion. At every meal Mildred dished up, Rolf was given the choicest bits. When he'd cleared his plate, his mother asked if he'd had enough. She was concerned about everything he did. She bought most of his clothes for him and washed and pressed them too. She was ready with advice on any subject he brought up. She kissed him goodbye every time he went out, though Rolf could look a bit embarrassed by that.

In fact, Cathy would have said Mildred loved Rolf more than she did her husband. During the first months she'd taken up with Rolf, Cathy had felt she was allowed in their home but only as an outsider. The best dishes and tablecloths were used as though to enhance the family's status. When she and Rolf became engaged, she'd felt a few steps closer to Mildred. Now they were married, she hoped she'd be accepted.

Rolf, who'd always had the mother love she and the girls at the Orphanage had longed for so much, seemed not to value it.

'Can be suffocating,' he'd said with a shrug.

That had shocked her. 'Don't you love your mother?' But she could see he did.

'Yes, of course. I know I come first with her, but it's not easy. When I was small we were very close, and she came first with me, but as I grew up and made other friends, she said I was growing away from her and resented it. She gets upset and hurt if I don't spend a lot of time with her. She says she needs me and I have to keep her needs in mind. Sometimes I feel she's taking me over. I have to do what she wants. She doesn't give me space to love anyone else.'

'Oh!' It had never occurred to Cathy that the bonds of love could be too close, but that's how Rolf felt. She asked herself if all mothers were like Mildred.

'And now we're married, which means I love you and I put *you* first.' His dark eyes were serious. 'Don't forget that. Mam and I had a little talk about you. I told her I loved you both but in different ways.'

'I've always hoped she'd give some of her love and care to me. In time, you know.'

'She will,' Rolf had said. 'Love and care spill out of her. She won't be able to help herself.'

And now, it seemed, she had. Cathy walked home from the market with Mildred, hugging the little parcel of pink satin. That was proof she cared about her, wasn't it?

Cathy helped Mildred cook a dinner of liver and bacon. Otto got dressed and came home to sit in front of the fire that Rolf had lit. They'd eaten and were having a cup of tea afterwards when Rolf again brought up the need to change their name.

'I can't understand why you're so against it, Dad. Surely after what's happened here, you can see why I want it changed?'

It was his mother who answered. 'We can see that all right. But it isn't easy.'

'Yes, it is. I've been asking how it's done. I can see to it.'

'I meant there are complications,' Mildred said finally.

There was a long-drawn-out silence. Cathy couldn't take her gaze from her father-in-law, who looked acutely uncomfortable.

'What sort of complications?' Rolf wanted to know.

Mildred said heavily, 'We'd better tell them, Otto. Rolf has a right to know, he's an adult now.' Cathy could feel the growing tension. 'You tell him.'

'It's like this . . .' The old man looked dispirited, without energy. It took him a long time to get going.

Rolf tried to help. 'You're German and you want to remain German.'

'*No!*' It was almost a shout. 'I left Germany thirty-five years ago, back in 1880. I had to get away, start a new life somewhere else. I happened to pick on England.' A fit of coughing overtook him. His voice was steadier when he went on. 'It could have been anywhere for all I cared then. I loved my country, but . . .'

Mildred seemed as tense as a tiger ready to spring.

Rolf asked, bewildered, 'Then what drove you out?'

'My life was falling apart. Personal problems, I suppose you'd say.'

'Dad!' Rolf looked taken aback. 'You said you'd had a happy upbringing.'

'I did, but this was a long time after that. I was working in a butcher's shop in Hamburg, one of three assistants. I'd been married for six years.' His German accent had become stronger.

'Married? You were married before?' Rolf stared at his father, then at his mother.

'My wife Irma was a beautiful girl who worked as a cashier in a bank,' Otto went on. 'However, she was ambitious. She wanted to be a singer and from time to time she performed in bars and nightclubs.'

Otto gave a long sigh. 'We were saving. I was determined to set up in business on my own, buy my own butcher's shop. I didn't allow any pleasures. I wanted a family, I thought that might settle Irma, but a child didn't come. I know she found our life bleak.

'Both my parents were dead by that time, but I came from a big family. I had two brothers and a sister as well as aunts and uncles, who'd never taken to Irma. They'd warned me against her – said she was flighty, not the sort of girl who would make a good wife for a butcher. I didn't listen, I was in love with her, but they were proved right.'

He looked Rolf in the eye. 'To cut it short, she left me for a more exciting man and drained our joint bank account. All at once I lost my wife, my life savings and my will to live. I got no sympathy from my family, who said I should have expected it. *They* certainly had.'

'Dad, you must have felt dreadful losing everything like that. It made you turn your back on your home and country,' Rolf said. 'But once you came here, you were all right?'

'Not really. I brought my problems with me, you see. I found the same sort of work and started scrimping and saving again. What else could I do? I knew nothing else.'

Cathy felt moved by his sad story. 'But eventually you saved enough to get your shop and were able to settle down here.'

'Yes, I bought the shop.'

'And you met Mam.' Rolf looked puzzled. 'You managed to get a divorce?'

Otto closed his eyes and said slowly, 'No.'

Cathy asked, 'Something happened to Irma?'

Otto was downcast; he shook his head.

'She died,' Rolf said. 'Must have done if you and Mam . . .'

'No. I never heard anything of her again.'

Rolf's tongue moistened his lips. 'Then how did you manage to marry Mum?'

Mildred moaned softly, sounding distressed.

'I couldn't marry her. I was married to Irma. I didn't dare, it would have been bigamy.'

There was a long silence. Rolf seemed paralysed. Eventually he stirred. 'You mean . . .?'

'Irma was twenty-eight when I last saw her, healthy and seven years younger than me, full of life. She had tremendous energy, real bounce. I couldn't suppose her to be anything but alive and well.'

'Not even after, what would it be? Ten years?'

'Twelve,' he said, 'before your mother and I met.'

Cathy had never seen Rolf look so shocked. 'You mean you're not married?'

'No,' Mildred whispered. 'It's my dearest wish that we could be.'

There was another painful silence. Cathy was screwing up her face and trying to think. 'I'm sure I've read somewhere that after hearing nothing for seven years, you can assume that someone is dead.'

'But I left her in Germany – how could I hear? She didn't know I'd come to England.'

'Your family might know,' Cathy suggested. 'They might have heard something.'

'Dad, that was thirty-five years ago!' Rolf burst out. 'A lifetime ago!'

Cathy tried to help. 'She'd be what age now?'

'Sixty . . . sixty-three.'

Cathy looked round at the agonised faces. 'She'll be a different person to the one you knew.'

After yet another silence Rolf said, 'And what about me?'

Mildred caught at his hand. 'This is raking everything up.' Cathy heard the catch in her throat. 'It was a bad time for me. I was in domestic service like you, Cathy – a cook, too. Well, more a general maid of all work, a drudge. I was the only servant in the house. I did the shopping, the cooking and the cleaning. I used to buy meat for my employer from the shop where Otto found work. I made a point of waiting until he could serve me . . .'

'You fell in love,' Rolf said. 'And after that you settled down and were happy?'

'I suppose you could say we supported each other,' Mildred mumbled.

'But you never married? You've always seemed married to me.'

Otto said, 'We have lived together as though we were.'

'I've always thought of us as a family. Not married – I suppose it does make a difference . . . Well, there was a reason why you couldn't.'

Otto's head lifted until he could look Rolf in the eye. 'I'm not your father, lad.'

Cathy caught her breath. She could see the colour draining from Rolf's face. She herself felt deeply shocked by these revelations.

'I was already with child when we met,' his mother whispered. 'I'm so ashamed.'

Rolf looked astounded. 'Who *is* my real father, then?'

'A sailor. He was off faster than a frightened hare when I told him you were on the way. I was left to fend for myself.' Cathy could hear the anguish in Mildred's voice.

'Your mother didn't know which way to turn,' Otto said, trying to help.

'I had a living-in job, you see, and was afraid I'd be turned out once my employer knew. I had nowhere else I could go. Otto came to the rescue and offered me a home.'

'It seemed the best thing to do,' the old man said, his eyes on Mildred. 'To pretend we were married. For the sake of propriety and the business.'

'You had this shop then?'

He sighed. 'The situation pushed me into buying the lease. Time was not on our side then, but we've been happy here. We made a success of it.'

'You see, Rolf,' his mother explained, 'your dad . . . I mean Otto is afraid that if we try to change his name, all this will be dragged up. They'll want to see birth certificates and marriage lines and all that.'

'But my birth certificate gives me the name Rolf Gottfried. I've seen it.'

'I went down and registered your birth,' Otto told him. 'It seemed the least I could do for your mam. It was what she wanted. Even if we weren't married, I could do that for her, have my name on the certificate.

'I took the law into our own hands, you could say. But now it'll rebound on our heads.'

'No,' Cathy said. 'I don't see how it could. Who would question that?'

20

'It might all come out, I'm afraid, if we draw legal attention to it.'

'If you hadn't given me your name, what would it have been?' Rolf wanted to know.

His mother said, 'It would have been my name – Morris.'

'Very English,' Otto sighed. 'If I'd registered you under that, you wouldn't have this deed-poll problem now.'

Rolf said, 'I still feel half-German.'

'See what I've done to you?'

'Where did my natural father come from?'

'Liverpool,' his mother said shortly.

'And his name?'

'Onslow, but he didn't want you and me to have that.'

Cathy watched Rolf turn to Otto. 'You've been a good father,' he said quietly. 'I couldn't have had better. I'll always think of you as my dad.'

Otto smiled for the first time. 'I'm glad to hear that. We wanted more children, but they didn't come. For me, I don't think they could.'

Cathy met Mildred's burning gaze. 'I suppose you think I'm shameless,' the older woman said. 'Having Rolf out of wedlock.'

'No, no,' Cathy said, but in truth she *was* shocked. She'd been taught that it was the most damning sin a girl could commit, and the cause of much suffering for the child. But Rolf hadn't suffered like the girls at the Orphanage: he'd had a proper home and two parents to love him.

Mildred's voice was hardly audible. 'I've felt guilty, of course. I've hidden it, never talked about it to anyone. It's a secret locked away inside me, never to be shared.'

'We deliberately kept it from you.' Otto told Rolf. 'I didn't want you to know I wasn't your real father. After living together for twenty-three years, it seems like marriage to me. Mildred's been a good wife to me.'

'In everything but name,' she agreed.

'Everybody round here, all the customers believe we're married,' Otto said fondly.

'It's just that I know we're not.'

'I'm afraid it's preyed on your mother's mind – she has felt it deeply.'

'Mam, you mustn't upset yourself.'

'But you . . .?'

'I'm not going to let it upset me,' Rolf said firmly.

'And now there's this war.' Otto shook his head. 'England against Germany – I can't think of anything worse. It tightens me here.' He tapped in the region of his heart. 'To hear you talk, Rolf, of going to fight – you'll be fighting my nephews, your cousins. One half of the family trying to kill the other.'

'Don't go,' his mother pleaded. 'Stay here, get yourself a job in some reserved occupation.'

He said, 'Conscription is coming, it says so in the papers. It won't be long now.'

'Not for those in jobs that are important for the war.'

'I feel I have to go,' Rolf sighed. 'So many of the boys I knew at school are already in France. It seems cowardly not to.'

Long after they'd gone to bed that night, Rolf continued to whisper to Cathy about his parents' revelation. It had been an enormous shock, and he could scarcely take it in.

'I can't understand why Dad didn't consult a solicitor about marrying again,' he fretted. 'Surely he'd have seen one when he bought the shop?'

'Don't forget, this was a foreign country to him,' Cathy said. 'He wouldn't know anything about English law. Perhaps he didn't understand so much English in those days. As he said, he didn't want to draw attention to the situation.'

'But after thirty-five years of hearing nothing of this Irma, surely it would be legal for them to marry now?'

'I don't know.'

'Tomorrow, I'll go to see a solicitor about changing our name and ask about that too. These are things I need to do before I join up.'

Cathy said, 'You promised you'd stay home with me for a few weeks.'

'Yes, but without some means of earning a living, it's going to be difficult.' Cathy felt her heart sinking. He went on, 'You married me for better or for worse and so far it's been for worse.'

She kissed him impulsively and whispered, 'No, I've got a family now and we had a good honeymoon. We both enjoyed that.'

'But things don't look too rosy now. I thought I had a means of supporting you, but I haven't. What are we going to live on?'

'What about a munitions factory? That's war work, and they're always advertising for staff. You'd earn a good living there.' Even as she said it, Cathy knew she shouldn't try to persuade him to stay at home. Other young men were fighting in the front line; other wives were left behind. She and Rolf shouldn't stay safe and let others make the sacrifice. But it was so hard.

She heard his long sigh of frustration. 'I'm torn in two, Cathy. I want to stay with you but I feel it would be wrong.'

'You're going to volunteer?'

'It's one way of earning a living. There's an allowance for wives.'

'I'll get a job. Save for when you come back,' Cathy told him. But what if he didn't come back? The thought left her rigid and wouldn't go away.

'Mam will want to look after you, Cathy. She'll want to do it, she'll take good care of you.'

She shivered. It was almost as though he knew what she was thinking. 'I know, but I'm able to work. It's only right I should.'

The next day, Rolf asked Otto for the name and address of the solicitor he'd used when he bought the shop.

'He was an old man then,' Otto said. 'He'll have retired long ago.' But he remembered the address.

Cathy went with Rolf. They found two solicitors were practising in the same suite of offices, in a rather grand Georgian house in Argyle Street. The rooms were large and full of expensive-looking furniture. They saw several formally dressed clerks in an office as they passed an open door.

An elderly gentleman seemed to be acting as receptionist. He said, 'If you care to wait, Mr Dyson will see you when he's free.' He offered them a seat.

The atmosphere was very different from that in the butcher's shop, and Cathy could understand why Otto might have felt in awe of these men with their middle-class accents and white hands.

At last they were led up a lovely curving staircase with a mahogany balustrade to a spacious office on the first floor. Mr Dyson, who was middle-aged and bald, sat at a large partner's desk on which papers were laid out in little heaps, some tied with pink tape. Cathy was offered one of a pair of very elegant mahogany chairs.

She listened while Rolf explained that they wanted to change their names by deed poll, and so did his parents. Mr Dyson listened to the reason and said he saw no difficulty.

'I'll draw up an affidavit for each of you, then you'll all need to come in and sign them. It's usual to place notices in the local papers to say that in future your name will be Godfrey. My clerk can see to that, it won't take very long to arrange.'

Rolf said, 'There's something else. My father left Germany thirty-five years ago, after his wife deserted him. He was very upset. He's heard nothing of her in all that time and would like to remarry. What is the legal position?'

The solicitor steepled his fingers. 'If a wife wilfully absents herself from her husband without his consent and with the intention of forsaking him, it's known legally as Desertion.'

Rolf nodded. 'Can he marry again?'

'He's a naturalised British citizen, you said? And he's no idea of his wife's whereabouts?'

'He assumes she stayed in Germany, but it's thirty-five years since he had any contact. Can he presume the marriage to be over?'

Mr Dyson was shaking his head.

'Or that she's dead?'

'A foreign marriage is a complication. No, he'd have to go to Court to prove his case.'

'Oh! I was hoping he'd be free.'

'I can draw up a document setting out the details for your father, and arrange for a hearing. It would be up to the Court to decide what efforts should be made to establish the facts and what enquiries need to be made.'

'We're at war with Germany, Mr Dyson. How can enquiries be made at this time?'

'Quite so. But it's up to the Court to decide.'

'Do you think it's likely they'll decide the marriage is over? Logic says . . .'

'It is complicated. I would be hopeful but can't say definitely.'

Cathy could see Rolf was disappointed. 'And it could take a long time?'

Mr Dyson said, 'Quite possibly. If your father wants to go ahead with this, perhaps you'd ask him to come in and see me? In the meantime, I'll arrange to have your names changed by deed poll.'

He was scribbling the details on his pad. Looking up, he said, 'If your parents never married, then legally your mother's name isn't Gottfried?'

'No, it's Morris.'

'And she wants to change that to Godfrey?'

'Yes,' Rolf said, making the decision for her.

'Right, I'll draw up the necessary documents for you, and you'll all have to come in to sign them on oath. Bring your birth certificates and marriage lines with you. You can make an appointment with my secretary for that, let me see – in five days' time.'

Mildred was getting their midday meal ready. She'd been feeling low since the rioters had invaded their premises. It made her feel a fool that she'd done nothing to change their name, especially as Rolf was saying it was easy. If he could do it, she should have been able to. She should have been able to avoid this crisis.

But some good might come of it. Rolf also thought it would be possible for her and Otto to be married. To hear him talk of it had reawakened her old longing. To be married and legally entitled to wear her wedding ring would be a huge relief. For years, she'd gone in dread of somebody finding out and exposing her.

When Otto had first taken her into his home, she'd been so grateful to him, she hadn't been able to do enough to repay him for his kindness. She'd worked hard for him, helped him build his business up, though butchering was not really to her taste. Even now, she didn't dare think where she and Rolf would be if he hadn't come to her aid.

At first, she'd thought living with Otto a very daring thing to do, but in time, she'd come to accept it as the status quo. Otto had repaid her by treating her as his wife. He'd been faithful and kind, and everyone had assumed they were married. But she knew that wasn't the case; it had been something she and Otto had had to hide and must never talk about.

She knew Otto had hankered for marriage too. He was so much older than she was; he'd been a man of status with his own prosperous business. Years ago, he'd seemed a man of the world to her, a man who knew everything. He'd certainly known a lot more than she had, but he was a gentle person, never forceful, and now he was growing old his energy had gone. He was leaving the decisions to her. Relying on her and Rolf more and more.

Perhaps she should have insisted on them getting married years ago. Unlike Otto, she'd never seen it as impossible. He could have described himself as a bachelor; nobody would have known. It wasn't as though Irma would ever find out, or care if she did.

But Otto wanted to keep to the letter of the law and he didn't understand how things were done in this country. And she'd been a nervous wreck when Otto had taken her in and she hadn't wanted to upset him, hadn't dared to ask him for anything more.

Not that she'd needed to ask. Otto had been very generous. Of course, she'd known he was in love with her. For her, love hadn't entered into it. She'd thought herself in love with Rolf's father and look what that had done for her. She'd been too fraught to think of anything but survival, but deep affection for Otto had developed over the years despite the bad start.

The dinner was ready to dish up when Mildred heard the shop door slam and footsteps coming up the stairs. She could feel little currents of excitement running through her. It would be wonderful to be able to plan their wedding now. She'd make herself a really smart outfit and they could have a honeymoon, just like Rolf and Cathy. It would cheer Otto up, make them all feel better. He was pulling himself upright in his chair to hear the news.

Rolf and Cathy were taking their coats off on the landing. Mildred called, 'Rolf, what did the solicitor say? Can it be done?'

They came into the living room. 'The name change, yes. He's putting that in hand.'

'What about the other?' One look at Rolf's face warned her it wouldn't be as easy as she'd hoped. Mildred felt deflated.

He explained what the solicitor had said they must do before they could marry.

Otto sighed heavily. 'And how much will it cost to go to Court?'

'I didn't ask that,' Rolf said. 'I'm sorry, I should have done.'

'Yes,' Mildred flared. 'You should have.' She knew Otto would take it no further.

'Don't fret, love,' Otto pleaded.

Cathy said, 'Mr Dyson seemed to think enquiries would have to be made in Germany, but the war makes that impossible. Perhaps when it's over . . .'

Mildred burst out, 'Wait until it's over? Don't you think I've waited long enough? It's all right for you, Cathy. You've had everything legal right from the start. You don't understand what it means not to have your union blessed by the Church.'

'Mam,' Rolf was protesting. 'Don't take it out on us. We'd love to see you and Dad married.'

Cathy was biting her lip. 'We're sorry,' she said. 'Very sorry but that's how things are.'

Mildred wanted to scream with frustration. Her hopes had been raised only to be kicked down again. 'There's not much I ask for. I would like to find out if it's possible for us to be married. It might not cost all that much.'

Otto put his arm round her shoulders. 'It makes no difference what it costs. We can't afford solicitors.'

'We can, to change our name.'

'We have to – a German name will attract bad feelings while we're at war. Now the business has gone, our savings won't stretch to Court cases. I know you want to make it legal, love. I do too, but I don't think we can.'

'It's what I want,' she insisted. 'A church wedding.'

'Mam,' Rolf said gently, 'all your friends and neighbours think you're married already. How would you explain that?'

'We've been all right up to now, haven't we?' Otto said. 'We can go on the same way.'

Mildred burst into noisy sobs. Her dark eyes had a frenzied glitter. 'Does that solicitor know what he's talking about? It's thirty-five years since you saw Irma. She's hardly likely to come looking for you, is she? I never heard of anything so ridiculous.'

'Come and lie down for a little while,' Otto urged, taking her to their bedroom. 'You'll feel better if you do.'

Cathy dished up the food Mildred had prepared, but no one was very hungry. Afterwards, when she started to wash up, Rolf came in the kitchen to help. After closing the door carefully he said, 'You mustn't let Mam upset you. She feels very strongly that she should be married, you see.'

'Your dad said she was highly strung.'

'He also said it had preyed on her mind and he's right. Most of the time she seems very controlled and can think faster than the rest of us, but sometimes it gets on top of her. I shouldn't have raised her hopes as I did.'

'Rolf, you were trying to help.'

Cathy thought Mildred more than a little unreasonable.

Chapter Three

For Cathy, the early days of her marriage were racing by. She'd always hankered to be part of a family, but now she was, she longed to spend more time alone with Rolf.

Otto was a little better and pottered about the premises. His cuts had healed. They'd finished cleaning the shop and the rooms above, but the walls had been marked and some redecoration was needed; also, some of the furniture had been damaged.

Mildred was houseproud and wanted her home to look the way it used to. Rolf had no sooner offered to redecorate the living room, than his mother was scouring the town for wallpaper and paint. Cathy worked alongside him. Mildred found a shop with a few rolls of lino and they relaid that too.

'I used to be so proud of my dining table,' she mourned as they moved it back to its place. 'On Sundays, after we'd had our dinner, I used to take off the cloth and put on this runner and the aspidistra in its brass pot. A lovely polished table it was, early Victorian.'

'One of the first things I bought when your mother came to live with me,' Otto nodded.

'The rioters pushed their way in here.' Mildred shuddered. 'Tossed our things about, deliberately damaging them, bumping bookcases over to tip all the books out and throwing chests of drawers on their corners and tearing off knobs and handles.'

'They've hacked off a piece of your table,' Cathy said, running her fingers across the deep gashes in the wood. 'What a pity.'

'Ruined Otto's cleavers and my table at the same time,' Mildred said with a spurt of anger.

Otto raised his head and looked at Rolf. 'A heart-stopping moment, that was. Your mother tried to stop them. Shouted at them, called them thugs and vandals.'

'A lot more besides. It was a breach of the peace, wanton destruction . . .'

'It made them turn on her, and one of them sent her flying.'

'Mam!' Rolf was shocked. 'They could have hurt you.'

'I know. I realised that when Otto pushed himself in front of me.'

'I thought they were going to beat me up,' he said. 'But one of them shouted that I was an old man and they should leave us alone.'

'Thank goodness,' Cathy said.

'A nasty moment that,' Mildred nodded, 'and it made them really vent their hate against my table.'

'Keep the cloth on,' Otto growled. 'We don't have to look at its wounds.'

Cathy could see he was reminded of the hostility the local population had shown towards him.

'It wasn't personal, Dad,' Rolf pointed out. 'They didn't know you.'

'The table's spoiled. We'll look out for another, get something similar if we can.'

'Have you still got the piece they hacked off?' Rolf asked.

'Yes, your mam couldn't bear to throw it away.'

'Perhaps it could be glued back.'

'I can't keep the cloth on all the time,' Mildred objected, taking it right off now. 'Where else can I do my cutting out?'

She took out the pink satin she'd bought to make a nightdress for Cathy. 'I must be careful not to let it catch on the rough edge; it could pull the threads.'

'Your mam can't bear to be idle.' Otto smiled at Rolf.

'I have a whole drawerful of paper patterns,' she said, taking them out. 'Several for nightdresses. Come and choose the style you want, Cathy. I can adjust any of them to fit you.'

Fifteen minutes later Cathy watched her snipping into the new cloth, fully absorbed in the task.

After lunch, knowing she must be willing to do her share of the housework, Cathy started the washing-up. Rolf came into the kitchen, picked up a tea towel and began to dry.

'Let's go out when we've finished this,' he said. 'We could look round the secondhand shops and see if we can find Mam a table. Or we could try and find someone to mend this one.'

Cathy welcomed any opportunity to be alone with him, and set off happily, clinging to his arm. Most of the secondhand shops were clustered in Exmouth Street at the top of town, quite a walk from Market Street.

'Junk shops most of them,' Rolf said, looking in the windows at the collections of broken chairs, battered books, brass pots and old vases.

'This shop has mostly furniture.' Cathy could see several tables through the window. 'And look at this notice. It says they do French polishing and repairs.'

'It's a cut above the others.' Rolf looked up at the name over the shop window. 'McLelland's Antiques. I had a friend once whose name was McLelland. Let's go in.' He led the way.

A young man with straight brown hair swept back from his forehead came from the back of the shop.

Rolf gave a gurgle of pleasure. 'It *is* you, Danny! Hello, how are you doing?'

'Rolf! Haven't seen you in ages.' Danny clasped his hand, then gave him a hug.

'You're keeping well?'

Danny was nodding. He was taller than Rolf and had a wide smile that showed strong, even teeth.

'We're looking for a dining table for my mother,' Rolf told him. 'Oh, by the way, I'm married now. This is Cathy, my wife.' He drew her forward. 'Are you spliced yet?'

'No, you've beaten me to that.'

'Cathy was at St Mary's School in Priory Street, too.'

'I don't think I remember you.' Laughing brown eyes looked into Cathy's; honest, trustworthy eyes.

'She's three years younger than us.'

'She's a good looker,' Danny approved. 'A real dazzler. How long have you been married?'

'About a fortnight now.'

He laughed. 'Oh, you're still the bride and groom. Congratulations, Rolf.'

He led them round the shop and showed them the three dining tables he had. None were as handsome as the one that had been damaged.

'How much?' Rolf wanted to know.

Danny told them.

'A bit expensive.'

'Everything's expensive now,' Danny said. 'No new furniture's being made – so there's scarcity value too. Business has looked up since the war began. Done us a favour.'

'More than it's done for us. Ours has gone down the drain,' Rolf grimaced.

'It's a shame. Look – I heard what happened to your dad's shop. Saw a picture in the local paper, too. You've got to change your name, Rolf.'

'Don't I know it. It's in hand now.'

'After the horse has bolted?'

'Afraid so. You've got a good shop here. When did you move from Pilgrim Street?'

'Quite recently. Went up in the world with this place.'

'Danny was my best friend at school,' Rolf told Cathy.

'And for quite a few years afterwards.'

'We used to go to each other's houses to play,' Rolf went on. 'Lived in each other's pockets, didn't we? How's your mam and dad and your brothers and sisters?'

'Mam's fine now.' Danny pulled himself up straight; his smile had gone. 'There's just me and her left.'

Cathy watched Rolf's pleasure at meeting his friend fade. 'Oh Lord, Danny! Is that all? You had a terrible illness in the family, didn't you?'

'Yes, TB.'

'There were four children younger than you?'

'Yes, two brothers and two sisters. They all caught it – and our dad too.'

'That's dreadful. We lost touch then, didn't we?'

Danny's dark eyes were agonised. 'Mam and I had a few hard years.'

'We didn't lose touch exactly.' Rolf pulled a wry face at Cathy. 'Mam forbade me to go to Danny's house. "Don't you dare cross the threshold," she told me. "They've got TB there. There's no cure if you catch it. His brother's ill and his little sister's dead. You risk your life if you go there. You must have no more to do with Danny." '

'And you stayed away?' Cathy asked, disbelievingly.

'I did argue about it. I said Danny was my best friend and anyway, he hadn't got it. "Not yet," she said.'

'Actually, you'd been coming for some time when we found out what was wrong with our Grace.'

'My mam didn't trust me to stay away. She went round and asked your mam not to let me in.'

'I know. We had an awful time. Those years were terrible.' Danny was biting his lip. 'It didn't help that you were banned. I felt like one of the untouchables, but I never caught it, and neither did Mam.'

'The last I heard was Margaret, the older of your two sisters, was getting better.'

He shook his head sadly. 'She died, like the others. They were all dead within three years.'

That caused an uncomfortable pause. Then Rolf said, 'I'm glad things are looking up for you now.'

'Never had it so good,' Danny smiled. 'Come and say hello to Mam. She'll be made up to see you again.'

'Hang on – didn't we see each other in Hamilton Square the night war was declared?'

'Yes, there was a real carnival atmosphere that night, wasn't there? Fools, we were – thought it would all be over by Christmas.' Danny chuckled.

'You were dead keen to go and fight.'

'So were you.' Danny grinned at him.

'I'm surprised to find you still here.'

'Well – you're still here too. We didn't know what war was, did we? We all thought it would be a bit of a lark, a chance to get away from dull routine and see something of the world. We're a bit wiser now. I'm no longer burning to go to France.'

'Rolf is,' Cathy told him.

'No, I'm not,' Rolf denied. 'But I feel I should, instead of leaving the dirty work to others.'

'Idealistic,' Danny said to Cathy. 'He always was, not like me. I have to look after me and mine. I can't very well leave Mam to get on with the business, can I?'

'But you didn't have a business like this when I knew you.'

'Built it up since,' Danny said proudly. 'My dad worked in house clearance but he always worked for someone else.'

'You've done jolly well here.'

'Rolf, your family always had a thriving business.'

'We haven't now. The war is finishing off the food shops.'

'I used to love being invited to tea at your place. Your mother's sliced roast pork was delicious. The crackling was . . .' He kissed his fingers. 'We couldn't afford to buy it though.'

He led the way to the room behind the shop. It was fitted out with a carpet and fine furniture.

'Mam!' he shouted from the bottom of the stairs. 'Come and see who's here.'

Danny's mother came running down. She was slim and had a lot of thick brown hair like Danny's. She was in her mid-forties, and still a pretty woman. Despite the tragedy in her life she looked younger than she was.

She smiled. 'Rolf Gottfried, I'd know you anywhere. You haven't changed a bit.'

'I hope I have,' he laughed. 'Mrs McLelland, meet my wife, Cathy.'

She offered Cathy her hand to shake. 'Little Rolf married. Fancy that!'

'You've made this room look very smart.' Rolf was looking round him. 'My mother would love it.'

'I put the best of our stock here,' Danny told him. 'It's a showroom, part of the shop. We live upstairs really.'

'Danny's idea,' his mother said. 'He's taking us up to a better class of shop: we're stocking antiques these days. I'll put the kettle on, you must have a cup of tea.'

'Now that's a nice table,' Cathy said, looking round the back room.

'My mam would love that,' Rolf said. 'You can tell us the price, but I don't think we can afford it.'

Mrs McLelland brought the tea down on a tray and they sat round the table.

'I could French polish your old table, if they've scratched it,' Danny suggested. 'Put it right for you.'

'It needs more than that,' Rolf told him. 'They hacked a piece off one end. Just to spite my mam.'

'D'you still have the piece?'

'Yes, a nice plank of mahogany.'

'Perhaps I could glue it back.'

'Would you come and see if you can?'

'I'd be glad to. Let me walk back with you. You're going home now?'

'We are.'

'You'll mind the shop, won't you, Mam? I'll just collect a few things to take with me. I'll need a brace and some linen strips to hold the wood in place until the glue's dried.'

They walked back together. 'Are you sure you're not going to join up?' Rolf asked him.

'Mam's begging me to stay here. For the first time in our lives we're making a reasonable living. I'm afraid our business couldn't operate without me. I feel I'd be letting her down if I walked out on her now.'

'I'm going to volunteer soon,' Rolf said. 'I thought I'd have the shop to run, but with that gone . . .'

Danny said, 'To start with, everybody thought going to war would be a big adventure, but now we all know what it's like, there aren't so many rushing to volunteer.'

'Conscription's bound to come.'

'I've heard there may be exemptions for small businesses like ours, but even so . . .'

Otto and Mildred welcomed Danny. Mildred was quite excited to find him setting to work on her table. He tried fitting it together, filed it down in several places to make it fit better. Then he smeared glue on both sides of the join, tied the end piece in place and tightened the linen strips to keep it there.

'Don't use the table tonight, Mrs Gottfried,' he said. 'I'll be back tomorrow. It'll need some infilling here and there where there are splinters missing. The top will have to be French polished after that, but you'll hardly see this join when I've finished. I can make it look like new for you.'

'I'm very grateful,' Mildred beamed at him. 'How much do we owe you?'

'Nothing. Let's say this is for old times' sake.'

Otto said, 'You can't spend your time and not charge, lad. It's your livelihood.'

'Course I can,' Danny grinned. 'You did it for us. We owe you a lot. My mam's always saying how grateful she was for what you did for her.'

'Then I'll do the French polishing,' Rolf said. 'Can't expect you to do it all.'

'You wouldn't know where to start,' Otto scoffed.

'If you tell me what to do, I'll make as good a job of it as you.'

Danny laughed. 'He hasn't changed a bit, has he? He was always a bighead. Always thought he could do everything better than me.'

'Just some things.'

'See you tomorrow then,' Danny said, collecting his tools together. He grinned at Cathy. 'Don't let him order you about the way he did me,' he warned her jokingly. 'He can be a bit of a bully sometimes.'

'Rolf wouldn't hurt a fly,' she laughed.

When he'd gone, Otto said, 'Isn't he a pleasant lad?'

'Always has been,' Rolf agreed.

Danny McLelland walked home with a spring in his step. His own family had always looked up to the Gottfrieds. When he was young, they'd seemed to have a good business and so much more money.

In those days, he and his siblings had run around in bare feet. His mam had not been above buying him shoes and respectable clothes for school, then making him change completely when school was over for the day. She'd sent him out to play in bare feet during the summer. He'd been ashamed to go round to the Gottfrieds' like that, since Rolf always had boots.

'What's the point of it?' he'd flared at his mother. 'If I don't wear them out, I'll grow out of them.'

'They'll come in for our Sydney if they're too small for you, won't they?'

Mrs Gottfried would sometimes offer him a parcel, tied up securely with brown paper and string. 'Rolf wanted me to put some things together,' she'd say. 'Ask your mother if she can find a use for them. If she doesn't want them, you can give them to the rag and bone man.'

Danny remembered saying, 'If the rag and bone man gives me goldfish or balloons for them, I'll share with Rolf.'

But his mam was always grateful, and wanted to keep the things. Usually the parcels contained clothes Rolf had grown out of. Danny couldn't wear them because he was much the same size, or taller, but his younger brothers had fallen on them.

He could also remember Mrs Gottfried coming to ask his mother not to let Rolf into their house. 'He's my only child,' she'd said, near to tears. 'I couldn't bear it if Rolf caught TB.'

Danny had felt defeated at that time. Not that the Gottfrieds hadn't been good to his mam after that. The shop used to stay open until late on Saturday nights. They sold off most of their meat then, because it might not keep over the Sabbath. It was always busy at that time, since many customers hoped to get cheaper meat. Danny used to go with his mother to help her carry their bags home. Mr Gottfried always kept them a good roasting joint and never charged her anything.

'Your order, Mrs McLelland,' he'd say across a crowd of customers when they went in the shop. 'Hope to see you again – we'll have more of that liver you like on Wednesday.'

And Mam always had a pan of broth on the go, made with good marrowbones and scraps of meat that Otto said were too small to sell. The Gottfrieds had understood that a nourishing diet was the only hope Mam had of beating the disease. They'd been really poverty-stricken when Dad had become too ill to work. Mam had had to take in washing to bring in a little more money.

Danny had felt envious of Rolf all his childhood. It was only now he could see that every family had their ups and downs. He and Mam were up now, and the Gottfrieds had gone down.

Except that Rolf had got himself a very pretty wife. Danny had felt a terrible urge to pull one of those dark silky corkscrew curls that hung about her face – and straighten it out. But she'd have thought him a cheeky monkey to do that when he'd only just met her.

Cathy thought Danny very relaxed and at home in Mildred's house. He came several times over the next few days to work on the table, and he was showing her and Rolf how to French polish out the scratches on the other pieces of furniture.

'You're better at this than Rolf,' he joked with Cathy. 'You take more care over it, you're more meticulous.'

'Better than *me*?' Rolf pretended to be shocked.

'Danny, you've made a lovely job of my table,' Mildred told him. 'I can hardly see where all that damage was. You've learned a good trade.'

'I enjoy it.'

Cathy was pleased when Danny asked Rolf if he'd mind his shop for him so that he could attend one or two sales with his mother.

'I'll pay you the going rate,' he'd grinned. Later, he gave Rolf other work so that he might earn a little money. Cathy hoped it would be enough to keep him at home instead of volunteering for the army.

Cathy put on her hat and coat. It was an important day for the family but the joy had been taken out of it. They were going together to the solicitor's office to sign the forms he'd drawn up, and swear on oath that the information they'd given was the truth.

They'd all been wary of Mildred since she'd flared up over the bad news about Otto's remarriage. They'd been handling her with kid gloves, and were all a little nervous that she might make a scene in the solicitor's office.

They walked there in silence, Mildred holding firmly on to Otto's arm. Rolf took his other arm to help him along. Cathy followed behind, since the pavement wasn't wide enough for them all to walk abreast.

Once inside the solicitor's office, she thought both Mildred and Otto seemed intimidated by the grand surroundings. It was not a world they'd seen before. As they were led up the fine staircase, Mildred looked round, taking it all in. Cathy knew Rolf was on edge when he introduced his mother to Mr Dyson; however, she shook the hand he offered but said nothing. When it was Mildred's turn to make the oath, she did it in a whisper and signed her name where he indicated.

They none of them relaxed until they were back home. Then Rolf opened the large envelope he'd been given and spread the contents over the table.

'It's official now, Mam, our name is Godfrey.' he said. 'Just look at these. To prove it, we each have the original document we signed, as well as several copies.'

'For the bank manager,' Otto said gently. 'We have to let him know we've changed our name.'

'And the landlord: we have to change our name on the lease,' Rolf added.

His mother said slowly, 'I thought it would be a lot more trouble than that.'

'I'm right glad our Rolf took it on himself to do something about it,' Otto said. 'We'll be left in peace now, I hope.'

Mildred's mouth drooped in misery. They all knew she wanted something else. Cathy felt it as a weight; it hung over them, blighting the day.

The family were having their breakfast porridge when the morning post brought a large brown envelope addressed to Rolf in a very ornate script.

'Is it something else from that solicitor?' Mildred wanted to know.

Rolf tore it open and took out a single page of notepaper. Out fluttered a white feather.

'Glory be!' Mildred almost dropped the tea pot. 'Oh my goodness!'

Cathy felt her heart turn over as she watched the colour drain from Rolf's face. They all knew what a white feather meant.

Rolf opened up the note and read, ' "Why aren't you in uniform and fighting for your country? Isn't it time you were pulling your weight instead of gadding about having a good time? Only yellow-bellied cowards leave it to others." '

'You aren't a coward, Rolf,' Cathy said firmly. 'Nobody who knows you would ever think that.'

'Somebody does.' He was tight-lipped. 'I've got to join up, Cathy.'

His mother scooped up the feather and the note and threw them both on the fire. The bright yellow flames curled round them and the smell of burned feather was acrid in Cathy's throat.

'Don't take it to heart, lad,' Otto said. 'It's thoughtless nonsense. Who sent it anyway?'

'It wasn't signed, there was no name on it.' Rolf buttered his toast stoically.

'They haven't the decency to sign it. They don't want you to know who they are.'

Cathy examined the envelope it had come in. 'It's post-marked Liverpool. Who do you know there?'

Mildred snatched it from her and tossed that into the flames too. 'Could be anybody. Only have to go over on the ferry to post it, wouldn't they? Don't let it upset you.'

'But it has,' he said. 'People see I'm fit and healthy and twenty-two. They think I haven't the guts to go and fight, and they're right. I should be in the trenches now!'

He slammed his tea cup down on its saucer and strode to the door.

'Where are you going?' his wife and mother chorused in unison.

'Where d'you think?'

Cathy knew she must look as shocked as she felt.

'Oh Mam,' he said. 'I'm sorry. You too, love.' He gave Cathy a quick hug and dropped a kiss on her forehead. 'I'm going to volunteer. I can't put it off any longer. I feel a coward.'

'You're not,' she insisted.

'Yes, I am. I'm scared stiff of going. Denis McGrath from the grocer's on the corner – I saw his name in the paper yesterday. Killed in action.'

'Who wouldn't be scared?' Cathy said.

'I shudder every time I pass one of those posters saying *England Needs You* with the finger pointing at me. I'm letting others go, aren't I, while I'm enjoying myself with you. Not that there hasn't been trouble coming at us from everywhere.'

'Take no notice, love,' his mother said. 'You wait for Conscription, like Danny's doing. It'll be here before you can turn round. They won't be getting many volunteers now, not when we all know what it's like over there.'

'No, Mam, I must go. I've hung back long enough.'

When he'd gone, Mildred sank back in her chair and let her head fall on her hands. 'I'm so afraid for him. He means so much to me and Otto. To them he'll be just another soldier to be ordered over the top.'

Cathy was fighting tears.

'And you, dear, I know he means a lot to you too.'

They sat around waiting, restless and edgy. It was almost midday when Mildred got up to cook their usual hot dinner.

'I've left it too late,' she said, suddenly putting down the carrot she was peeling. 'It'll never be ready in time. We'll have bread and cheese now and eat our dinner tonight.'

Rolf didn't come home to share his news with them. They were left to speculate about what was happening to him. The afternoon dragged on. Cathy couldn't settle to anything. Towards teatime, she helped Mildred cook a hot dinner of stew and dumplings followed by rice pudding, but dinnertime came, the meal was ready and still there was no sign of Rolf.

'We'll wait,' Mildred decided. She was coming to the living room every ten minutes or so to consult the clock on the mantelpiece. It was six-thirty when she gave up and started dishing up.

'What can he be doing till now?' she fussed. 'Surely it doesn't take this long to volunteer and sign up.'

Cathy felt drained when at last she heard Rolf coming upstairs. He burst into the kitchen, elated and flushed.

'I've done it, Mam. Had my medical and passed A1. I'm in a yeomanry regiment.'

Cathy felt her spirits sink. This was what she'd been dreading since the war began. She choked out, 'When d'you have to leave?'

'Next Monday. There's an army camp at the Oval Sports Ground in Bebington. I'm to report there.'

'At least it's not far.'

Cathy was fighting to keep her tears under control. She could see Mildred was struggling too. 'We'll be able to see something of you if you're that close.'

'I won't be allowed home for a month. We're all confined to camp – so we can settle in.'

'What are we going to do without you?' Mildred asked.

Cathy echoed the same thought. She'd given up the job she'd had since she left school. It had taken her some time to find her feet at Halesworth Hall, but eventually she'd settled down and been happy there. The trouble was, she'd thought she'd be even happier living with Rolf. Now, it seemed, that was not to be.

Chapter Four

Cathy found the month of Rolf's initial training long and empty; it felt as though he'd been ripped from her. They wrote to each other every day. She thought he seemed quite homesick.

She didn't feel altogether comfortable about living with his parents when he wasn't there. They had always been kind to her, generous with meals and small gifts. They accorded her the same dignity she'd seen them give their customers but they asked nothing of her. That made her feel an outsider.

Before she was married, Cathy had yearned to belong to a family. She thought she could adopt Rolf's family as her own, but she hadn't grown up with them, didn't really know them, and was always on her best behaviour. She wasn't sure how to get on more comfortable terms with them. She felt she'd missed out on part of childhood's learning.

But I still need them, she wrote to Rolf. *The Home gave up contact with me when I was married.*

Mam will look after you, he wrote back. *She'll want to. Don't you worry about that.*

Cathy now realised she was only truly at ease with Rolf himself and couldn't bear to think of what the future might bring.

She knew she needed to get on better terms with her in-laws. She must make more effort, be friendlier towards them, get to know them better. She noticed at the breakfast-table that Mildred looked enviously at the letters that arrived from Rolf. They were all addressed to Cathy. She started to share them with her, when they weren't too personal. Some mornings she read out paragraphs, on others she handed some of the pages round.

Mildred spoke of him often and how acutely she was missing him. Cathy tried to comfort her, saying, 'At least he's in no danger yet.'

They both knew he soon could be and felt low and anxious. Cathy tried to keep herself occupied. She went shopping for Mildred and waited in line to buy food. She finished off the painting Rolf had left undone, and French polished more of the furniture so that the home regained its old sparkle. She could put her husband temporarily out of her mind, if she kept busy.

She'd often seen Mildred kiss Rolf when he left the house. He'd told Cathy he'd gone off that at about thirteen years of age, but it upset his mam if he made it too plain. Now Mildred began kissing her and she quite liked it. There had been no kissing at the Home, no sign of affection shown by the adults for the children.

The first time Rolf came home on a forty-eight-hour pass, they were all excited. He looked tanned but leaner.

'Are you getting enough to eat?' his mother asked.

'I'm fitter,' he told her. 'It's all the square bashing I have to do.'

Cathy said, 'You look handsome in your uniform.'

Mildred felt the cloth between her fingers. 'It's coarse, rough material.'

'It's itchy.'

'It'll keep you warm,' she said, 'when the winter weather bites.'

'It feels too hot and heavy now, but don't get me wrong, I'm proud to be wearing it.' He was a private in the Cheshire Yeomanry. 'At least nobody spits on me now as I walk past them in the street.'

'Did they do that?' Cathy was shocked.

'Disgusting,' his mother added. 'They shouldn't do such things to strangers. They don't know people's circumstances.'

'We'll try and have a good time this weekend,' he said to Cathy when they were going to bed. 'I've been looking forward so much to being home with you.'

'And when you go back, what will happen then?'

'We're being sent to Catterick for more training.'

'That's Yorkshire?'

'Yes. I'll be given a forty-eight-hour pass every alternate weekend.'

'But you'll be a long way from home.'

'Yes, but I'll come.'

'How long will your training take?'

'They're not saying. Cathy, I've done the right thing.'

'You said that about us getting married.'

'That was right too.' He beamed at her.

Rolf did come home from Yorkshire whenever he could, but the trains were crowded and no longer running to time. Travelling took up a large proportion of his leave.

'I have to come,' he whispered to Cathy when they were alone. 'Seeing you keeps me going.'

'Keeps me going too,' she confessed. She really needed him here. As soon as he returned to camp, she was crossing the days off the calendar, living for his next visit.

Mildred was always sewing. Her treadle sewing-machine stood beneath the living room window where she could catch the light. Cathy watched her, as she made the wheel buzz and the needle fly.

When Mildred bought some flannel shirting to make new shirts for Otto, Cathy offered to help her and was given some tacking to do. She made an effort to talk to Otto, who was doing little but sit by the fire these days. She told him about her years at the Orphanage. He watched her thread her needle and said, 'It's very nice for us to have you here, Cathy.'

'I've nowhere else to go.' She was blinking back the tears as she realised he was making a special effort to show friendliness and kinship. She warmed to him. 'I'm grateful you've taken me in, but I should be paying my way, finding myself a job.'

Otto cleared his throat. 'Bide your time, lass.'

'I feel I'm battening on you. Rolf will be away for a long time, possibly years.' She couldn't stop the thought jumping into her mind – *possibly for ever*.

'Tell her, Mildred. We want her to feel welcome.'

'Of course we do,' Mildred said. 'You're one of us now, part of the family. We have to look after each other.'

'I've got plenty of shirts,' Otto said. 'You should be sewing for the lass, not for me. Her trousseau was looted, wasn't it?'

Cathy said, 'I love the nightie Mildred made for me, it's beautiful, but she mustn't spend all her time sewing for mc.'

Otto's moist eyes smiled at his young daughter-in-law. 'You lost a lot more than one nightdress. Mildred likes to sew.'

'I do,' she agreed. 'Why don't we go round the market now? Do us good to get a breath of fresh air.'

Cathy was glad to be out. The market was always busy with people trying to buy the necessities of life. Mildred led her to the stalls that sold remnants of cloth, saying, 'Is there anything here you like? Not that there's much choice in remnants these days.'

'This blue silk . . .'

'I don't think it's real silk.' Mildred was opening it out, assessing the amount between hand and chin. 'Not enough for a nightie. A petticoat perhaps? We'll have it.'

'Let me pay.'

'No, I'm paying. We'll try again next week, they may have more in.'

'You're very kind doing all this for me.' Cathy felt touched.

'Who else do I have to fuss over now?'

They were both missing Rolf acutely; it made Cathy feel closer to his mother.

Mildred was cutting out again on the living-room table.

'You can help by doing the hand-sewing to finish them off,' she told Cathy.

'I can do more than that. If you're sewing for me, I'll take over the shopping and the cooking.'

Cathy began to feel more at ease in Rolf's home after that. Otto liked to talk to her, tell her anecdotes from the past about the way he and Mildred had managed to pull themselves up by thrift and hard work. Cathy filled her evenings listening to him.

On his next visit, Rolf came home looking subdued. Mildred had saved up ingredients to make tastier meals while he was home; they were finishing a supper of black pudding on his first night, when he said, 'Next time I come on leave, it will be for two whole weeks.'

Cathy gripped the edge of the table; she could guess what that meant. 'Embarkation leave?'

He nodded. 'We're going to France.'

'Oh my God!' Mildred was clutching at her throat.

'I'll be all right, you'll see. I'll volunteer to take care of the horses.'

'Will you be able to?' The hope in his mother's voice was obvious. His smile broadened but he didn't assure her that he could.

When it was time to go to bed, Cathy said, 'We should make the most of your time at home, Rolf. Do something different. Especially in this heatwave.' August had been unusually warm and sunny. 'What about a trip to New Brighton beach tomorrow? We could take a picnic lunch.'

He was all for it. 'We could take the ferry over to Liverpool and then catch the New Brighton boat. Much nicer than the bus on a hot day.'

Cathy saw the look on Mildred's face and understood how she felt, and although she would have loved to have Rolf to herself, she added, 'All of us. As a family.'

'What a good idea.' Mildred was keen now. 'Tomorrow?'

'Make a nice change,' Otto said. Even he seemed pleased at the thought of leaving his fireside chair. 'It's not as if we have to keep the shop open any more.'

'I must look for the Thermos.' Mildred was off to the kitchen. 'I think we still have that. If I can get a new loaf . . .'

But very early the next morning Cathy was awakened by hammering on their bedroom door.

'Rolf, are you awake?' Mildred was calling, her voice croaking with fear.

'Yes, Mam.'

'Get up, will you?'

'What's the matter?'

'It's your dad, he's quite strange.'

Rolf was sliding out of bed. 'How d'you mean, quite strange?'

'Come and see.'

Cathy got up too. When she saw Otto, she had a sinking feeling that something had gone terribly wrong. He was looking at them with a puzzled expression on his face as though he didn't know who they were. His voice sounded queer – they couldn't understand what he was trying to say. Rolf tried to persuade him to get back into bed, but he wanted to get dressed.

'No,' Mildred was telling him. 'You need to rest, you should be in bed.' As he was resisting that, she found his slippers and wrapped him in one of her shawls.

'Run for Polly Weaver, will you, dear?' Mildred asked Cathy. 'She'll be up – they have to open the shop on Saturdays.'

When Cathy rang next door's bell, Mrs Weaver came to answer it, her mouth full of toast. 'I'll come back with you now,' she said.

Mildred had got Otto to his armchair in the living room, with the eiderdown across his knees. He was trying to tell them something.

Cathy caught one word of his speech. 'He says he feels chilly.'

'His hands are frozen,' Mildred said. 'Feel them.'

Cathy could see them trembling too.

'Should I light the fire?' Rolf wanted to know.

'Looks like a stroke,' Polly gulped. 'I hope I'm wrong, but . . .'

'Oh my God!' Mildred's face went as white as flour.

'When my father had his stroke, he went like this. You'd better send for the doctor, Mildred.'

'I'll go round for him now,' Cathy said. 'I know where he lives.'

She wanted to make herself useful and knew Mildred needed Rolf with her. Cathy was worried about Otto, anxious about how she and Mildred would cope when Rolf went back.

When she returned, Mildred was helping Otto to drink a cup of tea. Rolf had lit the fire, even though it was hot outside. Mildred went to make breakfast as usual but for once she looked distracted. Otto would eat nothing. Rolf and his mother were questioning him, but it wasn't easy to understand his replies.

The doctor didn't come until his morning surgery was over; by then they were all very worried.

'Yes, he's had a stroke,' he confirmed, after he'd examined Otto.

Mildred looked shaken. It sounded ominous to Cathy. 'What's that, exactly?'

'A clot in the arteries on one side of the brain. You see his mouth has dropped a little on this side?'

They all watched horrified as the doctor checked how much strength Otto had left in his limbs. 'It's possibly not a major episode.'

'Will he get better?' Rolf wanted to know. 'Recover his speech?'

'Most people do. They can sometimes recover as much as ninety per cent of their strength – unless they have another stroke, of course. There's always the danger of that.'

Cathy saw Rolf shudder. 'What's caused it?' he asked. She knew he was afraid he'd brought it on. They were all dreading him being sent to France.

'Who's to say? Your father's no longer a young man.'

That afternoon, Mildred pushed her and Rolf out. 'Go to New Brighton on your own,' she told them. 'I'll sit with Otto. He'll need looking after now.'

Cathy felt terrible, because last night it was what she'd wanted, to be on their own. It was pleasant to sit in the sun and watch the children enjoying donkey rides, but Rolf was worried about Otto, and in a sombre mood.

When Rolf had to return to camp, Cathy was filled with foreboding and knew his mother was too. Otto was a big man and they didn't have the strength to lift him about in the way Rolf could. Fortunately, he already seemed slightly better and was able to help himself a little.

The following week, Rolf's letters were full of woe. All the upset he'd felt on learning that Otto wasn't his father surfaced again. He was guilt-ridden because he'd left Cathy and his mother to look after him, and sure his imminent departure for France must have added to the distress Otto was feeling.

Cathy passed her empty days walking Otto round the flat. 'It's to keep your legs going,' Mildred told him. 'You must keep moving.' The doctor had advised that.

'Out,' he said. 'Out for walk.'

It was another pleasant sunny day, but Mildred whispered to Cathy that she was afraid if they got him downstairs they wouldn't be able to get him up again.

'Better if you stay indoors until you're stronger,' she told him.

The evening Rolf came home on embarkation leave, he sat talking to Otto for an hour.

'You're getting better, Dad. Cathy wrote and told me your speech was clearer.' It still sounded queer but at least they could communicate again.

Rolf announced over tea, 'Cathy hasn't exactly had a great time since I married her, so I want to take her away for two or three nights. Then we'll come back and spend most of my leave here with you.'

Cathy's heart lifted at the prospect. 'Where will we go?'

'Not too far. What about Chester? Or would you rather go to Southport?'

'Either would be lovely. I just want to be with you.'

'Chester then. There'll be lots to do there even if the weather turns bad.' Autumn had brought rain.

Cathy was determined to enjoy every minute of his leave but she couldn't shake off her dread of the future. The days were fleeting past, far too quickly for comfort.

When the day came on which he had to return to camp, the family ate an early breakfast of porridge in near silence. They'd said their farewells over the previous day. Rolf stood up and brought his kitbag into the living room.

'Goodbye, Dad.'

'Take care of yourself, son.'

Rolf hugged him quickly and turned to his mother. 'Goodbye.'

'Just make sure you come back to us.' She was blinking hard.

Cathy went to Woodside Station with him to see him off. She found it a very emotional parting, and wanting to be alone for a little while, she walked back to Market Street. When she got there she found Otto alone looking woebegone. She made a pot of tea for them and they both had a little weep.

Cathy knew Mildred must be feeling just as bad as she was. She came home white-faced and looking drawn.

'Rolf got away all right?' she asked pointlessly.

Cathy could do no more than nod.

'Lamb chops for dinner today,' she told them. 'I had to stand in line for half an hour to get them and they cost the earth, but we all need a treat.'

Cathy knew the only treat she wanted was to have Rolf back. Otto tried to push two half-crowns into her hand. 'Go round the market. Buy yourself – something – a dress-length,' he told her haltingly.

She didn't want to take his money, and she could see by Mildred's face that she thought he was being too generous. 'You give me more than enough already, Otto. You're having to keep me.'

'Go on,' he said. 'Give you – something to do. Take your mind off – Rolf. Go out and choose – something nice.'

'Depends if there *is* anything.' Mildred sounded rather acid. 'Dress-lengths are not so easy to come by now.'

'I'll get something to eat if I can. Eggs?'

'Bacon too, or sausage,' Mildred added. 'Anything that's there.'

Cathy washed her face and pulled herself together before going out. Crowds thronged the market, though there was noticeably less to buy now than there had been in May when she first came to live here. The stall from which she'd previously bought eggs and cheese had closed down.

She was turning away, when a woman examining crockery at the next stall caught her eye.

'Botty? Fancy seeing you!'

'Cathy, how are you? We've been wondering how you were getting on.'

It was Harriet Bott, the housekeeper at Halesworth Hall where Cathy had worked until her marriage. Because of the status of her job, the housekeeper should have been called Mrs Bott, but the staff there prided themselves on being friendly and had given her the pet name of Botty.

Her iron-grey hair was looped against her cheeks to hide the scar which ran down one side of her face, before being taken into a bun in the nape of her neck. Her plain, no-nonsense straw hat made her look rather demure.

'I'm all right,' Cathy said, although in reality she felt low.

'And your new husband? How's married life?'

Cathy felt her lip quiver as she told her she'd just seen Rolf off after his embarkation leave.

'You poor thing.' Botty gave her a hug, but sympathy was the last thing Cathy felt she could cope with. Her tears were perilously close.

Mrs Bott was nearing retirement age. She always wore black and dressed in a style that had been fashionable twenty years earlier. That made her look older still – but Cathy had found her the very opposite of the authoritarian Superintendent and her helpers at her Orphanage. Botty had always treated her with the utmost kindness.

Botty said now, 'The place hasn't been the same since you went. We've missed you, especially me. I've had to work twice as hard.'

'But you hired a cook to take my place.' She'd started a couple of days before Cathy had left. 'I explained everything to her, told her what Major Fleming liked to eat and left her some recipes.'

'She didn't stay. Nor did the next woman we tried. You see, they can earn more in the munitions factories these days. I advertise from time to time, but nobody wants a job in domestic service any more.'

'I do,' Cathy said. It seemed such a good idea, she couldn't understand why she hadn't thought of it before. She'd been happy at Halesworth.

'D'you mean you want to come back?' Botty's eyes beamed at her, full of goodwill.

'Yes, if you'll have me.'

'Of course! We'll all be delighted to have you back. In fact, I was wondering whether I should call and see if you knew somebody who'd come.'

Mrs Bott had family who lived not far away in Cooper's Yard. She always came into town when she had time off.

'How's Major Fleming?'

'No better but no worse, unless he's a little weaker. Life goes on for us all.'

The major was elderly and very disabled by a disunited fracture in his right leg. His femur had been shattered by a bullet during the Boer War, and the highest ranking surgeons in the medical profession had been unable to knit the pieces together. Rheumatism and gout added to his discomfort. He'd had difficulty in walking since, and these days the duties of Jackson, his valet, were more those of a nurse.

They stood talking by the stall. Cathy was keen to catch up with what had happened at Halesworth since she'd left.

'Come home with me and say hello to my in-laws,' she said. 'I want to tell them I can have my old job back. They're very sweet and generous, but I can't let them keep me. They aren't that well-off.'

Cathy knew Mildred would welcome Mrs Bott with a cup of tea; she offered one to all callers. 'But you know them already, don't you?'

'I have met them,' she murmured.

Every year the Orphanage had sent a report form for the housekeeper to fill in, regarding what they called Catherine Tanner's progress. When Cathy had told her she wanted to get engaged to Rolf Gottfried, Botty had asked to meet him and his family. She'd asked a lot of questions about them and over the years had visited more than once.

Afterwards, Cathy had asked her, 'Do you approve of him? D'you think Rolf will make a good husband for me?'

Mrs Bott had smiled. 'I don't really know. He comes from a respectable family, and if it's what you want . . . Though I do wish you were a little older. Nineteen is so very young to get married.'

Mildred remembered the housekeeper and welcomed her warmly. 'There has been a great change in our circumstances since you were last here. My son has gone off to fight in France, and poor Otto hasn't been well.'

Cathy went to the kitchen to get the cups and saucers. She could hear them talking.

Mrs Bott said, 'I was very shocked when I read about vandals overrunning your home and business. They went wild that day. I do wish they'd stopped to think about what they were doing.'

'I can't tell you what I felt.' Mildred was choking.

When Cathy returned with the tea pot, she could see Botty's eyes were full of sympathy. 'You must have been terrified. I thought of Cathy coming home from her honeymoon to that and my heart went out to you all. I knew, of course, that you did not have German sympathies, and that you and she were as English as the rest of us.'

Cathy could see Mildred was touched by her understanding.

Mrs Bott said, 'I've told Cathy we would all be delighted if she came back to work at Halesworth. When we're left in the lurch, I have to do the cooking as well as my own work. It's almost impossible to get staff these days.'

'Don't you have to speak to the major first?' Mildred asked.

'No. He told me to find a cook for him, but I can't find one who'll stay. He knows Cathy – she worked for him for five years and gave satisfaction. I'd like to take her back with me now.'

'I'd like to go,' Cathy added, 'if you don't need my help with Otto.'

'No, he's so much better. Slow to move, but he can get around by himself now.'

'I can't sponge on you for ever.'

'You aren't sponging,' Otto said. 'I don't like to think of you going.'

Mrs Bott put in, 'It's only to Oxton, a tram-ride away. She's not going far.'

'Rolf would want you to stay,' Mildred told Cathy. 'We do like having you. You cheer us up.'

'Like the daughter – we never had,' Otto added from his seat by the fire.

'But I need to work. Rolf and I, we'll need money to set up home when the war's over. And it will fill my day so I don't miss him so much. Here in his home, everything reminds me of him.'

'But you want that? You want to stay close to him?'

'Of course, but it's painful too, knowing where he is.'

'She'll be all right at Halesworth where she's kept busy,' Mrs Bott said. 'I know. My husband was a soldier, and when his regiment was sent to India I was very fearful for his safety. There was the climate and I was always hearing of native uprisings. Having work does help.'

'I thought you said . . .'

'Yes, I've been a widow for years. I was right to be worried, since my husband was killed on the North-West Frontier. When that happened, I had to find some way of supporting myself and my two sons. As I said, being busy helped.'

Cathy could feel a tight ball of dread in her throat. Botty's words had driven home the fact that Rolf's position was dire. That men had always gone off to fight wars and mostly they lost their lives doing it.

She went to pack her suitcase. When she came back with it, Mildred said, 'Mrs Bott has written the address down for me. I'll redirect Rolf's letters to you until you can tell him where you are. Ask him to write to me too, won't you? I'll want news of him.'

'I will,' Cathy promised as she kissed her and Otto goodbye. 'I'll come and see you when I have a day off. We can bring each other up to date with the news.'

'Come in time to have your dinner with us,' Otto told her.

Mildred was glad when they went. It had been an effort to talk to that woman, Mrs Bott. She went to her bedroom and lay down on her bed, feeling shattered. It had been a most awful day.

This morning, she'd hardly known what to do with herself. To see Rolf leaving for the station on his way to France had unnerved her. She couldn't remember when she'd felt so agitated, so afraid that she'd never see him again.

She'd washed up the breakfast dishes in a frenzy. She had to go out, get away from Otto and her home. The fact that Rolf had wanted to say goodbye to her and Otto here, yet take Cathy to the station for a last private farewell had felt like a knife cutting into her side.

She'd done her best to make a friend of Cathy, but the feeling that she'd been ousted from Rolf's affections wouldn't go away. It was like a weeping sore inside her. Mildred had never loved Rolf more, but she was no longer the person he loved most; the thought was making her feel sick.

She felt jittery and cold inside. She hadn't felt this bad since she'd been a girl and expecting Rolf; dreading the time when her pregnancy would become noticeable and she'd lose her job. She'd had nowhere to go and not much money and had felt she was looking disaster in the face.

That same feeling was with her now; she was afraid she'd never see Rolf again. He'd gone off to the trenches and they all knew how many were being killed in the fighting. Mildred had that cold certainty in her stomach that Rolf would meet his end there.

She'd wandered round the market looking at nothing and seeing less, but she'd needed to buy something for their dinner. She saw a long line of waiting housewives by a butcher's stall and was told he had meat. She stood in line too, glad to be doing something definite.

Lying on her bed and closing her eyes, she began to feel better. It helped that Cathy had gone. It was one thing having her here with Rolf and quite another having her on her own. And the girl was right, there was no reason why she should sponge on her and Otto. They'd had to retire sooner than they'd intended and wouldn't have much to spare. Cathy was young and healthy; for her to go back to her old job was the best thing for all of them. Since the war, married women had had to work – there was nothing wrong with that. Mildred had had to work all her life.

Mrs Bott was nice enough. Mildred couldn't help but notice how Cathy had responded to her. She'd spoken of her many times in the past, and said how kind she was. It was good that her daughter-in-law had other friends: she didn't need to lean on her and Otto.

Chapter Five

For Cathy, returning to Halesworth Hall made her remember her roots. The day she'd first been taken there by one of the Orphanage staff would always be engraved on her mind. She'd been fourteen and very nervous – in fact, downright afraid of leaving the Home. It was all she'd ever known.

She couldn't say she'd been happy there, but she'd learned to survive. The rules were strict and woe betide any child found breaking them. Silence was golden, no chattering allowed except in play areas, and punctuality meant being ready five minutes early. She'd seen girls whipped for being late back from school. The Superintendent had believed in the maxim 'spare the rod and ruin the child'.

Cathy had been careful never to break a rule except when she was reasonably sure she wouldn't be found out. Like all the other girls, she'd been forced to conform: it was the only way to survive.

They were all trained to be domestic servants, hard-working, obedient and knowing their place in life. Every minute of every day was filled with some activity. Even as a very young child, there had been bedmaking and tidying before breakfast. The Home must shine and the children be spotless at all times. Cleanliness was next to Godliness in importance. There were prayers in the Home morning and evening, and on Sundays they went to church twice, as well as to Sunday School.

Cathy had been there since her birth, though other girls came and went. As a young child, she'd been told, as most of the other girls were, that both her parents were in Heaven, but some had visits from their families. Others were taken out on trips. All of them dreamed of the time when a mother or a grandmother, an aunt or an uncle would come and take them away for good.

Like many of the girls, Cathy had never had any contact with her family, but she'd been quite certain that somebody would come and claim her one day. Every year on her birthday, she received a present addressed to her personally, and she believed it came from a family member. There was never a card or a message, but Cathy had received soft toys, teddy bears, dolls, games and books which were the envy of the other girls in the Home. She really believed she was loved and cared for by somebody who would come back and claim her, and they'd live happily together in their own small house. She'd never given up hope.

On her last birthday, she'd gone to the Superintendent's office to ask if she might write to thank the person sending the gifts. She'd hoped to get her family's address.

'You may write a note and say how pleased you are with the book but I will post it on for you in the usual way.'

'But p-please,' Cathy had stammered, 'I-I'd like to know who this person is. If it's m-my mother . . .'

'It isn't, Cathy. The person is a well-wisher who prefers to remain anonymous. Someone who thinks of you.'

Cathy didn't believe her though she knew all about well-wishers. They came in fur coats and pearls at Christmas and brought a parcel for each of them. They paid for Punch and Judy shows and the magician and could be picked out at church services on Sundays.

The Home was in a handsome Georgian building, much of which was out of bounds to the girls. It had a beautiful garden, but they weren't allowed to play in it; there was a concrete playground for that.

Cathy had one close friend who had risen with her from the baby group to the senior girls, one confidante who'd made it all bearable, and her name was Lily Payne.

During their last year, the girls took over the cleaning and cooking in the Orphanage, as it provided a sound training for domestic service. Their first placements were found for them and they were sent off in strict age order as jobs became available.

When Lily, who was six weeks older than Cathy, was given her placement, she was told her employer had asked for two girls and that Jean Brown would be going with her.

Cathy and Lily were both angry and tearful. They'd been good friends through all their years at the Orphanage and wanted to stay together now. It would make all the difference to the way they'd be able to settle down. They went together to ask the Superintendent if Cathy could go instead of Jean.

'No,' she was told. 'Work placement is given in strict age order and Jean must go first because she's a fortnight older than you, Cathy. You will get your placement soon.'

She'd felt bereft without Lily but had heard within the fortnight that she'd be going to Halesworth Hall. The morning she was leaving, she'd received a letter from Lily, saying she hated her job, and that Jean was talking of running away.

They'd been sent to a Liverpool boarding-house and were kept on the go from morning to night. Their employer was more ferocious than the Superintendent at the Home, and she found fault with everything they did. They had their meals when the boarding-house guests had already been served and there was never much left for them. They were always hungry.

Cathy was sorry for Lily and worried about her, but the letter left her quaking and expecting to find herself in a similar situation.

She remembered her first meeting with Mrs Bott. She had striking dark eyes, and Cathy thought there was an intensity about her gaze when it rested on her. Her back was ramrod straight and she didn't look very different to the women who ran the Home.

'A cup of tea,' she'd offered her escort. 'And we'll have a little chat.'

Cathy knew the chat would be about her. That Mrs Bott would sign papers agreeing to supervise Cathy's care until she either married or reached the age of twenty-one. Cathy was afraid she'd be exchanging one tyrant for another.

When Mrs Bott had turned back to her, she'd noticed the scar down the side of her face which she was trying to hide under her hair. It was faded to a silvery streak but still spoke of violence. Yet her manner was at odds with that; she was prim and proper and her expression was benign, even kindly.

'Come and meet Lizzie, our parlourmaid. You'll be sharing a bedroom with her. Take Cathy up, Lizzie, and show her where she'll sleep. Help her unpack. Look after her, show her where things are and introduce her to the others.'

That had sounded friendly enough. Lizzie was only a few years older than Cathy and quite bubbly. She said she'd worked here for years and Botty was all right but fussy about the dusting.

'D'you call her Botty to her face?'

'Yes, everybody does.'

Cathy was reassured when Lizzie said she was as happy here as she could be in a place of work.

Half an hour later, Cathy found herself sitting at the kitchen table between Lizzie and the very ample Mrs Arrowe, the cook, with a cup of tea in front of her. Big cake tins were being passed round from which they all chose a slice. Cathy had never tasted such wonderful chocolate cake.

She was to be the tweeny, spending her mornings cleaning with Lizzie, and her afternoons and evenings helping the cook. She'd been given plenty of work to do but she'd expected that. Of course, there was a bigger staff then, but more work to do. Major Fleming's mother and her sister lived there too. On Sunday mornings, Mrs Bott in a big black hat with feathers in it, with her prayer and hymn books held piously to her chest, took Lizzie to church; on Sunday evenings, Mrs Arrowe took her.

At mealtimes when they were all round the table, the staff asked her questions about the Orphanage. 'You all went to church morning and evening on Sundays?'

'Yes, and Sunday School in the afternoons as well.'

'Goodness,' Lizzie said. 'Couldn't you sneak off somewhere else?'

'No, we'd have been missed and punished for it.'

'Punished how?'

'We'd get no playtime and be given bread and water instead of supper for a week, with a good beating as well.'

'Good Lord! What sort of a beating?'

'A cane across our bare legs.'

The questions went on. Had she been taken out shopping, or on trips to the seaside? What sort of uniform had she worn? That it was usually secondhand, they expected. What had they given her to eat?

Jackson, the major's valet, had been shocked at the unchanging weekly cycle, the paucity of the food and the fact that the older girls did the cooking.

'You poor thing,' Lizzie said. 'It sounds a terrible place. What happened to your family that they couldn't look after you?'

'I was told my parents were dead and I had no family, but . . .' She told them about the gift she'd received on her birthday every year. 'It's always intrigued me. Somebody must be thinking of me but I don't know who.'

Mrs Bott's eyes looked at her with their hot intensity. 'Somebody cares about you,' she said. 'That's proof.'

Cathy felt she got on well with the staff. There had been less regimentation in her life at Halesworth and fewer strict orders to obey. Provided she did the work expected of her, which was no more and no less than the others had to do, she'd been treated fairly and kindly and had been able to relax.

Going back at Halesworth Hall seemed almost like going home. Today, Cathy found nothing had changed in the vast Halesworth kitchen since she'd left; everything was comfortingly familiar. That struck her as odd when so much had happened to *her*. Botty had to bustle round to get the evening meal ready. It was known as high tea in the kitchen, but called supper by the major.

Jackson was there setting a tray with the cut-glass tumbler and a carafe of water ready for the major's evening whisky.

'You're coming back?' he greeted Cathy. 'That's champion. I'm very glad to see you. Now perhaps I'll be properly fed.'

'You have been properly fed!' Botty rounded on him. 'Only have to look at you to see that.'

Jackson had plump cheeks and sparse mouse-brown hair with no sign of grey. He was short and as a young man had been of slight build. His legs were bandy – due, he said, to having had rickets when he was a child and not having enough to eat. It had given him an enduring preoccupation with food. He'd told Cathy that good cooking and heaped plates were his prime interest in life. It was beginning to show in his pot belly and disappearing waistline.

'You're a glutton,' Botty told him.

Cathy set up the mahogany trolley for the major, while Botty warmed some soup and set out a baked egg custard to follow.

The major had a suite of rooms on the ground floor, and because he couldn't walk he used a bath-chair made of basketwork to get around. When Cathy pushed the trolley in she found that Jackson, who was never far from him, had told him she was back.

'I'm delighted to see you, very pleased to have you back,' the major said warmly. 'You know what I like to eat, and what you cook suits me. The two women we tried weren't half as good as you.'

The poor man was thin to the point of emaciation and seemed incredibly old to Cathy. She could remember when he'd been stout but now his flesh hung off him in flaccid folds. She thought he was beginning to resemble a tortoise; his head was almost devoid of hair, his neck stringy, his eyes were heavily lidded and his skin brown and scaly.

However, his mind was still as sharp as it had ever been. He remembered everything and read two daily newspapers to keep abreast of current events. He used to have regular visits from an old friend who brought him books to read, and once a week three old gentlemen used to arrive together so they could enjoy a game of bridge. But Jackson had told her his social life was virtually over now.

Seeing him again made Cathy pray every night that Rolf would not be wounded in a way that would render him an invalid for the rest of his life.

When Rolf received her letter telling him she'd returned to Halesworth, he wasn't pleased. He said he was sure she'd have been better off staying with his parents. He didn't like to think of her having to work hard and couldn't understand how she could say she was happy at Halesworth.

He wrote: *You're living amongst the elderly and very elderly. What can you have in common with them? What pleasure do you find there? Do you get time to go out?*

You know I do, she wrote back. *I always go out on my day off. Didn't I come to Market Street to see you before we were married? The only difference now is that you're no longer there. Instead we talk about you.*

In his next letter he said, *But you'll sit round the table talking to Mam and Dad – more old people. Don't you want to be with people of our own age?*

The Orphanage was full of them, she wrote again, *and I was glad to get away from there.*

She tried to explain what Halesworth meant to her. *When I first came here as a tweeny, I was by far the youngest, but there were many more staff. The cook was called Mrs Arrowe. She had a heart-attack in the middle of a dinner party because Major Fleming sent the beef back saying it was tough. He was very upset because he thought he'd caused it and was kind to her afterwards. Poor Mrs Arrowe, she survived but couldn't leave her room in the attic for a long time. It was my job to look after her, take her food up and make her comfortable.*

We had a parlourmaid called Lizzie. I liked her, but she refused to do any cooking. She went to a munitions factory at the beginning of the war.

The cooking sort of came down on me. Mrs Arrowe would explain what I must do. If I got in a fix, I'd rush upstairs with a cup of tea and ask her to explain over again. She taught me a lot. I missed her when she went to live with her sister in Ormskirk.

The major used to do a bit of entertaining when I was first there, but gradually less and less. Then he wanted his dinner served at lunchtime, followed by a light supper in the evening. He found that better for his digestion.

I don't think there was ever a Mrs Fleming; he was an army man. Jackson, his valet, used to be his batman and has always looked after him. He's devoted to him. I like Jackson, though he teases me. His name is Jackson Jackson, his given name identical with his family name: what a strange thing for parents to do. Nowadays, he's the next youngest after me. He's fifty-four!

Rolf wrote back: *He'll soon be an old man too, Cathy!*

Cathy was fond of the staff at Halesworth and felt she'd grown up with them. She tried to explain her feelings.

Jackson is kindly, they all are. They're very caring, but if there's a needle to be threaded, then I'm asked to do it, as my eyes can see more easily. Same if something needs fetching from upstairs: my legs are younger. I've always felt needed there, especially when Mrs Arrowe collapsed. They said they couldn't have managed without me.

They're like my family in a way. We are three for most meals in the kitchen, four at lunchtime. George the gardener has that with us. He has a cottage in the village and is over seventy now. He's always complaining of his rheumatics. The young gardeners volunteered at the outbreak of war. Once there were three of them as well as a man to look after the horses.

There's only one horse left now and George looks after him and puts him in the governess cart when the major wants to go for a drive. But he hasn't wanted to for this last year. They think it's too much of an effort for him to get into it. Nowadays, he'd rather stay at home.

They all look after me. They gave me advice about not letting my admirer – meaning you – take any liberties before you put a ring on my finger. I told them I didn't need to as you'd never tried, but their opinion of youth is as bad as yours of the aged.

Rolf wrote asking about the major.

I don't think he minds that the house isn't kept to the standard it used to be. He knows there's only half the staff, and he doesn't want to do all the things he used to. He's kindly too but gets a bit impatient when he doesn't feel well, which is pretty often now.

Rolf wrote back, *At ninety-two, I'm not surprised!*

Cathy settled back quickly into her old routine, except that the newspapers brought a new dread. She eyed them nervously when Jackson brought them from the major's room for the staff to read. These days, there was always a long list of names inside an ominous black border. She was afraid that she'd see the name of Private Ralph Godfrey listed there.

'It's all right, love, I'll check first thing in the morning for you,' Jackson told her. It was his job to collect the newspapers from the doormat in the hall and take them to the major.

'Not in,' he'd say cheerily when he came down to the kitchen to eat his breakfast. Soon he was telling her that the major was checking on her husband, too. In the evening, when Jackson cleared the newspapers from the major's rooms, Cathy couldn't help but check again to make sure.

She was finding it more difficult to buy the household supplies she needed. Previously, local shop-owners had called to take her order, vying for the trade. Now food was in short supply, they no longer bothered. If she was unable to buy enough eggs and bacon for them all to enjoy the usual breakfast, the major was served with his and the staff took turns to do without.

Within a month of resuming work, Cathy began to suspect that she might be pregnant.

To be expecting a baby felt momentous. Cathy decided to say nothing at Halesworth just yet. She'd led the major and Botty to believe she'd go on working indefinitely.

She wrote and told Rolf straight away. They'd talked about parenthood before they were married and he'd said, 'This war makes everything so uncertain. It's not a good time to bring a child into the world and I don't see how I can support a family. Even if I join up, the wages of a fighting man are anything but generous.' She'd seen him shudder. 'We none of us know what'll happen.'

Cathy knew what he meant. He was afraid he'd be killed in the trenches and she'd be left with children to bring up on her own.

'It would ruin your chance of finding someone else,' he'd said. 'Who would want to bring up another man's children?'

'I wouldn't want anybody else,' Cathy assured him.

'Then you'd have a hard life. A year or so ago, Mam was doing a lot in the shop and I suggested she found a washerwoman; she turned out to be a widow with a family to support. She came once a week to do our washing, and I know how hard she worked and how little she earned. I wouldn't want to inflict a life like that on you.'

'If it happens, it happens,' Cathy had said.

He'd remained silent, looking very serious. 'You're sure?'

'I'm quite sure, Rolf.'

And now it had happened. She knew his mother had advised him not to get married until the war was over, and it was one of the few times he'd gone against her advice.

Cathy was given Wednesday as a regular day off, which she considered generous. Before the war they'd had only a half-day each week, with a whole day once a month. She was happy with Wednesday because it was market day in Birkenhead and if she stood in line, she could often buy a few eggs or a little meat for Mildred.

By the time the following Wednesday came round Cathy was almost certain there *was* a baby on the way. She was excited at the thought of telling Otto and Mildred.

It was becoming routine for her to cook breakfast at the Hall on her day off just as she usually did. She also went to see the major to discuss what he would like for dinner and supper that day.

As usual, he was sitting up in his huge bed with the breakfast tray she'd set bridging his legs, the morning paper folded beside him. He always ate his breakfast in bed.

'It's not so much what I'd like,' he told her, 'as what you've been able to get.'

'I've got a nice bit of calf's liver,' she said. 'You'd like it braised for dinner?'

Cathy knew he liked soft mushy meals like stews, cottage pie and broth, because his teeth were reduced to a few broken stubs. He had false ones that he put in when visitors were announced, but he said they were uncomfortable and he couldn't use them to eat. She prepared as much of the meals as she could before leaving, so Mrs Bott would not have too much extra work to do.

It was just after midday when Cathy got off the bus and walked up Market Street. Now that no business was being carried on in the premises, Mildred had painted the inside of the shop window with whitewash so people couldn't see in. There were many such shops in the town.

She rang the doorbell, and after a long wait Otto came down to let her in. It took him ages to get back up again. He was much better, but Mildred said she was afraid he'd never be the man he had been. She was cooking in the kitchen. She came to the door to kiss Cathy.

'I couldn't get any fresh meat for dinner,' she said, shaking her head. 'I stood in line but it had all been sold before it was my turn. I've done bacon and sausage in the oven, I'll put some eggs in now you're here. How does it feel to be back at work?'

'Fine,' Cathy said. She felt excited. 'I've got some news for you.'

Mildred turned from the stove. 'About our Rolf?'

'No, about me.' She looked from one to the other. Mildred was hanging on her words. 'I think I'm having a baby. Almost certain.'

Mildred beamed at her. 'Oh Cathy! I'm so pleased, a grandchild!' She hugged her. 'That's marvellous, isn't it, Otto?'

He was hugging Cathy too. 'Such good news – I'm delighted.'

The dinner was forgotten in the pleasure of the moment. Cathy assured them she was delighted too and in a way she was. A child would be of Rolf's flesh and blood, something to remember him by whatever befell him.

'I'm thrilled.' Mildred was ecstatic. 'I can tell you now, can't I, that I was hoping for this. Rolf's child, our first grandchild. What could be more exciting?'

When she received Rolf's reply, however, it seemed to Cathy that he was quite shocked to hear about the coming baby. *You know it isn't what I'd have chosen for you,* he wrote. *All that advice I heard from my mates about it being safe if I withdrew before the end doesn't seem to be true, does it? Mam will look after you, though I ought to be there to do it myself. I wish I could be. She'll be delighted, but I'm not sure we've done the right thing.*

Jackson heard the major's bell tinkle; it sounded a long way away. He was fuddled with sleep but knew he'd have to get up. It rang again.

'I'm coming, Major!' He sat up and lit his candle, pushed his feet into slippers and pulled a jacket on over his nightshirt.

The major would have used his bottle and want him to take it away. It happened every night, sometimes twice. But the major was moving restlessly about his bed. 'The commode,' he said. 'Help me out.'

Jackson knew he ought to be used to this too, but it wasn't easy to wake up from a deep sleep and find the strength to manhandle the major about. He pulled the commode nearer, opened the lid and then turned back to the bed.

'Ready, Major?' It took a huge effort, for the old man could do little to help himself. Everybody said he was nothing but skin and bone, but they wouldn't if they had to lift him.

Jackson got him on and draped his dressing-gown round him so he wouldn't get cold. He turned to pull the sheets straight on his bed. 'Anything else, while I'm up?'

He'd probably ask for some hot milk whether he wanted it or not, in order to have a few minutes' privacy.

'Some hot milk, please. Put a little whisky in it.'

Jackson lit another candle and headed towards the kitchen. On the way through the major's sitting room, he helped himself to one of his Black Russian cigarettes. The old man didn't smoke much these days and his supply was holding up.

It was warmer in the kitchen. Before going to bed they banked up the fire in the range, so he could warm milk on it in the night and it would be quicker to get the fire going in the morning. While he was at it, Jackson decided to make himself a hot drink, too. He set the saucepan of milk on the trivet and sat down to enjoy his smoke.

Life at Halesworth was not as interesting as it used to be. Jackson could rarely go out, except for an evening stroll down to the Horse and Hounds, the nearest pub, after he'd settled the old man for the night.

62

The major had few visitors these days. Occasionally the doctor called, or Mrs Tynwald, his nearest relative. She was his heir, though only a distant cousin, and called round at Christmas and on his birthdays to take afternoon tea with him.

The vicar called in once a month, and the major always gave half a guinea for the church funds. This was put out on a little table by the door, before the vicar arrived. Jackson was instructed to hand it to him as he was showing him out. The vicar liked to conclude his visits with a prayer and a blessing and leave the major at peace.

Jackson waited outside the drawing-room door, except on the occasions when the vicar was giving Holy Communion, then he and Mrs Bott and any other staff who wished would be invited to partake with him.

Jackson smiled to himself. Nothing could be easier than exchanging the half-guinea for half a crown once the vicar had arrived. The major's attention was distracted by then.

Jackson always adopted a solemn voice, loud enough for the old man to hear, as he slid it into the vicar's hand. 'Sir, a contribution from the major to the church funds.'

The vicar always glanced back at the bowed head. 'The major will be blessed for his generosity,' he'd murmur, as he followed Jackson to the front door.

Jackson thought half a guinea over-generous for the church fund. It provided more than enough for Jackson to enjoy a regular glass of beer at the Horse and Hounds.

The old major was in a pitiful state now. Hard to believe he'd had a back as straight as a ramrod when they'd been in South Africa, but that was in the time of the Boer War, many years ago. He'd been in his prime then, giving orders, expecting everybody to jump to attention. Who would have thought he'd have come to this?

As his batman, Jackson had been close to him, and it hadn't taken him long to find out that the major was more interested in men than he was in women. It was something Jackson could sense in other men, though the major had never been much interested in him in that way. He preferred to find his partners amongst the officers.

Being in the army made it easy to find partners. Even Jackson had managed it there. Of course, it all had to be very discreet, because it was against the law. The major would have been cashiered at the first hint of anything like that.

For a year or two when they'd first come to Halesworth, the major had been coming to terms with his injuries and had had no one else.

Jackson had felt drawn towards him for a while, but feelings had not been all that strong on either side.

Years ago, the major had been bawdy and salacious, but that was all behind him, too. He'd quietened down, though he'd had a liaison with Mr Fellows until quite recently.

Jackson hadn't had a partner for years. He could live without that now, but the fact that once he'd preferred a man to a woman made it safer for the major to employ him. They'd always understood each other.

The milk was fizzing up the sides of the pan. He leaped to his feet just in time to snatch it away from the heat. He added a dessertspoonful of whisky to the major's milk, and poured double that amount into his own. He'd need it to get back to sleep. He had to put the mugs on a tray to carry them and the candle. He went to his own room first.

'Ready, Major?'

'Of course I'm ready.'

He was irritable, which Jackson knew meant he'd left him too long. Getting him off the commode was worse than getting him on it. There could be no dignity for a man like Major Fleming. He got him up and leaning against the bed; all that remained now was to lift him on to it. Jackson closed his eyes and put every ounce of his strength into the heave. The rest was easy, edging him into the middle and pulling up the covers.

Jackson was thankful now to climb back in his own bed and sip his milk. He wondered if Cathy would have egg and bacon for his breakfast. He was pleased to see her back: there was far too much work for Botty to do on her own. To have Cathy doing the cooking meant they could all be more comfortable.

Within a week or two Cathy felt she had to tell Mrs Bott about the baby. Mrs Bott looked disconcerted and by no means pleased at the news.

'I hope you won't leave straight away. It's hard work here if there's no cook.'

'I want to work on for as long as I can,' Cathy assured her. 'My mother-in-law would have me sitting about doing nothing. She wants to wrap me in cotton wool.'

Now, on her days off, Cathy was received in Market Street with open arms. She felt truly accepted by Mildred, who always cooked a good dinner for her and told her she must eat for two.

In the afternoons, Mildred took her shopping in the market for remnants of white flannel, flannelette and terry towelling. During the following week she'd make binders and baby gowns, and hem squares of terry towelling. By the time Cathy came on her next day off, she'd have them finished, pressed and neatly folded, awaiting her approval.

'It's a shame they all have to be white,' Mildred said, 'but there's no point in making anything in blue or pink until we know whether it's a boy or a girl.'

She tried to persuade Cathy to give up work. 'You mustn't overtire yourself.'

'I'm fine,' Cathy laughed. 'Never felt better. Frying eggs and bacon was a bit of a trial while I had morning sickness. It made me heave sometimes, but I'm over that now.'

'All the same, you shouldn't be working in your condition. What does Rolf say?'

'Much the same as you, but Mrs Bott would have difficulty getting someone else. I'd like to carry on for as long as I can.'

'You must come and have the baby here. It's only right that Rolf's child should be born in his home.'

'Oh yes, I've nowhere else to go.'

'I'll take you round to see the local midwife next week, so you can book her. She used to be one of our customers. People speak highly of her.'

'Thank you, you're a great help.'

'And the doctor, you'd better see him. I'm so looking forward to it, Cathy.'

Cathy wasn't sure she was looking forward to the birth. She wished the war would end and Rolf could come home and be with her.

He'd started by writing to her every day, but then said that when he was in the front line he was unable to find time to write and so she mustn't worry if the post brought her no letter. In fact, his letters tended to come in clusters of two and three and then there'd be several days without any. Eventually, he started keeping a diary, adding to it on the days when he could and posting it only once a week. Cathy did the same; it saved on postage. It gave her a real lift to receive one of his long letters.

He told her very little about his daily routine; there was never any mention of being under fire. He expressed no fear, but she was sure he must be terrified. Anybody would be in his position. He told her he worked a routine of two days in the front line, two days in the support trenches and two days in a rest camp behind the lines.

He wrote of games of football on his rest days, of swimming in the canal and of the French cafés and bars which were open for business very close behind the lines.

Cathy knew he was being guarded about what he wrote, and asked him for more details. She said she wanted to know what was going on, the bad as well as the good. He told her that being in the trenches was awful and they all hated it, especially in wet weather when they were waterlogged and full of mud, but he still didn't open up.

I long to be with you, to hold you in my arms again. Almost the worst thing about this life is being parted from you. Tell me every time you write if you are keeping well. I want to know how you feel. You shouldn't still be working. I'm beginning to think I've made a mess up.

Cathy kept her figure until her pregnancy was well-advanced. She was young and fit and her abdominal muscles were strong. Her uniform dresses had voluminous skirts and didn't fit well round her waist. In fact, some had been made for Mrs Arrowe. The big white aprons with straps crossing on her back helped further to hide it.

Even the major knew of her condition. He said, 'I'll be pleased if you'll work on. Nobody sees you in the kitchen. You mustn't overtire yourself, though. Tell me when you want to leave.'

The date she expected to give birth was still a month ahead when she told him she wanted to give a week's notice. Mildred had everything prepared for her and was getting cross because she was still working, but Cathy felt well able to carry on.

Chapter Six

As the staff ate their supper on the first Saturday in June, the last of the evening sun was brightening up the huge old-fashioned kitchen at Halesworth Hall.

Cathy was feeling relaxed; that morning, she'd received a thick envelope from Rolf containing many pages of writing. She'd read through it as soon as she could snatch a few moments, but now the day was almost over she was looking forward to rereading it slowly to savour his news. To have it brought reassurance that he was still alive and well.

For the pudding at lunchtime, she'd made rhubarb crumble for Major Fleming and a rhubarb tart for the staff. Just as she'd expected, the tart had been demolished and the crumble barely touched. She brought it to the table to be finished off.

'That looks good.' Jackson was watching every move she made. 'Rhubarb's my favourite and George can really grow it. Can I be greedy and ask for a large helping?'

'I know the size of your appetite.' Cathy was serving up generous helpings when the front doorbell rang.

'Who can that be now?' Mrs Bott looked round at them all, then pulled herself to her feet and went to see. Visitors at this time of day were almost unknown.

'Custard?' Cathy asked.

'Please, lots of that too, if you've got it.' Jackson had a ready laugh. The major called him a cheery soul.

'I knew you'd want a lot. You finished what I made at lunchtime, so I've made more.'

She was passing him a brimming jug when Mrs Bott came slowly back to the kitchen. Cathy knew from her shocked face that something was very wrong. Slowly, she brought out a bright yellow envelope from behind her back and put it on the table in front of Cathy. It was addressed

67

to Mrs Catherine Godfrey. Jackson sat with raised spoon over his plate, unable to move. They all knew what it meant.

Cathy took a deep shuddering breath. 'No,' she protested, flinging it from her. 'No!'

The scrubbed table with the plates from which they'd eaten cold beef and pickles began to spin round her. She fell back on her chair and covered her face with her hands. '*No!*'

There was a shocked silence. Then Botty put an arm round her shoulders. 'Cathy, it might just be to tell you he's injured.'

'Or some message from your in-laws,' Jackson added.

'Might it?' Hopefully she lifted her face, and reached for it. She could feel tears running down her cheeks; they blurred even the address.

'Jackson, open it for me.'

He didn't move; he was staring at it, transfixed. She pushed it in front of him. 'You open it. See what it says.' She could feel herself shivering; she was suddenly ice cold.

She watched him open it slowly, draw out the single sheet and open it up. His eyes came to meet hers and Cathy felt hope die within her.

She swallowed hard. 'Read it,' she whispered. 'Read it to me, please.'

' "We regret to inform you that Private Ralph Godfrey was killed in action at Arras on the twenty-third of May".'

It was what Cathy had expected but it stunned her. 'May the twenty-third? But it's June!'

'It's the fourth today,' Jackson said quietly.

'He's been dead for thirteen days and I didn't know!'

Suddenly, her tears were out of control. She could feel them streaming down her face. 'To think he volunteered for this! What am I going to do?'

They were both trying to offer comfort, but what comfort was there when she was more than eight months gone with Rolf's child?

'Would you like to lie down?' Jackson was concerned. 'That's the best thing, isn't it, Botty?'

Cathy knew there was no best thing. Without Rolf, she wanted her life to be over too. He'd been the pivot of everything she'd done over the last few years. But there was his coming baby to think of, too.

Botty helped her upstairs to her room. Steered her towards her bed, removed her shoes, put her to lie down on top of her counterpane and covered her with the eiderdown.

'Rest is what you need now. Sleep if you can.'

Mrs Bott drew the curtains, although outside it was as light as day. Cathy felt hysterical and began pouring out memories of Rolf to her.

How thoughtful he was for his parents, how he'd felt pressured into volunteering to fight while his family tried to dissuade him.

Harriet Bott sat down beside her, held her hand and tried to soothe her. Cathy talked herself out, wanting then to be alone.

'Your supper,' Mrs Bott reminded her. 'You must eat, think of your baby.' She went down to the kitchen and brought up her serving of rhubarb crumble, a fresh, hot cup of tea and a candle on a tray. There was gas in the main rooms downstairs, but it had never been installed up in the attics. Cathy was helped to sit up and Mrs Bott watched over her while she ate.

'Jackson has told the major. He says to give you his deepest sympathy, and George must take you home in the governess cart tomorrow. He thinks you'd be better off with your own people now. He asked if you wanted to send a telegram to let them know?'

Cathy shook her head in misery. 'Tomorrow will be soon enough.' She could give Mildred and Otto one more peaceful night.

But Botty lingered, her face full of compassion. 'Cathy, it would be easier for you if they knew about their son and were expecting you. Let's draft out a message and Jackson can send it tonight.'

Mrs Bott did the drafting and then said, 'I'll leave you. Get undressed and into bed, that's the best. Would you like your usual cup of cocoa later?'

Cathy shook her head; she didn't know what she wanted.

'I'll peep in before I go to bed. Try and go to sleep. Good night.'

She took the candle to light her way down. Cathy opened the curtains; the light was fading fast but there was just enough to undress by. She got into bed and tried to sleep but it wouldn't come. She was tossing and turning and wishing this was just a nightmare she was having. It was a dark night, heavy with cloud now and with the feel of thunder. There wasn't a star to be seen. Her room seemed filled with pain and black shadows.

It must have been an hour later that she got up and felt her way to the bathroom. It cleared her head, making her realise that the pain she was feeling wasn't entirely in her mind. Physical pains were racking her body. Surely it couldn't be the baby?

It was three weeks too soon for the child to be on its way. The thought that it might be was frightening. She couldn't stand it, not tonight. She was asking herself if it was possible, when her waters broke and gushed out on the bathroom floor. Her nightdress was soaked. She clung to the washbowl in a panic, unable to see exactly what had happened.

She straightened up to run weeping to Mrs Bott's room, but it was empty and in darkness. She felt alone, abandoned in this big house. Jackson went to bed early but he had a room next to the major's so that if the old man rang in the night, Jackson would hear it. Cathy knew she needed help. She'd have to go down to the kitchen to find Botty.

It didn't matter that it was pitch dark, she'd been travelling up and down this staircase for years; she could find her way blindfolded. She went down in her bare feet holding her wet nightie away from her shivering body. She saw the fluttering candle come round the bend in the stairs and stopped, clutching the bannisters, feeling a little unsteady. 'Botty?'

The next second, a plump body cannoned into her, upsetting hot liquid down the front of her nightgown and dropping the candle. She heard the cup shatter as the candle went out. She knew at once it was Jackson and threw herself at him.

'Cathy, are you all right? I was bringing you a cup of cocoa.'

'Help me,' she cried.

'Are you scalded?'

'I don't know. The baby's coming. I need help.'

'Oh my God! Are you sure? Let me find this candle, I've got matches in my pocket.'

Cathy was weeping with impatience. His manner was always slow. She and Botty could run rings round him. At last the match flared, and in the feeble light she pounced on the candlestick, righting the candle for him.

'Be careful of your bare feet with this broken cup.'

'Just get Botty . . . I think it's urgent.'

Cathy doubled up as another pain engulfed her, leaving him in no doubt she was right.

'Oh God! Go back to your bed. I'll get her for you. She'll know what to do.'

Cathy crept back to her attic bedroom in the dark and was rummaging in a drawer for a dry nightie. Mrs Bott and Jackson brought candles. They were holding a panic-stricken conference round her bed. She could feel their tension.

They didn't know what to do and that made her even more nervous. She was afraid they wouldn't be able to help her. At last, they agreed Jackson should go to George's cottage. His wife might know where the local midwife lived and perhaps he could fetch her. Mrs Bott was helping Cathy into a dry nightdress.

'Sit here for a minute.' She pulled up a chair for her. 'I'll have to get some newspapers,' she said, and ran downstairs.

She was puffing when she came back to unfold them and spread them thickly over the mattress. Cathy's bed was made up again, and cold and shivering she got back in.

'I need to make the kitchen range up and put some water on to boil.'

'Don't leave me,' Cathy pleaded, but Botty was already on her way downstairs. Cathy was frightened; every time she moved, the newspaper crackled. She had nothing for the baby here. Everything Mildred thought she'd need was waiting for her in the rooms over the butcher's shop. She wished with all her heart she was already there.

She could feel the baby coming: nothing was going to stop it. She called out for Rolf. She'd never needed him as badly as she did now, yet even as she called she knew he couldn't help her. He was beyond helping anyone. Then Botty was back, pushing a hot-water bottle to her feet, but it was almost too late for that.

Between the weight of mental anguish on one hand and physical pain on the other, Cathy knew she could do no more to help herself. What was about to happen would do so; she had no strength left to alter the outcome. The contractions were stronger now, more than she could bear.

'Botty, help me!' she pleaded, almost wringing the fingers off her hand.

'You're doing all right.' The voice was calm. 'I'm trying to remember . . . What happens, what I'll need to do, what I ought to have ready. Another push, go on.'

Cathy couldn't help herself: she pushed.

'It's here.' Cathy could hear relief as great as that she felt herself in Botty's voice. 'It's a girl.'

A girl! She pulled herself up to look. Would she look like Rolf? She could see a red and sticky baby kicking on the soiled newspapers. She had a crumpled face, not like anybody she knew, and was letting out wails of distress at being propelled into the world.

Mrs Bott wrapped her in a towel and lifted her up onto Cathy's belly. 'Look – a lovely plump baby. Oh, she's still joined to you. What should I do about that?'

'I don't know.' Cathy's voice sounded faint in her own ears. She wiped the sweat from her brow on the sheet and lay back exhausted.

The baby quietened; she was aware of her breathing. She reached out to touch her hair; it was wet and sticky. Cathy could hear Botty's heavy breathing gradually becoming quieter.

She could also hear footsteps on the stairs and another light came in.

Botty got to her feet and said, 'It's come. It's here already.'

The newcomer held her lamp high, peered at Cathy and prodded the baby. 'What about the afterbirth?' she asked in a strong rough voice.

Botty was defensive. 'I don't know anything about that.'

The woman was introducing herself. Cathy was beyond registering names, but felt she could be in experienced and capable hands at last. The midwife was lifting the baby away and giving it some attention before wrapping her back in the towel and putting her down near Cathy's face.

'Must be seven pounds or more, that one. Strong baby. What are you going to call her?'

'Rose,' Cathy gulped. She and Rolf had exchanged many letters before they'd agreed on that for a girl.

'That's nice.'

A cold hand was massaging her abdomen. 'How long since the birth?'

'Three-quarters of an hour or so.'

'Plenty of time yet. Oh, here it comes now, be all over in no time.'

The rough voice went on to tell her she'd delivered a hundred and thirty-four babies, and this was the one hundred and thirty-fifth.

'You can't count this one,' Mrs Bott objected. 'It came of its own accord. You did nothing to help.'

'Most will come when they're ready, whether we are or not.'

Cathy was being sponged down, then the woman called for another clean nightdress. Botty had to fetch one from her own room. The crackling newspaper was removed and Cathy felt better.

The woman said, 'Make a cup of tea, will you? I'm sure the new mother's ready for one now.'

Cathy could feel Botty's resentment at being ordered about. She was used to giving the orders, not carrying out those of others.

The woman was oblivious to Botty's feelings. 'We'll all have one, shall we? And I'll bath the baby. More hot water, Mrs Bott, if you please.'

Cathy could hear Botty's shoes clacking more quickly than usual on the stairs. She returned with a big enamel bowl and a jug of hot water. 'Jackson is making tea,' she puffed.

'Right,' the woman said, 'we'll need a cot. You haven't got one? Then you'll have to take out one of those drawers,' she directed Mrs Bott. 'If you put a spare pillow in as a mattress, it'll do for the time being.'

Botty drew back. 'A baby would wet the pillow and ruin it! No point in that.'

Cathy knew her two carers were in dispute as they faced each other across her bed.

Botty said, 'There's a basket in the kitchen we use for the laundry. We could put some hay in to make a mattress.'

The other relaxed. 'The very thing.'

Jackson came up with a tea tray and was despatched to the stables for hay to half-fill the laundry basket. Mrs Bott poured out a cup of tea for Cathy. It was hot and welcome on her tongue; she'd never enjoyed a cup of tea so much.

'Where are your baby clothes?' the midwife asked. 'Will you get them, so I can dress the baby when I finish bathing her?'

Botty looked at a loss.

'I haven't any,' Cathy said, 'not here.' She thought with longing of the lovingly sewn nighties Mildred had made. 'I was going home to have her. She's come too soon.'

'I doubt it – looks a healthy full-term baby to me. Did you get your dates wrong?'

Cathy shook her head.

'It was shock that brought it on.' Botty tried to tell her about the telegram.

'If this baby's early, I'd say it's not more than a week or so. What about nappies – got any of them?'

'No.'

'We've got some old towels,' Botty suggested, 'I was going to make dusters of them. They'd do for nappies.'

'Tear that one into four, if you would, and I'll wrap her in that big towel.'

An old sheet was torn to cover the hay and doubled back over the baby. 'All she needs now is a nosebag filled with hay to make an eiderdown,' the woman guffawed. 'Then she'll be really snug. A normal birth and a healthy baby. Now, miss, you've got to learn to feed her.'

'Mrs,' Harriet Bott corrected in shocked tones.

'It's Mrs, eh? Well, all the better for both of you. In my experience, young girl servants with nothing ready are usually Miss.'

Mrs Bott was able to explain then the tragedy of the father.

'Killed in action fighting for his country. Cathy only heard at suppertime, and look what the shock's done to her.'

Cathy listened to the words of sympathy and didn't know what to say.

'Let's have you sitting up then. We'll try her on the breast.'

Cathy cradled her daughter in her arms and the tiny mouth explored her nipple.

'Am I doing this right?'

'She knows what to do, she's sucking. She's keen, this one.'

Looking down at her newborn baby, Cathy felt the first tug of mother love.

'Oh, just look at her. Now pop her on the other side, dear. If you've got enough milk to fill her, you'll have an easy baby here.'

After a few minutes, the baby seemed to tire.

'There – that'll do for the first time. I think we should all try to get some sleep now.' It was three in the morning.

Cathy caught at the woman's hand. 'Thank you for coming. I'm very grateful.'

'I'll be in to see you again in the morning, to make sure you're both all right.'

'I'll be leaving tomorrow.'

'Oh, what time?'

'Not too early,' Mrs Bott said.

'Well, I'll come, but in case I miss you, you'd better pay me now. That'll be fifteen shillings.'

When she'd gone, Mrs Bott said, 'That was expensive, considering the baby was born before she got here.'

George had the governess cart clipping along at a good pace. Cathy felt numb as she watched the horse's rump moving rhythmically. At her feet, baby Rose was fast asleep in her basket.

There had been a long discussion between Botty and Jackson as to whether it was safe for her to travel so soon after the birth. Cathy felt she had to go, she had nothing to meet the baby's needs. Because she'd so recently learned of Rolf's death, it was decided the family would be better off together.

Tears prickled her eyes. Everybody at Halesworth had been so kind. They couldn't have done more for her. The major sent Jackson down with a gold guinea to cross the baby's palm, and a message to say he'd welcome her back as cook if she felt she could return.

'What about the baby?' Cathy asked. 'If I came back, would I be allowed to bring her with me? Ask him, Jackson.'

He was back a few minutes later, looking shamefaced. 'The answer's no, Cathy. The major thinks it would be better if you left the baby with a wetnurse.'

'He thinks you wouldn't have time to cook *and* look after her,' Harriet Bott said gently.

Cathy felt very let down. She'd expected to be filled with joy when she could hold Rolf's child in her arms. Despite the suddenness of her birth, it had gone well, but Rolf's death blighted everything. It had destroyed her world and all her hopes for the future.

George was pulling up outside what had been the butcher's shop in Market Street. She guessed Mildred had been watching for her because she came out on the pavement before George had found a lad to hold the horse for him.

Her eyes were red and her face woebegone. Cathy knew now that Botty had been right to insist on sending a telegram. It would be hard to tell her now when her own heart was breaking.

'How are you, love?' Mildred's arms came round her in a warm hug as soon as George had helped her down. He was reaching for the basket.

'What's this?'

'I had the baby last night,' Cathy told her.

'Oh my goodness! I should never have let you stay there so long. I knew it was wrong.' Mildred looked horrified.

'I'm all right,' Cathy protested, although she felt very weak. The jolting of the cart had made her bruised insides feel very sore.

'It was the shock that brought it on, missus,' George told her. 'Hearing the sad news about her hubby – a telegram arriving just like that.'

'So the baby's here? This is her?'

Cathy could see that even for Mildred, who had been looking forward so much to the birth, the news of Rolf's death eclipsed it.

'This is Rose,' she said. 'Rolf wanted the name, if it was a girl. How's Otto?'

'Much the same but he had a bad night. What can we expect with Rolf gone? He's breaking his heart. Well, we all are, aren't we?'

Otto was coming slowly down to greet her. 'How are you, Cathy?'

'I told you not to come down here,' Mildred scolded him. 'You know how the stairs make you catch your breath.'

'The baby's here,' Cathy told him, and went through her story again. Mildred lifted Rose from the basket, so George could take it back.

'Why, the poor child's wearing nothing but a napkin!' she exclaimed. 'And there's only a bit of old sheeting and some hay under her.'

'We had nothing else.'

'The baby'll be all right, missus,' George said, taking charge. 'Come on, Cathy, let's get you inside.' He helped her up the narrow stairs to the bedroom she'd shared with Rolf.

Mildred had made new organdie curtains for the secondhand crib she'd bought. She'd made it up and put it to stand beside the bed, all frills and furbelows and very pretty.

'Goodbye, George,' Cathy said. 'Thank you for bringing us home.' As she shook his hand, she found it difficult to hold back her tears, and when he'd gone, she broke down completely.

Mildred gave the baby to Otto to hold and her arms went round Cathy. She couldn't hold back her tears either.

'Twenty-three with a wife and new daughter. He had everything to live for,' Mildred mourned. 'And he's not even at rest in the local churchyard where we could put flowers on his grave.'

Cathy showed her and Otto the telegram she'd received.

'It says "letter follows". Major Fleming told Jackson that they'd probably tell me where he's buried.'

'But it'll be over there in France, where we can't go.'

'He said, after the war we'll be able to.'

'I dare say the likes of him could go, but we can't. Not all that way.'

'Killed and for what?' Otto asked.

Tears were pouring down Mildred's face. 'There's no sense in it. Dead and buried and us not able to say goodbye.'

Cathy wept with her. 'It's not just Rolf,' she said, trying to put a brave face on it. 'There are thousands being killed. Thousands of families losing their sons and husbands.'

'Not that it makes it any easier for us,' Otto said. 'Here, love.' He carefully placed baby Rose back in Cathy's arms. 'I'll make us a cup of tea,' he said as he left them.

'What am I thinking of?' Mildred said suddenly. 'You should be lying in, not driving round in a horse and trap the day after the birth. I've never heard of such a thing! Six weeks lying in – that was usual in my day. For the toffs anyway.'

'I feel all right,' Cathy lied. In fact, her legs would barely support her.

Mildred insisted she get undressed and into bed straight away. Nothing else would satisfy her.

'Goodness knows what effect this will have on you,' she fussed. 'Send your milk away, I shouldn't be surprised.' She stroked the baby's head. 'Isn't she lovely? To think she's Rolf's daughter! They say as one person leaves this world, another is born to take their place. How true for our family.'

She gently kissed the tiny head. 'Let's make you feel comfortable, shall we? A nice clean napkin, and then I'll dress you. I've made lots of clothes for you, little Rosie. And then you can snuggle up in your new crib.'

* * *

Over the next few days, Cathy felt the baby was her lifeline. Mildred insisted on her staying in bed and brought all her meals to her.

'I'm making such a lot of work for you,' Cathy said guiltily. 'I could easily get up and eat at the table with you and Otto.'

'You must rest and I need something to fill my time. I miss not having the business.'

Cathy filled her day by looking after her baby; by feeding and changing her, and nursing her in her arms. Mildred was never far from the cot. Cathy could see that she too was comforted by the child.

'She's Rolf's flesh and blood. It's all we have left of him.'

'No baby ever had more attention,' Cathy said. Even Otto liked to have her on his knee. Mildred was adding to her wardrobe by knitting her bonnets and jackets. 'She must be the best-dressed baby in town, too.'

'It takes so little wool or material to make something for our Rosie.'

As time went on, Cathy insisted on being up and about, but she was unable to throw off her grief and depression. Rolf was always in her thoughts. Mildred tried to persuade her to go out for little walks.

'It would do you good to get some fresh air,' she said, and contrived to send her out to buy food. However, this often meant Cathy had to wait in line because what they wanted was in short supply, and she'd come home overtired and occasionally empty-handed as well.

'We need a perambulator for Rosie,' Mildred decided. Since new ones were no longer being made, she went round the secondhand shops in Exmouth Street and bought one there.

'More like tenth-hand,' Otto joked as he watched Mildred oil the wheels and clean it out. She was really enjoying this and wouldn't let him help. 'Isn't that a bassinet? It must date back to Victorian times.'

The perambulator was made of basketwork and it reminded Cathy of Major Fleming's bath-chair. It had two wheels at the back and one at the front.

'Thank you,' she said. 'I think it's quite pretty, and it'll certainly be useful.'

'You'll be able to take Rosie for little outings and show her off,' Mildred said. 'And get some fresh air yourself.'

On wet days, Cathy took the baby shopping in the covered market, pushing the pram round the stalls. On fine days, she wheeled Rose up and down the nearby streets, occasionally going as far as the park.

* * *

Mildred couldn't get over the shock of Rolf's death. Bringing up her son had given her more satisfaction than anything else. He was her greatest accomplishment.

Ever since he'd been sent to France, she'd sensed his end would come, and come it had. He'd been her reason for living, the one person in this world she truly loved. His death, together with the thousands of others, seemed so pointless.

People had tried to console her by saying he was a hero who had died for his country, but what had his death achieved? She wanted him here with her. Alive and happy.

Her only consolation was his daughter. Mildred had been delighted at the news that Cathy had a baby on the way. She'd wanted to have the child born here in Rolf's bed, where she could be the first to hold her in her arms and look after mother and child. She felt she'd been cheated out of that when Rosie was born at Halesworth Hall, just as she'd been cheated out of so much in this life.

Cathy had not taken enough care of herself; it could have been dangerous for Rosie. Poor little mite – no midwife organised to bring her into this world, and nothing ready for her.

'She's come to no harm,' Cathy kept saying, but it was no thanks to her. Mildred felt more at ease with Cathy now. Her pregnancy had made Mildred feel better about her and Cathy had been so grateful for the help she'd given with the layette. Of course, it had been a labour of love.

Mildred knew she'd have to keep her mind on the baby from now on. She thanked God for her granddaughter. Without Rosie, she wouldn't have wanted to go on living.

Chapter Seven

Cathy was giving Rose her night-time feed beside the dying fire in the living room. She felt sleepy and Rose's eyes were already closing.

Mildred and Otto had not yet gone to bed. Otto looked ill; these days, he rarely stirred from his chair. Mildred told him firmly he was getting better and his speech was almost back to normal.

He looked up now and mourned, 'All gone. Nothing left of my business, after all our work.' Cathy saw him wipe away a surreptitious tear. 'Sorry, Mildred.'

'Otto, it's not your fault. You mustn't worry.'

'But what are we all to live on?'

'We've got our savings.'

Cathy felt driven to say, 'I'll get a job.' She knew Rolf's death meant she'd have to support herself and Rose.

Mildred asked, 'Would you like to go back to Halesworth Hall? I'll look after Rosie if that's what you want.'

Cathy had been considering it; she'd already talked about it to Mildred. Now her arms tightened round her daughter. She bent over to drop a kiss on the soft down of her head and caught her milky scent.

'I don't want to leave her,' she admitted. She couldn't. If she went back to Halesworth, she'd see her only on her day off. The thought was agonising. Rose was all she had left of Rolf.

Otto said haltingly, 'It's too soon for you to go back to work. You mustn't think of it yet.'

Cathy shook her head. 'If you'll look after Rose during the day, Mildred, I'll look for a different job – one where I can be here every night. I want to stay with Rose.'

'Of course you do.'

'In a munitions factory, perhaps?'

'There's no hurry.'

'I'm beginning to think there is. I can't put it off much longer.'

After a while, Mildred said, 'I've been thinking. We could open up the shop premises and run a little business between us. Then you'd be here all the time.'

That made Cathy sit up, full of interest. 'That would be marvellous! What sort of a business?'

'I was trained as a dressmaker when I was young and I've always done a lot of sewing.' Mildred closed her eyes and looked as though she was following a dream. 'I could set up downstairs. I'd have a room where clients could change when they came for fittings. I could hang a big mirror in it so they could see what their new clothes looked like. If I didn't get enough work to start with, I could make odds and ends and have them on sale – dressing-table sets and tea cosies, that sort of thing.'

Cathy felt disappointed. 'I don't know anything about sewing. I couldn't help much with that.' After a moment's thought, she added, 'It's getting harder to buy cloth. There's less and less on the market stalls.'

'I've got a few dress-lengths put by.'

'But you can't earn a living from what you've put by.'

'People could bring their own material to be made up, and there's secondhand clothes in the market. I could make new from old.'

'But you said yourself, the secondhand stuff is mostly party dresses. There's fewer good secondhand wool coats and dresses to be had.'

Mildred sighed. 'True enough.'

Cathy tried to think. 'I like the idea of running a business downstairs, but I'd like it to be something I know more about. I want to do a fair share of the work.'

She pushed her corkscrew curls off her face and yawned. 'What about secondhand stuff generally?' she suggested. 'I can varnish old furniture to make it look better. I'm not that good, but I can do a bit of French polishing.'

Mildred was sitting up straighter. 'Yes, there's nothing new being made. The secondhand market is strong.'

'That's what I mean. Mildred, we can each do our own part of it. They'd go together, wouldn't they?'

'They would. Tomorrow, I'll put a notice in the window to say I'll undertake dressmaking for private clients. I could cut down adults' clothes to make children's wear. Decent secondhand things are what we want.'

'And I'll have a look round to see if we can buy old furniture,' Cathy said, brightening up. She hadn't liked the thought of working in a munitions factory. 'We need a name for our business. What about Second Time Around?'

'I like that.' Mildred was enthusiastic. 'If we both work here, it'll be easier to look after Rosie. We can take turns.'

'If only we still had the butchery business,' Otto said sadly, unaffected by their excitement.

'It's time we went to bed. I should have put Rose in her cot ages ago.' Cathy stood up slowly, taking care not to wake her.

'This new business is a good idea. We'll try it, shall we?' Mildred asked. 'We've got to do something.'

The next day over breakfast they discussed it further, and from the local paper found that an auction was to be held in the Liverpool Sale Rooms the following day.

'I'll look after Rosie if you want to go,' Mildred told her.

'Yes, I'd like to. We ought to look into the possibility of buying our stock there. They hold sales monthly. But anything we bought would have to be sold here at a higher price and there'd be the cost of bringing it over. Knowing what to pay will be the problem.'

'But look what's advertised here.' Mildred's finger came down on the paper. ' "Dick O'Mara, houses cleared to order. Domestic effects and equipment always on sale". I know where his shop is – just the other side of the market. We could go together and have a look at what he's got this morning.'

Cathy gave Rose her ten o'clock feed, put her into her bassinet and Mildred insisted on being the one to wheel her round to Dick O'Mara's shop. She pushed the pram to the threshold but the shop was so crowded with domestic effects she could get it no further.

'She'll be all right out there, missus.' Dick O'Mara was a broad-shouldered middle-aged man with florid cheeks. 'I'll keep my eye on her. What is it you're looking for?'

'I'm going to open a shop,' Mildred told him. 'I'm looking for furniture – small pieces and general household bric-a-brac we can smarten up and sell on.'

'A shop, eh? Well, there's plenty of stuff here to choose from.'

'Got any secondhand clothes?'

'Yes, lots. They're out the back. This way.'

Cathy let them go; she didn't want to go where she couldn't see her baby. She pushed her way between the furniture, being careful not to dislodge the smaller pieces piled on top, and began looking everything over carefully.

The owner came back, followed by Mildred with two wool coats over her arm. 'Most of his stuff is only good for the rag and bone man,' she whispered to Cathy.

'And most of this is junk,' Cathy said under her breath. 'But there are possibilities. This chair, there are six of them altogether. The joints are loose in all of them and one is broken, but I could fix that. A good polish up and some new seat covers, and they'd look quite smart.'

'I could make seat covers.'

'The seats come right out – look. It would be easy.'

'How much?' Mildred called to Dick O'Mara. He came over to see.

'Good chairs, those. Let's see, three pounds for the lot.'

'Good chairs? They might have been once, but they're battered. I'm not paying fancy prices like that.' Mildred sounded indignant. 'One of them's in bits. I'll give you thirty bob.'

He haggled and they settled on thirty-five shillings. For another shilling, Dick O'Mara agreed to put them on his handcart and push them round to her shop in his dinner-hour.

As they walked back home, Mildred chortled, 'We're in business again.'

Cathy felt quite excited; she spent the afternoon working on the chairs. The next day, she went over to Liverpool on the underground. Mildred had given her five guineas to spend on stock if she saw anything suitable. She'd never been to an auction sale before and felt a bit out of her depth.

She had to ask one of the porters she saw there, how the system worked, and how much it would cost to transport furniture across the river. He took her to the office where a clerk gave her a list of hauliers who would do it for her, but she couldn't find out how much they were likely to charge. In the end, Cathy decided she wouldn't bid for anything she couldn't carry back.

The quality of the goods on display was very different from that at Dick O'Mara's shop. She was very taken with what she thought was a small mahogany table, until she opened the top to reveal a large canteen of silver cutlery. It was far too heavy for her to carry – and anyway, it sold for twenty-five pounds.

She bid three pounds for a music canterbury that took her fancy and it was knocked down to her, but she knew she hadn't the knowledge to judge how much such things were worth, and what they could charge for it in their shop. The stand was difficult to carry, and as she lugged it home on the train, Cathy came to the conclusion that it was hardly feasible to carry on business this way.

A few days later, after a busy morning working with Mildred to set up the shop, Cathy pushed the pram up Grange Road to get some fresh air for herself and the baby. It was a warm afternoon and she was enjoying the sun as she looked in shop windows, though there were fewer goods on display even in the expensive shops. She was outside Robb's department store, when she saw Danny McLelland coming towards her. He was consulting a sheet of paper in his hand and didn't immediately see her.

Cathy sought some way to escape. He was Rolf's friend and would be sure to ask after him. She didn't feel sufficiently in command of herself to tell him without breaking down. But she left it too late, and his friendly brown eyes looked up to meet hers.

'Why, if it isn't Mrs Rolf! A baby? My, you two don't waste much time!'

His head went over the bassinet, and the sun lit up gold streaks in his straight brown hair.

'A girl? Must be, in that pretty pink bonnet. What have you called her?'

'Mary Rose – we call her Rose. Well, Mildred calls her Rosie.' She'd been against that to start with but was now accepting it.

'Rosie? That's pretty. How's Rolf?'

Cathy was expecting the question but even so she felt her lip quiver. Impossible to control it. 'He was killed in action.' The tears were coming, she couldn't stop them.

'Cathy!' His arms went round her in a comforting hug as she buried her face in his shoulder.

'Rolf killed? Oh my God!' He was shocked. 'How awful! I'm so very sorry. I was sure he'd come to no harm. I've been checking the names printed in the papers, but I must have missed his. When did it happen?'

Cathy did her best to tell him. 'He'd been dead for two weeks when I got the telegram. His letters were still coming and no big offensive was reported, so I was imagining him alive and well.'

'Do you know where it happened?'

'Near a place called Arras.' Cathy struggled free of his arms; she was embarrassed to see a damp patch on the shoulder of his blue shirt and she apologised for it.

'A shoulder to cry on. That's about all I'm good for.' He straightened his lips in an agonised line. 'My shop's just at the top of the road. Come and have a cup of tea with my mam. She'll be sorry to hear your news.'

Cathy didn't want to go, as other people's sympathy was hard to bear, but Danny had taken over the pram and was sweeping her along. Esther McLelland took her in her arms too and fussed and petted both her and Rose.

'My, she's lovely, and so like her father. They say one person leaves the world and another takes their place.'

Cathy nodded silently. How many times had she been told that?

Mrs McLelland comforted her. 'Rolf died a hero, gave his life for his country.' She went on asking questions, wanting to hear every detail, but Danny seemed inconsolable.

'I've lost a real good friend. I just can't believe I won't see Rolf again.'

After being refuelled with tea and biscuits, Cathy did feel a bit better as she set off for home. She felt warmed by their concern for her.

When Cathy had gone, Danny surveyed the screws and the beeswax he'd gone out to buy that afternoon. He'd meant to mend the hinges on a cupboard, but he couldn't settle to do anything now. He felt sick.

Almost impossible to think of Rolf Gottfried being in his grave for over two months, while he'd thought he was fighting for England. Rolf had been so full of life. Danny went up to the flat over the shop and threw himself on an armchair.

'I can't get Rolf's death out of my mind,' he told his mother, who was making a stew for their supper in the adjoining kitchen. 'He had so much to live for – a new wife and a baby daughter.'

'The poor girl! A widow at twenty.'

'He didn't have to go and fight.' Danny was angry. 'That's the worst part – he volunteered for it. He felt he ought to. Never gave a thought for himself.'

'Or for his wife and child.'

Conscription had come in at the beginning of the year and Danny had received his call-up papers. Restlessly, he got up now and took them out of the sideboard drawer. Exceptions were allowed for those running family businesses or working in jobs considered vital for the war effort. Danny had applied for exemption and his call-up was deferred while his case was being considered. He didn't know whether his application would be successful. An antiques shop was hardly likely to be considered an essential trade.

'I hope to God you won't have to go,' his mother said. He could hear the agony in her voice. 'I couldn't bear it if the same thing happened to you.'

Danny couldn't banish his anger. 'Rolf would have had a family business to keep up if it hadn't been for that senseless riot. We thought it a wonderful business before the war, didn't we?'

'The Gottfrieds seemed to live in comfort, yes. I was envious.'

'So was I. Then the local lads thought the Gottfrieds were Germans and finished it off. Yet Rolf went on to give his life for England.'

'I hope with all my heart that this business will keep you safe,' his mother said.

Danny sighed. 'Yes, and it makes me despise myself. I can't let it, Mam.'

'Don't be silly.' Anxiously, his mother came to the living-room door. 'This needn't change anything.'

'For me it does. I couldn't live with myself if I took the easy way out. I have no wife and child to grieve if I'm killed.'

'What about me?'

'Rolf had parents too.'

'Haven't I lost enough already? Your dad and four children?'

'Yes, I know. I'm sorry, Mam, but I still have to go. I'll go down to the recruiting office and tell them I've changed my mind about applying for exemption.'

'Don't be a fool, Danny! This business is your big chance – the one you thought would never come.'

'You can sell the stuff. You manage fine when I go out.'

'But what about the buying? We've got to have new stock all the time and I wouldn't know what to buy and what not to buy. And then there's doing the furniture up – the French polishing and all that. Without you, everything would come to a halt.'

'It needn't. I'll find someone to help you – Arthur Benbow, perhaps? I'll ask him if he'll buy for us.'

'Old Benbow? Surely he's past it? He's getting on a bit.'

'We won't want him fulltime. I see him at many of the sales I go to.'

'He's just killing time. Got nothing better to do,' she said. 'That's why he comes round here, for a gossip and a cup of tea and to look over the stock you've got.'

'He's interested in old furniture, passionate about it, in fact.'

'It'll take time to make arrangements like that. Don't rush into anything with the army just yet, please.'

'I'm made up my mind, Mam. I've got to do it.'

Now it was his mother's turn to be angry. 'Well, I think you'll be throwing away the one chance you've ever had to make something of yourself. That's if you don't throw away your life at the same time.'

Cathy had just finished washing up the tea things when the doorbell rang. She ran downstairs to see who it was and found Danny on the doorstep.

'Hello. Yes, twice in one day. I was wondering if you were ready to take on a job?' His gaze was steady and penetrating.

'A job? Come in, Danny. Mildred and I have been busy setting up her shop. We've made one of the rooms at the back into a changing room for her dressmaking clients. I found a dressing-table and a full-length mirror for it in the market yesterday.'

Mildred was coming downstairs to greet him. Cathy had already told her and Otto she'd met Danny that afternoon. 'What is it you want made?' she asked him.

'I meant a job for Cathy.' He looked a little embarrassed. 'In my shop.'

'But Cathy and I have already agreed to set up a business here.' Mildred was indignant.

'Let's go upstairs,' Cathy said, leading the way.

Otto was dozing; Mildred woke him up. 'Say hello to Danny, Otto.' She pulled out a seat for him, then turned on Cathy.

'You didn't say anything to me about taking on a job! I thought you didn't want that. You'd be doing too much, working too hard, just as you did when you were having Rosie – and look what happened then.'

'What did happen?' Danny wanted to know.

'Born before she was due, that's all. Cathy had her up at Halesworth Hall. Nothing was ready for her.'

Cathy changed the subject. 'You want me to help in your shop?'

'More than just help,' Danny said slowly. 'I've decided to join up.'

'No!' Cathy rounded on him sharply. 'Don't do that.'

'I feel I have to.'

She noticed how resolute and determined his chin was, and for the first time saw that it had a small cleft in it. 'You're not being forced to?'

'No, but I can't let Rolf give his life while I stay here safe and sound, having a grand old time building up my business.'

'Yes, you can,' Mildred said, her indignation forgotten in her fear and hate of war.

'Don't even think of it,' Cathy pleaded. 'Rolf was careful not to say much about life in the trenches. I think he was afraid he'd frighten us, but reading between the lines, I'm sure he found it hell on earth.'

'They send them over the top, straight into the enemy fire,' Mildred gulped. 'I wouldn't like to think of you doing that.'

'I've made up my mind,' Danny said quietly. 'Mam's said all these things already. I came to ask you, Cathy, if you'd help her run the business, keep it going for me until I come back? You needn't keep strict hours, not while your baby's so young.'

'What a good idea,' Mildred said, changing her mind suddenly. 'It would give you a regular wage and definite work to do.'

Cathy thought about it for a moment. 'I thought we were setting up this shop together so I could work from home? So I wouldn't have to leave Rosie?'

'Cathy, what we're planning isn't off the ground. It'll be ages before it earns much. Wouldn't it be better if I started it and you worked for Danny for a while?'

Cathy was torn both ways. 'I don't want to leave Rosie, but . . .'

'I'd love to look after her.'

Rose still slept solidly between feeds. She'd miss her mother less now than she would when she was older and running about. Danny tried to point out the advantages to both of them.

'But I don't know anything about antiques,' Cathy said.

'It'll give you a chance to learn. You seemed interested when you came round with Rolf, and you made a good start at French polishing.'

'A start is all it was. Danny, I bought a piece of furniture at auction the other day. It's down in the shop – will you come and see it? I'd like your opinion.'

Mildred followed them down. Cathy knew she'd thought three pounds a lot to pay for the canterbury; she was afraid it was a mistake and they'd never get their money back.

'I like it,' Danny said as soon as he saw it. 'Nineteenth-century, mahogany, well-made. You did well to get it at that price. I could sell it in my shop tomorrow for five or six pounds.'

'Cathy bought it for *our* shop,' Mildred said pointedly. 'We'll sell it here.' She led the way back upstairs.

Cathy smiled. 'There you are – I liked it, too. Good, so I was right to buy it.'

'I'm impressed,' Danny said.

'Beginner's luck.' Cathy laughed. 'I don't really know what I'm doing and I can't rely on my instincts all the time. I can't do what you do.'

'I realise that. I've hired a man called Arthur Benbow – he's got a good eye for furniture and knows what can be sold on at a profit. Arthur's spent years in the trade, but he's an old man now and hasn't much energy and he can't work fulltime. I thought between you . . .'

'All the young men are being called up,' Otto said from his chair by the empty grate.

'Exactly, so I wondered if you'd do it, Cathy? The shop's got to stay open and without help, it would mean long hours for Mam. You'll need to push her and Benbow along. Press them to make decisions. Mam seems to like you, I'm sure you'd get on.'

'Can't you get somebody who knows more about your business? I mean . . .'

'I don't know of anybody off the top of my head. I'd have to feel I could trust them, and it would have to be somebody Mam could get on

87

with. I don't want to advertise for a stranger – I don't think I've got time for that anyway. How about it, Cathy?'

She turned to Mildred. 'You think it's a good idea, don't you?'

'Yes, for a while. Until we get our own business running properly.'

'It would help with the housekeeping.'

'Yes. Everything's getting so expensive.'

'It would mean you'd have to do more for Rose. Look after her while I'm gone.'

Mildred smiled. 'You know I'm more than happy to do that.' The smile of satisfaction on her face was evidence. 'Nothing I'd like to do more.'

'Thank you. I'll be able to pay you for it out of my wages.' Cathy turned back to Danny. 'Right, I think working for you might suit me, but you'll have to explain exactly what you want me to do.'

'Come up tomorrow morning and I'll show both you and Mam how I keep the accounts. Mam says she won't remember, which is why I want to show you too. And I've got some books I can lend you about antiques.'

The following day, after giving Rose a farewell kiss, Cathy set off for McLelland's Antiques. Danny's mother had cleared the living-room table so that Danny could spread his accounts out.

'I'm relieved you've agreed to help,' she told Cathy. 'I was afraid he was going to leave me to cope with everything.'

'I'm glad to be offered the job, Mrs McLelland.'

'Oh, you must call me Ettie. I mean, we're going to see a lot of each other from now on. It's Esther really, but I've always been called Ettie.'

She wore a summer dress of pink cotton, and with her pretty brown hair, looked too young to be Danny's mother. Danny was very patient with his explanations. For Cathy it took a lot of concentration. The only account she'd kept up to now was a record of what she'd spent on food at Halesworth. It was a long session.

'Do *you* understand what all these figures mean, Cathy?' Ettie looked up at her with a worried frown. It surprised Cathy how lacking in confidence she was.

'I think so. Danny, I'd better start keeping the books now, then you can check that I'm doing it right while you're still here.'

'I'd be glad if you would.' Danny went round fixing price tags on everything in the shop.

'Old Benbow can't be beaten on prices,' he said. 'Leave him to price any new stock you get. Well, until you get the hang of things. He's also got an excellent memory. He can tell you if he's seen a piece of furniture before, where it was and the price it made.'

One afternoon, Danny took both Cathy and his mother to an auction in Liverpool.

'That's Old Benbow standing on the other side of the room.' He pointed him out to Cathy. 'He's the old chap with a lot of white hair and whiskers.'

She smiled. 'His beard is brown round his mouth.'

'That'll be all the tea he drinks,' Ettie whispered behind her hand.

'Or the beer.'

'He looks a real gentleman.' He was dressed with great formality in striped trousers, waistcoat and jacket with a bowler hat.

'You'll like him,' Danny said. 'He's as gossipy as an old woman, always wants to know the whys and wherefores of everything. Let's go over and I'll introduce you.'

Cathy could see now she was near him that his grey eyes were alert and shrewd.

'I'll be working with this young lady? As well as Mrs McLelland? I consider myself very fortunate. An honour indeed.' He gave Cathy a stiff little bow.

'What d'you think of this desk?' Danny asked him, gesturing at one of the items on show.

Benbow studied it with his head on one side, running his gnarled fingers over the polished top.

'Nice one. A mahogany partner's desk, unusual blind fretwork decoration. Early Victorian, I'd say. If you can get it for six or seven pounds you'll be all right.'

Danny laughed. 'Be all right for a bit more, I'd say.'

As the days went by while Danny awaited his call-up, he gave the three of them an intensive course in how he wanted his business run in his absence. Cathy was finding the antiques business much more interesting than her former job of cooking.

The day that Ettie McLelland had dreaded finally came, and Danny announced he'd been told to report to camp at the beginning of the next week.

'At least you'll be in the district for a while,' his mother said shakily. 'You'll be able to come back and see how we've got on and give us more help.'

'I hope I will, Mam, but I could be sent to a camp at the other end of the country quite soon.'

Danny wasn't allowed out of camp for the first month, but as it happened, he was able to come home on a forty-eight-hour pass every other week after that. When he did, he pored over the accounts Cathy was keeping for him.

Arthur Benbow often came to the shop and Cathy would arrange to meet him at auction sales at private houses. He'd greet her with the words, 'Well, young lady, what are we going to buy for Danny McLelland from this little lot?'

He'd lead her round, pointing out items of special interest. Sometimes he said, 'That's a lovely piece, but it'll be too expensive for Danny.' And when it went under the hammer, Cathy found the price he'd suggested was never far out. She knew she'd be wise to defer to his greater knowledge.

Over the following months, the shop did well; sales began to increase over those of the year before. Cathy was pleased they were able to find new stock to bring in.

She could see Ettie McLelland felt able to cope with serving in the shop; she'd been doing it for Danny when he went off to auctions and viewings. Cathy tried to concentrate on all the other things.

Benbow was buying some furniture for them that was in need of repair and French polishing. Cathy did some of the work on it, but often Benbow had to show her what was needed.

When she went home from work in the evenings, she ate the meal Mildred had ready and played with Rose, feeding her and getting her ready for bed. Then she opened Danny's books and studied the descriptions and pictures of antique furniture.

It was Ettie who told her Danny was coming home on embarkation leave and expected to be sent to France within days of returning to camp. She was very upset and Cathy found it difficult to console her.

'Make him take you out and about,' she told Ettie. 'Have as good a time as you can. Forget what's ahead. That's what Rolf and I did.'

But then she worried that she had said the wrong thing. It made them both think about what had happened to Rolf. 'I couldn't bear it,' Ettie said, 'if I lost my Danny, too. He's all I have left, Cathy.'

When he came home, Danny seemed even more resolute and determined than before, and spent a good deal of his leave working in the business, making sure everything was up to date.

He said, 'You're doing fine, Cathy. I'm very grateful. Now I can go away knowing my business will continue to provide for Mam.'

'And for you,' she said, blinking hard. 'You'll need it when you come back.'

Chapter Eight

As the weeks were passing, Cathy loved her job but found her daily routine tiring. She was still breastfeeding Rosie. The early-morning and evening feeds were easy to arrange, though they cut down on the time she had for sleep. Mostly she managed to rush home in the middle of the day to feed her again. Mildred liked her to express a little so that she had something to offer the baby if she became fractious.

'It'll be easier once she's weaned,' she comforted her daughter-in-law. 'But it's a bit early to start yet.'

Cathy knew Mildred took the baby regularly to the chemist's shop in Argyle Street to be weighed. The chemist said Rosie was gaining weight exactly as she should, not too much and not too little.

Mildred recounted everything Rosie did, when she took her naps and her outings, and exactly how long they lasted. Cathy also heard that both Mildred and Otto played with her every spare moment they had. Rosie wasn't going short of love, but Cathy felt she wasn't seeing as much of her daughter as she wanted, and that made her feel sad and a little envious.

Mildred was now making their main meal in the evening because it suited Cathy better. There were days when she couldn't come home at lunchtime. This evening, she'd been greeted by a good meal of lamb chops followed by bread and butter pudding. Rosie had watched them eat, propped up in her bassinet, and had chortled throughout the meal.

Mildred said when they'd finished, 'Otto and I will do the washing-up. You have a little play with Rosie.'

Cathy picked up her daughter, feeling guilty that she left so much of her care to Mildred. The fact that she was so well cared for made her feel worse, for she doubted she could do it so well herself. Rosie was kept clean and beautifully dressed. She seemed happy and was sleeping through the night.

'Bring her down to the shop for a minute,' Mildred said when she'd finished in the kitchen. 'I want to show you what I've done.'

Cathy knew Mildred had carried on with her plans and had reopened the shop. Her sewing-machine had been taken down to the back room, where the meat had once been cut up. She knew Rosie spent a lot of time down there in her bassinet.

Mildred had commissioned a signwriter to paint Second Time Around over the plate-glass window. She'd cleaned and polished that and arranged the articles she'd made in artistic groups.

'How d'you like these cushions?' she asked. 'I made them today.'

'They're beautiful. Lovely brocade.'

'It was a remnant I bought in the market, and that green silk came from Rostances; it was the end of a roll.'

'I love your tea cosies and these novelty pot-holders with chicken heads on them.' Mildred seemed to have more energy than Cathy did herself.

'I can use up all the scraps, as they only take a few inches of material.'

'They should sell fast.'

'*If* we could get the customers to come in. Second Time Around is slow to take off.'

'It's only been open a few weeks,' Cathy said. 'It'll build up when people hear of it. You've got to have patience.'

'D'you think my cushions and things would sell through McLelland's shop?'

'I'm sure they would,' Cathy assured her.

'If I gave Danny's business a small commission, would he be agreeable, d'you think?'

'I'll write and ask him if you want me to, but wouldn't it be better to keep them here? You'd have more to show the customers who did come in.'

'I need to sell them, Cathy. I need some money back to buy more material.'

'I see. In that case . . .' Cathy made a point of writing to Danny at least once a month telling him how his business was faring. He always replied promptly. Now, when she wrote to explain her mother-in-law's problem, he wrote back to say Mildred could send along her cushions and counterpanes – anything Cathy thought suited to his shop, and she mustn't charge her for it. He didn't want a commission on her bits of sewing.

Like Rolf, Danny revealed very little of what life in the trenches was like. When she asked directly, he told her he'd been given a new job working for the quartermaster and was seeing very little of the front line.

Cathy showed all the letters he wrote her to his mother, knowing she was hungry for every little detail of news from him. Of course, Danny wrote to Ettie more often, and sometimes she read out a few sentences, but she didn't give his letters to Cathy to read.

Arthur Benbow straightened his aching back. He had to admit old age had brought him a lot of good things, his house and all this lovely furniture. But he didn't like the loss of strength and energy that came with it.

He rubbed his duster into the tin of beeswax and applied it to a Regency satinwood Pembroke table he'd bought at last week's sale.

He'd grown up knowing what it was like to be poor. His father had had steady work from a nearby stable, driving a horse-drawn public omnibus, but he'd been unable to stay away from drink. The first home Arthur could remember had been one room in a cheap rooming-house.

He remembered his mother always sitting by the window to catch the light as she endlessly stitched collars and cuffs on shirts to put food on the table to feed them all. Arthur had been the eldest of four children and they'd all slept and lived in that small space, and all of them had been frightened of their father when he rolled home drunk.

As a lad, he'd roamed the streets half-wild, looking to pick up a penny in any way he could. Arthur had been ten years old when, one very wet morning during the rush hour, one of the horses pulling his father's omnibus had slipped on some old manure and had gone down in the shafts. Soon there was a traffic jam and Mr Benbow, rather the worse for drink, had got down from his seat on top of the bus to urge the animal to get back on its feet. He received a kick from the horse that sent him into the path of another, which trampled on him. He died soon afterwards from his injuries.

Their neighbours told his mother she'd have one less mouth to feed, but it hadn't worked out quite like that. Poor Mrs Benbow found she couldn't earn enough to take care of her family, so all four of her children were taken into an orphanage, while she had to take a live-in job as a maidservant in a house in Hamilton Square.

Arthur couldn't say he'd found the orphanage all that bad. They'd given him enough to eat and sent him to school. He'd been to school when he was younger, off and on, but it was only after he'd turned ten that he learned to read, write and add up. They taught him a bit of history and a lot about the Bible.

By the time he was fourteen and old enough to work, his mother had found a job in the Woodside Hotel, and was able to rent a room and take her children out of the orphanage.

Arthur was working as a porter in the Liverpool Auction Rooms and loved it. From the start, he'd really enjoyed sale days. It was his job, amongst other things, to lift up smaller items to show them before bidding started.

He was amazed to learn how much the rich were prepared to spend on tables and chairs and other furnishings that were secondhand. Until then, he'd thought new furniture much superior. He started to look more closely at what was being sold and began to appreciate the difference.

Books were provided to help auctioneers and the more senior staff to price sale articles; they needed to know as much as they could about them. Arthur started reading the books and found antiques utterly fascinating. He took the books home to study and even purloined some of them. He had to have them.

Soon his taste altered and he wanted that sort of furniture for himself. He wanted to live in the sort of house the stock had come from. It became an obsession that had lasted all his life. He sought for the best and bought it, whatever the price. Like this lovely table. The scent of the beeswax brought up visions of luxury living. Well, luxury after his early years.

He looked round his sitting room. It was enormous, compared with that single room which was the best his mother had been able to rent for them. He also had a dining room and a library and five bedrooms upstairs. His home was now something Arthur could glory in.

Of course, Clifton Park was no longer considered the best part of town and that made it more affordable. The smart villas had been built back in 1840, the intention being that it would become the premier residential district in Birkenhead.

To provide domestic and street lighting, and to add to the luxury of these villas, the town gasworks were built in the same year. They were sited just the other side of Argyle Street South, close to the perimeter of Clifton Park. The inhabitants soon complained of the stench and 'intolerable nuisance' of the gasworks, and those who could afford it, moved further away to Claughton and Oxton. Arthur had no intention of doing that. In Clifton Park he was within easy walking distance of the centre of town, the big shops, the theatres, the bars and the eating-houses.

He finished his polishing by putting a blob of beeswax under the table; that way, his house always smelled nice and fresh, provided he kept his windows closed.

Old Benbow was proud of what he'd achieved. He loved to wander from room to room, admiring the furniture he'd made his own. There wasn't a better collection of antiques in the town. Now he went to his vast, well-equipped kitchen to look for Ena Smith to tell her he'd be back for his lunch at one o'clock.

To employ a daily woman to keep the place clean and look after his needs was the pinnacle of high living for Arthur Benbow. He really felt he'd risen socially when he was able to afford that. Ena was a middle-aged woman who came at eight in the morning and left at five. He liked having the place to himself in the evenings.

She was busy making a steak and kidney pie for him. 'I shall look forward to that, Ena,' he told her. She was a good cook.

It was ridiculous, of course, to have a big house like this with five bedrooms just for himself. But he needed the space for his furniture, and space was what he'd longed for as a lad.

He went upstairs to his own bedroom. The staircase was particularly fine in this house, curving up from the hall with mahogany bannisters and rails. He brushed his hair and beard with a silver-backed brush. He had the full set; it was sterling silver, but the monogram and crest showed that originally it had belonged to someone else.

He changed his jacket to a smarter one – no need for an overcoat this morning – picked up his bowler hat from the hall-stand and set out for Exmouth Street. He always looked back at his house as he latched the garden gate. It was built of white stucco and had been described as 'a gentleman's residence' in the sale literature.

The shop bell of McLelland's Antiques clanged as he went inside. They used beeswax polish here, too – he could smell it. Danny McLelland had made a good start in the business, but he'd had luck. The war meant that nothing new was being made so there was a good market for even poor quality secondhand furniture. Danny knew how to make it look better, mend it and polish it up, so he'd done well.

But to join the army when he wasn't being forced to, and to leave his shop in the hands of those two girls was asking for trouble. Both were still wet behind the ears!

'Morning, missus.'

The mother was wielding a feather duster over the furniture. Esther McLelland was a pretty woman, but she had no idea what anything was.

'Good morning, Mr Benbow.' She had a sweet and gentle smile and was generous with cups of tea. He couldn't help but like her, but those rogues in the sale rooms could rob her blind and she wouldn't even know they were doing it.

'Cathy's gone over to the warehouse. She'd like your advice about what to do with that Davenport you bought in Liverpool the other day.'

'I'll go over right away,' he said. Cathy was too young to have learned anything, but she had a bit more about her. He reckoned Danny had hired her to help his mother because he was sweet on her. The lad had no business sense, unfortunately; he was far too trusting, hiring him to buy for his shop. Most of the antique dealers he knew were rogues. They could all make a mint here – he could himself. It would be easier than taking sweets from children.

One morning, a few months later, Cathy was setting the table for breakfast when she heard the post coming through the letter box downstairs. She ran down to see a letter addressed to her. Tearing open the envelope, she found it was from Mrs Bott.

You'll be sad to hear the major has died, she'd written. *He'd been quite chesty since you left, and last week he was taken so bad he could hardly breathe. In a way, it must be a relief to him. He hasn't had much of a life these last few years. His funeral will be at St Saviour's at 11 o'clock on Friday.*

Cathy decided she would like to pay her last respects to the major. He'd always been kind and considerate to her.

On the day of the funeral, she reached the church in time to see the Halesworth staff going in through the door. She followed and sat herself down in the pew next to Jackson.

'How are you?' she whispered. He looked grey and quite ill. He shook his head, unable to speak. Seated beyond him, Mrs Bott gave her a smile of recognition.

It was a long and solemn service. At the graveside, Cathy noticed that his cousin, Mrs Tynwald, wore a magnificent black hat swathed in lots of veiling.

When it was over and Mrs Tynwald had been escorted to her chauffeur-driven motor car, George said, 'It was a good service. They said some lovely things about him.'

'And all of them true.' Jackson blew his nose on a new black-edged handkerchief. 'I'm going to miss him.'

'Unfortunately, my dear,' Mrs Bott said to Cathy, 'we can't ask you back to Halesworth for refreshments. You see, we're not allowed.'

Jackson explained angrily: 'Mrs Tynwald said she'll invite his few remaining friends to her place, but she has no thought for us.'

'We don't need refreshments from the likes of *her*,' George muttered.

'You can come to our place,' his wife said. 'I'll make you a cup of tea even if her ladyship won't.'

'Sherry, they're getting,' Jackson sneered. 'I heard her ordering two cases.'

'D'you know, Cathy, she's going to close Halesworth? We must all be packed and out by the end of the month.' Botty's lips were trembling.

'Doesn't give us much time,' Jackson sighed. 'Not when it's been my home for the past fifteen years.'

'You've been packing all this week,' George pointed out.

'You'll not be feeling it, you've got a place of your own, George,' Mrs Bott told him.

'And you've got folks at Cooper's Yard,' George retaliated. 'It's not as though you're without a home.'

'But *I* am,' Jackson lamented. Nobody took any notice. 'That woman has no consideration for the rest of us.'

Mrs Bott said, 'I understand she doesn't want Halesworth. The Hall is going up for sale.'

'She's the old man's heir but she's already got a better house of her own.'

'The major let the place go these last few years, that he did.' Jackson shook his head.

'It's got a lovely garden,' George said. 'I've looked after it all my life.'

'Well, you can sit back now,' his wife said. 'The new owner's retired you. I don't know what you've got to grumble about. She's told you the major's remembered all the staff in his will. All those still working for him, that is.'

'You lost out there, Cathy. Left a bit too soon.'

'And she thanked you for looking after him, Jackson. Not many would do that. Now, are you coming round to my place for a cup of tea or not?'

'Thanks, but I can't,' Cathy said. 'I need to get back to work.'

'Eh lass, we didn't ask about your new job,' Jackson said. 'Are you cooking for another family?'

Jackson felt he wasn't over the shock of the major dying like that. He and Botty had gone on year after year, saying the major was going downhill, that he was looking more frail, but giving no thought to the possibility that his life might ever come to an end.

The night he died, Major Fleming had said he felt light-headed and a little dizzy, but Jackson had thought nothing of it. He knew the old man often felt unwell.

The major had been reading through letters and documents all day – his bed was covered with them. When Jackson had suggested clearing them away so he could have his supper, he'd been more than usually irritable.

'Put this pile of papers on my tallboy,' he'd ordered. 'You can burn that pile there. Tip them into the grate now and set fire to them.' Jackson had done as he'd asked, knowing his every movement was being watched.

There were a lot of documents, and they left the hearth full of fluttering ash.

When he'd brought his supper up, the major had hardly touched it, just had a few mouthfuls of soup and had taken an age to get that down. He'd called for coffee and brandy, but left the coffee to go cold in the cup.

Afterwards, Jackson had said, 'We're quite late tonight. Shall I bring you some hot milk and put out your light?'

'No, I'm not tired. Take out that bottom drawer, will you? It's full of letters. I'll sort through them now.'

Jackson had wanted to get off to the Horse and Hounds, so he'd said, 'It's time you went to sleep, Major. Wouldn't you rather leave the sorting till tomorrow?'

'No, dammit. I'll want you to burn more papers for me in the morning.'

Jackson had stifled a sigh. The drawer was packed tight with letters, most still in their envelopes. He took out two handfuls.

'No, no, I want them all. Take the drawer right out of the chest – bring it over,' the dying man had panted. 'Push my lamp closer. What did you do with my spectacles?'

He returned to his reading and Jackson accepted that it wasn't his night for the Horse and Hounds. Instead, he sat by the range in the kitchen reading the morning papers. When Botty went up to bed, he did likewise. It was gone eleven, later than usual, and he was tired.

He'd got himself ready for bed, but before getting in, he put his head round the dividing door to see if the major wanted anything else.

'Perhaps a dose of my physic – before you go to sleep.'

That done, Jackson asked, 'Shall I put that drawer on the floor? It must feel heavy on your bed.'

'No – couldn't reach it there.' He was still reading, sorting his letters into two heaps. 'You could put this pile over on the tallboy – to give me more room.'

'Very well. Good night, Major.'

'And my bell, bring that to hand. Good night.'

Jackson left the door slightly ajar as he always did, and could feel himself drifting off within minutes of putting his head on the pillow.

He knew the major was calling him. 'Jack-son,' and again, in his rather querulous voice. 'Jack-son.' But the major always rang his bell when he wanted him. Jackson yawned; he felt fuzzy with sleep. '*Jack-son?*'

He forced his eyes open. More awake now, he could see by the glow round the dividing door that his employer still had his light on.

'Coming, Major,' he answered, and struggled out of his warm bed to find his slippers.

At first glance, he couldn't believe the bed was empty. He went round the other side and found the major lying in a crumpled heap on the bedside rug. That shocked him to full wakefulness.

'Major! What's happened? Are you all right?' He couldn't rouse him. The elderly man was breathing stertorously. Jackson tried to lift him back into bed, but couldn't, not from the floor. He was a dead weight.

Jackson felt himself panicking. He pulled the major's nightshirt down, made him decent. Moved the drawer from the bed so he could lift the eiderdown over him to keep him warm, then he'd run upstairs to wake Botty.

It had been like waking the dead to get her moving, but at last he managed it. He lit her candle and left her to follow him down. It felt quite wrong to leave the major on the floor.

He bent over him. 'Major, did you call me?'

Once he'd fallen to the floor he wouldn't have been able to reach his bell, but he seemed to be in a sort of coma; it was impossible to rouse him. Jackson couldn't say whether he'd really called him, or whether it was telepathy, or had he just imagined his voice? At the time it had seemed real enough. If it was telepathy, it was some measure of how close they were, that he'd got up to him. Or was it simply that he was conditioned to getting up to his employer in the night?

Jackson slid the drawer back into the chest. He blamed that for making the major fall out of bed. Next he collected up the letters and pushed them into it. When Botty came, between them they managed to lift the old man back into bed. He was still breathing but it didn't sound normal; it was deeper and his breath rattled in his throat. They still couldn't rouse him.

'I'd better go for the doctor,' Jackson worried. 'He looks real bad.'

'Will you put the horse in the governess cart?'

'No, Botty. I'll take my bike, it'll be quicker.'

'If you had the trap, you could bring the doctor back here in it. That'd save time.'

He'd said, 'Don't be bossing me round. You'd better sit with him.'

Botty had been nervous. 'Don't be long.'

He'd gone on his bike. The doctor would have to come in his own gig, otherwise he'd want to be taken home again. He'd know the way, he came often enough. Jackson was wide awake by the time he'd ridden into the village. It took a lot of hammering to get the doctor down to the door in his dressing-gown.

'The major's took bad, sir.' He told him what had happened. The doctor peered out into the road. Jackson had left his bike propped up against his gate.

'Right, I'll come straight away.'

Jackson pedalled back to find Botty in a nerve-racked state.

'He's unconscious. Is this the end, d'you think?'

That scared him. 'I don't know. Perhaps they'll take him to hospital.'

'Where's the doctor?'

'He'll be here in a minute. Listen for the doorbell.'

'I wish he'd come. I'll make some tea.'

He took her place in the chair by the bed, feeling sorry for the old man. Despite his money, he'd not had much of a life since the Boer War. Jackson noticed then there was a pause between each breath he took, and it was getting longer. A dart of fear shot through him. The breath came rattling out of the major's chest and Jackson found himself holding his own until he heard him take another. He clasped the old man's cold hand between both of his warm ones.

'Major, how d'you feel?'

There was no answer, no sign that the sick man had heard. Jackson squeezed his hand but there was no answering pressure. He could feel himself sweating, sure now that the old man wasn't far from death. It would mean some big changes for him and Botty.

On the table behind him was a chased gold snuffbox decorated with enamel flowers. The major had been fond of snuffboxes; he'd told him this one was French and dated from 1745. Jackson slid it into his pocket against the day when he'd have no job, no home, nothing. He was afraid that day could be near at hand now. He could feel panic rising in his throat.

The major had stopped breathing when Botty came back with the tea, and she came long before the doctor arrived.

Jackson was shivering with cold and shock before he was able to return to his bed. He didn't know what was to become of him now. He'd been here with the major for almost sixteen years. Before that he'd been in the army where he hadn't had to worry about having a roof over his head or finding something to eat.

Without the work of washing and shaving the major and seeing to his every need, the next few days seemed impossibly long to Jackson. He couldn't keep out of the major's rooms. He saw the small heap of letters that the major had sorted, on the tallboy. He'd wanted them destroyed. It was one last service Jackson could do for him.

He took the drawer to his own room and settled down to read through the rest. Many were from Mr Winter, who'd signed himself Frederick;

he'd been one of the old man's partners and a regular visitor for many years. Jackson was fascinated by his letters, but he did what the major had wanted and burned all of them.

There were other papers and letters which were not incriminating in any way, but they were of no value and would be of no interest to anyone else. Jackson decided to keep them, for no particular reason other than they'd remind him of the major.

He also helped himself to four other snuffboxes. The major had a very nice pocket-watch with a chain and albert that he'd very much have liked, but everybody had seen the major wear that. Very few came into his rooms these days; fewer still knew about the little things lying around. Jackson took a small carriage clock, the silver cigarette box still half-full of cigarettes, and some guineas he found in a leather purse. He hid them in his room amongst his own things. Nobody was going to give him much from now on.

He couldn't make up his mind what he should do. Jackson had been born in Shoreditch but he'd had no contact with his family for years. No point in going back there. He'd have to find himself another job, preferably one where he could live in.

Botty too was upset and hardly knew whether she was coming or going. Life at Halesworth had been unvarying and orderly, and now suddenly they'd been jerked out of their comfortable routine.

'At least you've got a home to go to,' he told her. 'I don't know what's to become of me.'

'You'll have to find something. It's not impossible.' Botty had always been very direct, she didn't mince her words.

'I'm trying. I went after a room in Park Road West but somebody beat me to it, and I looked at another in Romilly Street, but the place needed doing up and I didn't like it.'

Botty's intense gaze rested on him for several moments. 'You could come to Cooper's Yard with me if you like. There's plenty of space.'

'Rent a room, d'you mean?' He was relieved at the thought.

'I'm not offering to support you, Jackson.'

That made him smile; she was smiling, too. He'd always thought her a kind and caring person. They'd worked together for so long, he probably knew her better than anyone else in this world.

'There's three or four attic rooms that haven't been used in donkey's years. They'd need a good clean and some paint, but they'd fix up all right. You'd have space and be far enough away from the family.'

'I don't want to be away from your family.' Jackson was afraid of being lonely and left to his own devices. He wanted to be with other people.

Botty was half-smiling again. 'There's youngsters. Grandchildren. You'll be glad to have some escape from them. There are times when I need it.'

Jackson was pleased when Botty suggested taking him to Cooper's Yard the next day, so he could see the rooms. He'd already decided he'd take them whatever they were like; he felt a need to be settled. They went down on the tram together.

He was surprised at the size of the house. It was solidly built, too. The attic rooms were not big and had sloping ceilings. They were full of dust and cobwebs, and odds and ends of furniture had been pushed in to get it out of the way. But they were dry, they could be made comfortable, and he could see himself living in them.

He was introduced to the family, Botty's nephew Frank, her son Jimmy, his wife Iris, and their two little boys Billy and Georgie.

'You'll be looking for a job too?' Frank asked.

'Yes. There's not many needing a valet these days, but I'll have to find something.'

Jim said, 'There's always jobs want doing here – horses to feed, stables to muck out, loading and unloading the vans.'

'I could do that.' Jackson felt a spurt of pleasure and looked at Botty, wondering if she'd asked them to make this offer.

She smiled. 'I know you need a stopgap, Jackson. I told them you'd do enough work to pay for your room and board.'

He felt a flush of relief run up his cheeks. 'That's right kind.' He hardly knew how to thank her.

Frank said, 'If you do find a job that's more your line in the meantime, well . . .'

'It'll be all right. You can move on,' Jim added.

'And if not, we could come to some arrangement about pay when you've found your feet and we see how much you can do.'

'That's very fair.' Jackson was beaming. 'Very fair.' He liked the look of Iris's wide smile and red hair, and was delighted when she said: 'You must stay and have your tea with us now.' He didn't even mind the company of the two noisy little boys.

Tea at Halesworth had been a cup of tea and a piece of cake at four o'clock. At Cooper's Yard it was served at six and was high tea. Jackson was given a seat at the scrubbed kitchen table surrounded by the family. Iris brought two large baking tins from her oven. One contained a large toad-in-the-hole, and the other was full of potatoes baked till their skins were hard and crisp. There was apple pie and custard to follow.

'I'll come down tomorrow if I may, and start cleaning up,' he said.

'Those bits and pieces of furniture up there are junk mostly,' Frank told him. 'There's plenty of room in the stable-loft for what you don't want.'

Jackson was well pleased. It wasn't Halesworth Hall, nothing grand, but a solid middle-class house. Iris was a good cook and he reckoned he could get along with the lads.

Going back on the tram with Botty he tried to tell her how grateful he was. He could see a future for himself now.

'A new life for us both,' she said, 'Reckon we'll not find it that easy to settle, either of us.'

'I'm going to try. I think I might like it. We're both due for a change, aren't we?'

Jackson went back to Cooper's Yard the next morning and on the way, bought two large tins of white distemper. Botty was busy up at Halesworth and only Iris was at home. The sun sparkled on her bright ginger hair as she showed him the nail in the coal-house where the key to the back door was hung when everybody was out.

'So you can come and go as you please. Mother-in-law says you're to be treated like one of the family.' She followed him up to the attic.

'It'll take a bit of cleaning up,' she said cheerfully. 'You'll have to get the cobwebs down and the dust out before you start on that distemper.'

Looking round again, Jackson decided that a living room and a bedroom would be more than enough space for him. 'I won't want to use all four attic rooms.'

'Which two do you want?' Iris asked. 'I'll fetch a couple of brooms and give you a hand.'

First, she helped him drag the furniture out onto the landing. Botty had told him he could use what was here and he thought it would polish up and look quite good. It was just neglect and the dust of ages that made it look so shabby.

The bathroom was on the floor below and he'd have to share that with the family, but even so, the size of the house amazed him. He saw a large living room downstairs for the first time – comfortably furnished, too. It made him curious about Botty. Why, when she owned all this, did she work as a housekeeper? She seemed on close terms with her family; it couldn't be that she wanted to get away from them.

Iris cooked a big dinner for one o'clock and called him down to the kitchen. The two men of the family were there and one of the ten-year-old horse boys.

'This is Duggie,' Jim said. 'Mam thinks he needs feeding up.'

They employed four other youths. 'They bring sandwiches and eat them in the stable,' Frank told him. Jackson counted himself fortunate to be invited to eat with the family. Iris had made stew with mashed potatoes and red cabbage, and it gave him the energy to start distempering.

With one coat on, he looked again at the pieces of furniture he and Iris had carried out to the landing. There was a nice chest of drawers – nothing wrong with that. It was just what he'd need to keep his clothes in.

He opened the top drawer. It was stuffed full of papers. He'd seen some empty boxes in the room next door and he fetched one, so he could empty the drawers into it.

He'd had his fill of clearing out drawers and cupboards since the major's death, and this belonged to Botty, his friend and ally, who was very much alive. He'd tell her what he'd done.

As he tipped the first drawer out, he came across some photographs and took them to the window to see them more clearly. He expected them to be of Botty and her family, but he didn't recognise these people. He was flashing through them when he saw one of Cathy.

The face smiled up at him but he knew immediately it wasn't her. The sepia picture had been taken years ago. The dress looked more the sort of thing Botty would wear than Cathy. But this girl had her corkscrew curls and much the same smile.

Jackson was tired and decided he'd done enough for one day. What was here was none of his business, anyway. He almost pushed the photograph back into the box with the other papers, but curiosity made him take it downstairs to show Iris. 'Who is she?' he asked.

She peered into it, then slowly shook her bright head. 'I don't know.'

He took the photograph back to Halesworth with him, and when Botty was dishing up the soup and Welsh rarebit she'd made for their supper, he put it on the table in front of her.

'Who is this?'

'What?' She picked up the photograph and studied it.

He was surprised when she almost jumped out of her skin. She dropped everything to rush across the room and push it out of sight in the dresser drawer. Then she leaned back against it, breathing hard.

He said, 'She's very like Cathy.'

'Not really. It's just her hair – that's a bit like hers.'

'Who is she?'

Botty took a shaky breath and closed her eyes. 'Just somebody who used to live at Cooper's Yard before us.'

The words were a plea to Jackson to let the subject drop.

Chapter Nine

Jackson decided to walk down to the Horse and Hounds after they'd eaten. He stuffed the major's carriage clock into one pocket of his jacket and his cigarette box, now empty, into the other. They bulged heavily, but he'd feel safer if he could get rid of them.

It made him nervous to have them here amongst his possessions. Mrs Tynwald was coming to the house almost daily now and he was half-afraid she'd ask what had happened to them. He'd taken the snuffboxes down to Cooper's Yard with some of his clothes and he'd burned the major's purse in the kitchen range. He had to take what steps he could to keep out of trouble.

He'd been comforting himself with the thought that she hadn't visited the major all that often when he'd been alive, but she'd been in his rooms and could have seen the things he'd taken.

It was raining a little as he walked down but he was cheered by the buzz of voices as soon as he opened the Saloon Bar door. He stood for a moment letting his gaze move from one group to the next. He knew most of the regulars here and counted himself one of them. This was where he came to relax.

He saw the man he was looking for drinking at the bar, and went to stand beside him.

'Evening, Mr Jackson.' The barmaid came to serve him right away. 'The usual?'

'Yes, Ida, thank you.' The man turned to greet him; he was middle-aged and bald. 'What about you, Alec? What you drinking?' Jackson asked.

'Thanks, I'll have a pint of bitter.'

'I've got something for you,' Jackson said quietly, holding his tankard in front of his mouth.

'Let's find somewhere to sit down,' the other man responded, heading for an unoccupied table near the door. They both sat with their backs to the room. Jackson knew Alec was a fence, he'd used his services before. The carriage clock and cigarette case changed hands. Alec checked for the absence of monograms, crests and engraved messages, and the presence of hallmarks.

Jackson saw the items glittering in the half-light on Alec's knee and knew he was being offered less than a third of their value. He took what was offered but felt he was being done.

He was fed up with Alec but knew of no other way to dispose of what he had acquired. 'I might be able to bring you a snuffbox,' he tried.

Alec didn't seem all that interested. 'Snuffboxes are two a penny, for them that wants them,' he said. 'The stuff often comes in a handy box.'

'But that would be tin, wouldn't it? I mean a valuable snuffbox,' Jackson said. 'Gold.'

Alec pulled a face. 'I'll have a look at it. Perhaps it could be melted down.'

That soured Jackson still further. He walked back to Halesworth feeling full of resentment. He needed to find some other way of realising the value of those snuffboxes. He wasn't aiming to make a fortune for Alec.

A few weeks later, Cathy saw a handbill blowing about in the market and picked it up to read.

It announced *Important Furniture, Fixtures and Fittings for Sale by Public Auction*. She read on and found it was about the sale at Halesworth Hall.

It was only then she noticed the posters up inside the market-hall and in several other places about town. Suddenly, she was gripped with excitement and wrote to tell Danny about the sale. From what she remembered of the furniture at Halesworth, a good deal of it would be just right for his shop. She told him Major Fleming had had a lot of nice things, though some of them might be too expensive. He replied:

Take Old Benbow with you on viewing day. If prices are right, buy as much as you can. It might be an opportunity to stock up with better quality items. If storage is a problem, ask Mildred if she's got room to keep some of it in her shop. That's if she doesn't need the space herself.

I'll write to Benbow about this and also to Mam. She might need to release capital if Benbow buys a lot. Talk to her about it, Cathy, and get him to discuss it with her. She likes to hang on to the money and sometimes it isn't the right thing to do.

The week of the sale set in cold and wet. Viewing day turned out to be a dark day of driving rain. Cathy took Mr Benbow up to Oxton on the tram.

'Couldn't be better,' he chuckled, pausing on the Halesworth steps to knock the raindrops off his bowler. 'Say your prayers for an even worse day tomorrow. We want the buyers to stay away.'

'The dealers will come, won't they?' she asked. 'A sale in a big house like this?'

'Possibly, but a rival firm of auctioneers have set the same date to hold a sale in a shipowner's house in Mossley Hill. Liverpool isn't all that far away, and dealers might find that sale more attractive than Halesworth. We'll be in luck if they do.'

When they went inside there didn't seem to be many viewers. While Cathy bought a catalogue, Mr Benbow took a quick look round the ground-floor rooms. His sharp eyes sparkled; he was so excited he could barely get the words out.

'A beautiful extending dining table, Regency mahogany with four pedestals, and twelve matching chairs.'

'Too big,' Cathy pointed out. 'Not many people have room for a table of that size, and who would want a dozen chairs?'

'The quality, it's top class. Look, there's a matching sideboard.'

'They're so big,' Cathy gulped.

'I love it, but for Danny's shop perhaps not. Mersey Antiques would take it like a shot: I might contact them.'

'What about this?' Cathy asked. 'Botty called it a bureau. It's small enough and very stylish.'

'Chippendale,' Arthur said. 'Again top quality, first-class stuff.'

'Let's start listing what you think would be good for Danny's shop.' Cathy opened the catalogue. 'What price would you put on this bureau? I mean, how much should we bid, so that there'll still be profit in it?'

Cathy led him through the rooms feeling very much at home. Although she'd spent most of her time in the kitchen, she knew her way round all the main rooms of the house. When she'd first come here, she'd helped to keep them swept and dusted and she'd visited Major Fleming's private quarters daily.

Cathy had asked his permission to borrow books from his library and so had gone there often in the evenings. Most of his books were beyond her comprehension, but he had old guidebooks, from which she'd learned a great deal about the history of Merseyside, and there were complete sets of Dickens, Thackeray and George Eliot, some of which she'd read.

Cathy kept remembering things she had thought attractive when she worked here. There used to be two sofa-tables in the entrance hall and a love chair in the drawing room. In Major Fleming's own rooms she'd much admired a rolltop desk. She took Old Benbow in to see it.

'There's a pair of large mirrors missing from in here!' she exclaimed. 'And there was a bust of Napoleon on a black marble stand over there.'

'The family will have taken them.' Arthur Benbow scratched in his beard.

'There was a lovely picture over the fireplace in here too.' Cathy was looking at a rectangle of unfaded wallpaper where it had hung. 'A group having a picnic.'

'A family portrait perhaps, but Danny doesn't sell fine art and I don't know much about it.'

They went steadily round the rooms making notes on the catalogue. Cathy made sure he missed nothing that Danny would consider suitable. Benbow was clearly thrilled with the quality of the goods on offer.

'All depends on the bidding tomorrow,' he said.

Cathy took him to the kitchen quarters and stood in the middle of the main room. All the brass fish kettles, colanders, saucepans and jelly moulds that had hung on the wall were laid out in lots ready for sale. The endless kitchen crockery, mincing machines and flatirons, all of which she'd used, were set out on the tables she used to scrub.

But there was no fire in the range, and the grate had been cleared out. The place was silent except for the drip of a cold-water tap that had been dripping for years. There was no life here any more, no Botty and no Jackson.

'We'd better bring Mrs McLelland with us tomorrow,' Benbow said. 'I won't be able to sign the cheque if it comes to more than fifty pounds. If the prices are right, we should buy more than usual.'

When they'd seen all they wanted, Cathy suggested they go back to see Ettie and discuss it with her. They were walking back down the drive when Cathy was surprised to see Mildred, coming up.

'Hello, Cathy. I was curious to see where you used to work and I thought I'd come and see if they have any curtains in the sale. Or any bedspreads or old clothes I could make over.'

Cathy opened the catalogue to show her. 'There's a lot of old fabrics, but I don't know whether you could do anything with them. Where's Rose?'

'I put her down for her rest in Polly Weaver's. Went out like a light, just as usual. Polly will keep an eye on her till I get back.'

'Mildred, I was wondering if you'd look after Danny's shop tomorrow? He'll be glad to pay you. We'll need his mother here with us and she won't want to close it.'

'What about my cloth?'

Old Benbow said, 'You make a note of what lot numbers you're interested in and what you're prepared to pay, and we'll bid for you.'

'Well, all right. I'd better go and see what's on offer.'

The first thing Ettie McLelland said when they told her they wanted her to come to the sale was, 'I can't just close the shop. Danny would be dead against that.'

'Mildred says she'll stand in for you. She can bring Rose with her.'

Ettie looked doubtful. 'Will she be able to manage?'

'Mildred can manage anything,' Cathy said with some force and realised too late she was showing how she felt about her mother-in-law. Mildred would push herself to do anything if she was being paid.

In a more relaxed tone Cathy added, 'She's very capable and she's used to serving in a shop, though yours is very different to a butcher's. I'm sure she'll manage.'

Arthur Benbow told her, 'We don't get many chances to buy stuff of this quality – high-class furniture and domestic bric-a-brac of all sorts. If prices are not too high tomorrow I think we should stretch ourselves.'

'If you're sure, Mr Benbow.'

'It's what Danny would want us to do,' Cathy said.

She wrote to him that evening and told him Old Benbow had been like a child in a sweetshop, rushing from one find to the next.

The next day, as they went up to Oxton on the tram together, the weather was equally bad. It had rained all night and the gardens looked sodden. The rain was still rushing in the gutters and the slate roofs gleamed dark and sombre.

Jackson was almost the first person Cathy saw as they went through the entrance hall. He greeted her as though she was his nearest and dearest.

'What changes for us all,' he said. 'And so sudden. This old house is in its death throes. Sad really, isn't it? I miss the old major. It's quite lonely without him.'

'Have you come to buy something?' Cathy asked.

'No, there's nothing I need.' He gave them a wry smile. 'I've taken a couple of rooms in Botty's house.'

'If you've got her company, you won't be lonely.'

'Yes, I'm her lodger now.' He looked round and sighed. 'I'm just curious, I suppose, as to what it'll all fetch.'

Ettie and Benbow moved Cathy on. 'There are more people here today,' she observed.

'But I don't see the big dealers,' Benbow murmured as they reached the double drawing room where the sale was to be held. 'We could be all right.'

The auction started. Cathy saw George the gardener and his wife in the crowd, but she couldn't do more than wave. Old Benbow was bidding for the lots they'd marked on their catalogue yesterday. He seemed to know almost everybody here. Many stopped for a word with him, while others waved their greeting across the room.

'There's somebody over there I'd like a word with,' he said to Cathy and Ettie more than once, and went across to them. Cathy couldn't help but notice he didn't take her and Ettie to be introduced.

Once he was away such a long time, Cathy was afraid he'd miss the next item they'd agreed he should bid for. She sidled up to remind him. Before the morning session was half-over, Ettie was plucking at Cathy's arm. 'He's buying an awful lot of stuff.'

'We showed you all the things we wanted to get. If they're being knocked down to him, that's all to the good, isn't it?'

Then Cathy noticed Old Benbow had a second catalogue and had started to bid for a lot they hadn't ticked.

'That's too expensive for our shop.' Ettie was tapping Old Benbow's arm, wanting him to stop. 'That Regency dining suite is too big. You'd need a house this size to take it.'

'Shush,' he said and went on until it was knocked down to him.

'Are you buying for somebody else as well?' Cathy wanted to know.

'I've always done a bit of dealing.' He held the catalogue against his mouth as he spoke. 'That's how I met your Danny in the first place. I told him I'd want to carry on. I mean, why not, when I'm at the sale anyway?'

'I'd better keep a running total of the money you're spending for Danny.' Cathy was concerned. 'We don't want any mix-up, do we?'

The total on her catalogue grew and grew, with lots comprising of china and glass, and small items of silver and plate. They purchased tea caddies, tankards and scent bottles, as well as the furniture Danny specialised in. They bought several side-tables, a card-table and a tea-table, two Pembroke tables and a drum-table, every variety of chair too, with whatnots, chests and desks.

Cathy managed to acquire three lots for Mildred, too. One was a great bundle of heavy velvet and brocade curtains, another was bedlinen, and the third – the biggest – consisted of old clothing of every sort, from the well-worn servants' uniforms to garments that had belonged to the major and his family.

Ettie was growing increasingly nervous. 'Where will we put all this stuff?'

'There's plenty of room in the warehouse,' Arthur told her, 'and Danny asked if we could keep some in Mildred's shop if things got tight.'

When the sale was coming to a close, Cathy knew they'd bought a prodigious amount of stock. Together, she and Benbow escorted Ettie to the cashier, where she very carefully checked the figures on the account made out to McLelland's.

Ettie then wrote the cheque and said she'd never written one for such a high figure before – and neither had Danny.

Cathy paid for Mildred's fabric lots and Old Benbow asked her to check the amounts he was asked to pay. She was quite surprised at the number of items he'd acquired for other people.

'A good day's work,' he said as they trooped out to the tram-stop. 'Danny's got some good stuff at very reasonable prices. He should be mightily pleased.'

Cathy felt triumphant. Back at the shop, Mildred reported that she'd had a good day, too.

'I've sold a bookcase and a set of chairs, and I've really enjoyed myself,' she beamed at them. 'Rosie's been no trouble. Shall I make a cup of tea for us, Mrs McLelland?'

'I'd be glad if you would. It seems to have been a long day to me and we've spent so much.'

'You'll never get better value for your cash, missus,' Benbow told her. 'Think of it as putting your son's capital into high-class stock.'

Arthur Benbow walked home feeling he'd had an excellent day. He was well pleased with what he'd bought: there'd be a good commission from Mersey Antiques. He'd also bought two or three items for himself – Major Fleming's sword, with other military objects, some silver bowls and candlesticks and some nice Bohemian glass. He'd clean everything up so it sparkled and decide whether he liked it well enough to keep, or whether to sell it on.

The young girl Cathy had surprised him. Of course, she'd worked in the house for years and knew the furniture, but only as a housemaid. Yet she knew which pieces were good – she'd pointed them out to him. Like him, she had the eye for it. In her case, it must be instinctive, because she said she'd never had anything to do with antiques until Danny had hired her.

Arthur had thought she'd be a pushover when it came to cheating on the bills, but she'd followed two steps behind him all day, writing down exactly what each piece was knocked down for and totalling it up afterwards. He wasn't sure whether she was suspicious of him or not.

She was certainly keeping a close eye on what was spent on Danny McLelland's behalf.

He'd expected her to add the few items bought for her mother-in-law to Danny's bill. After all, the old girl was minding his shop so his mother could come with them, and the bundles of old clothes and curtains only made a few shillings. But no, he'd seen her pay for those personally.

These women were painfully honest, and therefore he must be, too. They'd expect it. He must gain their trust, appear whiter than white.

That evening, on the way home from Exmouth Street, Cathy called on Ezra Boardman, the carter Danny had always used, to ask him to fetch their purchases from Halesworth. She'd been before; it wasn't much out of her way.

'We bought a great deal in a sale,' she told him. 'It'll take at least three trips, maybe four to Exmouth Street.' She was using Benbow's estimate. 'And we'll want one load to go to Market Street.'

But Mr Boardman was shaking his head. 'Can't do a big job like that. Not four or five loads. Not this week.'

'But we have to move what we've bought from Halesworth Hall. We can't leave it there.'

'Sorry, miss. I can't help you. There's no petrol to be had anywhere.'

Cathy felt desperate; she hadn't foreseen a problem like this. 'It's for Danny McLelland.'

'Yes, you told me.'

'He's a regular client of yours.'

'I know, but I can't run my lorries without petrol. There's two of them standing idle over there. I'd do one trip as a favour to a regular, but four or five – no. Sorry, I can't. This war's going to ruin my business.'

Cathy was shocked. She'd have to find somebody else to move their purchases, but if there was a petrol shortage, wouldn't they all be in the same position? What on earth was she to do? Then she remembered Mrs Bott's family: they were carters. She'd go straight round to Cooper's Yard and try them. If she had a word with Botty, she might be able to persuade them to take the job, especially as the goods were coming from Halesworth.

Cathy had never been to Cooper's Yard, although she'd heard Mrs Bott talk about it often enough. She knew it was off Price Street, further out of town, but not too far to walk. She found a plain but substantial house fronting the street and a six-foot fence enclosing the yard.

Cathy banged the heavy knocker on the front door but nobody came. She tried again with the same result. Alongside the house were double metal gates wide enough to admit commercial vehicles, and alongside them, a narrow gate for pedestrians. She went through into the yard and found it bigger than she'd expected, with a water trough for horses.

The yard was bounded by buildings. Mostly they seemed to be warehouses used for storage. Some were open at the front; in one she could see a motor lorry half-covered with a tarpaulin. But there were several stables, a hay barn and even a cottage.

'Anybody home?' she called. She walked towards the cottage meaning to knock on the door, but as she got closer she could see it was uninhabited. She called out again, but there was no answer.

Feeling frustrated, she was heading for home but she'd hardly gone a few paces when she heard a horse clip-clopping down the street. Behind it was a covered van with the name Bott Brothers, Reliable Carters and Removal Agents painted on the side. A boy of about ten jumped down and ran to open the double gates.

The driver waved to her. 'Hello there, can I help you, miss?'

'I'm looking for Mrs Bott,' she called. 'Is she here?'

'Isn't she in? Isn't Iris there?'

'No, nobody.'

'Oh, I remember now, the kids are off school. They were taking them to get new boots.'

He had a tanned face, with rosy cheeks and a cheerful smile. The horse went through the gates and Cathy followed before the lad could close them again.

'I'm Cathy Godfrey,' she said. 'Did your mam ever mention me?'

He jumped down from the van. 'Not my mam, my aunt. So you're Cathy the cook? She talks about you all the time.' Suddenly his smile went. Cathy guessed he must have heard what had happened to her husband.

'I'm working for McLelland's Antiques now,' she said hurriedly, 'and I came to see if you could move some furniture for them.'

'Of course.' The smile returned. 'We'd be glad to.'

'You must be Frank? I've heard quite a lot about you all.'

'That's right.' He offered his hand. He was a big man with shoulders like a bull, strong and muscular from lifting heavy furniture about.

'Botty said Jackson had moved in with you?'

'Yes, he went out with Jim on a job this morning. He's looking for something to fill his day.'

Frank was in his mid-forties with tousled brown hair and looked as though he spent a lot of time outdoors.

Cathy explained that McLelland's had regularly used Ezra Boardman to cart their furniture but now he had no petrol and couldn't do it.

'Oh, petrol! We can't get any either but we kept our three horses. Hay and oats are not as plentiful as they were, but we can manage.'

'That's great news.' Cathy laughed. 'For a while I thought I was in real trouble.'

'No, we can start tomorrow but it'll be afternoon.'

'Excellent. We bought furniture at the Halesworth sale and want it moved. Our Mr Benbow reckons there'll be about four and a half loads.'

'Old Benbow? Not Arthur Benbow?'

'D'you know him?'

'Yes, we've had dealings with him from time to time.' Frank shook his head. 'He's been around a long time. Still working then, is he?'

'Yes, he knows the business.'

'Should do by now. Four and a half loads? That suits us, we've got other stuff to fetch from there. Where's yours to go?'

'Some to our shop to Exmouth Street, some to a warehouse close by and some to Market Street. Mr Benbow will go with you and sort out what's to go where. What time d'you want him here tomorrow?'

'Two o'clock would be fine. Fancy . . . Old Benbow still at it.'

Cathy had been working all afternoon at Ettie's living-room table. She saw the shadow move across the window and got up to see what it was. The Botts' van was so high the roof came level with the first-floor windows. She saw Old Benbow climb stiffly down and come towards the shop. She ran down and found he'd brought a lad with him; they were helping Ettie clear a passage to the back room.

When Frank Bott came to the shop door, Cathy said, 'Have you met Mrs McLelland, Mr Bott?'

He gave Ettie a broad smile. 'Frank,' he said, offering his enormous hand.

'You know Danny McLelland – well, this is his mother.'

He said slowly, 'I've seen Danny about but I wouldn't boast I know him.'

Cathy noticed he kept hold of Ettie's hand for longer than was usual, and his eyes were reluctant to leave her face.

'Nice to meet you, Mrs McLelland, and I'm pleased to have your business. The young lass says you need the services of a carter from time to time.'

'That we do, Mr Bott. We're very pleased you could help us.'

To Cathy, it sounded very formal but she could see an unaccustomed flush on Ettie's cheeks.

An hour or so later, when the van had been emptied, Ettie provided cups of tea for everyone. When the men set off again to Halesworth for the second load, Cathy helped her wash up the cups.

'You know the Bott family, don't you?' Ettie asked. Her cheeks were still flushed. She was showing great interest in her tea towel.

'Only Frank's aunt. I worked with her for years but I only met him last night.'

'You like her?'

'Very much. She was always kind to me – sort of mothered me when I started at Halesworth. She was wonderful when I had my baby – I'll always be grateful to her. But I don't know her family at all.'

Cathy had finished work for the day when Bott Brothers furniture wagon pulled up in front of the butcher's shop. Old Benbow had travelled into town on it.

'I've brought you enough stuff to set out a sitting room and a bedroom,' he said. 'Mrs McLelland says she'll send customers down from her place. You agreed to all this?'

'Yes. My mother-in-law is going to sell it if she can.'

He was in the shop pacing out the size of it. Mildred had cleaned through again this morning in readiness.

'It's all to go into the shop area,' she said. 'Mildred's fitted up the two back rooms for her sewing.'

'It'll be tight.' Arthur stroked his chin thoughtfully.

'We decided it would be best to have the bedroom display at the back of the shop.'

'Yes, you told me. I've got the van loaded so the bedroom stuff will come off first.' He went to the door. 'Come on, lads. Let's have it inside.'

She following him out to look in the van. Jackson was there, lifting a dressing-table down to a helper on the pavement.

'Have you settled in at Cooper's Yard?' she asked.

'Yes. The Botts have been real saints,' he told her. 'I'm helping out on the vans now.'

'I'm glad I'll still be seeing you around.'

'Where d'you want this?'

'Against the back wall, please.'

'You tell them, Cathy,' called out Benbow. 'They'll arrange the furniture where you want it.'

A few moments later Mildred came bustling out to join them. 'Whatever are you doing, Cathy? I don't want that wardrobe there.'

'I thought you said the bedroom furniture was to go at the back of the shop.'

Mildred was impatient. 'I meant here, near the stairs. Look – you go up and finish your tea and I'll see to this. It's better if I make sure they put the stuff in the right place. We don't want to have to move it round ourselves, do we?'

Cathy smiled her thanks and told herself she should be glad of all the help Mildred was giving her. She couldn't understand why she didn't feel more grateful.

Mildred didn't offer to help carry anything in: the lads were paid to do that. Old Benbow didn't either.

'Too old,' he said. 'Haven't got the strength for wardrobes any more. I'm going home for my tea.'

But he stopped to look at a small sofa-table she'd had in her shop for a few days. He was taking out the drawers and examining them minutely, getting down to look underneath.

'You want to buy that?' she asked, none too politely.

'No, missus, just interested. Where d'you get your stuff?'

'I have two dealers who bring it for me.'

'Bring it here? You don't go to their premises to choose it?'

'They buy for me, as you buy for Danny. I've got my work cut out here, can't get out much.'

'Oh! And who would they be?' He looked at her with a disarming smile. 'I mean, no point in me bidding against them at sales, is there?'

'Tobias Smith and Dick O'Mara.'

'House-clearance traders.' She heard the scorn in his voice.

'I get the cream of what they get.'

'So I see – nice little table. What you asking for it?'

'If you don't want to buy it, what's it got to do with you?'

'Keep your hair on, missus. Just interested.'

'Four pounds,' she said grudgingly.

Old Benbow lifted the leaves at each end to extend it. 'It's worth more than that. Might make six in Danny's shop. Get this from Dick O'Mara, did you?'

'Yes.'

'I'd watch him, if I were you. Bit of a rogue.'

'What d'you mean?' Mildred was indignant. She'd been congratulating herself on finding O'Mara. He was bringing her just the sort of thing she wanted.

116

'Be careful about what you take from him. I mean, where did he get this?'

'You said it yourself, house clearance.'

'Missus, stuff from house clearance is what's left when everything decent has been sent to the sale room. This looks like it's Regency but it isn't. The style was copied in the last century but it's good quality rosewood. Doubt anybody would be daft enough to think it worthless.'

Mildred bristled. This fellow was talking down to her. Making out he was cleverer than she was. She kept a record of what she bought and from whom. She fished the book out from behind the counter now and ran her finger down the entries she'd made.

'He bought it in a sale at the Liverpool Auction Rooms in June. I told him I wanted better-class stock.' She'd paid him two pounds ten shillings. It was a nice table, a bit too posh for round here, maybe.

'Did you ask him to show you the catalogue for that sale?'

She hadn't. 'Why should I bother about catalogues?'

'The description of the lot would give you the auctioneer's opinion. I might have a copy at home. I'll look for you, if you like.'

Mildred was losing patience. 'Don't bother.'

'Missus, if it wasn't in the catalogue, either Dick O'Mara didn't get it from that source or it was put into the sale after the catalogue had gone to the printers. Either way, you need to be careful.'

'Why, for heaven's sake?'

'Because a well-tried way of disposing of stolen property is to put it in an auction the day before, as a late sale. That means it misses the catalogue and there are fewer records. The thief is using the auctioneer as an agent but he can be innocent. If the booty is listed in the catalogue, the auctioneer can be charged with receiving stolen goods – or even theft. As I said, you be careful. I wouldn't put too much trust in Dick O'Mara if I was you.'

Mildred was glad to see the back of Old Benbow. He'd got up her nose, showing off, pretending he knew everything about the trade, and inferring she didn't know what she was doing. Interfering old busybody. She'd rather liked Dick O'Mara. He was plainspoken, he'd never pressed her to buy from him; in fact, it was the other way round. All the same, the conversation left her feeling a bit uneasy.

Chapter Ten

Cathy was making up the account books on Ettie's table and thinking about Old Benbow. Danny had said she'd like him and she had to admit he had great charm. Over cups of tea in Ettie's kitchen, he could be the life and soul of the party. He was fond of telling anecdotes about the antiques trade, and was always deferential to Ettie, but Cathy had the feeling he wasn't entirely open and honest.

Ettie said she liked him and her whole manner showed she accepted him at face value. Cathy felt uneasy because he bought things for other people, though he'd agreed to buy regularly for McLelland's Antiques and they were paying his travelling expenses to go to the sales. She checked with Danny, who wrote back saying Old Benbow had refused to work fulltime for him; he'd insisted on retaining the right to buy on his own account. He'd said it would take all the fun out of it if he couldn't do a bit of dealing for other people as well.

Something about Benbow aroused Cathy's suspicions, although she hated herself for looking at him in that light. She asked herself what she suspected him of doing, and the only answer she could come up with was that he might be having his goods moved and the cost put on Danny's bills.

It was her job to check the bills that Danny's business incurred. It made her look several times at what Danny was being charged by the Botts for haulage, but all seemed in order.

One morning, she went with Benbow to the warehouse to work on some of their cheaper items.

'Did you get your stuff moved from Halesworth all right?' she asked him.

'It's on its way,' he grunted. He'd made a bit of beading to match a piece that had broken off an occasional table and was concentrating on getting it glued on absolutely straight.

'Bott Brothers do it for you?' she asked.

'Some of it.' Benbow straightened up. 'Ezra Boardman took that big dining set down to *Mersey Antiques*.'

Cathy was surprised. 'He did that for you? You're a more valued customer than Danny, then.'

'Been dealing with him longer,' he smiled. 'Half a century now. Our Danny's a relative newcomer to the trade.'

Cathy thought about it. 'You must put a lot of business Boardman's way.'

'Too much,' he said, 'and he can't do all of it any more. Can't get the petrol.'

The very next day, Frank Bott was delivering furniture to their warehouse and he came round to the shop afterwards. Ettie took him upstairs to have a cup of tea with her. Afterwards, she gave Cathy two bills.

'Frank left these,' she said. 'One's for Old Benbow – will you give it to him?'

She did the next morning. 'You been buying more stuff for Mersey Antiques?' she asked.

Benbow stroked his beard. 'No. I got Botts to box up some items and take them to the railway station to be sent to London.'

'Oh!'

'I often send things down to the big London salerooms,' he told her. 'They hold speciality auctions. If I get my stuff into the right sale it can make a better price than in a general sale up here.'

Cathy decided the suspicions she'd had about Old Benbow were unfounded. He was not trying to dodge his bills for haulage, but all the same, she felt he was hiding something from her.

Jackson was pleased. It was the first time he'd been allowed to make a delivery on his own.

'I know the way, mister.' The lad who was to hold the horse swung himself up beside Jackson. 'Been before lots of times.'

It was a busy Saturday afternoon and Frank and Jim were out with the two big vans. They'd loaded the few items for Arthur Benbow on this small cart. It was only a short distance across town but Jackson was a bit nervous about being in control of the horse. He'd had nothing to do with horses since he was a young man, but after the first hundred yards he began to relax. This one seemed docile enough.

They crossed into Clifton Park with its beautifully laid-out streets lined with big houses, some of which were near-mansions. They'd left the traffic behind.

'It's that house there.' The lad pointed to one of a pair of white stucco houses with large gracious windows.

Jackson was surprised. There were terraces of smaller houses round the perimeter, and he'd expected it to be one of those. 'It looks posh.'

'It is.'

He'd already met Old Benbow at Halesworth and seen him about the yard. Jackson didn't equate him with a house like this. He pulled up in the road, got out and walked up the path, admiring the neat garden before ringing the doorbell.

The middle-aged woman who came to the door was wearing the uniform of a housekeeper. Jackson thought the lad had made a mistake, but he said, 'I'm looking for Mr Benbow. Mr Arthur Benbow.'

Her eyes went to the cart waiting at the gate. 'Another delivery, is it? I'll tell him.'

Jackson was left on the doorstep, marvelling at Benbow's domain.

He came out. 'Hello! You've brought what I bought at Halesworth? Good. I'm looking forward to seeing it again.'

He sauntered out to the cart and Jackson followed. 'Carry the chairs in for me, lad,' he said. 'I'll hold your horse. Dobbin, isn't it?'

'Yes.'

Each chair was protected under a grey blanket. Old Benbow pulled one off. 'Chippendale-style, good quality. Take them to my sitting room – Ena will show you.' The housekeeper was hovering at the door.

'I know, mister. I've been before.'

'So you have. I don't know why lads like you get the best jobs, while old codgers like me are expected to heave the big stuff about. Can't do it any more,' he told Jackson.

They sat on the cart until the lad had carried in the chairs and some small bundles.

'Thank you,' Benbow said when he returned. A large bundle wrapped in another blanket remained. 'We'll carry this between us.'

Jackson got down and pulled one end on to his shoulder. 'What a weight! What on earth is it?'

'Military bits and pieces and the major's guns.'

Once inside, the blanket was pulled from around them, leaving them on the carpet. Jackson picked up a rifle and squinted along the barrel.

'Enfield percussion,' he said. 'Standard stuff. Takes me back a bit. I was in the army too.'

'This is what I like.' Benbow was withdrawing a sword from its scabbard. 'I can just see your major on his horse leading his troop into battle wielding this at the enemy.'

Jackson laughed. 'He never did that – it's a ceremonial sword. He'd wear that with his dress uniform on big occasions. It still has some of the original polish on it. D'you know, I think I could even tell you what he paid for it. I have the bill somewhere.'

'The bill? How d'you come by that?' Benbow's watery blue eyes were sparked with interest.

'Did you know officers have to buy all their own stuff? I had to clear up after the major, see – he had a lot of papers he wanted me to burn – but I kept some as I wanted something to remember him by. Papers are worth nothing anyway.'

'Some are. Anything signed by a famous person, for instance.'

'I don't think . . . They're mostly bills or notes from the major's friends, and none of them were famous.' Jackson could see the old man looking at him intently, and wondered if he was telling him too much.

'I'd like to see those papers, especially the bill for the sword. Bring them round – I can tell you whether they're worth anything. Maybe sell them on for you.'

'All right.' Sell them on for him? Benbow might be able to do him a bit of good. 'But a bill – what good's that?'

'It's called provenance – makes the sword more valuable if I can prove its origin. Course, it would be more valuable still if it belonged to a famous soldier.'

'Like Kitchener?'

'Exactly. If you wanted a sword, you'd pay more for one that had belonged to General Kitchener, wouldn't you?'

'More than I'd pay for one that had belonged to Major Fleming. Nobody will have heard of *him*.'

'That's right.'

Jackson said, 'When d'you want to see these papers?'

'Could you bring them round tonight? I won't be going out.'

Jackson drove the cart back to Cooper's Yard at a spanking pace, his mind pondering on Arthur Benbow. He couldn't believe he lived in such style. He'd been inside houses belonging to the major's friends, and Old Benbow's property wouldn't be out of place amongst them. He was sure Benbow hadn't been born a gentleman. He wondered how he'd come by such luxury; just to think of it made him fizz with curiosity.

By the time he'd taken the horse from the shafts, high tea was nearly ready at Cooper's Yard. Jackson climbed to the top of the house where he was working on two of the attic rooms. By now he'd whitewashed the walls, ceilings and woodwork; it had taken three coats but it had made them light, bright and clean-looking. He'd bought the bed he'd been sleeping in at Halesworth and some of the furniture from his bedroom there. Botty had found him some curtains for his bedroom and he didn't need them in the other room. He was high up and enjoyed looking out over the town to the Mersey and the Liverpool shore. All in all, Jackson was very pleased with his new home.

The major's papers were in a cardboard box under his bed; he dragged it out now. Yes, here was the bill made out to Lieutenant Fleming for a dress sword. Ten guineas he'd paid, but that was a long time ago.

There were other bills, one for a snuffbox – oval, gold-chased and set with diamonds. He'd paid sixty pounds for that. Jackson took a deep breath; snuffboxes then were worth more than swords. Slowly, he unwrapped the other boxes from their tissue paper. They all looked expensive. Two seemed to be made of gold and the others partly of gold and materials he didn't recognise. He didn't want to keep them – they were not the sort of thing a man in his position would have.

As far as Jackson was concerned, the snuffboxes were worth a small fortune. Alec wouldn't pay him more than a fraction of their real value. He sat on the end of his bed and wondered if he should show them to Old Benbow. Perhaps he'd buy them from him? Or he might know somebody who wanted them.

He was afraid Benbow would ask how he'd come by them, felt certain he would. He could say the major had given them to him, but would he be believed? He put one in his pocket. He'd wait and see how he got on with Benbow before he brought it out. He had to be careful.

After the high tea of cold ham and salad, he borrowed a shopping bag from Iris, filled it with the letters and documents and walked back to Clifton Park. When he knocked, Old Benbow himself opened the door.

'Come in, Jackson. What about a glass of beer?' He led the way to a vast kitchen where there was a firkin on tap. He filled two tankards and put one in Jackson's hand, then led him to the sitting room he'd been in before.

'Have a seat while I glance through your papers.'

Jackson took a sip from his tankard. It was silver and must be worth a mint. He looked round. It was an impressive room, must be all of thirty feet long. The furniture looked as good as, if not better, than that at Halesworth.

Old Benbow had found the bill for the sword. 'This is very interesting. As I have the sword it refers to, would you mind if I kept it?'

Jackson wondered if he should try to get him to pay for it. Why not? Benbow could afford it, but he had no idea how much it would be worth to him and his nerve failed. 'All right.'

'D'you also mind if I hold on to the rest of these papers for a day or two? There's a lot to read and it takes time.'

Having brought them, Jackson felt there was no point in refusing.

'I have a few autographed letters and programmes here. Would you like to see them?' Jackson could hear the enthusiasm in Benbow's voice. He got up to fetch a big folder from a drawer. Inside, each document was protected between sheets of tissue.

'This is a letter to a client signed by Lloyd George. He was a solicitor at one time. And here, look – I got Harry Lauder to sign a programme for me when he came to the Argyle Music Hall a few years back. They're my two best, but autographs of little-known people are worth keeping.'

Jackson looked through the documents, pretending to be more interested than he was. Should he show him the snuffbox? Everybody said Old Benbow was clever with antiques, but was he above board? He must surely have bent the rules a little to acquire all these treasures? If he had, he wouldn't be shocked to hear how he'd come by the snuffbox. But if he was honest, he might want nothing more to do with him.

Benbow was pointing out another signature to him. 'He was a General, but I'd never heard of him. You're an army man – have you?'

Jackson shook his head and fingered the snuffbox in his pocket. His mind made up, he brought it out and unwrapped it. 'What d'you think of this?'

'A snuffbox?' He could see by Benbow's face it was very special. 'How d'you come by this?'

'The major gave it to me some time ago. What d'you reckon it's worth?'

Benbow whistled through his teeth. 'It's old . . .'

'The bill for it is amongst those papers.'

'Is it, by Jove?'

'Could you help me sell it?'

'It's gold.' He was turning it over and over in his hands. Suddenly, his shrewd eyes came up to meet Jackson's.

'If I'm to sell it, I need to know whether Major Fleming really did give it to you, or whether he left it lying around in his house and you picked it up.'

Jackson felt his stomach turn over. He'd already imagined ten times how he'd deal with that question. It had come and it floored him. How could he admit he was a thief?

Old Benbow sighed heavily. 'It's like that, then – you picked it up?'

'Yes,' he admitted.

'Let's have some more of this beer.'

Jackson followed him out to the kitchen to get it. 'I've got four more of them at home.'

'What? This quality?'

'I think so.'

Benbow straightened up, looking pensive. 'Who else knows the major collected snuffboxes? Do you remember him showing them to other people?'

Jackson shook his head. 'He didn't want me there when he had visitors. I used to go and sit in the kitchen until he rang for me.'

'He had a lot of visitors?'

'No. At one time, a Mr Winters used to come quite a lot. There were two others; all three came to play bridge on Tuesday afternoons. He might have shown the snuffboxes to them, I don't know.' Jackson paused reflectively. 'They were all old. Mr Winters was ill and went to live in London with his daughter. One of the others died, and the major was past playing cards anyway. For the last few years he hardly had any visitors – just the vicar and a woman he didn't care much for, his cousin.'

'I'll need time to think about it,' Benbow said. 'This sort of thing brings a better price when sold in a speciality sale through a London auction house. And there's less chance of somebody recognising them as Major Fleming's property down there. If we could add some provenance, something that looks like proof that they're really yours . . .'

'There's the bill in amongst those papers I gave you from when Fleming bought that one. He paid sixty pounds for it.'

'Excellent. Where did he buy it? And when?'

Jackson couldn't remember.

'No matter, I'll look it out. Then a card from the major to you . . . a Christmas card perhaps, mentioning the gift of a snuffbox. With that, nobody would need to ask if you owned it.'

Jackson was surprised. Old Benbow had said he needed time to think, but it seemed he could think on his feet.

'I also kept a few of the major's unused postcards, envelopes, writing paper, that sort of thing, but I haven't brought them. There could be the odd Christmas card amongst them; he usually ordered more than he sent. Not that he could be bothered sending any, the last two Christmases.'

'Just what you need. Let me see them.'

Jackson had his doubts. 'He never wrote any cards to me, he wasn't that sort. I don't know if I could write one that would look genuine.'

'I'll do that for you, no problem.'

'Thank you.'

'I work on commission, you do know that?'

Again he felt Benbow's eyes studying him. Jackson gulped. 'How much?'

125

'In this case, forty-five per cent of what they fetch.'

'That's almost half!'

'And you pay all the costs. The usual terms for stolen property.'
Jackson flinched.

'A nice collection of five snuffboxes – if the others are like this –
should fetch a good price in London. Do it my way and they'll sell for
the full market value.'

'So I'd get more cash your way?'

'Yes, but you'd have to promise not to mention my name in connection
with the sale. I'll set it up for you, but only your name goes on the
records.'

'Hang on, we're in this together.'

'No, 'fraid not. It has to be this way if you want me to help. None of
us in the trade can afford to touch stolen goods. If I once got a name for
doing that, I'd get no more commissions to buy for firms like Mersey
Antiques, Danny McLelland would give me the push and nobody would
touch anything I wanted to put in an auction. I'd no longer be able to
make a living.'

Jackson felt thoroughly alarmed. 'But the major never gave me much
of anything. These are valuable. Perhaps his cousin . . . She's his heir,
perhaps she saw them on show in that cabinet in his sitting room. They
were there for years, so she probably did. Perhaps she'll ask where
they've gone.'

'Don't worry, I can see this sale going through with no questions
asked.' Benbow's calm made him feel worse. 'If she accuses you, you
wouldn't want them found in your possession, would you? Better for you
to sell them on. It's probably what she'd expect of you.'

'She's a bit of a tartar. She might ask why he'd want to give such
valuable things to me.'

There was a silence, then Benbow sighed. 'Well, Jackson, you'd have
to whisper that they were gifts of love. Explain that you and Major
Fleming had an aberrant relationship.' He smiled slowly. 'That should
shut her up. She wouldn't want anything like that attaching to the family
name.'

Jackson felt his guts turn to water. 'How d'you know about that?
What makes you think . . .?'

Benbow's shrewd eyes were assessing him. 'I guessed.'

Jackson folded up. He knew he'd confirmed that guess as correct.
'The major was very discreet and anyway, not for years . . . He was past
all that and so am I. What made you guess?'

'Put it down to my age. I've seen a lot of the world and its ways. To

make my living as I do, I have to have eyes in the back of my head.'
Benbow smiled.

'But what if others, Botty and Cathy, guess too?'

'They won't. When Cathy introduced us on the day of the sale, I asked
her about you. She likes and trusts you.' Benbow smiled. 'I doubt she
knows as much about you as she thinks she does. Don't you worry about
her and her friends, they won't know men like you and the major exist.'

Thursday was half-day closing and usually Cathy went home when the
shop shut at one o'clock. But today she'd had a sandwich with Ettie and
worked on for an hour or so to bring the books up to date after acquiring
so much new stock.

It was a sunny afternoon and she was sauntering home down Grange
Road. Though all the shops were closed, Cathy couldn't help but be
interested in those selling furniture and soft furnishings, comparing what
she saw with what Mildred and Danny had on offer. There was less on
display in their windows now. She didn't see Botty's unfashionable long
black skirt and black straw hat until she spoke to her.

'Cathy! Hello, aren't you working today?' Her iron-grey hair was
arranged too obviously close down one side of her face to hide her scar.

'It's early-closing day.'

'Of course!'

'I've actually worked overtime but I'm on my way home now.'

'Yes, you're at McLelland's Antiques – Frank did tell me. Quite a
change for you. I always knew you had a good brain.'

Cathy thought Botty looked a little down in the mouth. 'What have
you been doing since you finished?'

'Very little, although I haven't settled to a life of idleness yet. Jim's
married, you see, and Iris has always done everything in the house. It's
her kitchen, and I don't feel I can push in now. It makes me feel at a
loose end sometimes.'

'So you've retired?'

'Well . . . If I could get another job to suit me, I might take it.'

'Botty, you have grandchildren. Don't they keep you busy?'

'Yes, two boys, and they're lovely at this age, but out at school all day.
When they're home they'd rather be out with the vans or grooming the
horses.'

'But you have a big family, another son?'

'Not any longer. Peter was killed years ago.'

Cathy saw her lips twist with pain. Botty shuddered and could no
longer look at her.

'I have a nephew who's been like a son to me – he's lived with us for many years.' Her words were tumbling out as though to avoid questions. 'I thought Frank was a confirmed bachelor – I'm still darning his socks, in fact – but perhaps now . . .'

'He seems quite smitten with Danny's mother.'

'Yes, Ettie McLelland. I'm pleased for him.'

'And you have Jackson with you. He says he's fallen on his feet and he's very happy with his new lodgings.'

'Yes, he's enjoying working for my lads, but I don't see much of him except at mealtimes.'

Cathy had been fond of them both, but particularly of Botty.

'Jackson's out and about now,' Botty went on, more cheerfully, 'meeting lots of people. Things are definitely better for him. He must have had a dull life, being at the major's beck and call all the time.'

'I do see him when he comes with the van. I'm glad we haven't lost touch.'

'It's you I hardly see these days.' Harriet Bott smiled at her. 'If you're not in a hurry, why not come home with me now? Meet Iris and have a cup of tea. Do you have time?'

Cathy knew Rosie would be having her afternoon nap.

'Thank you. Yes, I'd like that.' She fell into step beside the older woman.

'I suppose I'm just missing work,' Botty confided. 'Never had time to go for walks before. Never needed to – I got plenty of exercise walking round that house.'

Cathy smiled, feeling a little sorry for her. 'To give up before you choose to must make things feel a little flat.'

'That's just it.'

Cathy had seen Cooper's Yard and Botty's house from the outside, but now ushered into the large hall she was surprised.

'You've got a lovely house, Botty.' The grandfather clock was chiming the quarter hour.

'Come to the living room.'

It was like no other living room Cathy had seen. A fire burned in a Victorian grate that had fancy green tiles down both sides. Every inch of the oak mantelpiece was covered with china ornaments. An armchair in maroon plush sat on each side of the fender. Cathy had spent enough time in Danny's shop to recognise them as Victorian, one designed to accommodate a lady's crinoline, the other for a gentleman. The two women sat down on a sofa of the same vintage that didn't quite match.

'My goodness, this is quite grand.' Cathy was looking round. The ceiling was heavily decorated with plaster laurel leaves. There were rich drapes at the two big windows and a matching curtain that could be pulled across the door to keep out draughts. The room was comfortable, but somewhat over-furnished with whatnots, aspidistras in brass pots, and books. It was the sort of room that was no longer in fashion. Cathy felt she'd stepped back into Victorian times.

Botty didn't seem quite at ease. She said, 'It's too big. Not cosy.'

'*I* think it is.' A young woman with red hair came in from the kitchen. 'It needs to be big,' she added. 'There's a lot of us.'

'This is Iris, my daughter-in-law,' Botty said.

'I heard you'd been round.' The young woman was smiling at Cathy. 'Sorry I was out last time. What about a cup of tea?'

'And some of your fairy cakes, Iris, if we may.'

'Of course. Will you come to the kitchen for it?'

Cathy followed them down the passageway. Their kitchen was in the same Victorian style and seemed as big as the one at Halesworth. Iris was jolly and quite a chatterbox. Cathy found it hard to believe Botty could feel depressed in this house.

When she was leaving, Cathy told Botty she must come to Market Street next Thursday and have tea with Mildred. 'She'll be pleased to see you again,' she said.

Walking home, Cathy pondered again on Botty's circumstances. She'd always thought it strange that she'd worked as a housekeeper when she had her own family and a business. Now she'd seen the house Botty owned she found it doubly incomprehensible. It seemed she wasn't altogether happy there, and Cathy couldn't understand that either. Iris appeared jolly and easy to get on with, and there had been something protective about her manner towards her mother-in-law.

When she got back to Market Street, Cathy told Mildred all about Botty's opulent home in Cooper's Yard. The two older women seemed to like each other. Botty had shown great sympathy and understanding when vandals had overrun Mildred's home and business, and Mildred had spoken of Botty as a friend ever since.

The following Thursday, Cathy was home in time to make scones and set out afternoon tea on the living-room table before Botty was expected. She came promptly at three. Otto put aside his newspaper to talk to her.

'There's a big article about the royal family in it today,' he said. Since early in the year, reports had been appearing that they were about to change their name. With war casualties mounting, feelings against the Germans were growing.

'Copying our example,' Mildred said tartly.

'It's taken them long enough,' Otto grunted.

'They must feel unpopular,' Botty frowned. 'If anything, the anti-German feeling is stronger now than it's ever been.'

'Saxe-Coburg-Gotha – I mean, it's an awful mouthful!'

Mildred snorted. 'George the Fifth, King of England with a name like that. How can we think of them as British?'

Cathy had heard many suggestions regarding what they should change their name to, some not very polite.

'It's announced today that the royal name will be Windsor from now on,' Otto said.

'Windsor?'

'After the town. That should please most people.'

'We can all pretend they're English now,' Mildred said sharply.

'It proves we did the right thing.'

'Course we did.' She rounded on Otto. 'We haven't had our home overrun by troublemakers since, have we?'

Cathy stood up. 'Isn't it time we woke Rose up? She won't sleep tonight if—'

Mildred leaped to her feet and rushed to do it. 'What am I thinking of?' She pushed Cathy aside in order to reach the cot first. Rosie was flushed and sleepy after her nap. They all fussed over her.

'How pretty she is!' Botty exclaimed, taking her in her arms.

While Cathy made the tea and handed round her buttered scones, Mildred launched into a detailed account of how much arrowroot and porridge the baby could eat, the daily care she gave her, and how sweet-tempered she was. 'Only the best is good enough for our Rosie,' she said. 'We are all quite besotted with her.'

Mildred transferred the baby to Otto's knee so their guest could drink her tea in comfort, and started to tell her about the new business they'd set up. She spoke with enthusiasm about Second Time Around and about her sewing.

Nothing would do but that Harriet must go downstairs to have a proper look round their shop. Their animated voices drifted up, and Cathy knew Botty was feeling more cheerful. They came back for a second cup of tea, Mildred carrying an armful of sewing that needed to be finished off by hand.

'Clear these things off the table, Cathy,' she said. 'So I can spread my work out.'

Cathy did so, and Mildred spread out a child's scarlet dress and began working on the buttonholes. 'Mrs Bott has promised to come round again to help me,' she said.

'Such beautiful things from all that old fabric from Halesworth,' Botty marvelled. 'I can hardly believe it's possible. I could help you now while I drink this.'

'I'd be really grateful,' Mildred said gladly. 'It's the hand finishing that takes the time.' She gave Botty another dress and a card of buttons to sew on.

'I like sewing,' Botty said. 'I'm not up to your standard, but I can do simple things like tacking and putting up hems.'

'Tonight, I need to get the dust of ages out of those curtains,' Mildred sighed. 'I can't do anything with them until that's done.'

'I'll give you a hand with that,' Cathy offered. She was pleased to see them getting on so well. She thought Mildred was taking on too much work, and if Botty really wanted something to fill her day, she need look no further. She hoped they'd become good friends.

She could see Otto had tired and Rosie was becoming restless. He was glad to let Cathy take her on to her own knee. Mildred began to outline her plans to wean her in the future. Botty put forward her own views on how it should be done. Cathy listened to both, knowing she lacked experience, and the baby became again the focus of attention.

'How she's grown,' Botty said. 'I haven't seen her since the night she was born.'

Cathy thanked her again for her help on that night. 'Couldn't have managed without you and Jackson. I'll always be grateful.'

'You kept us young at Halesworth, and we've never thanked you for bringing the McLelland business to us.'

Cathy smiled. 'I'm sure McLelland's needed you more than you needed their business. It isn't easy to find a firm to do carting these days. So many of them have changed to motor vans.'

'They were in too much of a hurry to get rid of their horses. For us, business is booming. War has removed some of the competition.'

Mildred was frowning. 'Some are lucky and some are not. So much depends on what the business is.'

'You were unlucky,' Botty sympathised.

'Very, but you always had a good business. You were always the biggest firm of hauliers in town. I remember when it was being run by a fellow called—'

'Is that the time? I really must go.' Botty leaped to her feet. 'Iris, my daughter-in-law, cooks a meal for us all so I have to be home on time for it. Can't keep them waiting. Thank you for the tea.'

'You'll come again next week?' Mildred asked.

Cathy thought Botty's enthusiasm for that was fading.

'All right, two o'clock, next Thursday.'

Botty was already heading for the stairs. Cathy rushed to open the shop door for her and see her out. Slowly, she climbed back up the stairs wondering what had made her old friend depart so abruptly.

Mildred had started washing up. Cathy picked up the tea towel. 'What were you saying? What made her leap up and leave like that?'

'Just that the Botts had always had a good business, that they were always the biggest carters in town.'

Cathy shrugged. Perhaps she'd imagined Botty was rushing away.

Then Otto said, 'I remember . . .'

'What?'

'It wasn't always the Botts who owned it. It used to belong to a family called Cooper.'

'Before the Botts bought it?' Cathy asked. 'When did they take over?'

Otto shook his head. 'I wish I could remember.'

Chapter Eleven

Cathy sat alone in the living room upstairs at Exmouth Street, working on the books. Rain was spitting gently against the window. She kept the doors open, since the sounds drifting up from the shop made her feel part of it. She knew Old Benbow had arrived, he was talking to Ettie.

Just then, she heard the clip-clop of horse's hooves. Bott Brothers' van cut some of the light from the room as it pulled into the kerb outside. Moments later, Ettie's voice was louder and full of pleasure, which meant Frank must have come with it.

The shop was giving the Bott family business regular work. Today, the van had come to pick up furniture that McLelland's Antiques had sold and would deliver it to the homes of their customers. Benbow would be tying on blankets to protect it while it was in transit.

Cathy got up and set the kettle to boil, knowing that Ettie would offer cups of tea. Meeting Frank Bott had really made her sparkle. She hoped their new relationship would continue to develop.

Cathy had barely returned to her ledgers when she heard a crash followed by a shout. She put her pen down and listened. There was a jumble of voices all talking at once and all full of alarm. Panic-stricken, she ran down to see what had happened.

'Oh, my goodness!'

Old Benbow was on the floor, pinned down by a large wardrobe. Frank and his lad were trying to manoeuvre it off him.

'What happened?'

Ettie was frightened. 'He slipped. He shouldn't be moving heavy furniture, not at his age.'

The wardrobe was upright again, and Old Benbow was freed. He took in a huge breath of relief.

Cathy knelt beside him. 'Benbow, are you hurt?'

He grunted, his eyes were closed. Then he gasped, 'I'm all right, don't worry. Just banged my head when I went down.'

'You're bleeding. You've grazed it.'

'Come and lie on the couch,' Ettie said.

Getting him up from the floor wasn't easy. He stood holding on to Frank, yet still swaying on his feet.

'Better throw one of those grey blankets over it,' he joked. 'Don't want to bleed on the upholstery, do I?'

Frank provided a white handkerchief and Cathy staunched the flow that was matting his white hair. It seemed a chaotic moment; they were all crowding round, even a customer who had come in.

'What happened?'

'The wardrobe door opened against him.'

'He slipped. The floor's wet – it's tramped in on people's feet.'

'I need something to bathe this cut,' Cathy said.

'There's iodine and dressings in the kitchen.' Ettie ran for the stairs. 'I'll get them.'

'And some boiled water!'

Benbow was calmer than any of them. 'Just let me lie here for a moment,' he said. 'I'll be all right.'

Cathy attended to the graze on the back of his head. Once the blood was wiped off it didn't seem too bad. She saw him wince as she dabbed iodine on. 'It's turning your hair brown,' she told him.

He whistled through his teeth. 'I'm not worried about that, but it really stings.'

'It'll stop any infection,' Ettie said. 'It's better to be on the safe side.'

'Are you hurt anywhere else?' Cathy asked.

'My chest . . .'

Willing fingers were removing his tie and opening his shirt. There was blood on his vest. Ettie lifted it gently.

'Another graze,' Cathy said. 'It'll be where the wardrobe caught you. I'll bathe that too.'

'No iodi—' he ordered, but he was too late. It made him wince again.

The shop quietened down. 'Is the wardrobe all right?' Benbow asked faintly.

'Not a mark on it,' Frank assured him. He and the lads loaded it and the other items for delivery. Ettie made tea and they all perched round Benbow on the couch as they drank it.

'Frank,' Ettie said, 'could you take Mr Benbow home on your van? He won't be up to much after this.'

Old Benbow protested. 'It's viewing day – that house sale in Rock Ferry. I was going to see if there was anything—'

Ettie interrupted firmly, 'You said you didn't think there'd be much, and with all this stuff from Halesworth, we've plenty of stock at the moment. Forget it.'

'But there might be something interesting there.'

'You can go to the sale tomorrow if you feel up to it.'

'Come on,' Frank said, keen to do anything Ettie suggested. 'We'll take you home, Mr Benbow, before we start delivering.' With some care, the shaky old man was helped outside and up into the passenger seat, before the van moved off into the rain.

By mid-afternoon, Cathy had brought the account books up to date and looked after the business while Ettie went out to get some shopping.

On her return she said, 'Cathy, do you think you could leave early and look in on Old Benbow on your way home?'

'Yes, of course. He lives alone, doesn't he? He took a nasty tumble for a man of his years.'

'Yes. I don't like to think of him lying there on his own. I've bought a few things you can take to him – a slice of ham and a couple of fairy cakes for his tea – so he doesn't have to go out to get something.'

Ettie sent Cathy off before four o'clock. She took his address from the records and looked it up on the street map they kept in the shop. Clifton Park was quite near but as it was entirely residential, and she knew nobody living there, she'd had no reason to go there before.

She was surprised to find it a quiet backwater. The roads were lined with big houses. When she found the right number, she looked up at the white stucco house with large gracious windows and thought perhaps Benbow had rooms here, though she'd understood him to say he had a house.

The front door was rather grand and the woman who answered her knock was middle-aged and looked like a housekeeper. 'Does Mr Benbow live here?' she asked. 'Mr Arthur Benbow?'

'Yes, but he's not very well.'

'I know, that's why I've come.'

The door opened a little wider. 'I'll tell him. Who shall I say is calling?'

'Cathy Godfrey.'

She was left to wait in a lofty hall, with a magnificent staircase winding round it. Pictures in ornate frames hung on the walls. She was amazed to find Benbow lived in a place like this.

The woman went into one of the rooms and she could hear her talking to Old Benbow. She came back. 'He'll see you,' she said, waving her in.

Cathy found herself in a beautiful room quite thirty feet long, furnished with the sort of antiques Danny would give his eye-teeth for. Two big windows overlooked the garden at the back. Benbow was on the couch, pulling himself up into a sitting position.

'Don't get up, Mr Benbow,' she said. 'Ettie and I were worried about you. She sent me down to make sure you were all right and I've brought something for your tea.'

Even as she handed the bag to him, Cathy realised the woman could provide as good with no trouble to Benbow.

'I'm feeling much better,' he said, opening the packages to see what she'd brought and exclaiming with pleasure when he saw the slice of ham, a ripe tomato and two fairy cakes from the Exmouth Street Bakery.

'We didn't realise you lived in such a grand house.' Cathy let her eyes go round the room. 'Or that you had somebody to look after your needs.'

'It's very kind of you both. I'm touched.' Benbow was smiling tremulously at her. 'Stay and have a cup of tea. Keep me company.'

He rang a bell and the woman reappeared. 'Tea for two please, Ena.'

When the tea was brought in on a silver galleried tray ten minutes later, Cathy almost gasped aloud. It came in a Georgian silver tea pot, with china cups and slices of fruit cake set out on a starched doily in a silver dish.

'You pour, Cathy.'

'My goodness! This is how we served tea to the major,' she said. 'How posh you are, Benbow.' She lifted one of the dainty tea cups. 'You use all these lovely antiques every day?'

'That's modern, my dear. I wouldn't trust Ena with antique china.'

Cathy laughed. 'You live in great style, like a millionaire.' She thought of the thick pottery cups in which Ettie provided tea, and how gratefully he always seemed to drink it.

'For an old man living alone, it provides a touch of comfort. Put it down to fancy,' he told her. 'I like old things.'

'We thought your circumstances were the same as ours. Do you eat quails' eggs and smoked salmon for your supper?'

'Can't get luxury food like that, Cathy. Not since the war. I shall eat Ettie's ham tonight and be very glad of her kindness. Thank her for me. On second thoughts, I shall be back at work tomorrow, I can thank her myself.'

As she walked home, Cathy felt ashamed that she'd suspected Benbow of making a bit of cash at Danny's expense. Clearly, he didn't need to. She'd got the old chap all wrong.

When Cathy had gone, Benbow lay back on his couch. He'd got over his fall and felt pretty much back to normal. Ettie and Cathy couldn't have been more kind, and he felt grateful. They'd seemed genuinely concerned for his welfare. Arthur couldn't say that about many people these days.

It made him feel a heel that when he'd accepted Danny McLelland's offer, he'd done so with the express idea of using his shop to make profits for himself. He'd been waiting for the right moment, but now he knew he couldn't take advantage of them. They were nice people.

The next morning when he went back to work, a customer was in the shop, and Cathy was serving him. Ettie was there too, polishing up a Pembroke table. He thanked her for the food she'd sent and for looking after him so well.

'A nice bit of ham, that – I really enjoyed it,' he told her. 'Very kind of you to think of it.'

'How are you today, Mr Benbow? No ill effects?'

'No, I'm fine. What d'you want me to do this morning? Go to that sale in Rock Ferry?'

'Better leave that,' she told him. 'Will you go to the warehouse and work on those pieces we bought cheap?'

Danny rented a ramshackle building round the back of the shops that had once been a stable. It was hardly a warehouse, but it was convenient and they did a lot of the work there.

'The pieces from the Halesworth attic? Yes, they'll need a bit of doing up. Is there still room to move in there?'

'Not a lot,' Cathy said, 'now we've had our mammoth loads delivered.'

Ettie looked dreamy. 'Lucky that Cathy found the Botts would do it. They did a good job, didn't they?'

Benbow said, 'They did what we asked them to do, and why shouldn't they? That's their trade.'

'Have you used them before?'

'No, but I've seen them about, fetching from the sales. They've been at it a long time.'

'Frank Bott seems a nice fellow.'

Arthur smiled; it was clear Mrs McLelland was sweet on him.

'Do you know him?' she persisted.

Was she fishing for information? 'Seen him about.'

Ettie turned to Cathy. 'Tell me about his business.'

For once, the girl seemed at a loss. 'They are just about the biggest hauliers in town.'

'I know that.' Ettie showed a touch of impatience.

Cathy was casting about. 'I knew Botty well, of course, but she never talked much about their business.'

Just then, a customer came in asking for a Windsor chair. She took him to see the two they had at the other end of the shop.

Ettie said with some asperity, 'Why does nobody want to talk about them or their business? Somebody said it used to belong to a fellow called Cooper. That's why it's called Cooper's Yard.'

Benbow said slowly, 'The Bott lads worked for him. They grew up in that yard. They are hardworking lads, I'll say that for them.'

'I don't understand why Mrs Bott worked as a housekeeper up at Halesworth Hall. Surely she'd have wanted to stay home to keep house for her sons? Especially as they were running a prosperous business.'

Cathy came back in time to hear some of that. 'I've wondered that myself.'

'So the Botts bought the business?' Ettie mused.

'Missus, if you want to know, you'd better ask Frank.' Arthur reached for his coat. He knew by the way the women were looking at him that they thought there was more to tell about the Bott business than he was giving away. 'I'm going to the warehouse,' he said. The shop bell clanged as he went out.

Arthur knew the Botts wouldn't want their private business discussed. There were a lot of unsavoury facts they'd prefer to have forgotten. He'd be doing Mrs McLelland no favours by telling her. Gossiping about it wouldn't help; it would be much better if Frank told her himself.

Like most people, Arthur had things in his past that were best kept there. He had his secrets, too: he wouldn't want people to know he'd been in prison for adding false provenance to antiques. It was years ago when he'd lived in the back streets of Liverpool. He'd come to Birkenhead to make a new life for himself, and he had succeeded: nobody knew of his past.

Arthur knew well enough why he liked to live in style with expensive antiques all round him. His term of imprisonment had made him hanker for the comforts and luxuries of life. They were necessary to him now.

A few days later, he was sitting at the front of the van as Frank Bott eased it back down the drive of Ivy Cottage towards the road. He'd had to get it as close to the door of the cottage as possible, otherwise the pair of them would have had further to carry the heavy pieces they'd picked up.

Usually, there was no problem. In big houses the gates were built wide enough to take a horse and carriage. But this was not a grand house, and though the drive was wide enough to take a horse and trap, Arthur could hear the trees brushing along the side of the van. The gate was narrower still.

'Whoa there,' Frank muttered to his horse, his face stiff with concentration.

Today they were alone. With only a couple of pieces to collect, Frank had said it wasn't worth bringing a boy. He'd taken most of the weight on himself.

'Nice Welsh dresser we got there.' Benbow was watching the gatepost now only two inches away. 'You'll be all right this side,' he told him.

Once they were out on the road Frank could relax. Benbow looked at him and saw a man in his prime, with thick dark hair and a ruddy complexion.

'You've got the pretty widow interested in you,' Arthur told him.

'What?' Frank spun round, and his dark eyes looked into his.

'Mrs McLelland – she's asking questions.'

'What?'

'About you and your business. You'd better tell her before someone else does.'

Frank shook the reins so they snapped against the horse's flank. It made the animal quicken his pace. 'Thanks,' he said. 'It's not easy.'

'No. She's a nice woman – you could be all right there.'

'Yes,' he sighed.

'Difficult for us old bachelors. Not used to the ways of women.'

Old Benbow sat back then to enjoy the drive. Everybody had their little secrets, he thought again, skeletons in their closets, things they didn't want discussed by one and all. He didn't believe in passing on that sort of gossip. Also, if Frank handled it himself, he couldn't blame anyone else if it put the pretty widow off.

Cathy went home feeling weary after being on her feet all day. She climbed the stairs to the flat and found Otto dozing beside the fire. She could hear Mildred in the kitchen.

'I'm home!' she called out.

'Hello, dear, you're back. Dinner's nearly ready.'

Cathy went straight to Rose who was in her high chair finishing off her evening meal with a hard biscuit. 'Nanna,' she said clearly. 'Nanna.'

Mildred shot out of the kitchen, her face shining with triumph.

'Did you hear her, Cathy? She's saying "Nanna"! Here I am, pet. Here's your Nanna.'

Rose giggled and smiled radiantly at her mother.

'Aren't you clever?' Cathy choked.

She'd heard her babbling 'Mam mam mamma,' and 'Dad dad dadda,' and a lot more besides, but she didn't seem to attach any meaning to those words. Not in the way she seemed to know 'Nanna' meant Mildred. It was ridiculous to be jealous. Cathy knew she ought to feel glad Rose was so well stimulated.

'Mam mam mam mamma,' Mildred said to the child, tickling her chin. That made Cathy feel worse: did Mildred realise how she felt? Was she making it that obvious?

'Mamma mamma,' Rose chortled.

'This is your mamma, my pet. Dad dad dadda.'

Cathy had to lift Rose out of her chair and give her a cuddle. Bury her face in the child so as not to show her jealousy. Rose was all she had left of Rolf and she wasn't seeing nearly enough of her. The baby had bonded more closely with her grandmother than with her.

Cathy told herself she had to earn a living for them both. She was lucky Mildred was willing to do so much for her baby. But it had been Mildred who'd discovered Rose could sit up unaided. No doubt, it would be Mildred who saw her first tooth and found she'd learned to crawl and then to walk.

'Must get the meal dished up, or it'll spoil,' Mildred said, going back to the kitchen. 'Have you had a good day, Cathy?'

All right up till now, she thought. 'Yes, Mildred. Not bad at all,' was what she said.

The war years were dragging on; years of slaughter in the trenches, grief and shortages at home. Another summer came and went, another autumn, another sparse Christmas.

In the last days of 1917, Cathy was working her regular stint on the McLelland accounts. She'd drawn up cheques to meet the end of the month bills and during a lull in the shop, Ettie had come up to sign them. They were pushing them into envelopes when the shop door pinged and Ettie ran down, thinking it was a customer.

All was silent below; she was gone a long time. Cathy carried on with her work, only putting her pen down when she heard Ettie coming back slowly as though she was having to pull herself up the stairs.

She staggered back to her chair and sank down with a little moan, her face paper-white. It was only then that Cathy saw the orange envelope. It was one of the dreaded telegrams.

'Ettie!' She sprang to her feet and put an arm round her shoulders. 'Oh Ettie!'

'I feel sick,' Ettie said. 'Oh Danny, Danny!'

Cathy felt snakes of fear crawling over her. 'It might be to tell you Danny's been injured,' she said, remembering what Jackson had said to her when she'd received a similar telegram. But Jackson had been wrong.

She waited, feeling an explosion was imminent. 'Aren't you going to open it?'

Ettie was sobbing. 'I can't.'

Cathy understood. Until she opened it, there was still hope. 'I'll put the kettle on.'

'You open it,' Ettie said when she came back.

Cathy swallowed hard and prayed, *Please let him be all right*, as she tore open the envelope. She liked Danny; they'd got on well together. He was young with all his life in front of him. She was afraid he'd been killed.

At first she couldn't read the message for the film of tears across her eyes. When she did, she burst out laughing – not far from hysteria.

'Danny's been injured,' she shouted joyfully. 'A bullet wound in the thigh. He's in hospital in Calais nowhere near the fighting now. He's safe, Ettie – *safe*!'

Ettie lifted her face; it was wet with tears but mirrored huge relief. They were laughing and crying at the same time.

Cathy said, 'A bullet wound in the thigh doesn't sound too serious.'

The kitchen was full of steam when she went back to make the tea. 'By way of celebration now,' she laughed, while Ettie mopped at her eyes.

'It's such a load off my mind. I saw my life crashing down. Every one of my five children dead before me. All this buying and selling for Danny – it would be pointless if he were killed, wouldn't it?'

'No,' Cathy said, and wept again. 'It's for you too.'

Within three days of having the telegram, Ettie received a letter from Danny himself. When Cathy arrived for work, she was excitedly waving several pages of closely written notepaper at her.

'Listen to this. "I'm all right, Mam. Don't you worry. It's the sort of wound all us Tommies dream of. I got a bullet in my thigh from a sniper while I was helping to unload bully-beef stew from a cart. With ship's biscuits, cheese and tea, it was dinner for the troops in the front line. Everything has to be carried by hand up to them. It's only a flesh wound, and it's missed the bone. It is earning me a rest in hospital here, then I'll be sent back to Blighty to convalesce. So I'll be home with you in a few weeks' time".'

'That's wonderful news!' Cathy said, giving Ettie a little hug. 'I'm so pleased for you.'

141

'I just wish this awful war would finish. How much more of it can we stand? Danny seems to have had a charmed life to survive this long. Just think of all those who haven't, including your poor Rolf. I shall dread him going away again.'

'It'll be ages before he has to,' Cathy comforted her. 'Think of all the things we've got to show him, and all the things we've got to tell him.'

A week later, Ettie had another letter and was able to tell her that Danny was back in England. He'd been moved to a hospital near London, but they would have to wait another four weeks before he was able to come home. An ambulance was going to bring him and four others up North.

Cathy finished work one afternoon knowing Ettie was expecting Danny to arrive at any moment. She'd been like a cat on hot bricks since midday.

The next morning, Cathy set off to work early. She was really looking forward to seeing Danny again. Ettie had already turned round the notice on the shop door saying it was open. She let herself in, and when the bell stopped jangling, she called, 'Morning, Ettie – it's Cathy!'

'Come on up,' came the reply.

Cathy ran upstairs to find Ellie eating her breakfast alone.

'Didn't he come?' She was disappointed.

'Yes.' Ettie's face was all smiles. 'I told him to stay in bed for his breakfast, but he said he was getting up.'

'Here I am – it takes me a bit longer than it used to. How are you, Cathy?'

That made her spin round eagerly. Her first glimpse of Danny shocked her. He was on crutches and wearing a uniform of hospital blues.

'Cathy,' he said, taking both her hands in his. 'How lovely to see you. You're looking well.' She watched him anchor one of his crutches under his arm. The other slid to the floor with a clatter and she picked it up for him.

'Sorry, I'm not very good with them yet.'

'I hope you won't need them for much longer,' his mother said. 'Come and sit down. I'm doing egg and bacon for you. You need feeding up.'

Cathy could see Danny had lost a lot of weight. His face was thinner and his brown hair had been shorn in an army haircut. His broad smile had gone and his brown eyes seemed full of pain.

'Pour him some tea, Cathy, and have a cup yourself,' Ettie said happily. Cathy was pouring it when the shop bell rang. 'I'll get it,' she said and ran down, glad to get away for a moment to pull herself together. She was afraid her face would tell Danny how shocked she was by his appearance. She'd expected him to be over the worst by now.

The customer asked if they had a desk but didn't like the one she showed him. There was another in the back room; she took him to see it but he didn't like that one either. She saw him out then went back upstairs.

'I had the bullet taken out in a field hospital in France, but my wound went septic,' Danny explained. 'I had to go to theatre again when I got to London and have it opened up. They washed it out with saline twice a day.'

'That sounds painful.'

'Yes, but it's much better.' He smiled and for a moment seemed his old self. 'The doctors tell me it'll heal now.'

'They've finished with you?'

'No, I've got an outpatient appointment at the Borough Hospital and I have to go for physiotherapy.'

'We'll soon have you on the mend,' his mother said. 'Though I hope you'll be able to spend a long time here with us.'

When Old Benbow arrived, he came up to see Danny.

'I'll go down and look after the shop,' Ettie said.

The three of them had a long discussion round the table about what had been done in the business and what they hoped to achieve in the future.

Cathy warmed to Danny. She hadn't realised he was ambitious, that he wanted to expand his business until he owned a chain of shops. He was alert and asking questions, full of enthusiasm to start with, but within the hour he flagged and was soon finding it an effort to concentrate.

'This injury has taken it out of him,' Old Benbow murmured as he and Cathy went downstairs together.

Danny felt a physical wreck. His mother moved like a dancer while he hadn't mastered the crutches and hadn't the energy to keep trying. His leg was so painful he found it difficult to move at all, and he was having nightmares about the trenches. He had never been able to get over his terror of them.

When he'd first gone to France with a group of new soldiers, Danny had tried not to think of them as being replacements for those killed in battle.

After a long slow journey from Calais in ancient cattle trucks, he'd climbed stiffly down to find himself in a surreal world dark with smoke.

The battle was raging uncomfortably close, with constant thunder from heavy guns. The countryside had been devastated. Buildings were reduced to rubble, trees were split and uprooted. There were craters everywhere, and the smell of cordite stung his nostrils.

They were taken to the rest camp which was said to be behind the lines and put in charge of a Sergeant Miller. He looked both tough and hardy and told them he'd survived here for eighteen months, and they'd better listen carefully to what he told them if they wanted to do the same.

In a barn with only half its roof in place, they'd each received a packet of cigarettes, a dollop of bully beef hash into their mess tins and had their mugs filled with lukewarm tea. Sergeant Miller had them on their feet soon afterwards. It was starting to rain.

'I'm taking you to see the trenches,' he bellowed. 'You won't be staying and you won't be going up to the front line today. It's just to get you acquainted, so you'll know what to expect when the time comes.'

'I'll never get used to this,' Danny heard someone whisper behind him. 'Are these British soldiers? Just look at them – they're more like scarecrows.'

They were all shocked at the sight of wet and bedraggled men wearing Balaclavas, sacks and old coats over their mud-stained uniforms, anything to keep out the rain and the cold.

'We had spit and polish drummed into us,' someone else whispered. 'No sign of it here, now they're in action.'

'Single line now as we go up this trench,' bawled the sergeant. 'No talking from here on, and it's very important to keep your heads low – well down below the top of the parapet. If you don't, you could be picked off by a sniper.'

Danny was slithering on the muddy duckboards, third in line behind their leader and finding it hard to keep up. He heard the whine of the rifle shot and the sergeant, who was turning to remind them of something else, just keeled over against the side of the trench and slid down into the mud with a look of surprise on his face.

Danny was totally paralysed. He heard the stunned gasps from behind and the shocked comments. 'What's happened to him? Has he been shot?'

Then another said, 'Should have practised what he preached, shouldn't he?'

A bedraggled corporal took charge. The new recruits were ordered to turn round and retreat. 'And keep your bloody heads down!'

Danny, shivering and terrified, joined the stampede to get away. This wasn't for him; he'd never cope here. He should never have let himself in for this. He didn't calm down until they'd all been back in the barn with half a roof for a couple of hours. He looked round then and realised they were all in a state of shock. Like him, they were all utterly appalled. He spent an uncomfortable and almost sleepless night.

The next morning, he went on parade with the other recruits to be allotted to their places in the regiment.

'First ten to A Company,' the officer shouted, and began reading off the names. 'Next twelve to B Company.' Danny listened attentively to another list of names. He heard his name at last. He was ordered, with two other men, to report to the quartermaster.

Waves of relief washed over him. The other two were all smiles, he could see they felt the same. In the quartermaster's office, he was told he would be helping to deliver meals to the men in the trenches.

The cookhouse was behind the lines. Food was loaded on to carts, and horses pulled it as far as the support lines. From there it had to be manhandled up to the front.

Countless times, Danny had had a heavy insulated container strapped on his back and had to grope his way along endless trenches up to the front. Sometimes it was stew he carried, sometimes it was tea; in the evenings it was usually soup. It had to be dished out and the container returned to the cookhouse. In addition, great boxes of ship's biscuits and tins of jam had to be carried up. Always there was the ration of cigarettes and the rum toddy to fortify the spirits.

Often there were inches of muddy water on top of the greasy duckboards. Enemy shells and gunfire frequently caused the sides of the trenches to collapse, and then he'd have to slither through thick mud. Danny counted himself lucky he didn't have to stay in the front line and fight. He was so pleased to have been given a job he could cope with, and he never forgot how essential it was to keep his head well down. But he'd have preferred to work fulltime in the cookhouse.

When he first got the bullet in his leg, the pain had seemed bearable when it could be offset against home leave. Danny felt his luck had held up until his wound became infected. Still, he was home, away from all that now.

His mother kept putting large platefuls of food in front of him, hoping to build him up, but his appetite had gone and he couldn't eat. He'd got into the habit of sliding part of his meal onto another plate before he started. He knew that upset her.

'Eat it, Danny, it'll do you good.'

'Food's scarce, Mam, and I really can't finish all this.'

The physiotherapy was painful to start with and his leg ached for hours afterwards, but Danny knew it was helping to get him moving, bringing him back to life.

Chapter Twelve

1918

Danny was spending a lot of time with his mother. She was humming a tune as she made a pie for their tea. He couldn't help but notice that she seemed happy.

'Tell me about Frank Bott,' he said. 'You have a new friend.'

Ettie spun round and flushed like a young girl. 'I don't know him very well myself.'

'He's attaching himself to you.'

'What makes you say that?'

'He was here this afternoon.'

'Only to deliver a hall-stand and desk that Old Benbow bought in Widnes.'

'He stayed longer than was necessary.'

'I asked him to have a cup of tea.'

'He managed to leave Jackson down in the shop talking to Cathy. You like him?'

'Yes.' Again she hesitated. He marvelled that at forty-four she could look so young, especially after the traumatic life she'd had. There was a new sparkle in her eyes. 'He's trying to persuade me to go to a show at the Argyle with him.'

'Go, Mam. Why not? You never have any fun.' He saw her flush again. 'You and me,' he said, 'we have to snatch at pleasure when we can. We only just survived, didn't we? But we're over all that now. You've got to look forward, not back.'

'I'm trying. I'll ask him to come and have Sunday dinner with us, so you can get to know him too.'

Sunday came and Danny couldn't help but notice his mother was going to great lengths to have everything just so for Frank Bott. She'd been quite upset that she hadn't been able to get a leg of lamb. She'd had to buy chops instead and was afraid they might be tough.

Frank arrived exactly on time, wearing his best suit. He presented Ettie with a large bunch of daffodils, wrapped in newspaper. Their sharp fresh scent filled the living room.

'Lovely,' Ettie said, burying her face in them. 'Have you grown these yourself?'

'From our garden,' he smiled. 'They come up every year. We don't do much to help them.'

He towered over Danny, and had a chest as broad as his horse's. He lowered his bulk awkwardly on to a chair, exuding good humour and good health. Mam was busy in the kitchen, so Danny tried to talk to him. He thought this strong man of twice his age was rather shy, so he tried to put him at his ease.

'I hear Cathy Godfrey knows your family,' he said. 'And when Ezra Boardman let us down, you were able to move furniture from Halesworth Hall for us.'

'Yes,' he said. 'My aunt knows Cathy.'

'We were very glad to have your help. You have the largest carting business in the district, don't you?'

'So I believe.'

Danny could talk about his own business for hours on end and couldn't understand why this fellow found it so hard to get a word out. But during the meal, his mother managed to get him talking about Cooper's Yard.

'My mother was an invalid. She died when I was thirteen, but from the age of ten I spent a lot of time in Cooper's Yard with Aunt Harriet and her family. She was Herbert Cooper's housekeeper and we lived in that cottage in the yard. You know my Cousin Jimmy – well, we had a happy childhood with the horses to groom and feed. We rode them sometimes, bareback. There were two cats and a dog and always something happening, carts coming and going.'

Danny had to chew hard on his meat. Mam was right about the chops, they *were* tough. He could see Frank sawing at his.

'The men used to take me out on the vans to hold the horses. I liked doing that and when I left school I was employed by Mr Cooper. I've worked in the business ever since.'

It was only when the meal was over and the dishes washed, that he heard Frank suggest to his mother that they should all go for a walk on Thurstaston Common. Danny knew he wouldn't be able to cope with the steep climb or the rough paths, and declined. He was sure they wouldn't want his company anyway.

It was late when his mother returned home. Danny was just thinking of going to bed.

'Have you had a good day?' he asked.

'Yes.' She sat down, looking bemused. 'Frank has been telling me how Cooper's Yard came to belong to his family. He said he thought I should hear it from him.'

Danny waited for more; it didn't come. 'There was a difficult court case, wasn't there?' he prompted.

'Yes, it caused a huge scandal. Once he started to talk about it, I did remember. Not the details, but . . .'

'And?'

'It's better forgotten, Danny.' She looked up at him and smiled.

Danny was pleased she'd found somebody who could make her happy.

After a few weeks, Danny was told he could start putting a little weight on his leg. He decided he would manage without crutches in the house.

'You're doing well,' Cathy told him when she saw him limping from one piece of furniture to the next.

He couldn't tell Cathy he wanted to be fit and well for her; that he'd thought of her through all the terrible months he'd been in France. Even harder to say he had dreamed of her tiny black corkscrew curls swinging round her face and that at this very moment he felt a strong urge to put his arms round her.

She flashed a smile at him. 'A bit more practice, that's all you need.'

'I want to get up and down the stairs.' He was fretting that he couldn't. 'I feel shut away from life. First it was in France and then in hospital. I want to see people and talk to them. I want to get up and down to the shop, and see how it's getting on, and what stock you've got coming in.'

When he did, he was full of praise for what she and Benbow had chosen. Cathy laughed and ran her fingers along the beading on a bureau.

'I lived amongst pieces like this for years at Halesworth, helped dust and polish them too. They're like old friends to me. I'm not sure I like seeing them sold.'

That made him smile. 'Selling them is the only way I know of making a living. Mam says our stock is going like hot cakes.'

'Yes, and Old Benbow's put high prices on them.'

'Between you, you've taken McLelland's Antiques another notch into a higher class. Mam never stops singing your praises.'

Cathy beamed with pleasure. 'Mildred's selling quite a lot in the old butcher's shop, too. She acts as though she's opened a branch for you. You know she's charging you commission?'

'You wrote and told me. That's fine – it gives her something and I don't have the cost of setting a shop up and employing someone.'

'Mildred needs to feel she's earning a little. She looks after Otto and Rosie but she's brimming with energy.'

'How is Rosie?' Danny saw her face soften.

'Growing up; very well cared for and much loved by us all.'

He'd kept all Cathy's letters and read them through many times. He'd longed for news of her rather than of his business and had even asked for it. It hadn't come. Her letters were really business reports, though she often mentioned his mother and Old Benbow.

Now he was home and seeing more of her, he'd been having dreams about Cathy he couldn't mention to anyone. She was lying in bed beside him, naked. It was what he craved for, but even in his dreams, somehow he never managed to make love to her. The fact that she'd been Rolf's wife and was likely to be more experienced in lovemaking, made her seem more exciting. One day, when he was no longer a cripple, he'd tell her he loved her and ask her to marry him. Even if his dreams didn't go that far, he was determined he'd do it in real life.

When Danny felt he could manage the stairs, he said, 'I'd like to start going out. I want to walk about the streets and see people, but I'll need an arm to lean on to start with. Will you take me?'

Again her smile flashed at him. He knew she wanted to do it.

'You need a walking stick,' his mother told him. 'You shouldn't put all your weight on Cathy.'

'Otto has several,' she said. 'I'll ask him if he'll lend you one.'

She'd brought Danny a stick the next morning. 'Is it the right height for you? He said you can chop an inch off if it's too long.'

It was a bit long. Otto was taller than he was, but Danny didn't like to cut it down. He hoped he wouldn't need it for long. He told Cathy it was just right. Every day now, he asked her to take him out.

'I feel alive again. I love to see the shops open and the crowds bustling about.'

What he didn't say was that hanging on to her arm and having her chatting to him was utter bliss. That was something else he'd fantasised about while he'd been at the front. Now it was giving him huge pleasure, lifting him up. He could feel her warmth and was dazzled by her. She had perfect teeth and a lovely smile and he'd never seen such fair, almost translucent skin. Each day she let him walk a little further, taking on the role of nurse.

'Tomorrow,' he said after a couple of weeks of this, 'I want to get all the way down to Market Street.'

'It's further than you've walked before.'

'But I'll be able to have a rest before we walk back.'

'Then the best time to go is in the lunch-hour when the shop's closed. Mildred says she'd like to see you and I must bring you in for a cup of tea.'

'Good, we'll have a sandwich here before we go.'

Cathy loved her little outings with Danny and had to laugh when he spoke of them as being work for her. 'I enjoy them,' she said. 'It's the best job in the day.'

She thought Danny enjoyed the walk down to Market Street but he looked daunted when he saw the steep stairs up to the flat. She knew he was tired and found the climb hard. They were halfway up before Mildred heard them. She flung open the living-room door and beamed down at them.

'Hello, Danny. Good to see you. Come on up, lad.'

He'd stopped by then to get his breath but that made him struggle on.

'Hello,' Rosie said, ducking under Mildred's arm to see who was coming. 'It's Mammy and . . .'

'Danny,' he puffed.

'Mr McLelland,' Mildred corrected. 'Children have to be brought up to show respect to their elders and betters. What's this gentleman's name, Rosie?'

'Mr Lello.'

Danny laughed. 'My, you've grown since I last saw you. How old are you now, Rosie?'

'Two.'

'Nearly two,' Mildred said. 'She's twenty months and very forward for her age.'

'Very pretty too,' Danny said, 'and I think your dress is lovely.'

Rosie was wearing a new outfit because Mildred was expecting them. She was holding up the blue wool skirt of her dress to show a white voile petticoat trimmed with wide bands of lace.

'Lubbly here too,' she lisped.

'You little minx.' Mildred knocked her hands away from her skirts. 'Young ladies don't do that.'

Cathy gathered up her daughter and gave her a hug, while Mildred was ushering Danny to an armchair. Otto occupied the one on the other side of the fire.

'Hello, lad. Glad to see you home again.'

'How are you, Mr Gottfried?'

'Godfrey now,' Mildred corrected.

151

'Of course, I'm sorry. Force of habit. I'll sit on a straight chair if I may.' Danny sat at her table. 'Easier to get up from here.'

Cathy watched him looking round the room. There was a silence that was vaguely uncomfortable. Mildred had prepared and decorated two varieties of cup cakes for the occasion, and arranged them on two cake-stands on the table.

Danny said, 'Those cakes look good.'

She pressed him to have one.

'How's your table standing up to it?' he asked.

'Fine.' Mildred lifted the corner of her best damask cloth to show him. 'You'd hardly know it had been damaged, would you?'

She poured tea for them all and handed the cakes round again. 'I'm glad you've been able to get here, Danny, because I want to talk to you about business.'

'By all means. I see you've had a sign-writer round recently.'

'Yes, we decided to call our shop Second Time Around. All secondhand stuff, you see.'

'Cathy wrote and told me. But she didn't tell me what a very smart shop you've made it, Mrs Godfrey. I must congratulate you on that.'

'Business is beginning to pick up. I'll show you round on your way out.' She got up and proffered her cakes again.

'They're delicious,' Danny told her, 'but I couldn't possibly eat another.'

'What I wanted to talk to you about,' Cathy saw her mother-in-law cast an anxious glance in her direction, 'is the commission. Cathy wanted me to charge you five per cent on what I sell for you, but I had to insist on ten – and really that isn't enough. I'd like fifteen.'

'Mildred!' Cathy was incensed. 'You could have mentioned this to me first. I had no idea—'

'No point in talking to you about it, you wouldn't agree.'

'But I do,' Danny told her. 'I don't think fifteen per cent is too much. Not for what you do.'

'I do,' Cathy said obstinately. 'We're supposed to be partners, Mildred – in business together, that was the arrangement.' She was burning with indignation. 'You shouldn't ask Danny for more commission without consulting me first.'

'It's me that has to earn it. You're out all day.'

'But you're taking over, doing almost everything without even talking to me about it. I was going to see to the furniture, but you're taking over that too, deciding whether to buy or not without reference to me.'

Rosie was pulling on Otto's hand, and her baby voice asked, 'Has Nanna been naughty?'

That brought Cathy to an abrupt stop. The atmosphere seemed suddenly electric. Danny levered himself to his feet, wanting to get away before any more was said. Mildred was stiff and tight-lipped. After her outburst, Cathy thought she'd have forgotten about her offer to show him round her business. But once downstairs, Mildred turned the sign round on the shop door to show it was open and led him round her premises.

'What a difference you've made,' he said. 'I'm more than impressed.' Cathy could see he really was. As well as the furniture and other household bric-a-brac, Mildred had a fine display of bedspreads and curtains. A large notice informed customers that eiderdowns could be recovered.

'I make all these small things from the bits that are left over,' she said, showing him a display of tea cosies, oven mitts, table runners, anti-macassars and dressing-table sets. 'I also do dressmaking for private clients, if they can provide the cloth.'

Cathy was still breathing fire as they set off back to Exmouth Street.

'I understand what she's doing to you, Cathy, but you have to give praise where it's due. Mildred's a good businesswoman. Got her head screwed on the right way. The place looks smart and prosperous.'

'She's pushing me out.'

He tried to soothe her. 'Well, you work hard for me, so you can't have that much energy left at the end of the day. Not with Rosie to look after, too.'

'I would have for that. I was going to take care of the furniture side, but Mildred's doing that now as well. She doesn't even ask my opinion. She just *tells* me when something needs French polishing or repainting.'

'You can't do everything.'

'And I think she was a bit pushy, asking for fifteen per cent from you. You were kind enough to say she needn't pay you anything when she was putting her sewing into your shop.'

'Yes, well perhaps she was, but she's been good to my family in the past, and you said her fancy cushions and bedspreads made my shop look rich.'

Cathy sighed. 'Customers did come in to buy a couple of cushions and sometimes saw a piece of furniture they liked and bought that too.'

'There you are, then. Also, my business is doing well now. I don't want to be mean to Mildred.'

'Neither do I.'

Cathy knew Danny felt very weary by the time they'd walked back to his home and he'd heaved himself up the stairs. He collapsed at the dining table and asked her to get out the account books.

'Let's work out how much Mildred has sold for me over the last year.'

Cathy sat beside him. It was she who picked out the items and added them up. They were both surprised it was so much.

He said, 'You mustn't worry about her, Cathy. She wants to do things for you.'

'I leave too much to her.'

'She's very efficient.'

'I know and I should be grateful. She does a lot for me. Wants to look after my every need, including some I didn't know I had. Is this what mothering is like?' She looked up and found him studying her.

He said, 'Now I'm grown up, Mam and I look after each other.'

'Rolf said his mother loved him *too* much – that he felt smothered by it. I didn't know what he meant then.'

Danny's hand came down on her wrist. 'It's Rosie, isn't it? Mildred's taking over the mothering.'

It surprised Cathy to find him so perceptive. 'I suppose I do resent that. Oh dear! Am I making it obvious?'

'Not you, it was the way Rosie turned to her. They're fond of each other, be glad of that. Mildred's her grandmother, after all.'

Cathy was pondering on that. Was she being unreasonable? She hardly noticed him moving closer until he put his arms round her and kissed her full on the lips.

She jerked away from him, startled, but her heart fluttered wildly. He was reviving memories of passion she'd had to suppress. His dark eyes gazed into hers, full of love. She was shocked; she'd never thought of Danny in that way.

She watched him draw back. 'I've embarrassed you.' He was horrified, apologetic. 'Look – I couldn't stop thinking about you, Cathy, when I was in France.'

She had to stop him. 'No – *no*, Danny!'

'Thinking of you took me from the desolation to a more tranquil world. I couldn't have managed without it.'

'Danny, I'm not over Rolf yet. I'm so sorry.'

She saw the light go out of his face. He shook his head in despair and turned away. 'It's me that should be sorry. I'm rushing you. I wanted you to know how I feel.'

'But I don't think—'

'I love you, Cathy. When Rolf introduced you as his wife, I was envious, d'you know that?'

That hadn't occurred to her. His hand came up to touch her hair.

'What did you think of *me*?'

She shook her head; she'd had eyes only for Rolf. Now she saw that day as being perfect because she'd been with him.

'Tell me.'

'You were Rolf's friend. He'd mentioned you, he was fond of you.'

'But that's what Rolf thought. What about you?' His eyes were searching into hers.

She had to be truthful. She'd been prepared to like Rolf's friends, share them.

'I had eyes for no one else, not then. Rolf was the first person to love me. In my whole life, I mean. He meant everything to me.'

'It must be hard for you now he's gone.' Danny attempted to put his arm round her shoulders again but she moved away. She couldn't answer.

He looked stricken. 'Couldn't you think about me, just a little? You're still young . . .'

'I'm twenty-one.'

'Your life's still in front of you.'

Cathy felt she had a fair amount behind her too. She'd believed she'd found deep and everlasting love from Rolf. To lose it again so quickly had been a profound and moving experience. She'd known that marrying him would change everything for her. It had, even if he was no longer with her. She was making her life round Rosie and her in-laws.

Danny was shaking his head. 'You're living in the past – you'll never be happy that way. You don't want to spend the rest of your life alone, do you?'

Cathy didn't know what to say. 'I haven't thought about it. Not like that.'

When she'd learned that Rolf had been killed, she'd had to take each day as it came in order to survive. Then it had been impossible to think about the weeks and months ahead without him. But she was stronger now and used to being on her own.

Danny patted her wrist again. 'I'll ask you again, if I may, when I come home for good. All right?'

She nodded; tears were smudging her sight. She liked Danny, was very much at ease in his company and they had shared interests. But love him? She wasn't sure. Not in the way she'd loved Rolf.

Danny couldn't get away from Cathy quickly enough. What had he done? She'd been so relaxed and at ease with him before he'd opened his mouth. She'd been so outgoing and willing in what she was doing for him. Now all that was gone. She was tonguetied and wouldn't even look at him.

155

He'd done his best to get himself well as soon as he could. He'd exercised his leg and eaten more than his fill, but his whole aim had been to make himself fit enough to walk out with Cathy. Fit enough to propose to her. She wouldn't want an invalid for a husband. He'd hoped they could be engaged, if not married before he went back to France. He wanted to be sure she'd wait for him but in the end he hadn't actually proposed at all.

What a fool he'd been to rush in like that just because he felt well enough to cope. Well, he'd been wrong – he couldn't cope with this. She wasn't over Rolf!

He went to bed early, feeling very down. It seemed Cathy hadn't thought of him except as an employer and a friend of her husband. She'd taken care of his business, nothing seemed too much trouble to her in that respect. Mam was fond of her, but he hadn't asked himself what *she* wanted. Hadn't put himself in *her* place.

But perhaps it wasn't completely hopeless. She'd said she wasn't over Rolf yet; he wasn't sure he was either. Danny felt he'd be a proud man if he had a girl still hankering after him two years after he'd been laid to rest. Rolf had always had great charm.

But at least, while Cathy had nobody else in mind, he was still in with a chance.

Cathy walked home from work telling herself she really did need to think about her feelings for Danny. She couldn't get his face out of her mind – sincere, gentle, full of hope.

He'd said, 'Think about what you want from life.' Was it possible to have more than she'd supposed?

For two years, she'd been longing to have Rolf back, but that wasn't possible. She'd been looking back and grieving for what had gone for good. Danny was forcing her to look forward for the first time. He was right, she couldn't spend the rest of her life grieving for what she'd lost.

Danny had said he loved her. She couldn't get over that, so unexpected. It brought a warm feeling now, an inner excitement she hadn't felt for a long time. It hardly seemed possible he'd be interested in her. Rolf had thought a widow with a young child an unlikely burden for another man to take on.

Of course, Danny hadn't exactly proposed. Was she reading more into that than he'd intended? She didn't think so. Danny was straight, he wouldn't say he loved her unless he did. She'd upset him by shying off and he hadn't said all he'd intended. She couldn't say now why she'd done that. Loving a second time didn't mean being disloyal. Rolf would have understood, he'd have encouraged her to find another husband. He'd dreaded leaving her a widow to bring up his daughter on her own. He'd been fond of Danny too.

Although she'd told Danny she hadn't thought about him in that way, she'd felt a quickening of her heart almost straight away. She'd always liked him; she'd enjoyed his company these last few weeks and yes, she had grown fond of him. There were different sorts of love: what she'd feel for Danny would never be exactly what she'd felt for Rolf.

But she hadn't explained that to him. Instead, she'd knocked him back, kicked him down. She mustn't keep him wondering for weeks on end. He'd have to go back to the front when he was better. But if she let herself love him, it would mean living in dread that he, too, might be killed and she'd receive another of those awful telegrams. All the same, she felt life beginning to flow back into her veins.

Ten minutes after Cathy reached home, Mildred had dinner ready and on the table. Rosie was old enough to eat with them now. As Cathy played with her, she thought of Danny.

It was an evening like most others, except that she felt more alive, more optimistic than she had for some time. Otto, too, seemed less lethargic. He very rarely left his chair now. His hands were always cold and he wanted a fire even on warm days, but tonight his cheeks were flushed and he, too, was ready to play with Rosie.

'I want a ride, Grandpa. Be my pony. Be Dapple Grey.' She climbed astride one of his legs. 'Gee up.' Obligingly he bounced her up and down.

'Faster, Grandpa! Dapple-grey can go fast. He's a big pony.'

Otto did his best, but Cathy feared he tired of the game before Rosie did. He seemed glad when her bedtime came, but he wasn't his usual silent self even then. He and Mildred talked of the days when Danny was a lad and his family had been so ill, and without a breadwinner. It seemed Otto was fond of Danny too. Cathy went to bed still thinking of him. Tomorrow, she'd tell him how she felt.

It was still dark when she woke up with a start.

'Cathy, Cathy – wake up!' Mildred was in her room, ghostly in a long white nightdress. 'Please, wake up!' There was urgency in her voice.

'What is it?'

'Otto – come quick. His speech is slurred again. He doesn't know who I am.'

Cathy slid out of bed and followed Mildred back to her own room. The candle had been lit, and the clock told her it was half past four. Otto was agitated; she couldn't make out what he was trying to say.

Cathy asked, 'Aren't you feeling well?'

'He's confused, doesn't know where he is.' Mildred was panic-stricken. 'He was so much better last night.'

Cathy's heart sank. 'Is it another stroke, d'you think?' She'd understood that was the main danger.

Mildred was shaking her head. 'It could be, couldn't it?'

'Shall I go for the doctor?'

'I don't know. I can't think.'

'I'll get dressed and go,' Cathy told her.

It was a fine morning and the first light was just coming in the sky. The streets were empty. She ran most of the way and hammered on the doctor's front door. It seemed a long time before there was any response. He came at last, wearing a dressing-gown and looking half-asleep. She had to repeat Otto's name.

'Come in and wait,' he said. 'I'll get dressed and come back with you.' She stood in his hall until he came down carrying his black bag.

He walked with her in the cold light of dawn, and when they reached Market Street, Cathy took him straight upstairs. Mildred met them with tears running down her face. 'I think he's gone,' she sobbed. 'I think he's gone.'

Chapter Thirteen

Otto's death had come with little warning and was brutally swift. Cathy was shocked, she could see Mildred was too. It knocked the confidence out of her, changed her beyond recognition; her usual efficiency was gone, she was weeping uncontrollably. Cathy gave her a hug and tried to provide comfort.

It was only when Rosie woke up and came to throw her arms round her grandmother that she calmed down. Cathy busied herself making breakfast but only Rosie ate anything. Mildred wanted to sit by Otto's body but Cathy took her to her own bedroom and insisted she try to sleep in her bed.

Then she put Rosie in her push-chair and set out to do the tasks the doctor had told her must be done. She registered Otto's death and put the funeral arrangements in hand.

She called in at the shop in Exmouth Street. Ettie was serving there alone. 'Is Danny in?' she mouthed behind the customer.

'No, he's gone out with Old Benbow.'

Cathy sat down to wait and pulled Rosie on her knee, but more customers came in and she got up to serve them.

'Is something the matter?' Ettie asked when the shop emptied.

Cathy told her. 'I don't want to leave Mildred today,' she said. 'She's very upset.'

'Take a few days off,' Ettie told her. 'Danny would want you to. Until after the funeral, anyway.'

On the way home, Cathy knew that Otto's death was now in the forefront of her mind. It had pushed out the urgency she'd felt about talking to Danny. She went to the market and bought a bunch of flowers, but couldn't have said whether she meant them for Mildred or Otto.

It was almost lunchtime when the undertakers called to lay out the body and take the measurements for the coffin. The flurry of activity disturbed Mildred who came into the living room to discuss the funeral arrangements with them.

Cathy was busy in the afternoon too; she asked Polly Weaver to come in and keep Mildred company while she went out shopping. She stopped at the vicarage to ask the vicar to officiate at the funeral. He called on Mildred that evening.

It was when he'd gone and Cathy had tucked Rosie up in her little bed that Mildred began to talk.

'Otto was such a kind man. A very loving man. He couldn't do enough for me.'

Cathy had bought two bottles of sherry for the funeral tea, but now she opened one and poured them each a glassful.

'D'you know what he said last night? That I must look after myself from now on. It was as though he knew . . .'

'Perhaps we all know when we get close to it.'

'But he seemed so much better, more interested in things. He ate a good meal last night and he wanted to play with Rosie.'

'Perhaps he wasn't sorry to go, Mildred. He found it almost impossible to get up and down the stairs. He was a prisoner in this flat.'

Mildred mopped her eyes with a damp handkerchief. 'But I thought he was getting a new lease of life.'

'It was savagely sudden – we weren't expecting it.'

'I feel devastated.'

'Mildred, the doctor said he'd had another stroke, a much bigger one that would have left him paralysed. For him, perhaps this is the best way.'

'I'll miss him so much. He was very kind to me. I've always been grateful.'

'You've been extra good to him, these last months.'

'D'you think so?' Mildred's eyes were red and puffy. 'I've often felt impatient, you know. I hope I didn't show it. I should never have been impatient with him. He rescued me, as you know, when I was having Rolf.'

Cathy stared into the fire. 'Didn't you have a family to help you?' she asked gently.

'My mother died when I was nineteen. She'd been ill for some time.'

'You were grown up by then.' No need for Mildred to be sent to an orphanage.

'Yes. I'd looked after her and I kept house when she no longer could. But I was an apprentice dressmaker and I wouldn't be out of my time for two more years. My father married again quite quickly, and my stepmother wanted to do the housekeeping.'

'You didn't get on?' Cathy was trying to be sympathetic.

'I was cross with him – I thought he shouldn't have been in such a hurry to marry again.'

'And being newly wed, they didn't welcome a grown-up daughter living with them?'

'No.' Mildred sighed. 'Everything went wrong for me then. I'd talked to my mother about setting up a dressmaking business when I was out of my time. She was all for it, and encouraged me, but my stepmother didn't want me doing it in her home. I offered to work in my bedroom, but she said she couldn't put up with my customers tramping upstairs.'

'You could have got a dressmaking job.'

'That's what she said. I found a firm who were willing to take me on, but before I started I had a serious row with my father. He told me to get out.'

'Oh, Mildred!'

'There was nothing for it then but to go into domestic service. I had to have a roof over my head.'

Mildred began to cry again – harsh sobs of regret – and Cathy wordlessly took her hand.

The funeral was to be on Friday. Cathy wanted it over; the days since Otto had died seemed long drawn out. He'd been put in his coffin which was standing on a bier in his bedroom. On Mildred's instructions, the lid wasn't put on, it stood against the dressing-table. Cathy had made the bed up with clean sheets and dusted everything thoroughly.

There was a steady flow of neighbours and old customers calling to pay their last respects. Many brought flowers and every vase in the house had been filled. The room was heavy with their scent.

Mildred had wanted to sleep in the room and it was only with difficulty that Cathy persuaded her to share her bed.

She asked, 'All three of us in one small room?'

'Just until Friday,' Cathy said firmly.

The day of the funeral turned out to be dark and wet. Rosie was looked after by a friend of Polly Weaver's, because Polly wanted to come to the funeral. Otto was buried at Flaybrick Cemetery at eleven in the morning. Cathy saw Danny there with his mother, offering condolences to Mildred.

'Old Benbow's in charge of the shop this morning,' he told her. 'Don't you rush back to work – we're managing all right.'

'Thank you. I'll leave it until Monday, then.'

Cathy asked them back to Market Street for refreshments; the living room was crowded. Since Otto had died, to think of Danny had been her comfort, but she was very conscious of the need to clear the air between them. She had no time to talk to him today, however; her attention was taken up by Mildred and her guests.

161

* * *

On Monday morning, Cathy set off for Exmouth Street feeling sorry that she hadn't been able to ask Danny's forgiveness before now. She wanted to let him know she hadn't intended to show rejection.

It all seemed an age ago, almost another lifetime. She was afraid she'd let things grow cold between them. She'd tell him today that she'd thought it over and would welcome . . . welcome what? More attention from him? His affection? She didn't know how to say it, but she knew she had to make her feelings clear to him.

Danny and his mother were eating breakfast when she arrived. Cathy couldn't talk to him in front of Ettie. What she needed to say was very personal. Ettie poured her a cup of tea and told her how sorry she was about Otto.

'How's Mildred taking it?' Danny asked.

'Badly. She thought the world of him.'

They'd been talking about a house sale that was coming up next Wednesday. Danny picked up a brochure that had come in the morning's post.

'There's some good furniture here. A ladies' writing-table in rosewood, the top banded in satinwood. A pair of Regency tub chairs, Thomas Hope style. I can't miss this one.'

Cathy almost said, 'I'd like to come with you. It would be an outing, a nice change.' Over the past months he'd taken her to several sales.

He said, without looking at her, 'I'll take Old Benbow with me.'

That made her throb with hurt and disappointment. She swallowed hard and told herself it showed how much pain she'd inflicted on him. As soon as she reasonably could, she went down to the shop and opened up, hoping she'd have an opportunity to have it out with him quite soon. Danny was in the habit of seeking her out for a chat every so often.

But not, it seemed, any more. She heard him coming downstairs and looked up with a smile as he came towards her.

He already had his hat and coat on. 'I'll be back in an hour or so,' he said but didn't stop.

He was reaching out to open the door when Cathy flung herself in front of it. She couldn't let this go on; it was turning things sour. Now with his surprised eyes looking into hers, she didn't know where to begin.

'I want you to know,' she choked, 'you've brought me back to life. You told me to think about what I wanted. From life, I mean.' She knew she wasn't doing this right, but his lips were no longer turning down. 'You're right. I can't go on looking backwards.'

He was smiling. 'You do care about me? Love me?'

'Give me time . . .'

'Of course, all the time in the world.' He was bending to kiss her when Cathy felt a customer push the door against her back.

There was an elderly couple on the doorstep. 'Bit early in the morning for that, isn't it?' the woman teased. Danny was still wearing his hospital blues and everybody had a soft spot for an injured soldier. 'You are open for business?'

'Sorry, yes.' Cathy opened the door wider. 'Do come in.'

'I'll see you when I come back,' Danny murmured, slipping off.

Cathy's head was swimming with joy that she hadn't discouraged him completely.

The woman smiled at her. 'You said you might be able to get us a music canterbury.' Cathy recognised them; the couple came in every few weeks to see their new stock.

'Yes, we have two here at the moment. I brought them them down from the warehouse for you to see. Here we are. This one is mid-Victorian walnut.' It had three fret-carved divisions and a frieze.

'It's very fancy. What d'you think, Giles?'

He was shaking his head doubtfully. 'I don't like it much.'

'Or there's this Regency one in mahogany.'

'That's more what I had in mind. Yes, plain and practical. I like that. We're refurnishing our home,' the old gentleman beamed at her. 'Buying when we see something we like, investing in antiques.'

'We'll have it,' his wife decided. They were the sort of straightforward customers Danny valued.

Danny was on his way to the Borough Hospital, where conveniently for him, the army had taken over some of the beds. He had an appointment with a consultant to have his injury assessed. He felt jittery. Last time, a month ago, he'd half-expected to be passed fit to return to the front, and knew that sooner or later, that moment would come.

He was thrilled and excited about what Cathy had just said to him. She *was* fond of him – he'd felt that all along and couldn't believe he'd been mistaken.

Danny had to wait to see the doctor; the waiting room was full. He wished now he hadn't done his best to hasten his return to health because it also hastened his return to the trenches. He didn't want to go back; he was scared stiff, but that wasn't something a soldier dared admit.

The thought of leaving Cathy was truly painful, just when it seemed he could open up a whole new life with her. Nor did he want to leave his mother; he knew Ettie was dreading his departure almost as much as he was. And it had taken him all these weeks to feel on top of his own business again. Cathy, Mam and Old Benbow had changed it out of all recognition. They were earning more for him than he'd managed to earn for himself. He longed to be able to stay here, where everything was going well for him.

When his name was called, Danny felt the sweat breaking out on his forehead. He was getting used to having a nurse take him behind screens, telling him to take his trousers off so that both his legs could be seen. As he climbed on the examination couch to wait again, he kept his mind firmly on Cathy.

The doctor eventually came and prodded his wound. 'It's healed nicely. How d'you feel?' he asked.

Danny had considered swinging the lead at this point, but instead he told the truth. 'I feel well, sir. I can walk as well as I ever did.' He was told to get down and demonstrate that.

'Well,' said the doctor, 'I expect you could use another week or two's convalescence, couldn't you?'

'Yes, sir.'

'Right. Report for duty on the first of next month. D'you know the Oval Sports Ground in Bebington – the barracks there?'

The end was coming, but Danny wouldn't let himself be too down-hearted. He still had two and a half more weeks at home.

When he returned, the shop was closed for the dinner-hour. He took the stairs two at a time, just to prove to himself that he could. His mother met him at the living-room door.

'It's all right then? You're still on the sick?'

'No.' He saw her smile fade. 'Not any longer.'

'Oh! I thought you seemed pleased?'

'It had to come, but the good news is I don't have to go back until the start of next month.'

'That's something.' Danny knew she didn't think it enough.

'Where's Cathy?'

'She's gone home for her lunch today.'

Danny saw their table had been set for two; a large pork pie and pickles had been laid out in readiness. 'Might as well have ours then.'

'Right, I'll just make the tea first.'

While they ate he told her what the doctor had said, but all the time his mind was on Cathy.

'Will you be all right in the shop this afternoon?' he asked. 'I want Cathy to do something else.'

'Yes, of course.'

He knew Cathy would come back promptly at two, and he decided to meet her. He reached for his hat.

'It's raining,' his mother said. 'Take your oilskin if you're going out.'

Danny took the big umbrella from the hall-stand, too. He'd barely got it up outside the shop when he saw Cathy turn in from Claughton Road almost at a run. She had no umbrella. There were beads of moisture on her hat, and in the wet, her corkscrew curls were tighter than usual.

'I've told Mam she's in charge of the shop this afternoon,' he said. 'Come for a walk?'

'In this?' Her bright blue eyes smiled at him. 'Would you believe it was fine when I left home?'

Danny felt happy now he'd drawn her under his umbrella and was holding on to her arm.

'We need to talk,' he told her. 'I can't say what I want to in the shop. Mam's never far away and you're up and down to customers.'

Her arm tightened on his, and her hand felt for his. It was warm and comforting.

'I've been passed as fit, Cathy. I'll have to go back but I've been given another two weeks.'

'Did you go for a medical assessment this morning? I didn't know.'

'I tried to push it to the back of my mind. I knew this time, I was likely to be passed fit.' He stopped and turned to face her. 'Before I go, I want to settle things between us.'

'Danny . . .'

'I'm not going to rush you into any promises. I just want to know where I stand with you.'

'I feel as though you're bringing me back to life. As though you've wakened me up.'

'So I'm good for you?'

Her smile was radiant. 'You are. You were right – I can't grieve for ever.'

'I've loved you for a long time,' he murmured as they walked on. 'I'd like us to be engaged but I can wait, if you tell me there's hope.'

'There's definitely hope, Danny. I'm very fond of you. We get on well together.'

On the spur of the moment, he pulled her to a halt in front of a jeweller's shop window. Expensive rings sparkled up at him.

'Do you like diamonds? Would you wear my ring?'

'No, Danny, no!'

He felt a rush of disappointment. He'd thought all girls liked to wear jewellery.

She looked disconcerted. 'It's too soon. I need time to get used to the idea.' She was trying to explain. 'I was struck all of a heap when Rolf was killed. It overwhelmed everything. I've been only half-aware of what's going on around me ever since.'

'No, Cathy. Benbow says you're really alert in the sale rooms. Mam thinks you're great in the shop, and you keep all the record books up to date. I know you're efficient . . .'

'Emotionally, I mean. My feelings have been sort of frozen. I enjoy working for you. I'm looking forward to the future, and I want to spend more time with you. But I need to think about it all. It would mean big changes, a whole new life.'

'It would for me too. I've never done this before, Cathy. You're the first girl . . . I'd like to buy you a ring as a token of my love.'

'No, Danny! People would assume we're engaged.'

'Don't you want to be?' He felt cold inside; he didn't understand.

'I need time to think about it.' She was speaking slowly, giving it close thought. 'I'm not quite ready to get married again yet. That's what you're asking, isn't it?'

He nodded. 'Yes.'

'Getting engaged is total commitment as I see it.'

'Cathy, I feel totally committed to you. I want to marry you, be with you, be a father to Rosie.'

'I have to be sure I can give you enough love. I don't want to short-change you on that. Give me a bit more time.'

'Of course.' Danny could understand that.

'Mildred will need time, too. I mean, what would she think if I went home with an engagement ring tonight?'

That made him bristle. 'I don't care what she thinks. It's what you and I think that matters.'

'I have to consider her feelings, Danny. She thinks of me and Rosie as her family, and it's Rolf who binds us. The last thing she'd want is for me to get married again.'

'You can't let what Mildred wants run your life.'

'I won't, but she's just lost Otto. She's feeling raw . . .'

The rain was coming down more heavily, bouncing up off the pavement. Danny said, 'Look, there's a café down there. Let's go in for a cup of tea.'

As he was shaking the surplus water off his umbrella in the doorway, Cathy said, 'I hate the thought of you going back to the trenches. I couldn't bear it if you were killed, too.'

'Cathy, we none of us know what's going to happen. Marriage is a risk even in peacetime.'

She led the way to an empty table near the window which was all steamed up. There was a low buzz of conversation.

'Fancy a toasted tea cake, too?'

'Yes, please. I want you to think about what marriage to me would mean, Danny.'

'I know I'd be taking on Rosie too. She's a lovely little girl, and she's Rolf's. I'd count it a privilege to help bring up his child.' Danny could see now that persuading Cathy to marry him involved more than he'd first supposed.

He asked Cathy if she'd like to go out with him one evening and suggested they see a Charlie Chaplin film at the Queen's Hall.

'I'll have to ask Mildred if she would mind babysitting,' she said.

The following day she told him that Mildred had said, 'You go, Cathy. Rosie sleeps soundly; she doesn't wake up in the evenings.'

A few days later, Danny invited her to see a play at the Theatre Royal and once again Mildred had said she was happy to babysit. 'Rosie's no trouble. You go out whenever you like.'

Cathy said, 'Mildred, I feel you ought to go out sometimes.'

'Me? Wherever would I go?'

'You could ask Mrs Weaver next door if she'd go to the pictures with you.'

'I'd rather stay home and look after Rosie.'

Cathy told him she was a bit disconcerted because Mildred seemed to be pushing her out. She wanted to get Rosie ready for bed and read her bedtime story to her every night, whether Cathy was staying in or not.

The following two Sunday afternoons, Danny took Cathy and Rosie out. They went by bus over to the Dee estuary and walked over the downs, and the next time went along the promenade at West Kirby, ending up in a tea shop.

He was getting ready to go out again one night, when his mother said, 'You're spending a lot of time with Cathy. You seem quite attached to her.'

'You know I am.'

'You're serious?'

'Yes, but I'm not too sure how she feels. I'm hoping she'll come round to it.'

'I hope she does. She's a lovely girl.'

'Don't say anything to Mildred about it.'

'Why not?'

'Cathy was Rolf's wife. She won't want her to take up with me.'

'She can't help but notice. Cathy spends every day here and you're taking her and Rosie out a lot.' Ettie turned away, taking some of the dishes to the kitchen after their evening meal. 'Anyway, I hardly ever see Mildred.'

Cathy didn't confide her growing interest in Danny McLelland to Mildred, but she made no effort to hide it. However, her mother-in-law seemed to prefer to have Rosie all to herself.

'Rosie's a real comfort to me. A bit of company now Otto's gone.'

Mildred usually asked where Danny was taking her, and on hearing it was the Argyll or the Gaiety or the Theatre Royal, would enquire how she'd enjoyed the show when she came home.

Cathy thought about Danny and their future. Of course she wanted to marry him. Since he'd asked her to work in his business, he and Ettie had taken up the major part of her day. She wouldn't want to change that; she'd have a narrower life without them.

At the bottom of her heart she knew she was afraid to let herself love Danny. She was terrified he'd be sent back to the front where the carnage was continuing unabated, and he'd be killed as Rolf had been. She told herself it was illogical, that whether she married him or not, it would not affect Danny's fate in the trenches. She'd be heartbroken now if he were killed.

The day came when Danny had to report back to camp. It was only a short bus-ride away and he wrote to tell Cathy he'd be given a forty-eight-hour pass after two weeks.

He wrote every day, and she perused his letters quickly to see if he'd heard when he was being sent back to France. Then she read them again and was able to enjoy his news. Every morning, Ettie asked anxiously if she'd heard. Cathy knew they were both dreading it. She was working in the shop when Danny arrived home on his first pass. He was all smiles.

'Had some good news yesterday,' he said jovially. 'I won't be going back to France.'

Customers had followed him in. 'Tell you about it later,' he whispered, 'I'll just go up and see Mam.'

As she showed the customers a chest of drawers, Cathy could hear Ettie's delighted laughter. Other customers followed and she had to attend to them but she felt liberated.

At last, sparkling with pleasure, Ettie came down to relieve her. 'Danny wants to talk to you,' she said. 'I'm so relieved. It's the best news yet.'

Up in the living room, Danny was waiting to put his arms round her. 'The regiment's being relieved. It's done four years at the front and will be coming home to Salisbury Plain. We'll be training new recruits for the front instead of being there ourselves.'

It was a day of celebration. All three of them felt full of relief and able to look to the future.

When Danny walked her home that night, he kissed her and asked, 'Have you thought any more about me? Not that I want to rush you, I promised I wouldn't. But . . . have you had enough time to make up your mind?'

'Yes,' she smiled. 'I've made up my mind that I want to marry you.'

He was overwhelmed. 'That's marvellous.' He pulled her closer and his lips came down harder on hers.

Ten minutes later, Cathy whispered, 'Danny, can we keep this to ourselves for a while? Mildred isn't going to like it.'

'She likes me.'

'Yes, as a friend, someone to support her business and improve her furniture, but I don't think she'll want me to marry you. It changes everything, you see.'

'For us?'

'And for her. She won't like me and Rosie moving out, leaving her on her own.'

'Very well. It needs thinking about.' He gave her another lingering kiss. 'Now I know, I can be patient . . . but we won't wait too long?'

'No, not too long.'

Cathy felt everything was coming right for her. She'd always longed for a family; she had that already in Mildred and Rosie, but she wanted more – she wanted Danny too. She could see problems arising between him and Mildred and knew she'd have to handle her mother-in-law with care.

She was enjoying life again; her job kept her busy and she felt in the midst of things. Danny had a pass and came home every month. Working with antiques seemed a fuller, more varied life than cooking at Halesworth Hall. She was earning her own living and that brought Cathy a lot of satisfaction.

Danny wrote to her often. He asked how his mother was getting on and whether Frank was still taking her out. Cathy told him he was, and that Ettie was repaying him by inviting him round for his evening meal once or twice a week.

Your mam was always cheerful, she wrote, *but now she positively dances round the shop. It's lovely to see her so happy*.

Cathy occasionally saw Jackson making deliveries with Frank, and so felt she wasn't losing touch with her old friends either. Frank would often go upstairs to see Ettie, leaving Jackson to chat to Cathy when she wasn't busy with a customer.

'Shouldn't wonder if we don't hear wedding bells soon.' He nodded towards the ceiling. 'Frank seems very smitten.'

'It would be good for Ettie if we did,' she smiled.

Cathy was also pleased that Mildred and Botty had become friends. On Thursday afternoons, Botty came to help Mildred, and as this was Cathy's half-day she was seeing more of her too.

Mildred was throwing herself into a fever of sewing, making clothes for children, some of which ended up in Rosie's wardrobe.

'I really struck gold in those huge parcels of old clothes you bought in the Halesworth sale,' she told Cathy, holding up an old-fashioned chemise that had once belonged to the major's mother or aunt. 'Look at this – the finest lawn cotton and hardly worn at all. And this handmade lace – isn't it beautiful?'

She laundered everything carefully and found that one adult garment would make several for children. Mildred was turning out exquisite little nightdresses, petticoats and bloomers.

Cathy enjoyed sitting down with the two older women and helping with the tacking and the hemming. Botty's chatter made it fun and the afternoons passed in a flash.

On other evenings, Cathy had helped Mildred pick out the best of the staff uniforms; they'd washed and starched them so they looked crisp and fresh and hung them on hangers. They were selling very speedily to the middle-classes, who had started to come to Mildred's shop. There was nowhere else they could get uniforms for their maids. They often stayed to run their fingers over other items and frequently bought them.

In order to provide more variety in the shop, Mildred had turned to the velvet curtains. There were a great many of these in jewel-like blues and reds. She made dresses, smocks and even coats.

But it was the major's clothes which provided garments that were most in demand. From the melton cloth, merino, alpaca and barathea, she made trousers, jackets and coats for small boys. They were warm and durable and could be worn every day. Mildred had put up a notice in the shop, saying she could make clothes to order to fit children of any age. She was very pleased with the progress the business was making.

The shop in Market Street was showing a good profit and Cathy was delighted. It was giving Mildred an interest of her own, and a way of earning a living.

Chapter Fourteen

Mildred was losing patience as she carefully fashioned the umpteenth buttonhole in the child's velvet dress. Neither Cathy nor Harriet Bott realised just how irritating they were.

Mildred could do the machining quickly, but a backlog of hand-sewing could build up, making her feel pressurised. She'd encouraged them to spend their Thursday afternoons helping her with the hand-sewing in the little room behind the shop. They always enjoyed themselves, regarding it as a sewing bee and a social occasion. Today, Harriet was relaxed, her hair coming loose from its severe bun, making her look less prim. Their combined chuckles annoyed her even more.

Finishing off the last buttonhole, she flung the child's dress on the pile that needed only pressing, and jumped to her feet.

'Are you going to make the tea now?' Cathy asked.

She was not! She slammed the door and bounded up to the flat above. Mildred felt she had good reason to be irritable. Neither of them would attempt to make button-holes, though she'd shown them twice how to do it. They were more interested in gossiping than they were in sewing. Their tongues never stopped.

Mildred had counted Harriet as her friend and Cathy as her family, but together they had a rapport that was greater than she had with either. They talked about people she didn't know and it made her feel left out and hurt by the exclusion.

She could hear them laughing together now and didn't like it; she wanted Cathy to laugh with her. Now Otto and Rolf had gone, the only adult conversation she could have at home was with Cathy. She didn't want to share her with Harriet Bott.

There was something strange about that woman. She had a family of her own, a good home and a business, and yet for years she'd left them to go out to work as a housekeeper. It didn't make sense.

It was almost time to get Rosie up from her afternoon nap. Mildred went to the kitchen and filled the kettle; she needed tea more than they did. Then she went to lift her little darling from her cot. She knew

171

that would annoy Cathy. She liked to do it herself when she was at home.

It seemed to Cathy that the war would never end. In June 1918 the Germans were within 100 miles of Paris, but by August the tide had turned. When an armistice was negotiated and signed in November, she found it hard to believe it was all over. They expected Danny to come home straight away, but he wrote that it might be a few months before he could do so.

He was, however, coming home for a week's leave and Ettie invited Cathy to have supper with them on his first night. When the shop closed, she went home to change and to put Rosie to bed. When she returned, she found Frank had been invited too.

Danny kissed her as he took her coat. It was a quick and public kiss, but any kiss from him now could fill her with overwhelming tenderness.

'This is going to be Mam's big night,' he whispered. 'Our turn will come later.'

Ettie's face was wreathed in smiles. 'Cathy, dear, Frank has asked me to marry him and I've said yes.' She showed off her new diamond ring.

'Ettie! That's wonderful news.' Cathy kissed her. 'Congratulations, or should I be saying that to the groom?'

'Does it matter? We're both over the moon.'

'I want you to know,' Danny told Frank, 'that I'm very pleased you're taking Mam on. She really needs a better time than she's had up to now.'

'I'll try and give her that.'

'I hope you'll both be very happy,' Cathy said. 'When will you get married?'

'We've decided to wait until Danny's home for good. It's lovely just to be engaged. I'm thrilled to have another chance. It's like starting again.'

It was late when Cathy put on her coat to go home. Danny walked her through the empty streets with his arm round her waist. It was a moonlit night with a hard frost.

'At last,' he sighed happily. 'I can hardly believe the war's over. It's been like a black pall over us for years, spoiling everything. Another few months and I'll be demobilised. Then we'll all be able to get on with our lives.'

'And there'll be no more killing. It's such a relief to know that.'

When he gathered her into his arms to kiss her good night, it was very different from his first kiss of the evening. His touch made a thrill run through her. She could see passion and tenderness in his eyes.

'We're going to have a wonderful week,' he murmured into her hair. 'It'll have to last me until I can come back.'

'I'll see you in the morning,' she said breathlessly.

When at last Danny left her, Cathy ran upstairs, eager to tell Mildred the news. It was almost midnight but she was still working, arranging freshly starched and ironed petticoats over the maiden to air in front of the dying fire.

'Ettie McLelland going to marry Frank Bott?' Mildred pulled a face and seemed somewhat put out. 'I hope she won't regret it.'

'Why should she? She's very happy about it and Danny thinks it's marvellous.'

'Well, you know what the Botts are like.'

'Yes – nice people,' Cathy said. There were times when she didn't understand Mildred, but she was too tired to follow it up. She wanted to go to bed.

Jackson was very contented with his lot. He'd made his rooms comfortable and was on his own upstairs. The family never came up, but if he wanted company there was always somebody in the kitchen or the living room to talk to.

Last evening, Botty had called him into the office and he'd found Frank and Jimmy waiting for him. He'd sat down and they'd talked about what jobs he could do and how much they would pay him. He already received bed and board and knew he'd been treated generously. He counted himself lucky to have fallen on his feet like this.

Frank was trusting him to take the cart out to do jobs by himself. It was easier to manage than the big vans, and it usually meant he did the smaller jobs. He loved it and didn't mind the heavy lifting it usually entailed. Sometimes he was even given a horse-boy or one of the lads to help; it depended on the size of the job.

His last task of the day was to pick up a firkin of ale that Frank had ordered from the Lighterman's Arms. He'd just announced his engagement and said it was to drink his health and to celebrate the end of the war. But when Jackson had the cart at the door, he was told ale was in short supply and they couldn't spare Frank a whole firkin. Instead, he'd have to be content with half a dozen bottles.

Jackson drove back to Cooper's Yard and unhitched the horse. He was giving her a rubdown while she drank at the horse trough when Jimmy came out.

'I'll give you a hand to carry the ale in,' he said.

'I doubt if I'll need it.' Jackson showed him the bottles. 'That's all they'd give me.'

'Won't have much of a celebration on that,' Jimmy said, 'but it's better than nothing.'

He took them indoors while Jackson led the mare to her stall. One of the lads had mucked it out and put in a feed of hay during the afternoon.

When he went into the kitchen, he found most of the family had gathered there and were laughing together. Jimmy was filling their glasses and Iris pretended to be cross because he spilt a few drops on the floor. Within five minutes every man in the house had a glass in his hand and Frank produced a bottle of port and some lemonade for the ladies.

Jackson took his glass with him when he carried his daily workslip to the office. Iris made one out for each of them. It gave the name and address of each customer and listed what was to be delivered or picked up and the amount to be charged. It made for efficient working.

Iris liked him to mark how long he'd spent on each job as it was done. Often the client would pay there and then for the service. She was sitting at the desk making up the books.

'Got some money for you,' he said, counting out the coins from his pocket. 'Two people paid me.' She checked his workslip; he'd annotated it *paid in full*. 'Gave them both receipts,' he told her proudly. He felt he'd mastered the job quickly.

'Good.' Iris bent down to open the bottom drawer in the desk and lift out the green metal cashbox. He could see it was heavy. She counted the coins into their separate compartments, rammed the lid down and slid it back into the drawer. Jackson ran his tongue round his lips as he noticed she didn't lock the drawer. It seemed nothing in this house was ever locked.

The Botts were too trusting; to some that could be an open invitation.

Cathy folded up Danny's letter and danced round the kitchen. At last he'd been given his date of discharge from the army. He'd be home for good on 7 May 1919. Just two more months to wait.

When she arrived at work, Cathy found Ettie all smiles and even more excited than she was. Danny had written to her with the same news.

'This is what I've been waiting for,' she said.

'You'll set a date for your wedding now?'

'Yes. Frank's coming up this evening so we can talk through the arrangements. I want to get them started. Will you be my matron of honour, Cathy? And Rosie, could she be a little bridesmaid?'

'We'd both love that.' Cathy was delighted. 'Shall I ask Mildred to make our wedding outfits?'

'Yes, a good idea. I don't want a lot of fuss and a big wedding.' Ettie was gentle and self-effacing, the sort of person everybody wanted to take in hand and look after. 'I was married in St Mary's the first time round and I'd like the same sort of wedding again.'

At mid-morning, Frank had just happened to pop in after he'd finished a job and was returning to the yard. Ettie rushed him upstairs, and when they both came down twenty minutes later, Frank said he'd see if their wedding could take place at St Mary's Parish Church, shortly after Danny returned home.

It was two more days before Ettie could confirm the arrangements. 'It's to take place on a Thursday afternoon, six days after Danny gets back,' she announced. 'That means we can close the shop and invite you all.' It was easy to see Ettie was thrilled. 'Frank says Harriet is going to put on the wedding breakfast for us at Cooper's Yard.'

'I'll give you away, missus,' Benbow offered.

'That's kind of you,' she said, 'but I want Danny to do it. That's why we've waited this long.'

The following day, Mildred called on Ettie in Exmouth Street during her dinner-hour.

'I'd like to get started on the bridesmaid dresses,' she told her. 'It's difficult to get fabrics now, so unless you can get it, it's a question of deciding which you'd like of those I already have.'

'That's kind of you,' Ettie stammered. 'There's nothing much in the shops now.'

'Have you decided on your own outfit yet?' Mildred asked. 'You ought to, so we can pick colours and styles that go together. Have you bought it yet?'

'No. I've looked in the big shops for a smart two-piece but I haven't found anything.'

'I'll make it for you, if you like.' Mildred was enthusiastic. 'I've got some velvet. You could have crimson, dark green or royal blue. I could make you a two-piece from that, it'd look gorgeous.'

'That sounds lovely, thank you. I was beginning to think of a dress that's been in my wardrobe for years. Thank you very much.'

'My usual terms,' Mildred said.

'Of course. It's not going to give you too much to do all at once? With the dresses for Cathy and Rosie, I mean?'

'I'm a professional dressmaker,' Mildred told her tartly. 'I work quickly. Come down and see the velvet when you can. I've got some patterns too, but if you want to bring your own . . .'

'I'll come this afternoon, if that's all right? It makes it easier for me if you can provide the material.'

In the flurry of wedding preparations, the weeks passed quickly for Cathy. The dresses Mildred had made for her and Rosie were hanging in her wardrobe. They were of the same pale-green silk. Rosie's had a matching bonnet and Cathy had found a smart hat to wear with hers.

Danny wrote to tell them he'd be coming on a train that got in at five-thirty in the afternoon.

'We'll leave Benbow to close the shop so we can both go to meet him at the station,' Ettie told Cathy. They were both feeling very excited by then. The train was late, which only served to heighten their anticipation. When Danny arrived at last, he jumped out of the carriage and threw his arms round both of them.

'We're going to forget the war and all our other troubles,' he said, kissing them both. 'Put it all behind us. Everything is going to be tiptop for us now and we deserve a bit of fun.'

'You look the picture of health, so much stronger than you did when you were passed fit to work,' his mother marvelled. His eyes sparkled and his cheeks had a rosy glow.

Ettie had arranged a meal for them and Frank arrived with a bottle of sherry soon after they reached Exmouth Street. The foursome thoroughly enjoyed the little welcome-home party.

Ettie's wedding was on them in no time. After a busy morning at the shop, Cathy rushed home to change into her new matron-of-honour outfit. She felt very smart. Mildred had already dressed Rosie and she looked sweet in her green silk dress and bonnet.

Cathy enjoyed the wedding, especially as all her old friends from Halesworth were there – George the gardener and his wife, and Jackson who looked very spruce.

When Ettie appeared in the church, her wedding outfit, a two-piece costume of dark green velvet, drew admiring gasps. With it, she wore a big hat decorated with spring flowers. Everybody said it was a long time since they'd seen such an elegant wedding, and they didn't understand how it could be done when the shops were virtually empty.

Iris had decorated the house at Cooper's Yard with flowers from the garden. It was looking its best. Botty put on a splendid spread, even though most foods were still in short supply. She knew how to present food to make it look attractive. It wouldn't have disgraced the dining room at Halesworth Hall.

There were a lot of speeches. First came the groom, looking a little stiff in the suit that had been his best since the beginning of the war. He thanked them all for coming and praised his Aunt Harriet, then told them all he was delighted his bride had invited him to share her home in Exmouth Street.

When he sat down again, Mildred said to Danny, 'Frank's moving into Exmouth Street then?'

'Yes, Mam sees it as her home. It's what she wants.'

'What about you?'

He smiled. 'I'm keeping my room for the time being, but I'm not going to over-stay my welcome.'

'I see.'

Once Old Benbow stood up, there was no stopping him for half an hour. He finished by saying, 'I know you'll all join me in wishing the bride and groom great happiness. Let's raise our glasses to them and wish them luck as they set out in life together.'

The speeches went on, the wedding cake was cut and the last of the toasts drunk. With the wedding breakfast over, Iris began playing the living-room piano. The hall carpets had been lifted for dancing, and as Danny whirled Cathy round in his arms, he said, 'It's been a great success. Our turn next.'

Mildred had arrived at Cooper's Yard feeling very gratified. Everybody had praised the wedding outfits she'd made, but the guests were equally generous with their praise for the wedding breakfast.

Goodness knows where Harriet had come by the ham – she must have bought it on the black market. There'd also been an impressive display of jellics, trifles and blancmanges, with cakes large and small of every sort set out on the big table in the dining room for them to help themselves. Mildred tried the seed cake and the coconut sandwich, and knew she couldn't have done it so well, which didn't please her at all.

The speeches were going on too long, Mildred thought privately. Jimmy Bott was a bore and had nothing to say that Benbow and Frank hadn't already said. She wanted to see more of this house; it was a much bigger and grander place than she'd been led to believe. Harriet hardly mentioned her home. Good grief, why would a woman who had a magnificent house like this come to Market Street every Thursday afternoon, looking like a widow woman down on her luck who was glad to fill her day with sewing?

Mildred looked round the sitting room. Jimmy Bott was still holding forth and had the attention of her fellow guests. She happened to be

177

sitting by the door and on the spur of the moment, she put down her tea cup and slipped out into the hall.

Opposite was another sitting room: did Harriet have her own? Her embroidery was here. Mildred darted down a short passage to what seemed to be an office, containing a large desk covered with papers. Beside it was yet another room, a sort of bootroom, with old coats hanging on the walls. She went to the window, thinking it could do with a clean. The view of the yard took her breath away; it was such a big place. They must be making a mint here.

Just then, Mildred heard footsteps approaching and looked for some escape. There was none. Botty started with surprise when she came upon her cringing there.

'Can you help me, Harriet?' Mildred said quickly. 'I was looking for the lavatory.'

'Of course. There's one outside but we thought we'd leave that to the men. Let me show you to the bathroom upstairs.'

Mildred followed her, wondering how many bedrooms there were, but that wasn't something she could ask. The bathroom was as big as the bedroom Cathy and Rosie slept in at home. Her flat over the butcher's shop was not in this league.

'Can I leave you to find your own way back to the party?' Harriet asked.

'Yes, thank you.' It would give her the chance to peep into some of the bedrooms. When she went back downstairs Iris was playing a waltz on the piano. Rosie had her feet planted firmly on Danny's shoes and he was dancing with her.

Mildred sat down near Cathy. The older guests were starting to drift away. Mildred felt she'd had enough and when the tune came to an end she got up to go. 'Come on, Rosie, it's past your bedtime.'

But Rosie clung to her mother. 'Want to stay here,' she said. 'Want to dance.' She buried her face in Cathy's shoulder.

'We'll bring her home,' Danny said. 'We won't be long.'

Cathy didn't know Frank had bought a car until she and the remaining guests went out to see the newlyweds drive off on their honeymoon. They'd kept the destination a secret. Iris had attached a notice to the back, to let the world know they were *Just Married*. Jimmy had tied some old boots and tin cans to the bumper, which made a fearful clatter as the car pulled out of the yard.

Afterwards, Cathy and Danny walked back to Market Street. He had to carry Rosie on his shoulders; she said she was too tired to walk.

He said, 'Mam asked me if she and Frank could make their home in Exmouth Street. I had to say yes, of course.'

Cathy smiled. 'Why not? Ettie said Botty had just about filled Cooper's Yard – they're a big family now.'

'I'll tell you why not.' Danny's eyes smiled into hers. 'I rather thought you and I . . .' He was suddenly serious. 'Cathy, I don't want to wait any longer. I feel the time is right. I do love you.'

'I love you, too.'

'Then let's get married. Let's do it soon.'

Cathy felt thrills washing over her in waves. 'I'm ready now. I want to marry you, I really want to. I've been looking forward to it. I've missed you.'

He was beaming at her. 'Weddings are certainly in the air. Tomorrow I'm taking you out to choose an engagement ring. We're going to let everyone know about us.'

'If we're about to get married, I won't need an engagement ring.'

'Cathy, if Rolf gave you one, you'll have to have one from me. I can't let him upstage me.'

She laughed.

Danny was eager. 'When shall we tie the knot?'

'Soon. Let's give ourselves a week or two to get our breath back and then do it. There's a lot to think about.'

Danny pulled a face. 'Such as where we'll live. I'm sorry Mam wanted the rooms over my shop. I expected her to go to Cooper's Yard and leave that for us.'

'What d'you have in mind?' Cathy asked cautiously.

'A little house near the park, perhaps?'

Cathy was afraid that could be a problem. 'Danny, I'm a bit worried about Mildred. I haven't said anything to her yet, but I know she won't want me to take Rosie away. She dotes on her. She's practically brought her up. I've done very little for her.'

Danny's dark eyes looked into hers. He seemed shocked. 'She can't expect you to leave the child with her?'

That was exactly what Cathy feared.

'You won't do that?'

'No, I couldn't.'

When they reached Market Street, Mildred met them at the front door. She lifted Rosie down from Danny's shoulders and wanted to put her to bed.

'It's past your bedtime and you're tired, young lady. You'll only curl up and go to sleep on Otto's chair if I don't.' She took her off to get undressed.

'Let's have a cup of tea.' Cathy went to fill the kettle. Danny followed her into the kitchen. 'We'd better talk about where we're going to live. Get that straight for starters.'

When Mildred indicated that Rosie was ready for her good-night kiss, Cathy went in to her. There was just a mop of curls showing above the blankets; Rosie was almost asleep already. Feeling tense, Cathy went back to the living room and poured the tea. 'Mildred,' she said, putting a cup and saucer into her hands. 'Danny and I want to get married.'

'Married?' Mildred seemed astounded at the idea.

'Yes,' she said. 'You must have noticed we're together a lot?'

'That I can't get enough of Cathy's company?' Danny grinned.

'Well, yes, but she works for you. I thought you were friends.' She gave her daughter-in-law a reproachful look.

'We're a bit more than friends,' Cathy said gently. 'Tomorrow, Danny's going to buy me an engagement ring.'

'It's taken me some time to persuade her to marry me.'

'But you won't get married just yet? You'll want to be engaged for a time?'

'No,' Cathy said. 'We'll get married in a few weeks.'

'As soon as that?' Mildred looked bereft.

'What is there to wait for?' Cathy asked.

'The war's over,' Danny said. 'Everything's set fair. We want to enjoy life – why put it off?'

Mildred didn't look happy about it. 'Where will you live?'

'We have to talk about that,' Cathy said, knowing this was going to be the difficult part.

'I thought a little house near the park,' Danny said quickly.

'No need for that. There's plenty of room here. What could be handier for you? Cathy will want to keep her hand in at Second Time Around.' Mildred spread her arms wide as though willing to give them anything.

'I can't say my hand has ever been in at that,' Cathy told her. 'You run it.'

'You didn't have time – not with your job.'

'No,' Cathy agreed. She'd accepted long ago that Mildred preferred to run Second Time Around herself. She did almost all the work in it and Cathy felt more at home in the Exmouth Street shop.

Mildred turned to Danny. 'The best thing would be for you to move in with us. Cathy and I are very happy here, aren't we? No need to disturb anything. We can just put Rosie's little bed into my room, and you can move in with Cathy.'

Cathy could see Danny was a little shocked at that. He didn't know Mildred as well as she did.

'We'll have to think about it,' he said, sounding reluctant to commit himself.

'It would be very lonely if I were left here on my own,' Mildred mourned. 'Now that poor Rolf and Otto have gone.'

Everything came to a halt then, as though they had no more to say.

'I'll walk part of the way home with Danny,' Cathy said. 'I could do with a breath of fresh air before I go to bed, and it's a beautiful night.'

She knew Danny didn't like the idea of moving into Mildred's home, but it was exactly what she'd expected. She also knew Mildred understood they would have to talk about it.

'I'm not sure about this,' Danny said as soon as they were outside in the street. He was striding out quickly.

'Mildred will look after you, if you move in with us. She likes you.'

'Not as much as she did. I'm afraid I might get a knife in my back.'

'No, she'll soon see you as part of her family.'

'Is it what you want?' He pulled Cathy to a halt. 'You want us to live in Market Street with her?'

'Could you stand it?' Cathy asked.

He pulled a face. 'I can't let you walk home with me. You'd have to come back by yourself, and that's not right at this time of night.' He turned round and they strolled back towards the market-hall. It cast dark shadows down the side. Danny leaned back against the wall.

'It wouldn't be my first choice. I was thinking of a little place of our own, but if it's what you want . . .'

'It's not what I want exactly,' Cathy tried to explain. 'I'd rather be on our own, but Mildred's part of my family.'

'My mother's a part of mine.'

'But Ettie's got a life of her own – a new one. She doesn't need you.'

'Mildred does need you?'

'I feel she does.'

'Mildred will cope, Cathy. She'll be busy all day with her shop and she'll soon get used to being on her own in the evenings. She might even grow to like it.'

Cathy shook her head. 'I was very glad of Mildred when Rolf died. Couldn't have coped without her. Couldn't have worked without her, either – still couldn't. If we had a house of our own and I'm to continue working, I'd have to take Rosie round to Mildred before I could start.'

'Not a house near the park then,' he said. 'It would need to be between here and Exmouth Street. Couldn't Rosie just play in our shop? I mean, she's playing in Mildred's shop while it's open.'

'Mildred's talking of getting a girl to help, a school-leaver. I think she's finding she has too much to do.'

'So she should. I'm amazed she can concentrate with Rosie pulling at her skirts the whole time.'

'I don't think I could concentrate on doing your books with her around. In some ways it would be easier if Mildred lived with us. We'd have a permanent babysitter.'

Danny said, 'I can't hold out against you, if you think that's the best thing.'

'She's lost Otto. Rosie is the apple of her eye. Don't you think it would be selfish of me to leave her on her own?'

'No.' Danny's dark eyes looked into hers. 'This is one time when I think we should be selfish.'

Cathy didn't know what to say. Danny was leaning back against the wall, staring into the darkness.

'We could try living with her, I suppose,' he sighed reluctantly. 'If you really want to.'

'You know it's not what I want. Danny, you've always sung Mildred's praises until now.'

'She's a good businesswoman and very efficient. She works very hard, but is she easy to get on with?'

Cathy feared she might not be. She tended to want her own way most of the time. 'Let's try it, and see how we get on,' she urged.

'Right, we'd better start telling everybody there's another wedding in the offing.' She saw the flash of Danny's white teeth as he smiled. 'You go in and tell her I'll be glad to accept her offer.'

Cathy kissed him. 'Thank you. Mildred's getting older and she works very hard. It would be on my conscience if I pulled out and took Rosie away now.'

Mildred unhooked her whalebone corsets, laid them neatly on the other clothes she'd taken off and reached for her flannelette nightgown. It was bedtime but she'd never felt less like sleep. Her mind was whirling. She'd enjoyed Ettie's wedding more than she'd expected, and she'd been feeling perfectly content until Cathy brought Danny home with her.

Then, without any warning, they'd announced that they were going to get married. Mildred felt bewildered: they'd given her no time to think about it. She didn't know why she'd pressed Danny McLelland to come and live with them.

Now she felt cross and out of sorts. They'd gone out to discuss it, and Cathy had come back to announce that Danny would be happy to move in with them when they were married. Cathy had waited; her face told Mildred she was expecting her to say she was pleased, but she wasn't. This was going to spoil everything.

Mildred didn't want change. She'd arranged her household to her own satisfaction and the last thing she wanted was for Cathy to get married again. She didn't want Danny pushing in here and she didn't doubt Cathy had had to persuade him to come.

But it would be even worse if he took Cathy away, and if Cathy went, what about Rosie? Mildred knew it would feel like the end of the world if they took Rosie away to live somewhere else. But of course they couldn't. He'd want Cathy to go on helping in his business and she wouldn't be able to look after Rosie as well. Mildred could do it, but Cathy wasn't that well-organised.

It was all very upsetting. She'd known Danny was taking up more and more of Cathy's time when he was home. Ettie, too – they often invited Cathy up there for meals. Mildred had been so busy, she hadn't stopped to think where it might be leading.

Every newspaper she picked up reminded readers that the war had brought about the loss of a whole generation of young men. There would not be enough to father the next generation, and of necessity many women would have to remain single. Cathy had had one marriage; Mildred didn't expect her to be able to have another, not with Rosie hanging on to her skirts.

Why would a young man like Danny be willing to take on another man's baby? There were plenty of girls who were free and unencumbered. Mildred wanted Cathy and Rosie to stay here with her. They were getting on well. She'd been congratulating herself that they were happy and they were earning a good living.

She didn't want to be left here alone. Without Otto she'd be so lonely. And she'd miss her little Rosie. A house near the park, indeed! They'd take Rosie without any thought of what it would mean to her.

Cathy belonged to Rolf; she belonged *here*. This was his home and she'd been glad enough of it when he'd been killed. She'd expected better of Cathy. The ungrateful girl had been very quick to forget Rolf and all she owed to his family.

Chapter Fifteen

The next morning, Danny said, 'I'm going down to Pyke's to see if they've got any rings that would suit you.'

Cathy laughed. 'I'm sure they'll have lots to choose from. Now food costs so much, I've heard people are selling their jewellery to pay for it.'

He lifted her left hand. She was still wearing Rolf's rings: a plain narrow wedding ring, with an engagement ring of three red stones in a gold setting. 'You chose rubies from Rolf.'

'Actually, they're garnets: he couldn't afford rubies. We were very young, remember.'

'What would you like from me? Real rubies? Diamonds? Sapphires?'

'Not rubies.' Cathy hesitated. She didn't want Danny to give her a ring that could be compared directly with Rolf's. 'No need to spend the earth on it. I'll be pleased with anything.'

'I want you to have a ring you'll be proud of. I'm not all that young and you've helped me earn money from the business. It's only fair.'

Cathy took off Rolf's rings and put them in her handbag. She thought of it as a sign she'd put the past behind her for good.

'I'm delighted,' Danny told her. 'But I wouldn't be upset if you wanted to wear Rolf's wedding ring. He's part of your . . .'

'Past?' she asked. 'Perhaps I will when we're married, on top of yours. For now, no, I'm looking to the future.'

That afternoon, Danny asked Old Benbow to mind the shop for an hour or so, and he and Cathy walked down to the jeweller's. He was greeted with respect in the shop. They were both given seats and three trays of rings were brought out and put between them on the counter. Cathy saw them sparkling against the black velvet and knew immediately they were some of the most expensive in the shop.

'Diamonds would be best, I think,' Danny told her. 'Mam says it doesn't matter what you wear with them, diamonds enhance everything.'

With his help, she chose a ring with three big diamonds of equal size. 'It's absolutely beautiful,' she breathed. 'Look at the flashing colours in them.'

'Wear it,' he said, slipping it back on her finger. 'I want to make this official.'

When she got home that evening, Cathy didn't have to draw Mildred's attention to her new ring; she noticed it straight away and snatched at her hand to have a closer look.

'Where's your wedding ring? It's bad luck to take it off. What's put on in church should stay there always.'

Cathy snatched her hand back, affronted. 'It's safe,' she said. 'I thought it better to put it away now.'

'Oh no. You should wear both wedding rings on the same finger. That's usual if you marry for a second time.'

'No, Mildred,' Cathy said quietly. 'I couldn't wear Danny's engagement ring on top of Rolf's wedding ring. Better if I put Rolf's rings away.'

Mildred gave a snort of disgust. 'You think Danny McLelland can do better for you than our Rolf could. Money isn't everything, Cathy.'

Cathy was fighting to keep her temper. 'You know I was very much in love with Rolf,' she said, 'but he's been dead for three years. I can't live on memories.'

'I suppose the precious Danny said that to you.'

Cathy felt a flush run up her cheeks; that was exactly what Danny had said.

'The McLellands came from the slums,' Mildred went on, her face twisting with revulsion. 'The bottom of society. They'd have starved before the war if it hadn't been for Otto. He took pity on them.'

'Mildred, there was terrible illness in the family.'

Cathy hadn't expected her mother-in-law to come out with such a tirade against Danny. She felt as though she'd put her hand in a drawer and found a viper amongst her belongings.

'He'll be no good to you,' Mildred spat. 'He won't work! You and Old Benbow have built his business up, not him. You'll be looking after him for the rest of his life.'

There was hate in every line of Mildred's body. Cathy had always known she wouldn't want her to marry again, but she'd seemed to like Danny. She'd known him for years and had been full of good will towards him – until they'd told her they planned to get married.

'Mildred, stop it! You've invited Danny to come and live here with us. If you feel like that about him, it might be better if we rented a place of our own. Shall I tell him you've changed your mind about that?'

'No!' she gasped, looking deflated. 'No, I'll stand by my offer.'

'I know Danny would prefer a place of our own. I had to persuade him to agree to this.'

'No, no Cathy. Don't you turn against me. Don't let us quarrel about *him*.'

Exasperated, Cathy said, 'The quarrel is not of my making.'

She said nothing to Danny about Mildred's outburst, afraid it might turn him against her. She hoped Mildred would accept him in time. It was change that Mildred didn't like, the unknown. She decided the best thing to do was to bring them together as much as possible, so they could get more used to each other.

'Mildred,' she said, 'Danny's mother is still away on her honeymoon. Can I invite him to have his Sunday dinner with us?' Mildred pursed her lips with disapproval, but reluctantly agreed.

Danny arrived smiling, with a bottle of sherry under his arm. Mildred was making gravy. Cathy took him to the kitchen.

'Shall I open it now?' he asked, showing her the bottle. 'So we can drink to the future.' When Cathy found three glasses, he poured them one each.

'Right then.' He raised his glass. Cathy held Mildred's out to her, and they waited for her to raise it. She did so with marked reluctance.

Danny said, 'All the best of health and happiness to all of us.'

Rosie was pulling at his trousers. 'Want some.'

'It's not good for little girls,' he told her. 'You'll have to grow up first.'

'Want some, Mr Lello, please.'

'No, Rosie, little girls can't have sherry. You wouldn't like it.'

'Want to taste,' she demanded. 'Taste.'

'No, Rosie. Next time I'll bring you some lemonade.'

'Taste, taste . . .'

Cathy picked her up. 'Stop this, Rosie, we're going to have a nice dinner. Look, there's your favourite roast beef and there's rice pudding to follow. It's almost ready.'

Rosie began to kick against Cathy's legs. 'Don't want dinner, want taste of that,' she demanded. 'Nanna, want taste.'

Mildred swung round from the stove and snatched Rosie from Cathy's arms. She offered the child her glass. Rosie took a cautious sip and burst out, 'Don't like it. Don't like it.' She was spitting. Mildred held her over the sink.

'You're a naughty girl. Mr Lello said you wouldn't like it. You should listen to what he tells you.'

She set her down on her feet but Rosie clung to Mildred's skirt, hiding her face from Danny.

'Don't like Mr Lello,' she said. 'Don't want him to marry my mummy.'

Cathy was horrified. Mildred said with forced jollity, 'Of course you do. You like Mr Lello.'

187

Rosie began to scream and stamp. 'I don't, I hate him!'

Mildred said, 'I'll spank you, if you say things like that.'

Cathy could see Danny was devastated. He squatted down to the child's level and tried to take both her hands in his.

'I like *you*,' he said. 'You're a lovely little girl when you're good.' She pulled away screaming.

Cathy said firmly, 'Come along, Rosie, you're being naughty. You're in a bad mood. If you don't stop this noise I shall put you in the bedroom and you won't have a nice dinner with us.'

That brought even louder wails from Rosie. 'Don't want dinner, don't want Mr Lello.'

Cathy marched her to their bedroom. 'We asked Danny here to enjoy a meal together and you're spoiling it by being naughty. You can come out when you can behave yourself and not before.' She closed the door firmly and came back to her sherry, gulping down what remained.

Rosie bawled and howled, then suddenly there was silence. They were sitting down to their dinner when Rosie opened the bedroom door and came out.

'Are you going to be good now?' Cathy asked her.

'Want my dinner!' Rosie opened her mouth and yelled: '*Want my dinner!*'

'You must stop making this fuss,' Cathy told her. 'I'll get your dinner for you when you quieten down and ask nicely.'

Rosie screamed louder than ever. Cathy got to her feet, steered her back into the bedroom and closed the door. There was more screaming and a frenzy of kicks against the door. Cathy tried to close her mind to it, but found it impossible. She was embarrassed by such a display of temper in front of Danny. This wasn't likely to endear her daughter to him.

'Poor little thing,' Mildred said. 'I'll go and give her a hug, tell her she's forgiven.'

'No,' Cathy said firmly. 'Not while she's yelling blue murder like this. I've told her she can come out when she behaves herself. She's got to learn she can't get away with this sort of thing.'

Rosie kept up a lusty wailing throughout the meal. The noise was softened by the closed door, but was still clearly audible. It stopped all conversation, made it impossible for them to think of anything else.

Cathy was clearing the table when Rosie's noise lessened to an occasional racking sob. They were drinking tea when she finally quietened down and there was no more to be heard.

She went to see her. Rosie was curled up on the bedside rug fast asleep. Her face was tear-stained and her pretty dress crumpled. Cathy lifted her onto her bed and covered her with her eiderdown, then tiptoed out again.

'We'll warm up her dinner for her when she wakes up,' she said to Mildred. 'She'll be hungry by then.'

'You're too hard on her. Poor little thing.'

Cathy said through clenched teeth, 'If I'd thrown a tantrum like that in the Orphanage I'd have got a good hiding, and there wouldn't be any dinner being warmed up. Rosie has to learn to behave.'

'I think you'd better leave her to me,' Mildred said with a face like thunder.

Cathy had to get away. 'Right, I will.'

She couldn't get Danny outside quickly enough. 'It was awful for all of us,' she said, hurrying him through the shop. 'I went through agonies. Difficult to know how to handle it with you there.' She was really angry. 'Mildred knows that and makes things worse.'

She set off up the street at a furious pace.

'Why did Rosie turn against me like that?' Danny asked. He took her arm, and Cathy could see he was upset. 'Where are we going? Up to my place?'

'I don't want to be away long. I don't want to leave Rosie with her. Mildred will think she's won. But I didn't want to wake Rosie up either.'

Danny said, 'We'll go as far as the park, walk this off. Go back for Rosie when we're calmer. Take her up to my place for tea.'

There were few people about. 'I wanted us to have a nice meal.' Cathy couldn't stop fuming. 'I wanted you to get to know Rosie and Mildred. Instead, that blew up from nowhere.'

'It was very revealing.'

'In what way?'

'It's difficult to feel welcome when Rosie's screaming that she hates me. Does she really?'

'No, of course not. How could she? She hasn't seen that much of you. I've usually got her in bed before we go out. She loved dancing with you at Ettie's wedding.'

'Exactly. At other times she's seemed pleased to see me, happily showing off . . .'

'That was showing off too, but in a different way.'

'I can't have her calling me Mr Lello, either. I'm going to be her father. I'd like her to call me Dad.' He sighed. 'But I'm worried about how Mildred would take that.'

'She wouldn't like it. She'd think you were pushing Rolf out.'

'As if I'd have had a chance if he'd still been alive.'

Cathy said, 'If I let Rosie make a habit of doing that, she'll have us all at each other's throats.'

'I still think the wisest thing would be to get a place of our own. Take Rosie away, make it a fresh start for us all.'

Cathy frowned. 'Mildred said something not very nice about you the other day. I put it to her that it would be better if we moved away, but she was adamant that you must come.'

'All the same . . .'

'She loves Rosie: all the love she felt for Rolf has gone to his child. Rosie's fond of her, too. Mildred looks after her and the shop, keeps house, cooks and sews. She makes me feel I wouldn't be able to cope.'

'She's hired a girl to help her now.'

'Yes, Jessie. I've only seen her once. She's very pale, doesn't look well and is quite timid.'

'I bet she looks after Rosie.'

'No, I think she mostly serves in the shop. She seems scared stiff of Mildred. I hope she stays.'

Danny sighed. 'Cathy, we could get a girl to look after Rosie.'

Cathy shook her head sadly. 'Everybody would say her own grand-mother would do it better.'

On Ettie's first morning back from her honeymoon, Cathy went to work and found her flushed and happy, having breakfast with Frank.

'Has Danny gone?'

'Yes. He wanted an early start to get to Runcorn in time for a sale. He's told us you'll be getting married soon. I'm thrilled for you both. Cathy, if I'd chosen his bride myself, I couldn't be better pleased. Are you going to look for a house?'

Cathy shook her head. 'No, Danny's going to move into Market Street with Mildred and me.'

She saw Ettie's mouth drop open. 'Oh dear! Now I feel really guilty. I shouldn't have asked if Frank and I could make our home here.'

Frank looked embarrassed. 'We can still go to Cooper's Yard if you want us to.'

'No, no,' Cathy told them. 'It wouldn't solve the problem. I think it would break Mildred's heart to be separated from Rosie.'

'All the same.' Ettie was frowning. 'We've taken Danny's home.'

Cathy didn't let the problem get her down. She would have enjoyed every minute of her engagement, if it hadn't been for her worries about how Mildred would treat Danny when he moved in.

She tingled all over when she thought of him. Once, she'd believed she'd never love anyone half as much as she'd loved Rolf, but now she knew better. Seeing Danny, being with him every day made all the difference, and she couldn't wait to get married.

He had much more money than Rolf had had and was happy to spend it. One morning, he said, 'I think we should buy a car. Let's look round and see what we can get.'

'Isn't that extravagant?'

Danny laughed. 'You know how much the business earns. We don't have to set up house, so why not have a car?'

'You said you were saving to open another shop, that you were ambitious for your business.'

'I am, but all in good time. I need to learn more about antiques, so I can make my own judgements. I don't want to rely on Old Benbow for ever. I want to be able to run one shop with my hand tied behind my back first.'

'Well then?'

'We're well on track, Cathy. We've got to live and have a bit of fun too. I can afford a car.'

Cathy had no answer to that. They visited several garages. It seemed there were waiting lists for new cars, none having been made during the war, and although production was starting up, there was a backlog of demand. Danny decided on an 1913 Argyll, a white open tourer with a black hood and wire wheels.

'It'll be great fun,' he said. 'It'll make life easier and save so much time. I'll use it for going to country-house sales. It's often quite difficult to reach them, as they're usually at the end of a long private drive.'

Mildred was happy to go for rides in the car on Sunday afternoons and Rosie loved it.

Although they hadn't set a definite date for their wedding yet, Cathy wanted to start getting organised. Over tea one evening, she asked Mildred, 'Will you make my wedding dress for me?' She knew she still had some of the velvet curtains left.

Mildred was suddenly frosty. 'Do you really need another new outfit? I'd have thought the green silk you wore at Ettie's wedding would do well enough.'

'Mildred!'

'You've only worn it once and you've got a smart hat that goes with it. Rosie's outfit matches too.'

'No, Mildred, I'd—'

'You wouldn't be wanting a white dress, would you? Not when you've been married before?'

'I didn't have white the first time,' Cathy reminded her stiffly. She was having trouble holding back her tears. 'I'd like something new.'

Holding her head high, she went to her bedroom and closed the door firmly. Mildred was being horrible; it was almost as though she was turning against her. Cathy couldn't understand her.

Ten minutes later, she heard Mildred tapping on her door. 'Cathy?' She wiped her eyes.

'Cathy?' The door opened a few inches and Mildred's head came round. 'I'm sorry . . . Oh dear, you've been crying.'

She shot across the room to sit beside her on the bed. 'I don't know what came over me – I didn't mean to upset you.' Her arm went round Cathy's trembling shoulders. 'Of course I'll make you a new outfit. The royal blue would suit you.'

Cathy couldn't bring herself to accept Mildred's offer. It was what she'd originally hoped for, but she'd said some hurtful things.

Now it was Mildred's turn to be upset. 'You won't leave me, Cathy?'

'You know we're all staying, Mildred. Danny's said he'll move in with us.'

'I couldn't bear it if you left and took Rosie with you. You two are my life.'

Cathy swallowed. She didn't believe Mildred was all that concerned about *her*, it was fear that had made her turn nasty. Fear that she'd take Rosie away. Fear made people act very strangely.

'I'm sorry.' Mildred got up and headed for the door. 'Sorry I upset you.'

Cathy shivered. Danny was right, they'd be better off in a place of their own. She felt trapped, yet she'd promised Mildred yet again she wouldn't take Rosie away. She told Danny about their latest tiff and said, 'After that, I think I'll try and buy myself a new outfit for our wedding.'

'Why not?'

'I'm torn both ways over this just as I am over everything to do with Mildred. D'you think I should buy one, when she's apologised and said I can have the blue velvet?'

'Yes, I do. Look, she's twisting you round her finger and making trouble. I'll walk down to Robb's with you now to see if they have anything you'd like.'

New fashions were coming into the shops now. Cathy chose a summer outfit of cream shantung – a dress with a matching coat.

'I really like this – what d'you think?'

'It suits you,' Danny told her, 'and it's just the thing to get married in.' He carried the box back to Exmouth Street for her. On the way he said, 'D'you know, Cathy, the more I think about it, the more I reckon we should have got married at the same time as Mam and Frank.'

'A double wedding?'

'Yes. Here we are, planning it in the same church, on the same day of the week, and we'll mostly invite the same guests.'

When they got back to the shop, Harriet was there. She offered to put on the wedding breakfast for them in Cooper's Yard.

Cathy said, 'That's kind of you. I'd like to say yes, but Mildred's expecting to do it in the flat.'

'There won't be enough space there for us all though, will there?'

'No, but she'll be put out about it. I'll have to talk to her first.'

That evening, after Rosie had been tucked up for the night, Cathy sat down in the armchair opposite Mildred and made herself talk about her wedding arrangements.

'I bought my wedding outfit today,' she said and went on to describe it.

She saw Mildred's lips straightening in disapproval. 'I offered to make you a blue velvet two-piece,' she said.

'I didn't want to put you to the trouble.'

'Trouble? Sewing is no trouble to me. That's how I earn my living.' There was a flush of irritation running up her cheeks. 'Cream shantung, you say? You won't get much wear out of that; it sounds much too dressy. A waste of money, I'd have thought.'

Cathy said, 'You suggested I wore the green silk I had for Ettie's wedding.' Then she stopped. This was no way to placate Mildred. She went on quickly, telling her how similar the two weddings were going to be, and that Harriet had even offered to put on the wedding breakfast.

'Well, I never!' Mildred was indignant. 'That one's always pushing herself forward where she's not wanted. I told you *I'd* do that for you.'

'I'm afraid there won't be enough space here,' Cathy said apologetically.

'So my flat's not good enough for you now?' Mildred's dark eyes flashed with wrath.

'You know it's not that, Mildred.'

'Danny and the Botts are taking over. I'm not going to be allowed to do anything for you.' Mildred was getting really vexed now. 'I suppose they're going to make the cake *and* look after Rosie while you're away on your honeymoon, too?'

'No!'

'Oh, you'll take her with you, is that it? Anything rather than leave her with me?'

'No, Mildred!' Cathy felt agonised. She'd been bothered about what she should do on her honeymoon. She didn't want to leave Rosie behind – she knew she'd miss her – but it wouldn't help to have her sharing their bedroom during her first nights as Danny's wife.

Rosie rarely woke up whilst in her own bed at home, but who could say how she'd be when out of her routine and in a strange place?

She said now, 'This is Rosie's home, she's used to being here with you. Nobody else could look after her so well.'

'I'm glad you can see the sense of that, at least.' Mildred smouldered with anger for the rest of the evening.

The next morning, when Cathy told Danny how badly Mildred had taken it, he said, 'Mildred's close to you and feels she should be organising the whole thing.'

Cathy shook her head. 'It's a pity we can't just run away and get married without all this fuss.'

'We can,' he said. 'If that's what you want. We haven't set a definite date.'

Cathy knew he was serious. She smiled. 'Let's do that – have a secret wedding. Let's go off to the register office, just us on our own.'

'There have to be two witnesses, love.'

'Your mam and Frank – they'll understand.'

'Not even Rosie?'

'Oh yes, I'd like her to be with us.'

He laughed. 'Then this is what we'll do. Go down to the register office and fix the earliest date we can. Then we'll book our honeymoon and tell Mam. I'll get Old Benbow to mind the shop for the afternoon and instead of a reception I'll book a table at the Woodside Hotel for lunch.'

'Lovely.' Cathy sighed with relief. Keeping the wedding secret would definitely ease the pressure from Mildred. 'I'll have to think of some reason to take Rosie with me.'

'Bring her best clothes up to our place first – you can change her there. Do you want her to come on honeymoon with us?' Danny laughed. 'I can see by your face you do.'

'No, Mildred wants to take charge of her while I'm away. We'll take her home from the hotel and announce that we are man and wife.'

Danny had arranged for their wedding to take place in the middle of July 1919. Cathy opened her bedroom curtains on that morning, feeling keyed up with anticipation. It was going to be a momentous day. She laid out

Rosie's clothes for her, encouraged her to dress and wondered how she was going to take her away without having Mildred ask too many questions.

It was a lovely summer's morning. Cathy had to remind herself not to show too much excitement. It was a secret she wanted to keep.

Jessie, the girl Mildred employed, had been unwell the day before. They were having breakfast when a note was pushed through the shop door saying she'd had a bad night and wouldn't be coming to work today.

'You can't rely on anybody,' Mildred exploded. 'I've got a woman coming for a fitting this morning, and I need to work on her dress before she comes.'

Cathy saw the opportunity and jumped at it. 'Shall I take Rosie to work with me this morning?' she asked. 'It would give you a chance to get on with things.'

'That would be a help, yes – a great help.' Mildred bit into her toast.

Cathy felt a twinge of guilt. She shouldn't be hiding what she was doing from Mildred.

'I'll have to bring her back this afternoon, say around three. Danny – wants me to go out with him.' That was hardly the truth. Going out with Danny was miles away from going on honeymoon with him.

'Yes, all right.'

Cathy had already taken Rosie's green silk dress and matching bonnet up to Exmouth Street. Now she strapped her in her push-chair and set out. She worried that Mildred would feel excluded by not being asked to the ceremony. That instead of making things better between her and Danny, all this secrecy would make things worse. Mildred would think she was being underhand.

The wedding was no secret at Exmouth Street. Ettie was glowing with excitement. She insisted Cathy sit down and drink more tea with them.

'We can't expect either of you to work on your wedding day. I won't let you.'

Danny was all smiles, little laughs and tender glances. Cathy didn't feel capable of work; her head was spinning, she felt exhilarated.

Frank was going to drive down to Cooper's Yard to tell his aunt about the wedding. He took Rosie with him.

'Iris asked why I don't want bookings made for me to take the van out today,' he told them. 'I think she might have guessed.'

He came back with a wedding present from his Aunt Harriet. 'She said she had it ready and I must give it to you.' Cathy unwrapped a canteen of cutlery.

'It's very generous of Botty.' She hadn't expected to feel so emotionally high on her second wedding day.

'I'll look after the shop for you, for an hour or so,' Frank told Ettie. He took Rosie down with him and let her run round.

'Nanna got tables like this,' Cathy heard her piping voice. 'Nanna got chairs like this.'

When Arthur Benbow turned up at ten as he'd been asked to do, Cathy and Danny went down to let him into the secret.

'Getting married today? That's wonderful!' He seemed excited on their behalf. 'By Jove, you've kept that quiet.'

'We meant to. It's the married state we want,' Danny laughed. 'Not the big party.'

'What about the rest of us? We all had a great time when Ettie and Frank tied the knot.'

'That's not so long ago, and it would have been the same over again, wouldn't it?'

'I bet Mildred's thrilled with all this.' Benbow kissed Cathy's cheek. 'I wish you and Danny all the luck in the world.'

Cathy's conscience was heavy. Mildred would want to be with her on her wedding day and she hadn't asked her.

When it was time for them to get changed, Cathy found she'd forgotten to bring Rosie's best shoes with her.

Danny smiled and shook his head. 'I'll take her down to Robb's and buy her another pair. What about socks?'

Cathy covered her face with her hands. 'I've forgotten those too.'

'I'll get her more socks while I'm at it.'

'Oh Danny, I'm having second thoughts about not inviting Mildred. We should, shouldn't we? We'd got used to each other and were a happy little family until I wanted to marry you. Besides, I'm relying on her to look after Rosie while I'm away on honeymoon. I haven't even mentioned it yet.'

He pulled a face. 'I persuaded you we should be selfish once in a while, didn't I?'

'She'll be hurt and upset if we don't. Especially when she hears your mother and Frank were invited. It's a bit late in the day, but I can still ask her. I'll pick up Rosie's shoes at the same time.'

'Jump in the car, we'll both go,' Danny said. 'I don't want you worrying about anything today.'

As they went into Second Time Around, a customer was about to leave the shop. 'I'm very pleased,' she was saying to Mildred. 'It'll look lovely – it's exactly what I want. I'll come back on Monday, then.'

Mildred turned to Cathy. 'I thought you said this afternoon? Not that it matters now, that's the customer I was expecting for a fitting.' She looked at the car. 'Where's Rosie?'

Danny said, 'My mother's looking after her.' Actually, Ettie was washing and changing her into her wedding finery.

Cathy cleared her throat. 'Mildred, Danny and I are getting married today. We'd like you to be with us.'

Mildred's mouth opened. Cathy had never seen her look so shocked. 'Today? What time?'

'Twelve o'clock at the register office.'

'Good gracious! You've certainly left the invitations to the last minute.'

'We meant to be married in secret,' Danny explained. 'But Cathy isn't happy that you won't be there. Say you'll come?'

'Well, how can I? There's the shop . . .'

Cathy said hurriedly, 'I know Jessie's off sick, but if you asked Mrs Weaver next door, she'd stand in for you for an hour or so. It'll be closed for an hour over dinnertime, anyway.'

'Well, I don't know . . .'

'Go and ask her now, and I'll lay out the dress you wore for Ettie's wedding. All right?'

'It'll be a terrible rush.'

Cathy propelled her towards the next-door shop. 'She'll need to come here straight away.'

Another customer came in. Danny turned round to serve her, while Cathy rushed up to the flat.

Ten minutes later, Danny said, 'You get yourself ready, Mildred. We'll be back to pick you up at a quarter to twelve.'

'I don't know why you couldn't have asked me sooner,' Mildred complained. 'I wouldn't have told anybody.'

Cathy felt very smart in her cream shantung and she thought Danny looked very handsome in the new grey suit he'd had made.

Danny had ordered a spray of cream roses for the bride, and three buttonholes for the rest of the party. A red carnation for himself and Frank, and a cream one for his mother. Ettie was wearing the deep green velvet two-piece costume Mildred had made for her.

'I almost feel I'm getting married again myself,' she laughed. When she heard Cathy had invited Mildred at the last moment, Frank rushed out to get another cream carnation for her.

Rosie looked a little angel in her green silk dress and bonnet. Their excitement had communicated itself to her and she couldn't stop chattering. The wedding party was ready.

'There won't be room for Mildred if we all go in one car,' Frank said. 'I'll take mine too and we'll look after Rosie.'

Danny drove back to Market Street. Cathy sat beside him feeling she had a great deal to be thankful for. For her, the world had turned completely round. All the grief and misery of the war years were behind her; the future promised happiness.

She hadn't expected to have wedding nerves the second time around, but she was all a-fizz inside and almost overwhelmed by her love for Danny. Mildred was waiting for them just inside the shop and Polly Weaver stood in the doorway to watch Danny pull away.

Their marriage took place in a small wood-panelled room in the Town Hall. They signed the register and it was all over in twenty minutes. Ettie had arranged for a photographer to come and several pictures were taken on the steps of the register office. Then Danny swept them back to his car to drive down to the Woodside Hotel.

They had a bottle of champagne first and followed it with a substantial lunch of soup, roast lamb and roast potatoes, followed by apple pie and cream.

'No speeches,' Ettie said, 'but I'm going to tell you, Cathy, how happy it makes me to see Danny settling down with you. We hope you'll both be very happy.'

'As happy as I am with your mother,' Frank added.

They sat over their coffee for a good while, before Danny decided it was time to go. Rosie was a bit of a handful, but Mildred knew how to keep her occupied. Frank and Ettie escorted the bridal couple back to Danny's car to see them off and wish them well.

'We can drop Mildred back at Market Street,' Frank said.

'I could quite easily walk from here,' she told them. 'It isn't far.'

'No, no,' Cathy protested. 'Come with us. I have to collect my suitcase from my room anyway.'

Mildred climbed reluctantly into the back of the car, taking Rosie with her. 'Well, I hope you feel married after that,' she told them. 'I don't think much of a register-office wedding.'

'It's done the trick,' Danny told her. 'We're legally married. That's all I want.'

'You might have said – a bit sooner, I mean. It's been a rush for me.'

'I'm glad you could be with us,' Cathy told her stiffly, knowing now Mildred would have caused ructions if they'd kept to their original plan. They all piled out on the pavement in Market Street.

'I suppose you're off on honeymoon now?'

'Yes,' Cathy told her. 'I take it you'll be happy to look after Rosie for me?'

'You know I will. Where are you going? Or is that a secret too?'

'We're spending a week touring in the Lake District.'

Cathy ran upstairs to her bedroom to collect the suitcase she'd packed in readiness. She kissed Rosie goodbye and as she and Danny walked out to the car, she heard her pipe to her Nanna, 'Mummy's married to Mr Lello.'

Chapter Sixteen

These days, because he was on the go all day, Arthur Benbow enjoyed his evenings at home alone. Often he had a little snooze in his Victorian armchair. He felt half-asleep now and he knew he'd dozed for twenty minutes, but it never stopped him sleeping at night.

His eyes went round his sitting room, studying with satisfaction the expensive furniture that was his. The little ladies' writing-desk was his latest find. It was early nineteenth century, of rosewood banded with satinwood, and very pretty. Not that he had a lady to use it, but it complemented this room.

He pulled himself to his feet and went stiffly to his study. He preferred the large roll-top desk he had here for serious business. This was where he worked but even here he had furniture that would take pride of place in many antique shops. There was nothing more he needed: he loved the furniture he had and it enhanced his house. Perhaps he should turn his attention to silver or glass, knickknacks of some sort? But his real love had always been furniture.

He opened his desk. Jackson's snuffboxes had finally been sold. They'd had to wait for a specialist sale but he'd got a good price for them and no questions asked.

Knowing Jackson was bent, he saw him as another of the growing band of people he could call on for help should he need it. He'd done him a favour, after all. Not that Jackson hadn't done his best to return it. He'd given him most of the documents he'd lifted from Major Fleming.

Arthur took out the bill for the ceremonial sword he'd bought at the Halesworth auction. It provided provenance for it. He'd long since sold on the major's other bits and pieces – his guns, silver and glass. He had a steady turnover in things he bought and sold, but the sword interested him and he'd hung it over the fireplace. He got up now and took it down, slid it out of its scabbard.

He checked the details against the bill made out to Lieutenant Fleming. The sword had a blade of thirty inches, a copper gilt hilt, a guard chiselled with crown and laurel sprays, and had cost ten guineas in 1881. Arthur had seen this design before and knew the company had been making it for many years before it caught Lieutenant Fleming's eye. Since 1830, if he could rely on his memory.

But swords were not worth a great deal. The most desirable and therefore the most expensive had belonged to officers in the Confederate Army in the American Civil War.

This one would be more desirable if it had been worn by a famous soldier. Arthur had turned over the possibilities in his mind. He needed a personality long since deceased in order that his relatives and friends might be gone too, and would not hear of this sale. He didn't want the ownership disputed or another ceremonial sword produced.

Benbow had acquired books to furnish his bookcases at the sales he visited. On looking through them, he'd found one on the life and times of General Charles Gordon.

Known as Chinese Gordon, he'd found fame in China crushing a rebellion that had destroyed many cities. Later, he'd been made Governor of the Sudan and when Khartoum was besieged by numberless hordes, he'd held out against them for many months, trying to protect the Sudanese people. The city had fallen and he'd been killed two days before reinforcements had arrived. General Gordon had been a hero in his day and famous in several countries.

What captured Arthur's attention was that he'd been said to carry no weapon when he led his troops into battle. Instead, he armed himself with a small cane and used it to point to the places in the enemy ranks where he wanted his soldiers to aim their fire. He was said to encourage them with gestures and shouts. He would certainly have owned a ceremonial sword.

Arthur had been pondering whether to alter the date and name on the original bill, or make a new one. If doubts were raised about its authenticity, it would be the name and date that would receive special scrutiny. He decided an entirely new bill would be more likely to deceive.

The original bill was handwritten and gave him the wording and layout. He had some notepaper that dated from about the right period, and some early ink-powder. The main difficulty would be the printed bill heading, but Arthur knew somebody who could help him there. He'd sell it through one of the big London sale rooms.

For many years, Benbow had been adding provenance to articles he put into sales. He was taking a lot more care over it now. He didn't want to end up in prison again.

* * *

Cathy sat beside Danny, watching him drive on the last lap of their journey home. He was concentrating on the road and for once she didn't have his full attention. He'd put the car hood down and the wind was fluttering his straight brown hair. She felt full of love for him.

They'd had wonderful weather for their honeymoon and it was continuing hot and sunny. Looking back, it had been a blissful interlude away from real life. They'd motored round, stayed at different guest-houses, and enjoyed walking on the moors, climbing the hills and boating on the lakes.

'We've had a top-notch time,' Danny said, turning to glance at her. 'What did you enjoy most?'

'The luxury of having a car. Sitting here beside you as you drove through open country, seeing the sheep on the mountains and the cows in the fields.' She sighed with satisfaction. 'The lakes too, with all the different sorts of boats, all absolutely beautiful. And being able to think only of ourselves. What about you?'

'The nights, being able to make love to you at last.'

All too soon he was pulling into the kerb in Market Street. Mildred came bustling out to the pavement before Cathy was out of the car. Moments later, she was lifting Rosie up for a hug and a kiss. Cathy had really missed her; it was the one thing about her honeymoon she'd not enjoyed.

'Good to see you safely home.' Mildred pecked at her cheek. 'My, you do look well, both of you. I can see you've had lots of sun. Come on in.'

The flat was filled with the scent of roasting lamb. 'I've got a good dinner to welcome you home,' Mildred said. The living room was immaculate, the table set for four. Cathy couldn't help thinking how different things had been when she returned from her honeymoon with Rolf. She wondered if Mildred was thinking of it, too, for her manner seemed a little strained.

Rosie wouldn't let herself be put down; she was clinging to her. It made Cathy feel guilty, as though she'd turned her back on her. Danny brought their cases into her bedroom and looked round. 'Not very big,' he whispered.

Mildred called them out to have a glass of sherry, which she poured from the bottle Danny had brought weeks ago. She'd made lemonade for Rosie, but the child didn't drink it. Mildred drank that, too, so as not to waste it. The dinner was cooked to perfection and Cathy was hungry, but things were not relaxed. They were all on their best behaviour.

Once home from her honeymoon, Cathy's daily routine followed the same pattern as before. She went back to work with Danny. Using his car, it took only five minutes to get from door to door. The big difference was he now came home with her every evening and shared her bed.

Mildred set another place at the table and cooked an extra meal for him. It seemed he was going to slide smoothly into a place in the family.

During the first weeks, Mildred was more edgy, often moody and out of sorts. Cathy felt their evenings together were not as tranquil as they should be. Once she'd put Rosie to bed, Danny often suggested they go out. Often it was only for a walk, sometimes to the pictures or a theatre. Cathy thanked Mildred for babysitting, knowing they wouldn't be able to go out if she didn't do it.

'You know I like nothing better than to look after Rosie,' she said.

Cathy and Danny had discussed what effect their marriage might have on Rosie. Cathy thought very little, and that in time she'd accept Danny as her father. But almost immediately she noticed Rosie wanted to sit on her knee more than usual.

One evening when she got up to clear the dishes from the tea-table Rosie hung on her, throwing her arms round Cathy's legs.

'Sit,' she insisted pulling her back to her chair. 'Sit.' And when Cathy did so, she climbed back on her knee and curled up in a ball.

'Rosie missed you when you went away on holiday,' Mildred said, her voice disapproving, and Cathy felt another wave of guilt wash over her.

'It wasn't a holiday, it was our honeymoon,' Danny corrected. 'And it was only for a week.' He got up to help with the dishes.

'She's so used to being with you,' Cathy told Mildred. 'That's her routine. I didn't think it would bother her.'

Danny had done his best to make friends with Rosie. She liked to straddle his back and pretend he was her horse. He indulged her by giving her rides round the room. She loved to be lifted so high she could touch the ceiling and she also enjoyed going for rides in his car. He played with her almost every evening.

When the clock struck seven-thirty, Cathy said, 'Time for bed, Rosie. Come along, let's get you undressed.'

The little girl used to go to bed without any fuss, but now she howled that she didn't want to go. Cathy lifted her bodily and carried her to her bedroom. She'd just soothed her when Danny came in and opened one of her books to read her bedtime story.

'Mummy do it,' she said. 'I want Mummy to read, or Nanna. Not you.'

Cathy saw him flinch and knew how hurtful that must be.

'I'm your new father, Rosie,' he said gently. 'I want you to call me Daddy. I'd like to read to you.'

Mildred happened to hear that, and her face was like thunder. Cathy bit her lip. She'd warned Danny that as far as Mildred was concerned, Rolf was Rosie's father.

'But Rosie never knew him,' he'd protested. 'He was killed before she was born. She needs a father here in this world.'

'*I'll* read to her,' Mildred put in. Rosie's eyes gleamed in triumph.

'No,' Cathy said as firmly as she could. 'Either Daddy reads to you, or there won't be a story tonight.'

After more fuss and Mildred telling Cathy she was too hard on the child, Danny read *The Three Bears* while Cathy hovered nearby.

When he tried to kiss her good night, Rosie turned her face away and struggled to get away from him. 'Want my mummy,' she shouted. 'Not you. Want Mummy.'

That upset Cathy. 'I'm here, love,' she said. 'Your new daddy loves you very much. He'd like to kiss you, too.'

The rest of that evening spent with Mildred was anything but restful. Danny tried to talk to her about her business, but she was prickly. 'What's it to you?' she asked rudely.

Danny looked taken aback. 'I thought running a business was what we had in common,' he said. 'I was trying to make conversation.'

'Sorry, I'm sure.'

Cathy cringed and suggested an early night, mainly to get away from her. Once in bed with the light out, she whispered, 'You were right, I should never have pressed you to live here. We should have had a place of our own.'

'There's no privacy,' he sighed. 'I have to watch my tongue because she's always here. We could still go, couldn't we?'

'Wouldn't she find it even more hurtful if we left now? This was what Mildred said she wanted – us to live with her. It would mean we've tried it and want to get away from her.'

'How can any of us be happy here when Rosie's like this? I want her to be content.'

'It was a repeat performance of what happened that Sunday you came for your dinner.'

'Yes.' Danny put his arms round Cathy and pulled her closer. 'Is it me? Does she resent me moving in?'

'She used to like you.'

'I'm beginning to think Mildred's planting ideas in her head. Is Rosie being encouraged to say she doesn't like me? Is it Mildred who's taken the dislike and turned her against me?'

'Is that what you feel?' The same thought had occurred to Cathy. Again she was surprised at how perceptive he was.

'Yes. I think Mildred's jealous. She dislikes anyone who gets close to you.'

Cathy shook her head. 'It makes the atmosphere so tense.'

'And she never says "no" to Rosie,' Danny sighed. 'She gives in to her, lets her have her own way. She'll spoil her rotten.'

Cathy was afraid that was true.

'I need you at work,' he said, 'but I feel guilty. Do you want to stay at home with Rosie?'

'I'd rather be at work with you than at home with Mildred. She's unpredictable and totally obsessed with Rosie.'

'I'm beginning to wonder if it's right for her to be with Mildred so much,' Danny said rather grimly.

'I worry about what it's doing to her, too. She should spend more time with me.'

'That's what I think. We could take her up to our shop.'

'That's a good idea. She could bring some of her toys along.'

'Mam would be happy to have her about the flat.'

'Not all the time, surely?'

'It'll only be for a year or so until she goes to school. Mildred might even be pleased. Rosie's a handful and must be a distraction when she's trying to work.'

'We'll see,' Cathy said, but she wasn't hopeful.

When she told Mildred, she was immediately up in arms.

'Aren't you satisfied with the way I look after her?' she complained. 'Experience counts. I brought Rolf up, after all.'

'I'd like to see more of her, Mildred.' Cathy tried to keep calm. She ought to be used to the way Mildred flared up. 'Also, she's playing up, being quite a handful at times. I'm afraid she's tiring you out.'

'No, she isn't. She behaves herself for me. It's only when Danny's here that she shows off. She's frightened of him.'

'I find that hard to believe,' Cathy said firmly. To placate her, she went on, 'Why don't you let Rosie come up to Exmouth Street with me three days a week? She'd still be with you for the other three and you'd have more time for yourself.'

After a few weeks of this new arrangement, Cathy decided it was very distracting to look after Rosie while she was working. 'I don't know how

Mildred managed it all this time,' she said. 'I have to admire her for that.'

'We took her to one auction,' Danny laughed, 'but never again. She's too active, racing round, upsetting things.'

With Rosie tugging at her skirts, Cathy felt unable to keep up with her work. 'She's of an age when she needs to get out and about more. See a little of the world around her, perhaps be with other children.'

Danny said, 'Why don't we get a girl to keep an eye on her?'

Ettie heard them discussing it and said, 'I've heard one of my neighbours has a daughter who's looking for that sort of a job. She lives over the newsagent on the opposite corner.'

Cathy took Rosie by the hand and walked round to talk to the girl and her mother.

Peggy Ellis was sixteen years old and had been working for two years in a similar job, but her employers had emigrated to Canada. She had one thick brown plait going down her back and was bright-eyed and alert. She got down on the floor to play with Rosie, who took to her immediately. Cathy was delighted and offered her the job there and then.

Within days they seemed to have bonded. Peggy took Rosie out for walks and to play in the park. On the days Rosie stayed with Mildred, Peggy was happy to help in the shop.

Frank and Jackson sometimes took the two girls out with them for rides on the cart. On wet days, Old Benbow made a great fuss of them in the warehouse, while at other times, Ettie made scones and fairy cakes with them. Until, after a week or two, Peggy said that with Rosie's help, she could bake alone.

Rosie loved being taken regularly to Exmouth Street; she settled quickly into her new routine and begged to see more of Peggy. It became four days a week very soon, and then five, with only one day at home with Mildred. Rosie was out and about more, glad to go to bed after her tea and seemed happier. Nowadays, she threw her arms round Danny when he went to kiss her good night.

By the time Cathy had been married to Danny for six months, she knew that for them it had been the right thing to do. He was a loving and tender husband and they were more in love than ever. But Mildred was no easier to get on with, though she admitted she found her business easier to manage without Rosie's presence.

'She's growing up, Mildred, and demanding more attention,' Danny said gently. Mildred was still grumpy and at times she was even short with Rosie.

When they were alone, Danny said to Cathy, 'I suppose it's inevitable that Mildred feels excluded. You and I talk about our business and about people she doesn't know very well. We should try and include her more.'

Now he had a car, Danny was able to get round to more house sales. Today, he and Cathy were going to one in a house in Princes Park in Liverpool, but first he took Old Benbow to another house in Aigburth. They went in with him to have a quick look round. It was a large double-fronted Victorian terraced house.

'Nice dining-room suite,' Danny told Benbow. 'And I like that commode, but there's not much else to suit my shop.'

A pair of chairs caught Cathy's eye. 'They'd be fine for Mildred. She could do with more stock for her shop.'

'She ought to get somebody to go round the sales for her,' Danny said.

'She relies on those two house clearance men, but their stuff is shabby. Most of it needs mending or painting and there's never enough of it.'

Old Benbow said, 'That bookcase would be all right for Mildred too, and that whatnot. D'you want me to get them for her if I can?'

'What d'you think, Cathy?'

'Yes, it might please her.'

'Go for them, Benbow, as well,' Danny told him. He took Cathy's arm and led her back to the car.

'You're a very kind person,' she said. 'Willing to help Mildred when she's being so difficult.'

'The only help I can give is to her business.'

'She'll appreciate it, I'm sure.'

'Sometimes to show you care, that you're willing to help . . . it's enough to change people. Mildred would be all right if she weren't so jealous. She thinks I'm taking you and Rosie away from her and she's trying to fight me.'

That evening, Cathy was tucking Rosie up for the night when the Bott Brothers' cart drew up outside. She tiptoed out of the room and closed the bedroom door to find Danny and Mildred had gone out to the street. She guessed the furniture Old Benbow had bought was being delivered, and ran down after them.

Jackson and Old Benbow were unloading a pair of chairs; the bookcase was already on the pavement.

'Look – I just thought they'd suit your shop.' Danny was trying to calm Mildred. 'I thought you'd be pleased.'

Mildred was boiling with indignation. 'What d'you mean, suit my shop? You buy cheap stuff like this for me, and fancy antiques for your own place!'

'But that's the way it's always been at Second Time Around. When you and Cathy started up, it's what you decided.'

'Ah, but there's more profit in the better class of stuff, isn't there? You've always kept that for yourself.'

'And you've always taken furniture like this! Often it's in worse condition and needs a lot of work on it.'

'Well, I don't want this.'

'Cathy thought you've be glad of—'

'It's nothing to do with Cathy now. Hasn't been for a long time. She's thrown her lot in with you. This is *my* business.'

'We thought you'd like more stock.'

'These are good solid country chairs,' Old Benbow put in. 'Windsor chairs, years of use in them, comfy too. You'd make a fair profit.'

'Well, I'm not having them. I didn't ask for them and I don't want them.'

'Please yourself.' Danny was losing patience. 'Jackson can take them up to the warehouse. They can go to a sale room next week.'

'I'll have them,' Jackson said. 'I rather like them. Could do with more chairs in my rooms.'

'Cost price to you,' Danny said quickly.

Mildred was indignant. 'That bookcase is rubbish. Not good enough for your shop so you try to dump it in mine.'

Danny lifted one end. 'Let's have it back on the cart, Jackson.'

'I'll run my shop and you run yours. I don't want you interfering.'

'Don't worry, we won't in future,' Danny told her.

Cathy felt so shaken up, she didn't feel she could face sitting in the same room as Mildred after that. She suggested to Danny that they go for a walk.

'Mildred and I, we planned that business together,' she said. 'We're supposed to be partners. I know Mildred's done most of the work but it's as though she no longer wants me to have anything to do with it.'

'I'd swear she's afraid we're going to take it over.' Danny pulled Cathy's arm through his. 'It's the last time I try to help her.'

Mildred shot inside and slammed the shop door behind her. How dare Danny presume to buy goods for her shop? He was interfering with what was hers. She could feel the heat running up her cheeks. Then suddenly, all the fight went out of her. What on earth had got into her? As she looked round her shop, tears were scalding her eyes.

She should never have said such things to him and Cathy – in front of Jackson and Old Benbow, too. They'd think her a real vixen.

She stood panting slightly as she looked round. Cathy was right, her shop *was* looking bare. She'd never had so little furniture for sale and the place wasn't as attractive as it used to be. After the Halesworth sale, it had been full to the point of overflow. That stock had sold quickly and had given her a very profitable year but she'd never managed to repeat it. Danny had suggested a year or so ago that she ask Old Benbow to buy stock for her.

'He's going round all the sales anyway,' he'd said. 'You and I won't be in competition for what's on offer. We're at different ends of the market.'

Mildred hadn't liked that. She'd had her ambitions too, and had hoped to begin to sell real antiques. She was disappointed in the way her business had performed since the war had ended and was afraid the competition was getting tougher.

Last week, she'd taken a few hours off on consecutive afternoons to go round all the big shops both here and over the water, to see what they had to offer. Such a change in the last year; they were full of choice. The new season's clothes were elegant, crisp and the height of fashion. She saw plenty of spanking new pieces of furniture that would smarten up any home. And all at prices not so different to what she charged.

It had shocked her. With the scarcity war had brought, she'd found a niche in the market but that had gone now.

Mildred felt dead tired. Sewing as she did, day in and day out, was hard work, and she'd done her best to keep the place tidy and food on the table for them all.

She went slowly upstairs to her flat and peeped in her bedroom where Rosie was fast asleep in her own small bed. She looked a little angel; she meant everything to her.

Now Rolf and Otto were gone, Rosie was all she had left, but Cathy had changed Rosie's daily routine so Mildred was hardly ever in charge of her nowadays. That was her biggest complaint.

Tomorrow was Wednesday, the only day of the week she had Rosie at home with her. Mildred usually looked forward to Wednesdays but when she was getting up the next morning, she'd lost her usual bounce.

Cathy had always dressed Rosie in the mornings, made her bed as well as her own, and washed up the breakfast dishes before going off to work. She knew how much extra work she made by being here.

Rosie was growing more active as she grew older and since Cathy had been handing her over to that girl Peggy, she'd been demanding more and more attention, wanting Mildred to play games or take her out for a walk. She'd had to get Jessie to take her out so she could have an hour's rest. Mildred felt she hardly had peace to sew at all on Wednesdays.

When it was time to open the shop, she still felt tired. Rosie clattered downstairs behind her. She was a delight, of course. She had a mop of curls but they weren't so tight as Cathy's, and her hair was brown, as Rolf's had been. She had Rolf's brown eyes too, but today, Mildred felt it was hard work to have Rosie two paces behind her and to have to answer her everlasting questions.

'Who's this?' Rosie's piping treble drew her attention to Dick O'Mara's cart pulling up in front of the shop. There was no mistaking his squat figure and flat cap. He had a load of furniture to show her, and suddenly Mildred felt glad: she'd been right to stop Danny unloading the stuff Old Benbow had chosen on her.

'Mr Lello's naughty, isn't he?' Mildred said to Rosie.

'Is he, Nanna? He doesn't get his clothes dirty like me.'

'He wants to dump nasty furniture in my shop. Stuff he wouldn't sell in his.'

'Mr Lello's naughty,' Rosie was repeating as Mildred went out to see what Dick O'Mara had brought her. She'd asked him to find her some better quality furniture. She had to have it if she was to compete with the brand-new stock in the shops.

Dick O'Mara jumped heavily down from his cart. He was overweight with the fresh colouring of an Irish farmer, but his accent told her he'd been born and bred here on Merseyside.

'Morning, Mrs Godfrey. Got some good stuff for you today.'

'Let's see it then.'

It was impossible to see what he did have. The load was covered with old blankets to stop it being damaged and he'd roped the pieces together to prevent them falling off the cart.

'A nice display cabinet. Small enough for a modern house. A baby's rocking cradle with a hood. Nice quality, mid-Victorian. And what about this occasional table? Would you know what that's made of?'

Mildred shook her head.

'Papier-mâché, Victorian again, and the top's painted with a Highland scene. Isn't that pretty?'

'You'd better bring it inside,' Mildred said, 'so I can have a closer look – and I want to know what it's going to cost before I say yes.'

But she knew she'd take it. She liked what she was seeing and Dick O'Mara was reasonable in what he charged. He didn't have a boy to hold his horse; he got down and fixed a nose bag over her head.

'She'll munch away on her dinner while I unload,' he grinned at her.

When Mildred saw the load spread out in her shop, she decided she'd have it all, even the papier-mâché table painted with the Highland scene. She'd never seen anything like that before. It could do with a good clean but it looked as though it would come up like new. Somebody would like it. Mildred felt triumphant. The place looked well-stocked again. Several customers had noticed the new furniture through the window and had come in for a closer look. One had told her he'd come back for the display cabinet when he had the money.

'Isn't Nanna clever?' she asked Rosie. 'She doesn't need help, does she? Not from Old Benbow and Mr Lello.'

She took Rosie round the market that afternoon and bought a bit of cod; Rosie would eat that for her tea. There was smoked finnan haddock for the rest of them. She had the shop closed and the fish ready to cook by the time Danny was pulling up outside.

Rosie went tearing down to meet her mother. Mildred could hear them talking in the shop. She knew they'd stopped to assess the new stock.

'Aren't you coming up?' she asked from the top of the stairs.

'Just looking at the new furniture you've got in,' Cathy called. 'I like the little table with the picture on it.'

'You've got some good stuff,' Danny said as he came up carrying Rosie. 'Decent quality, this time.'

Mildred knew that meant he'd like it in his own shop, and gloated.

Chapter Seventeen

Cathy had been yearning for another baby for some time, and Danny was very keen. They'd talked of adding to their family, and the time seemed right now Rosie had turned four. By the late summer of 1920, Cathy began to think she might be pregnant again. She waited a few weeks.

'I can't stand the suspense any longer,' Danny had said that morning. 'Please go to see the doctor.'

He drove her to the surgery and waited outside to take her back to the shop.

As she came out, she was smiling. 'The answer's yes,' she told him happily.

'I'm thrilled.' Danny slid an arm round her shoulders and gave her a hug. 'Absolutely delighted. It's taken me a bit longer than it took Rolf but I've managed it.'

Cathy laughed. 'Are we going to tell your mother?'

'Up to you,' he said.

Back in the flat above the Exmouth Street shop, Ettie now cooked a dinner for them all in the middle of the day. Often Frank came home for it. Today he was full of the news that the telephone had been put in at Cooper's Yard.

Ettie said, 'Danny, we ought to have one here too. Keep the business up to date.'

'Perhaps we should. I'll think about it.'

'My aunt and Jimmy are very go-ahead,' Frank said. 'They're pressing me to order another motor van and get rid of the cart-horses. I think it makes sense and we'll do it. That'll be the next bit of news I'll be bringing up.'

'There's always something going on down there, isn't there?'

Cathy smiled. 'Things go on for us up here, too.' And she told them about the coming baby.

'That's the best news ever,' Ettie said, beaming round at them. 'It's just what Danny needs – a child of his own. I like the idea too. You're going to make me a grandmother.'

213

Since Ettie and Frank's wedding, Harriet Bott had been invited up to their flat quite often. She was now in the habit of dropping into the shop for a chat when she was at that end of town. She came that afternoon and Cathy told her, too.

Botty kissed her. 'How lovely for all of you. Better that Rosie isn't an only.'

'I'm going to make sure things go more smoothly for Cathy this time,' Danny said. 'She won't be allowed to work on for too long. Everything will be properly organised.'

'But in the meantime,' she put in, 'I'm going to carry on just as I always have.'

Within a short time, everybody at Cooper's Yard knew there was a baby on the way. Old Benbow wished Cathy well and Iris telephoned to congratulate her, asking if she wanted a son this time.

'I don't mind,' she said. 'And neither does Danny. Just so long as it's healthy.'

When Danny was driving home that evening, Cathy said, 'We shouldn't put off telling Mildred.'

'She won't like it, but it's better if she hears it from you.'

'Yes. With everyone at the yard knowing, one of them could let it slip.'

'They don't see much of Mildred any more, so I don't think it's very likely.'

'Jackson was there with the cart the other morning, Danny. One of her customers wanted something delivered. Anyway, she'd be furious if she thought she was the last to know. I'll tell her tonight.'

Cathy was silent for a few moments, watching the road ahead, then she said, 'There won't be room for another child in Mildred's place. It'll give us a good excuse to go.'

'Would you like a house of your own?'

'Of course – I'd love it.'

'Then I think we should start talking about it as a possibility. So it won't come as a shock to Mildred when we tell her we want to move.'

Cathy didn't reply.

'Do you agree?' Danny pressed.

'It hasn't been a great success, us living with her, has it?'

'I don't think Mildred's happy with it either,' Danny said. 'There isn't much room and we must make a lot of extra work for her. She might be glad to see us go.'

'She won't be glad to see Rosie go,' Cathy said.

* * *

214

With the ritual of putting Rosie to bed almost over, Mildred was glad to settle herself in Otto's old chair and pick up the evening newspaper Danny had brought home. She was tired but it had been a good day. For once she'd got the better of Danny. She could hear him saying good night to Rosie.

'Go to sleep, love. It's getting late.' He closed Rosie's bedroom door then he and Cathy came to join Mildred.

'Aren't you going out tonight?' she asked. She liked the peace of having her home to herself in the evenings.

'No,' Danny said. Mildred sensed a certain stiffness in the atmosphere; they were quieter than usual.

Cathy blurted out suddenly, 'I'm having another baby.'

Mildred felt the blood drain from her face. Hadn't she been dreading an announcement like this? A coal dropped in the grate. She looked up and found Cathy's eyes on her.

'When?' she croaked into the tense silence.

'April, next year.'

'We're very pleased,' Danny added.

'I am too, of course,' Mildred managed, but could say no more. Her mouth was dry.

'We've been thinking,' Danny went on slowly, 'that sooner or later we'll need more space. We should start looking for a house of our own. I'm sure you'll be glad to see the back of us.'

'No! It's not till April next year.' Anger was welling up inside her. Did they intend to take Rosie from her? 'And even then, another small baby won't make that much difference. We'll get Rosie's crib down from the loft when the time comes. Plenty of space in your bedroom for that. It was there before.' She was aware of the lengthening silence.

'Of course we'll want the new baby in with us while it's tiny,' Cathy said at last. 'But not for ever.'

'Babies soon grow,' Danny put in. 'It'll seem no time before we're looking for a bed for it.'

Mildred felt she had her back to the wall. Why were they doing this to her? They must mean to take the child away too and leave her on her own.

Danny said, 'In time, we hope we'll go on and have other babies; a proper family.'

Mildred knew if that happened they'd have to move out. She felt desperate and couldn't stop the words tumbling out, 'Will you leave Rosie here with me? I'll take good care of her.'

She heard both Danny and Cathy gasp aloud.

After a moment's stunned silence, Cathy said, 'Mildred, no. I couldn't do that.'

Mildred was overcome with anguish. She covered her face with her hands.

They all heard the bedroom door creak and Rosie's bare feet come padding towards them.

'What are you doing out of bed?' Danny asked, his voice sharper than usual. 'I thought we'd said good night to you, young lady. You know this isn't allowed.'

'Go on, back to bed, love.' Cathy looked fraught. 'You won't be able to get up in the morning if you don't go to sleep now.'

Mildred took a deep shuddering breath. 'Come to Nanna,' she invited, holding out her arms. Rosie rushed into them, and she lifted the child on to her knee. She couldn't let Cathy do this to her.

'Your mummy wants to take you to a new home,' Mildred told Rosie, kissing the top of her head.

'You love your Nanna, don't you, Rosie?' You'd rather stay here with me than go to a strange house that you don't know?'

Rosie was nodding. 'Stay here with Nanna,' she piped, beaming at her mother.

Danny was straight-lipped and severe. 'This is not the place to talk about it. Later . . .'

He was nodding towards the child, and Mildred knew he meant for them not to talk in front of Rosie. But she couldn't stop.

'You'll soon have other children, Cathy. You don't need Rosie the way I do. She's Rolf's child – my own flesh and blood. Please let . . .' Mildred knew she was wheedling now.

'She'll be going to school before much longer,' Cathy said. 'We'll all see much less of her then.'

'Don't want to go to school,' Rosie said defiantly. 'Want to stay with Nanna.'

Cathy was furious with Mildred and knew Danny was too. She could see he was biting back his anger. His gaze swept the ceiling in disbelief, before he got to his feet.

'Come on, Rosie. You know this won't do.'

Rosie was sullen. 'Want to stay with Nanna.'

He scooped her up in his arms. 'You can kiss Nanna good night again and Mummy too.' He held her out so she could. 'I'm going to tuck you up in bed, and if you promise to stay there I'll tell you another story. Goldilocks, yes?'

'No, Cinderella.'

'All right.'

Cathy got up to open the bedroom door for him. He whispered through clenched teeth, 'We can't let this go on.'

She pulled the door firmly shut behind them. Mildred was sitting back with what seemed like exaggerated ease, holding the newspaper in front of her. Cathy was determined to keep her temper but at the same time let Mildred know exactly what was upsetting her.

'Mildred,' she said, trying to sound reasonable. 'I do understand your position.'

The newspaper was slowly lowered; dark eyes glittered up at her.

'I'll always be grateful for your care and the generosity with which you took me into your home.'

'I'm glad you appreciated it.'

'I've tried to be a loving daughter-in-law, but you've turned against me.'

'Don't be silly.'

'You've turned against Danny too. I think it's because he's taken Rolf's place.' She watched Mildred purse her lips. 'You're putting ideas into Rosie's head, turning her against him. I've thought so for some time.'

'No!'

'Mildred, you've just done it in my hearing.' Cathy was growing more heated. 'You said, "You love your Nanna, don't you, Rosie? You'd rather stay here with me than go to a strange house that you don't know?" '

'And she said she would.'

'Only because you planted the idea in her head, and she knows it's what you want. We have to go. We're going to need another bedroom soon, and we aren't getting on as well as I'd hoped.'

There was bitterness in Mildred's voice. 'You mean you aren't happy here any more?'

'No, I'm not, and I don't think you are either. How can I be happy when you're deliberately turning Rosie against Danny and against the idea of moving out?'

Mildred was rigid with tension. 'I love her, Cathy. She's all I've got left. Leave her here with me, please. She's used to being with me; she loves me. You know she'll be well looked after.'

Cathy's cheeks were burning. 'I know it's what you've been fighting for all along,' she said quietly. 'I love her too, Mildred. I'm her mother. I can't do what you ask.'

'But you'll have another baby as well. I'll have nothing.'

'I didn't have a mother when I was growing up, and I've felt the lack all my life. For Rosie's sake as well as mine, I want to bring her up in a normal family. I'm sorry, but that's the way it's going to be.'

It was drizzling; not a pleasant night for a walk, but after that tiff with Mildred, Cathy needed to get away from the atmosphere. She knew Danny would be more than willing to come with her.

She hesitated in the shop doorway. 'On a night like this, we ought to go to the pictures or something.'

They were later than usual. 'The show will have started by now,' Danny said.

Cathy took his arm. 'The market's still open. We can stroll round there and be undercover.'

But she felt restless and it seemed pointless. They came out at the back of the market and Danny led her across the street to the shop window of an estate agent. He was reading the notices in the window.

'You know Fred Chesters,' he said. 'He comes into our shop quite a lot.'

'Yes, he bought a desk last week.'

'He specialises in commercial property. I got the lease for Exmouth Street through him. It might be worth thinking of premises in central Liverpool.'

'Open another branch, you mean?'

'Yes, we need to expand. We're not going to make a fortune from one shop, especially this one in Exmouth Street. We're earning as much from it as we're ever likely to. It's not in the best shopping area.'

'I thought you were in no hurry for that. You said you'd expand only when you'd learned all there was to know about antiques.'

He laughed. 'I doubt if I'll ever be able to boast of that. I'm in no hurry, but caution won't get us anywhere. If we could get a place with living accommodation too, we'd have a home of our own.'

'Not very likely if it's in the centre of a city. The upstairs is usually rented off as office space.'

'It's getting the right place,' Danny frowned. 'Next time, I want it right in the middle of the most prosperous shopping centre. It's worth paying a bit more rent to get a steady stream of well-heeled shoppers passing our windows. We'd sell much more.'

'If one came up now, would you take it?'

'It'd have to be exactly right. I'd rather leave it another year or so, but there's no harm in looking. I had a word with Fred Chesters last month, and he said he'd keep an eye out for something to suit us.'

Cathy could see someone locking up doors in the back of the shop. The next moment, Mr Chesters himself, portly and dapper, came out on the doorstep.

'Hello there, Mr McLelland, Mrs McLelland.' He tipped his hat. 'I was thinking about you only this afternoon.'

'You've got premises that would suit us?' Danny sounded keen.

'The very thing. Come inside for a moment, and I'll get you the particulars.'

Cathy felt cheered and followed them in.

Mr Chesters was rubbing his podgy hands together. 'This property has living accommodation too. There's a smart tea shop on one side and a jeweller's on the other.'

'Sounds about right,' Danny said. 'Where is it?'

'In Grange Road, not far from Robb's department store.'

'Here in Birkenhead?' Cathy heard the disappointment in Danny's voice.

'Yes. You probably know it, Mrs McLelland. It was a clothes shop – Pine's Fine Fashions. The lease was up and Mrs Pine decided to retire. It's in one of the best positions in Birkenhead, and it's a big shop. Why not have a look at it?'

'I'd be more interested if it was Liverpool or Chester,' Danny said. 'It's too near to Exmouth Street – only a few hundred yards away – and there's another ten years to run on my lease. I couldn't open another shop that close.'

'No, but I could sell the Exmouth Street lease for you.'

Danny shook his head. 'I was thinking of expanding to a second shop.'

'Take the particulars anyway. I'll be there about ten tomorrow to show a client round. Pop in at half past if you'd like to see it too.'

'I might do that, Mr Chesters,' Danny said, 'just as a matter of interest.'

They came out and headed back home. Danny said, 'It is a good position. I might as well find out what rent they're asking and see what the shop's like. But to move from Exmouth Street now . . . We're doing all right there; it would be a big step to take. I doubt if it would pay us to do that.'

'Maybe it's a bit soon to branch out anyway,' Cathy consoled him.

A couple of days later, Mildred was still feeling low. Now that Cathy and Danny would eventually be moving to a house of their own, she knew she was going to lose Rosie. For her, the future looked bleak. If she lost Rosie, she felt she'd lose her reason for living.

Mildred knew the best way to use what little energy she had left was to immerse herself in her business affairs. Most of the small shops nearby were family-run, without paid assistants. Now she employed Jessie Jones, her shop seemed to have grown in importance.

Not that the girl was up to much. She looked washed-out and wan, with a nose that wouldn't stop running. As well as serving behind the counter, Jessie kept the displays of tea cosies and oven gloves looking neat and tidy, and dusted the furniture in slack moments. Every evening, at closing time, Jessie swept through the shop. It generally looked well cared for, but she could always see something that still needed cleaning. She fetched the vinegar down from her kitchen, found some old newspaper and told Jessie to polish the shop windows.

The new furniture delivered last night was not looking its best. It all needed a good clean and plenty of polish. Mildred took the papier-mâché table and the baby's rocking cradle out through her sewing room to the back yard, rolled up her sleeves and set about it.

The table was encrusted with dirt; she had to take a damp cloth to it first. Buffing it up after a generous application of polish made her feel better and the painted scene on top was much brighter. She heard the shop bell clang but left Jessie to see to it. The girl came to the back door which she'd left open.

'Mrs Godfrey, there's a policeman here.'

'You can serve him, can't you?'

'He says he wants a word with you.'

Mildred followed her back into the shop feeling uneasy. What could a policeman want with her? He looked officious, towering over her with his helmet under his arm.

'Mrs Godfrey?' he asked.

'Yes.'

'I'm Constable Browning of the Birkenhead Police.' Mildred felt a cold shiver run down her spine. 'I'm making enquiries through the secondhand trade about stolen furniture.' He offered her a typewritten list. 'Have you seen any of these items?'

She fumbled behind the counter for the pair of spectacles she kept there, and was horrified to see the first item on the list was an early-Victorian papier-mâché tripod table with a painted Highland scene on top. There couldn't be many of those about. With the measurements quoted here, it was unmistakable.

Mildred felt the strength ebbing from her knees. The policeman was looking at her gravely. If he'd come in a few minutes earlier, it would have been standing right here. If he stepped through that open door to the yard, he'd see it now.

Jessie was leaning on the counter, picking her teeth and hanging on to every word.

220

He said, 'Most of the items were stolen locally. It's likely they'll turn up around here.'

The typescript danced before her eyes; dear Lord, the baby's rocking cradle with hood was here too. Oh goodness! So was that display cabinet. Constable Browning was standing right in front of it now and looking straight at it. She must keep her own eyes well away from it. She knew she was panicking.

'No,' she said, offering him the list back. 'I've seen nothing like this.'

'Are you sure? Please take the time to read it through.'

He opened a drawer in a chest she'd had here for weeks, peered in and slowly closed it again. 'There's a chest like this on the list, isn't there?'

Her mouth was dry, and Mildred felt dizzy with dread. She'd bought that from Dick O'Mara too! She pretended to take the list nearer the window to catch the light. It allowed her to turn her back on the policeman; her face must surely show the guilt she was feeling. She forced herself to study the list.

'Yes, here, mahogany chest of drawers, George the Third. That chest you're looking at isn't old, no more than twenty years. It isn't mahogany either.'

Her cheeks were burning. 'From a written description, one chest of drawers can sound pretty much like another. Most of what I sell has been factory made, so I see pieces that are exactly the same.'

That wasn't entirely true because she didn't have much throughput in her shop, but she'd heard Benbow say something like that.

'Even the makers of high-class furniture often used the same designs. It's very difficult to pick out one piece and say it was stolen.'

'Yes, so I'm finding,' he said. Her hand was shaking as she tried to give him the list back.

'Please keep that copy.' He was heading towards the door at last. 'I'd like you to study it and let us know if you see any of the items. They could turn up at any time.'

'Of course.'

Mildred stood with her hand pressed against her mouth, watching PC Browning stride away. What had she done? Why had she denied it? She'd bought the things in good faith, but she'd lied to a police officer.

She shivered. She had records but only those she made out herself. She didn't have a bill – Dick O'Mara never gave her one. She had nothing with his name on it, nothing to show she'd bought it from him or how much she'd paid. If she'd known it was stolen property she wouldn't have touched it.

Benbow had warned her, but he hadn't told her a policeman might come round asking about it. It had scared her stiff to see him walking round her shop, peering into everything. What was she to do?

She went out to the yard and could feel the sweat drying on her face in the cool air. Suddenly, she realised she'd left the list on the counter and she shot back to retrieve it before Jessie cast her eye down it. Even she, dim as she was, wouldn't fail to recognise the description of that table. Mildred didn't want her to know she'd lied. Didn't want anybody to know she had stolen property in her shop.

Jessie's dark eyes were watching her minutely. Thank goodness the policeman hadn't shown *her* the list – but perhaps he had, before she came to call her in? Mildred felt faint at the thought.

She had to hide that table. She carried it and the cradle back into her sewing room and covered them up with some dress-lengths. As she went back through the shop she dreaded hearing Jessie ask about it.

Old Benbow had told her not to trust Dick O'Mara and like a fool she'd taken no notice. She'd go round to O'Mara's shop immediately and get him to come and fetch his stolen property. She wanted her money back and she'd give him a piece of her mind. Mildred rushed upstairs to get her coat. When she came down again, there were two customers in the shop.

'I'm going out for a few minutes,' she told Jessie as she took her record book from behind the counter. She almost ran across the market to Dick O'Mara's shop.

There was one customer in, an old man looking through a collection of stained enamel bowls and buckets. Mildred waited. He was taking ages.

It was a scruffy shop. Junk of all sorts was piled up all round: cheap chairs and tables, odd stools, chipped crockery, glassware and books, some of which had lost their covers. Everything was shabby, battered or broken.

'Hello, Mrs Godfrey. It's an honour indeed to have a visit from you.' Dick O'Mara was in his shirt-sleeves. He wore no collar but the stud was in place ready to hold it on when he finished dressing. Ancient braces held up his trousers.

The old man had finally selected a washing-up bowl and a bucket.

'Threepence, sir, for those.'

O'Mara took the money and turned to her. 'I'm glad you've popped in,' he said. 'I've got a nice tea-trolley in the back that'd suit you. Come and have a look at it.'

Mildred waited, burning with frustration until the shop door shut behind the old man.

'I wouldn't touch anything more from you with a barge-pole,' she told him angrily. 'That stuff you brought round the other day was stolen.'

'No, missus! Whatever makes you think that?'

'I've had the police round, that's what.'

O'Mara straightened up. 'Did you say you got it from me?'

'The bobby didn't ask. I want you to bring your cart straight round and take it away, and I want my money back.'

'I can't do that.' He pointed a dirty finger at a disclaimer on the wall that read *Terms strictly for cash. Goods are sold as seen. Faults discovered later cannot be recompensed.*

Mildred felt the heat run up her cheeks. 'I'm not having your stolen property in my shop. I don't want trouble with the law.'

'I haven't stolen anything. I told you, I bought it at auction with you in mind. You said you wanted good quality stuff.'

'Not stolen property.'

'I don't believe it is stolen, I've—'

'It's stolen, all right.'

O'Mara's face turned ugly. 'Which pieces do you think are stolen?'

Mildred pulled the typed list from her pocket and pushed it in front of him. 'This papier-mâché table, this cradle – they're in my shop now. It was a miracle the bobby didn't see them.'

O'Mara held the list nearer the light. 'I don't know what you're talking about. I never took these things to your shop – I never handled anything like this. They've not been through *my* business.'

'Don't talk daft, you know you have.' Mildred opened her record book. 'Look here, on Wednesday the fourth: *Papier-mâché occasional table* and the price I paid you – two pound it was. Here's the baby's cradle and here's the display cabinet. Eleven pounds I paid you for that load. I want my money back.'

His finger stabbed towards his disclaimer again. 'Don't you understand? I don't give money back.'

'You buy stuff from anybody – there's another notice there that says you will.'

'I only buy what I want, or what I know one of my customers wants. I don't want stolen goods any more than you do.'

'I'll go to the police and tell them everything,' Mildred threatened, though she knew she couldn't, not after those lies she'd told. 'I'll show them my records.'

'But this isn't a proper record. You can write what you like, it proves nothing. The police will want to see bills and receipts.'

'You don't give either.'

There was a cunning sneer on his face. 'They won't believe that a businesswoman like you would hand over money without getting a receipt.'

Mildred remembered the bills and receipts she used to see going through the butcher's business, and knew she'd been very remiss.

O'Mara began to bluster. 'You knew what you were doing, must have. You weren't born yesterday. You can't be stupid enough to think you can buy goods of that quality for the few quid I charge. Not unless they're a bit dodgy.'

Two more customers were coming in. Mildred gave up, snatched up her book and pushed past the women. She slammed the door with such force the glass rattled in the windows.

She was fuming as she strode back to her shop. Frightened as well as angry. It had been a mistake to lie to that police officer, she could see that now, but he'd taken her unawares. She didn't know what the penalty might be, couldn't begin to understand the processes of the law. It was unknown territory to her. Otto too, had always been nervous of finding himself on the wrong side of the law.

She was sweating now and knew she'd have to get rid of that papier-mâché table. She'd chop it up and burn it rather than be found out. She counted as lost the eleven pounds she'd paid O'Mara. Dislike of him was rising like bile in her throat. He'd used her, deliberately fencing his stolen property through Second Time Around. Eleven pounds was an enormous sum of money. She couldn't afford to lose it.

Chapter Eighteen

Jackson had had a pleasant morning. He'd been out with the cart, but with only two calls to make he'd finished early. He had over an hour to kill before Iris would have the dinner on the table, so he'd told her he was going out to buy cigarettes.

Iris said, 'There's a few things I need. Will you get me a pound of butter? I'm running out.' She'd pushed a shopping bag into his hands. 'While you're in the shop you could get some biscuits too – ginger nuts and some Rich Tea – half a pound of each and a packet of Rinso washing powder. Shall I make a list for you?'

Jackson followed her down the passage to the office, and watched her take the cashbox from the bottom drawer of her desk. She opened it, and he could see lots of coins counted out into separate compartments. It fascinated him that the Botts kept all that cash on hand. As far as he could make out, they only went to the bank once a fortnight.

She pressed some coins into his hand, scribbled something on a bit of paper she tore off a pad and pushed that inside the box. Seconds later her red head went down and she'd slid it back into the bottom drawer. As usual, she didn't lock it. It was *never* locked. Dear oh dear. It was temptation itself.

Jackson was finding money a bit short. Living at Cooper's Yard was more expensive than living at Halesworth had been, because he now had to buy his own whisky and cigarettes.

'Thanks.' Iris smiled gratefully at him. 'Don't forget, dinner's at one.'

Jackson set off immediately, wanting to put some distance between himself and that cashbox. He couldn't take money that belonged to the Botts. They'd been too kind to him. All of them had shown him friendship.

He sauntered down towards the market. It took only ten minutes to buy what Iris wanted. The newsagent next door advertised Park Drive Cigarettes at ten for fourpence. He was coming out with two packets when he saw Mildred Godfrey with her head down, striding towards him at a furious pace.

'Hello, Mildred.'

She looked at him as though she didn't know who he was. Her eyes were fiery and her face red. She looked ready for a fight.

'Oh hello.'

'You are in a hurry.'

'Don't like to leave the girl alone in the shop for long,' she muttered.

Jackson fell into step beside her. He had to pass her shop on the way back to Cooper's Yard. 'You look worried,' he said.

'No, just bothered about selling enough to make a living. It isn't easy any more.'

'No, you're right.' Jackson didn't think Mildred knew enough about what she was selling. 'Those chairs Benbow bought for you the other week – I've got them in my rooms. They're good and strong, comfortable too. I'm very pleased with them.'

She stared at him, hostility in her dark eyes. 'I'm glad. Would you like a small table as well? I've got a nice one, might suit you. Come and see.'

Jackson followed her into the shop. It smelled of beeswax, just as Halesworth had.

The girl behind the counter was all smiles. 'I've sold that display cabinet, Mrs Godfrey,' she sang out.

'Oh good! Well done, Jessie.' It seemed Mildred was more than pleased at the news; he saw the glimmer of a smile on her face.

'Where is it then, this table?' He was looking round; there wasn't a lot of furniture here.

'Come this way.'

He followed her into one of the small rooms at the back, where she unearthed a small occasional table from under some silky material. He didn't like it. Tables shouldn't have pictures painted on them, not in his opinion. It was too fancy. 'It isn't wood.'

'It's papier-mâché. The painting is in oils and has a signature on it. Been lacquered over.'

'I don't know . . .'

'It's Victorian,' she told him. 'Good quality.'

It was. Jackson wondered if he could perhaps make a bit on it.

'I'm asking three pounds for it. It's excellent value at that price.'

'Make it two and I might be interested.'

'All right, two – guineas.'

He hadn't expected her to agree so readily. She must really be hard up. He felt in his pockets, knowing he didn't have that amount of money on him.

'I'll have to come back when I get paid,' he said, turning to go. 'I'm skint at the moment, sorry.'

'You can take it with you. Pay me at the end of the week.'

'Really?'

'You're a friend of Cathy's and I know where you live, don't I?'

'All right then.' He picked it up to see how heavy it was.

'You won't be needing a cart for that. Light as a feather, isn't it?'

'It's not heavy, but I wouldn't say it was exactly featherweight. I've got a bag to carry as well.' He'd picked it up and was making for the door.

'Hang on a moment,' she said. 'I'll tie a bit of paper round it, cover it up.'

'No need for that, I'll not scratch it.'

She was at the doorstep to see him out, her face screwing with worry. 'See you at the end of the week,' she repeated.

Jackson hurried his step. Everybody seemed to be looking at the table, but it was a pretty unusual thing to carry through the streets. He went faster still, telling himself he didn't want to be late for his dinner.

He couldn't help but guess there was some problem with this table. Mildred had had it hidden in her back room and she'd been very keen that he should take it out of her shop.

Probably, she'd found out it was stolen property. Benbow was always going on about the danger of being caught with that. Hadn't he warned Mildred not to buy from Dick O'Mara? Jackson wished he'd asked her where she'd got the table, but he was prepared to bet it was from him. He should have let her cover the top – what if he met a copper now? The only good thing was, he hadn't parted with any money for it.

When he reached Cooper's Yard, there was a buzz of chatter from the kitchen. He left the table at the bottom of the stairs and found Iris already dishing up.

'Here's your shopping.' He put the change down alongside it.

'Are you ready to eat?'

'Yes, always ready, you know me.' But first he shot upstairs to take the table up to his attic. Better if nobody here saw it. Just in case. As he ate his plate of scouse, Jackson decided he'd take the table round to Old Benbow sometime soon. He'd know if it was worth anything.

This afternoon, he was to go out on the van with Frank, so he'd not be able to do anything about it for the moment. It was nearly ten o'clock when they got back and he offered to stable the horse so the lads could get off home.

Mildred knew she'd wasted the whole afternoon. She'd spent it fulminating at what O'Mara had done to her. She couldn't settle to her sewing

227

– there was no way she could get on with it, even though she had two dresses to make for a customer.

Yes, she'd been relieved to hear Jessie had sold the display cabinet. Even more relieved when Jackson was persuaded to take that hateful table out of her shop, but she still had stolen goods in stock. She wasn't out of the woods yet. She didn't have the nerve to put the cradle out on sale.

She'd buy no more furniture, she decided, not from any source. She'd had enough of this. It had been Cathy's idea and not a good one. Mildred hadn't wanted to do it in the first place. In future, she'd stick to sewing. She could earn her living that way without all this trouble.

Mildred could think of nothing else. She was simmering, knowing she'd been done down. She hated anybody to get the better of her and O'Mara had been so callous, so rude when she'd asked for her money back. His face was before her now, twisting with contempt. Contempt for her!

Danny's car was drawing up at the kerb outside. She heard Cathy's laugh – it was another irritant. Mildred was not in the mood for laughter. Then Rosie came rushing into her arms, her face flushed.

'Hello, Nanna! I've been to the park. I fed the ducks.'

Mildred kissed her, but for once even Rosie couldn't cheer her up. She was glad to turn the card round on her shop door to show it was closed.

'Time to go home, Jessie,' she said briskly. The girl had got on her nerves all afternoon. It irked Mildred to see her standing about doing nothing, but it was a fulltime job keeping her busy. She couldn't see work when it stared her in the face. She wasn't worth the eight shillings and sixpence a week she paid her.

Mildred threw herself into Otto's old chair and sat tapping her foot.

'What's for tea?' Cathy asked, spreading the cloth on the table.

Mildred felt shocked. She hadn't given a thought to their tea! She covered her face with her hands, unable to believe she'd forgotten about it. She always had something prepared. She prided herself on her efficiency.

Cathy couldn't believe it either; she was staring at her in amazement.

It was Danny who laughed. 'I'm not surprised, Mildred, you're doing far too much. I'm always forgetting things too. I'll go and get us all some fish and chips.'

'I'm sorry,' Mildred said tartly, 'but you don't have to bother about me. I have a good meal at dinnertime.'

When Danny went, Cathy set the plates to warm on the range. 'I'll bring something home with me for our tea tomorrow,' she told Mildred. 'I've left all this to you for far too long.'

Rosie seemed to sense her mother's discomfort and helped her to bring out the knives and forks. Mildred felt as if she was sagging. She had no energy; she'd been doing less and less about the house, letting other things slide.

How she hated O'Mara! She wasn't going to let him treat her like this, she was going to get her own back. When Cathy called her to sit up at the table, she ate her fish and chips with gusto, suddenly aware that she'd had nothing at all at dinnertime.

The next hours she spent quietly rocking herself in the chair, silently dreaming up ways to make O'Mara suffer. She'd like to go back to his shop and shoot him. Or better still, tie him up under his pile of junk and let him slowly starve to death. She'd take him unawares, hit him over the head with that baby's cradle. To think of these things made her feel quite heady with vengeance.

It was only when she went to bed and lay listening to Rosie's soft and regular breathing, that she understood any revenge she took must be more down to earth. It had to be within her power and that narrowed her choice.

Mildred heard the clock on the living-room mantelpiece chime one o'clock and then two. By three, she had decided how she'd even up the score: she'd set his shop on fire.

With her mind made up she felt wildly exhilarated. It seemed a courageous thing to fight O'Mara, to show him he couldn't treat her like dirt and get away with it. She felt fluttery with excitement as she got up and dressed herself as quietly as she could. She knew she wouldn't wake Rosie, it was Cathy and Danny she must not disturb.

Stay calm, she told herself as she put on her hat and coat, found a torch and a box of matches. She shook it and found it half-empty, so took as well the spare box she kept handy. There was a half-used candle which she pulled free of the candlestick and put in her pocket. Then she picked up a good thickness of old newspapers and crept downstairs. She must keep her wits about her, not let herself get carried away with the joy of it.

Mildred kept a bottle of cleaning fluid and some rags in her sewing room. She'd needed them when she'd had to sew with secondhand material. She'd often found it easier to clean off a mark with the fluid than to wash the whole garment. She uncrewed the top; yes, it smelled of petrol and would be highly flammable.

It was a dark night, fine but heavy with cloud. There were few lights left on all night even here in the centre of town. During the war they'd been told to economise on lighting, and now they continued to practise thrift. Mildred needed her torch to see the edge of the pavements. To have the market square so empty of people and traffic seemed strange.

229

This must be O'Mara's shop. It showed not a glimmer of light either upstairs or down. She put on her torch for a moment to make sure. Yes, it was, and there was a letter box at waist height in the door. She counted it a bonus to see the door was ill-fitting and there was quite a gap under it. It was the last shop in the block. She went down the side street and looked at the back. No lights to be seen here either, and no sign of life. It was time she set to work.

She was going to wipe the contempt off O'Mara's fat face, and she felt heady with the thrill of it. On the front step, she shook out the newspapers to loosen them, then sprinkled them with cleaning fluid. Crumpling them slightly, she pushed almost all of them through the gap under the door. She soaked her three rags in the fluid and stuffed two through the letter box; the third she left hanging out.

She took a careful look round then, but nobody was about. There was a strong smell of cleaning fluid. She lit the piece of candle but the night breeze blew it out. She was more careful when she relit it, and the paper under the door blazed into life. She lit the rag then in the letter box and pushed it through with the candle, letting that fall inside too.

She was not prepared for the sudden roar as the fire took hold, nor the sight of the orange flames that were lighting up the street. She'd be seen easily now if anyone should look out of their bedroom window. She backed off into the gloom of the night, but turned when she judged she'd gone far enough to see the flames licking round the piles of junk inside. The shop door was well alight. Now it was smoke she could smell, not petrol; great black clouds of it were billowing everywhere.

She laughed aloud and wanted to dance. Her heart was throwing itself against her ribs and the feeling of utter satisfaction was balm to her injured pride. This would put O'Mara out of business; he was going to lose his stock and his premises. This would teach him not to turn nasty with *her*.

She reached her own doorstep without seeing anyone, and turned for one last look. O'Mara's shop was not visible from here, since there were other buildings in the way, but the sky above it was glowing with bright orange colour. She could hear the distant clang of a fire engine.

Mildred let herself in. She put the almost empty bottle of cleaning fluid back in her sewing room and, thinking she could smell smoke on herself, had a wash at the sink in the wash-house. Her finger felt sore and for the first time she realised she had a small burn on it.

She'd heard butter was good for burns and smeared a little on it in the kitchen before creeping back to bed. She was gloating at the success of her trip, thinking that now she'd exacted her revenge, she'd be content and able to sleep. But no, her feet were cold; she was chilled all over and couldn't stop shivering.

Another fire engine clanged through the night, and she heard somebody get up and open the window in the next bedroom. She hardly dared breathe. Suddenly she was frightened at what she'd done; she could feel the burn of acid bile in her throat.

Morning came before Mildred felt ready to face it. She didn't feel well; her head was thumping and she ached all over. It was only too obvious to her now that if the police found out she'd set fire to O'Mara's premises, she'd be in far greater trouble than if she'd admitted to telling them lies. Why hadn't she thought of that before she'd gone out last night? Arson was what they'd call it. Could they send her to prison for that?

Rosie got out of bed and tried to get in alongside her, as she did most mornings. For once Mildred couldn't be bothered with her.

'Go and tell your mummy I'm poorly,' she told her. She honestly didn't feel she could stand up if she tried. Cathy came in moments later and was sympathetic.

'Stay where you are, Mildred. You've been doing far too much and you need a rest.' She found her two aspirins and brought a bowl of porridge and a cup of tea to her bedside table.

'You've hurt your finger,' she said. 'How did you do that?'

'I think I touched it against the iron yesterday when I was doing some pressing.'

'I'll fetch the Germolene ointment, that should soothe it. Danny's lighting your fire for you. We'll stay until Jessie gets here and opens up. If you aren't better, ask her to make you something to eat at dinnertime.'

Cathy was on her way out when she turned to say, 'I think there was a big fire in the night. It must have been quite close – did you hear the noise?'

'No,' Mildred croaked. Whatever would Cathy and Danny think of her if they knew? She felt better when she heard them all going downstairs and knew she was alone. She dozed off for an hour and then got up and made herself more tea. She felt drained and hadn't the energy to do anything. She opened the living-room door and listened to the sounds from below. The shop bell clanged from time to time, followed by the murmur of voices. She hoped Jessie would sell that wash-stand.

At dinnertime she decided to boil herself an egg, and was setting about it when Jessie came up to ask if she could do anything for her.

'Just refill the coal scuttle for me, will you?' she said. 'I'll have a lazy day, a good rest. I'll feel better by tomorrow.'

Mildred slept most of the afternoon; it was nearly five when she woke up feeling fuddled and half-dazed. She felt her way down to the shop and sent Jessie out to buy the *Evening Echo*. She thought there might be something about the fire in it.

Jessie was away a long time, considering there was a newsagent just round the corner. A woman came in the shop and turned her tea cosies over. Mildred had to talk to her though she was sure she had no intention of buying anything.

The girl came back at last. Mildred opened the paper on the counter, groping below for her spectacles. The headline jumped out at her. *Arson Results in Ferocious Blaze. Victim Fights for his Life in Hospital*. Mildred felt the strength draining from her knees and had to support herself against the counter.

She could feel the girl's eyes on her, watching her. The sight of Jessie irritated Mildred, always had. She'd give her the sack at the end of the week. If she got out of the secondhand furniture trade, she wouldn't need a shop assistant.

'Did you know there was a fire last night?' Jessie asked. 'Just the other side of the market.'

'No,' Mildred said carefully. 'But I'm trying to read about it.'

'People have been talking about nothing else all day.'

Mildred knew she had to give the impression she knew nothing. 'Where was it exactly? Oh yes, it says here – in Alma Street.'

She was trying to read more. The police knew the fire had been lit intentionally; petrol had been poured through the door. Had she left any clues? Would they find out it was her? The print was dancing before her eyes. She was sweating; she took off her specs and wiped them.

Jessie said, 'You know that Mr O'Mara who brings furniture here for you? It was his place.'

'No!'

'And d'you know what I've just heard?' Jessie was keen to share the news. 'He's died.'

Mildred couldn't get her breath. He couldn't have done! 'Fighting for his life in hospital, it says here,' she gasped.

'In the paper shop they're saying he died. Somebody who knows him. Smoke inhilation.'

The shop began to swim round her. Did this mean she could be charged with murder? Mildred told herself she must not faint. She folded up the newspaper, tucked it under her arm and made unsteadily for the stairs.

Chapter Nineteen

The following morning, Jackson's workslip showed three small jobs he was to do on his own, using the flat cart. None would take him to Clifton Park where Old Benbow lived, but he was to collect two cabin trunks from an address not far away and deliver them to Woodside Station. It would not be much out of his way.

Before setting off, he ran back to his room with one of the grey blankets of shoddy they used to prevent furniture getting scratched, and tied the table in it. If he delivered it, it would save him the trouble of humping it round in his arms.

Benbow was unlikely to be in this morning, as it was the day of the monthly sale at the Liverpool Auction Rooms. When Jackson knocked on his front door, the housekeeper answered.

He said, 'Will you tell Mr Benbow that Jackson brought this table round and I'll come back this evening to see him?'

Jackson enjoyed his day. He spent the afternoon mucking out the stables and helping to unload a delivery of hay. When he went in for his dinner, the talk round the table was of a big fire last night over in Alma Street.

'I heard somebody died in it,' Jimmy said.

Jackson had heard talk of the fire when he went to Woodside Station. 'They said it lit up the sky. You could read a newspaper by it in the next street.'

'There were two fire engines there,' Jimmy's son Billy said.

'I heard it was Dick O'Mara's place.' Iris brought another dish of potatoes to the table.

'That fellow who does house clearance?' Harriet asked.

'Yes. Is it him who died?'

'So they say.'

Jackson was more interested in what Benbow would think of the small table. He'd been round to the man's house on several occasions and had always received a warm welcome. Benbow would provide a cup of tea or better still, some beer, and they'd stretch out in his comfortable chairs and have a long chat.

Tonight, when he arrived, the little table was in pride of place in his sitting room. The first thing Benbow asked was, 'Where did you get it?'

Jackson had already made up his mind not to say he'd bought it from Mildred. Benbow would guess, as he had, that she'd got it from some shady source and it could be stolen.

He said, 'It was Mrs Bott's. She doesn't like it, thinks it's a bit fussy, and said I could have it for three pounds.'

Old Benbow whistled through his teeth. 'A bargain at that price. It could bring six or seven in Danny's shop.'

'As much as that?'

'Maybe more. Not many of these about. Can't say I like it much, but plenty will. Lovely condition. I wish I knew who'd painted this scene on top.'

'There's a signature.'

'Yes, but I don't know enough about paintings and painters. If it was somebody famous, it would be worth more. I'll see if Danny wants it.'

'Danny?' Jackson didn't want it to go to McLelland's Antiques. 'I thought you'd send it down to London, like you did the snuffboxes.'

'I think Danny would take it. Haven't found much for him this month.'

Jackson tried again. 'I thought you said things brought more in a London sale?'

'Possibly this would, but we'd have to get it crated and pay for the carriage down. Small things like snuffboxes can go by post.'

Jackson hesitated; he almost confessed that he'd got it from Mildred. Benbow had warned her about having stolen goods in her shop. What if this was hot? He didn't want to get Cathy and Danny into trouble.

Old Benbow smiled. 'I'll get more than three pounds for it out of Danny. I'll ask for five – that'll give us both a bit in the pocket.' He pulled himself to his feet and went over to look at the table again. 'I might try to find out who this painter is first. If he is well known . . .'

Jackson felt the matter was out of his hands now. He asked, 'How would you do that?'

'I'd ask in the Art Gallery over in Liverpool, or even the library there.'

When he was walking home an hour later, Jackson felt a little uneasy.

Cathy and Danny were later than usual arriving in Exmouth Street the next morning. Ettie had already opened the shop and Peggy was there polishing up some new bookcases. There were not many customers for antiques at nine in the morning but Danny had always opened at the same time as the nearby shops. Rosie attached herself to Peggy and Cathy followed her husband up to the flat.

His mother called from the kitchen, 'Danny, we want a word with you.' She came out wiping her hands. 'Sit down for a minute, both of you.' Frank came from the bedroom and sat down with them.

'Aren't you going to work today?' Danny asked him.

'In a minute. Your mother and I have been talking things over. It's about these rooms.'

'You should be living here, Danny,' Ettie told him. 'I feel guilty – I should never have asked if Frank and I could have them. You've been very good moving in with Mildred, but I know you've got problems there.'

'We'll have to move,' Danny smiled. 'With another baby coming we won't have enough room.'

'So you said, and I don't like the thought of you renting somewhere else. It's not fair, you should be here.'

Frank said, 'We're going to move to Cooper's Yard.'

'I thought you didn't want to move there, Mam?'

'We didn't want to push ourselves into the house,' Frank told them earnestly. 'My family is large and noisy, and Harriet and Iris run the place between them. I was afraid your mam wouldn't settle after having a place of her own. And they've taken Jackson in too; so it would be a bit tight now.'

Cathy said, 'I'm very fond of Harriet, she's easy to get along with. She'll welcome you with open arms.'

'I know thcm all better now,' Ettie smiled, 'but we won't be living under the same roof. There's a cottage out in the yard.'

'Yes,' Frank went on. 'We Botts all lived there at one time, but it's been empty for years. I had a look at it yesterday, and I reckon there's not much wrong with it. Of course, it needs decorating throughout, and perhaps a new sink. I've had a word with Harriet and Jim, and they're more than happy to have us do the place up.'

'We're going to move out and leave this flat for you,' his mother said. 'Should have done it long ago.'

'You did offer,' Danny reminded her, 'but I felt we'd be turning you out.'

'I shouldn't have asked to stay on in the first place. You're a good son to me, Danny.'

'We've been through a lot, you and me. It makes us hang together.'

She nodded. 'But things are easier for us now. You'd be happy to live here, wouldn't you, Cathy?'

'Well, yes. Yes, of course. I'd love to, thank you!'

'There's two good-sized bedrooms and a small one, and without Mildred you'd have enough space.'

Cathy thought of a home without Mildred. She and Danny would glory in the privacy and peace.

'Danny, this is the centre of your business. It would be easier to run from here.' Frank smiled. 'And I have to say it would be more convenient for me if I were down at Cooper's Yard – really it would. I'll run your mother up here in the mornings.'

'Frank, I can walk, it will do me good. It's not as though it's far. It'll be very handy for you two, living here. There's a school nearby in the Woodlands for Rosie.'

'Thanks, Mam,' Danny was saying when the bell rang.

He'd fixed a bell-push under the counter in the shop to ring up in the flat, so that anyone serving alone and being swamped with customers could ring for help.

'I'll go.' Cathy got to her feet and gave Ettie a little kiss. 'I want you to know I'm thrilled. Can't wait to move here.'

Frank clattered downstairs behind her on his way to work. 'I'm getting the decorators in, Cathy. They say it'll take them a week. All being well, we'll move into Cooper's Yard at the end of next week.'

'As soon as that?' Cathy was excited.

'You've waited long enough.'

She found four customers in the shop and another coming in. Before she set to, she rang the bell again for more assistance.

All day, she was fizzing inside. Danny was excited too and said, 'I'll be so glad to get away from Mildred. She's been very difficult to live with.'

'We'll tell her tonight.' Cathy wasn't looking forward to doing that. 'She won't be pleased, especially as it'll come at a time when she isn't well.'

'Well or not, we're going – and the sooner the better. You've been very patient with her, Cathy.'

Within a few minutes, Danny's mind was on other things. 'You can change the furniture upstairs if you want to. Mam and I took what we needed from stock. When other things came in that we liked better, we swapped them round.'

Cathy could think of nothing else. Her head was spinning with plans. The move to a place of their own had come more quickly than she'd dared hope. She walked round the flat with Ettie, looking at everything with new eyes. She thanked her another half a dozen times that day.

She couldn't stop smiling and Rosie too seemed to catch some of her excitement about the coming move.

'You can have this bedroom,' Cathy told her. 'We'll go and choose new wallpaper together to make it nice.'

'What about Nanna? Will she be coming to share it?' Rosie asked.

'No, Nanna has her own flat and shop.'

'She'll want to stay there?'

'Yes,' Ettie told her. 'She'll want to stay there.'

'I hope so,' Cathy murmured. She was a bit worried about breaking the news to Mildred, but she didn't need to do it. As soon as Danny drove them home to Market Street that evening, Rosie rushed up the stairs to her.

'Nanna, I'm going to have a bedroom all to myself. We're moving to a new flat.'

Mildred's sharp eyes met Cathy's. 'What's all this about? Something new?'

'Ettie and Frank are moving down to Cooper's Yard so Danny and I can have the flat in Exmouth Street.'

Mildred was aghast. She choked out, 'I thought you wanted a house.'

'We'll have the extra space we need there,' Danny told her. 'There's two double bedrooms and a single. Mam thought we should have it.'

'That flat is a bit bigger all round than this,' Cathy added. She could see Mildred was not taking it well; there was an angry flush in her cheeks.

'It'll be easier for me to run the business if we're on the spot.' Danny was smiling.

'I can see you're delighted,' Mildred said frostily. 'But you won't be going just yet?'

'They'll be moving out in about a week, and then we want a bit of redecorating done. In a couple of weeks, if all goes according to plan,' Cathy said.

Mildred's mouth dropped open in astonishment. Her eyes flashed with resentment. 'That quick?'

'You've been very kind giving us a home,' Danny said. 'But you'll be glad to have your flat to yourself, I'm sure.'

'No,' she said angrily. 'No, you know damn well it's not what I want.'

Cathy was thrilled that she'd soon have a home of her own. Ettie and Frank had moved out of the rooms above McLelland's Antiques by the weekend. Danny brought in the same firm of painters and decorators from Cooper's Yard to work on the flat. They'd chosen wallpaper and paint and already the living room was looking quite different, but Cathy thought the new fresh paper would make the old curtains look shabby. When she got home that evening, she noticed Mildred had calmed down so she asked, 'Will you make me some new curtains, Mildred?'

She thought Mildred would be glad to earn some extra money, but Mildred had pulled a face.

'We don't expect you to work for nothing,' Cathy had been quick to say. 'We'll be glad to pay your usual rates.'

Mildred had agreed rather grudgingly, so she went out and bought the material. To help her get the size right, she took Mildred one of the old curtains, and was disappointed that she didn't start making them right away.

Danny urged her to buy new bedding and towels, too, plus new crockery and cutlery. They went together to choose a new crimson carpet for the living room and some lino for the kitchen. They were both keen to move in as soon as they could and they wanted to have everything just right.

By Thursday, Cathy had decided it was time she started packing up their belongings. She'd intended to use her half-day off for this, but when she and Rosie reached home, Botty was already there sewing in the room behind the shop.

Cathy picked up a dress that needed hemming and joined them. Mildred seemed restless; today she couldn't settle to her sewing. Instead she got out a game to play with Rosie.

Botty said to Cathy, 'It's such an exciting time for you. When are you going to move in?'

'When the decorators are finished. We hope they'll be gone by Saturday night. Danny's arranged with Frank to send the cart round here on Monday. It'll take up Rosie's bed and the rest of our things.'

'Only a few more days here then?'

'Yes. I feel I'm on my way.'

'It's easy to see that from the suitcases, cardboard boxes and the cabin trunk stacked at the bottom of the stairs.'

'Danny brought them down. We have Friday, Saturday and Sunday to pack them and sort ourselves out.'

'You sound as though you can't wait to get out of my house,' Mildred said bitterly. She was in a grim mood and put rather a damper on their usual chatter. Cathy was afraid she'd been carried away by her own happiness and hadn't thought enough about Mildred's feelings.

'It's just that the preparations are unsettling,' Harriet said gently. 'You'll all feel better when the move is over.'

When she got up to leave at the end of the afternoon, she said, 'I'll be a little later next week, Mildred. I'm going over to Liverpool with Iris and her boys.'

'But you will come?'

'Yes, I'll be here between half two to three. Will you be coming, Cathy? You'll be in your new home by then. I expect you'll have a lot to do.'

Cathy couldn't help but see Mildred's pleading eyes staring at her. She said, with more enthusiasm than she felt, 'Yes, of course I'll come. I enjoy our weekly sewing bee.'

Two days later, Cathy was alone in the shop when Old Benbow came in, followed by a lad carrying something on his shoulder wrapped in a grey blanket. Benbow lifted it down and said, 'Is Danny about?'

'No, he's gone to a sale in West Kirby. I thought you were going to take a look at that house in Claughton. Isn't it viewing day today?'

'Yes I am, but I've popped in with something Danny might like.' Benbow despatched the lad with sixpence and removed the blanket. 'It's an occasional table. Unusual, isn't it?'

Cathy stared at it in disbelief. 'I've seen it before.'

'Yes, and I know where. You've seen it in Cooper's Yard.'

'No, not there. How did *you* come by it?'

'I got it from Jackson. It was Harriet Bott's. She didn't care for it and sold it to him.'

'It was in Mildred's shop a few days ago.'

Benbow's old eyes stared into hers. 'Are you sure?'

'Certain. As you said, it's unusual.' She laughed. 'You're pulling my leg.'

'No! What makes you say that?'

'I can't see how Jackson came by it – or Harriet for that matter, unless Mildred gave it to her.' But Cathy knew Mildred wouldn't give anything away that was saleable. 'This was in her shop – I saw it with my own eyes. Danny will tell you the same when he comes back. He rather liked it.'

'What's this?' Ettie came down to the shop. 'That's a pretty little table.'

'It's a bit of a puzzle.' Cathy told her about its origins.

'Why don't you telephone Harriet Bott and ask her about it?' Ettie said to Benbow. 'Danny's had the phone put in upstairs. He decided we must have one when he heard Cooper's Yard had it.'

'Newfangled things,' Benbow sighed. 'Don't like them one bit. You do it for me, Cathy.'

'But I'm sure it was Mildred's.'

'Go on,' Ettie urged.

Within a few moments Cathy was through and asking Botty about the papier-mâché table.

'I don't know what you're talking about,' she said. 'I've never had a table like that. Jackson didn't get it from *me*.'

Cathy went slowly down to the shop again. Benbow was showing a desk to a customer with great enthusiasm.

'D'you know, I've just thought of something else,' Ettie said. She went behind the counter and started looking in one of the drawers. 'There's a policeman who comes round from time to time with lists of stolen property. Yes, here it is.' She pulled out a sheet of paper and perused it.

'Listen to this: "Early Victorian papier-mâché tripod table with a painted Highland scene on top".'

'Then it's stolen property.' Cathy felt her spirits plummet.

Benbow came striding across the shop to her, all smiles and rubbing his hands. 'I've sold that rolltop desk. You said you'd pay by cheque, sir?'

Cathy was afraid Benbow was trying to put one over on them. Ettie hurriedly wrapped the grey blanket round the table again, looking very straight-faced. Cathy thought she did too. The customer left when Benbow had taken the delivery address. He was pleased with himself.

'You got a good price for that desk,' he said. Then he saw the table had been covered up and his smile faded. 'What does Harriet say about that?'

'It's stolen property,' Cathy burst out. 'It heads the latest police list. Look,' she stabbed her finger at the item and pushed the list in front of him.

She'd had her suspicions about Benbow ever since he'd started working for Danny. He'd convinced her he was honest, but now . . . She felt he'd let her down. 'Are you trying to fence stuff through our shop?'

'No, of course not,' Benbow said, and she could see from his face that he was genuinely shocked. 'I wouldn't do that to you and Danny. I thought if it came from Mrs Bott it would be above suspicion.'

'It didn't come from her. She knows nothing about it.'

'But Jackson said . . . Cooper's Yard is full of furniture of that vintage. I didn't doubt . . .'

Cathy hesitated, confused now. Jackson had been giving her fatherly advice for years. She couldn't see him telling lies, he wasn't that sort of person.

'I wouldn't bring goods I knew to be stolen anywhere near you and Danny.' Benbow was indignant. 'I wouldn't want you two to get into trouble. Certainly not for the few pounds I'd be likely to earn from this.'

'You'll have to take it to the police,' Ettie told him. 'Hand it over. No two ways about that. We certainly don't want it here.'

Benbow looked so contrite so apologetic, so honest, that Cathy began to think she'd made a mistake. Could Mildred be up to something?

'I'll talk to Mildred tonight, ask her about that table,' she said.

Benbow felt churned up as he walked to the house in Claughton to view what would be auctioned tomorrow. He should never have made such a mistake. All morning, instead of concentrating on the furniture, he was turning over in his mind what Jackson had hoped to achieve by telling such a lie.

He was very careful about handling stolen goods. All right, he did it occasionally if he was almost sure he'd get away with it and there was a good profit to make it worthwhile. But he always found out all he could about the article first and took reasonable precautions.

His mistake was in believing what Jackson had told him. He knew what he was like even if Cathy didn't. Benbow was angry with himself for letting him get the better of him. Jackson was the sort who'd put a fast one over on his own father if there was a few bob in it for him.

By dinnertime, he'd ticked on the catalogue the items he thought worth bidding for and annotated the prices he thought they'd make in the sale. Then instead of going home he went down to Cooper's Yard. Jackson himself opened the door to him and Benbow said roughly, 'I think we need to talk about that table.'

He caught the delicious aroma of steak and kidney pudding and knew from the clatter of plates in the kitchen that it was being dished up.

'Now,' he said. 'I'm not waiting while you eat.'

Jackson went to the kitchen door and said something. 'I'll put it in the oven to keep warm,' he heard Mrs Bott tell him.

'Come on up to my room.' Jackson led the way at such a pace, Benbow couldn't keep up. He was puffing by the time he reached the attic and had to sit down to get his breath back.

When he could, Benbow told him what had happened in the Exmouth Street shop that morning.

Jackson was aghast. 'I'm in trouble from Botty too. She said, "Why bring me into it? As if there aren't enough rumours going round about me".'

Benbow said with a face like thunder, 'I counted you an ally. I expected you to be as open and honest with me as I am with you. You told lies in the hope of gaining an extra pound or two.'

He could see by his face that Jackson had suspected the table was dodgy. 'You didn't dare tell me where you'd got it. You knew I wouldn't touch it if you did. So you lied. I'm not having it, Jackson. I take great care my name isn't associated with receiving or theft, and now we have to go to the police with this story.

'You aren't clever enough to know what you're doing. You've acted like a bumbling fool and dropped us all in it, especially Mildred. And she doesn't have much sense either when it comes to the antiques trade.'

Jackson looked like a whipped dog with his tail between his legs. He said nothing and wouldn't even look him in the eye.

Benbow went on, 'I explained to you how I work. I've got to know the truth about where things come from, the whole story. D'you think I'd have taken it anywhere near Danny's place if I'd known it was on the stolen list?

'So come on, get your coat, Jackson. We'll go and pick it up and take it to the police station. There's nothing else we can do, now everybody in the shop knows about it. We'll all be in trouble if it comes out later that we knew about it and did nothing. I've got to keep my reputation and so have you.

'You're going to tell the police you got it from Mildred Godfrey and you brought it to me for my opinion. We both thought it was a clean piece until we took it to McLelland's Antiques and they showed us it was on the stolen list.'

'What about my dinner? Can't I go and—?'

'No! I'd like to have my dinner too, but eating will have to wait until we've sorted this out. Nothing will happen to you if this is your first contact with stolen goods. Be sure to tell them how shocked you are and that you'll be more careful where you buy in future.'

He made Jackson carry the table. It was a long and tedious interview in the police station, and they both had to make statements.

When they came out, Benbow said, 'That's the last business I'll ever do with you.'

Mildred was trying to pull herself together and get over the shock of Dick O'Mara's death. She'd intended to hurt him, make him suffer for what he'd done to her, but not to kill him. Nothing quite so drastic, even though he deserved all he'd got.

It was an accident, but the police were treating his death as murder and she was living in dread of another visit from them.

She'd got rid of Jessie, deeming it safer, because the girl knew what furniture Dick O'Mara had brought here. Mildred didn't want her talking to the police. Anyway, she'd had enough of her standing dreamily on a floor covered with customers' dirty footprints instead of washing them off. Jessie was completely blind to what needed doing. It saved her wages but it meant Mildred couldn't go shopping during opening hours.

When the shop bell clanged, she jerked her head round the sewing-room door to see if it was the police come to ask about her business connections with Dick O'Mara. Fear crawled up her neck, though it was only an elderly couple, clearly customers.

'We're looking for a baby's cradle,' the man said. 'Somebody told us they'd seen one here. Our first grandchild's on the way.'

Who could have said that? Mildred felt disconcerted, but they seemed genuine enough.

'Yes, I have.' Mildred fetched it from her sewing room to show them and they bought it straight off.

It made her feel better to be rid of it and have the money in the till. The wash-stand that had come from the same source was still in the shop, but it wasn't on the police list. The only other piece of furniture she had left was a chest of drawers. Once that had gone, she was going to stick to being a dressmaker. She might sell a few aprons and tea cosies, but only things she'd made herself.

Mildred had not yet closed the shop when Cathy and her family came home at teatime. She knew as soon as she saw Cathy's face that more bad news was coming. She looked tense and ready to do battle.

Danny said, almost before he was in the shop, 'You remember that papier-mâché table you had here last week? What happened to it?'

'Sold,' she said.

His tone was severe; it sliced through her confidence. 'Who to?' Mildred was reminded that Jackson hadn't come back to pay for it, though he'd promised he would. 'You sold it to Jackson, didn't you?'

Since it seemed Danny knew, Mildred decided there was no point in denying it. 'What if I did? He said he liked it.'

'Did you tell him you'd bought it from Dick O'Mara?' Mildred felt she was being backed up against a wall. 'We saw it here the day he brought you a load. There was a display cabinet and a cradle too.'

Mildred had to suppress a gasp; it seemed they were going to needle the story out of her. 'It might have come from him. So what?'

They were staring at her. Mildred said tetchily, 'There won't be any more. You heard he'd died in a fire?' That seemed a good line to take.

'It was stolen property.' Cathy was equally severe.

She had to stand up to them. 'How d'you know that?'

'Have you seen this list before?'

243

Mildred felt the strength draining from her legs. It was the police list that had so unnerved her in the first place.

'No, I don't think so.' She forced herself to reach for her spectacles and study it. 'Good gracious,' she said, pretending to be surprised. 'The baby cradle too.'

How had they found out all this? She was afraid she'd be ill again if Cathy and Danny kept on at her like this; she couldn't stand much more. She had to change the subject. She locked the shop door, turned over the sign to Closed, and led the way up to her flat.

She threw herself on Otto's armchair. Rosie came and climbed on her knee. She put her arms round the child and drew comfort from her small body, but there was no stopping Danny.

'Your papier-mâché table turned up in our shop today. Benbow brought it in, thought it would suit us.'

Mildred shivered. 'Did you buy it?'

'Fortunately, Cathy recognised it for what it was.'

She swallowed hard. 'You have to be so careful about your reputation.'

'And our pockets. We don't want to lose what we pay for our stock.'

She made herself ask, 'Is that what happens if stolen property is found on your premises?' Her voice shook.

'Yes. If someone else can prove it belongs to them, they get it back. But losing what you paid for it is the better option; you can also be charged with receiving or even theft. Depends on the circumstances.'

Mildred's mouth was dry. 'What sort of circumstances?'

'Well, you know. Whether your records look genuine. Whether you've got invoices, signed receipts, that sort of thing.'

She felt sick. She had nothing to prove she'd paid for that table. Nothing to prove she'd thought that load was all above board. 'Have you taken it to the police station?'

'We didn't buy it.' Cathy appeared at the kitchen door with a lettuce in her hands. 'I gather you'd sold it to Jackson, so he took it. Ettie said Old Benbow went with him.'

Mildred felt the blood rush to her face; she was sweating.

'You should have taken it,' Cathy told her. 'Instead of getting Jackson into trouble.'

'I didn't know it was stolen,' she lied. She was afraid the police could prove that she did. Would they keep records of where they delivered their lists?

Cathy was spreading the cloth on the table. 'I've brought pork pies and I'm making a salad to go with them.'

Tears were scalding Mildred's eyes. She buried her face in Rosie's curls. She mustn't let them show. Mustn't let them see there was more to it. She had to keep a firm grip on herself. She must give no hint that she had committed a far more serious crime.

'Right, we're ready.' Cathy put the tea pot on the fender to keep warm. 'Come and sit up to the table, Rosie.'

Mildred followed slowly. She had to make it appear she was still in control.

'The thing is,' Danny pulled out a chair too, 'it says in tonight's *Echo* that the police are treating Dick O'Mara's death as a murder. So they'll be casting round for leads and following up every connection they can find. With you buying that load of furniture from him so recently, they may well come round to talk to you.'

Mildred wanted to strike out at him. As if she couldn't see that for herself. It stood out like a neon sign! She stared down at her heaped plate; she didn't think she could swallow a mouthful of it. She was scared stiff.

'You mustn't worry,' Danny told her kindly, as he shook brown sauce onto his pie. 'It's not *you* they'll be searching for – it's the person who started the fire.'

That made her cringe. 'He probably deserved all he got,' she said.

'Not to die like that.' Cathy sounded appalled.

'He was selling on stolen property,' Mildred maintained. 'Getting others into trouble.'

She was relieved when they shut up. There was silence apart from an occasional chink of cutlery against a plate. She found it a struggle to get her food down.

After all she'd done for Cathy, she was turning her back on her. Worse, she was taking Rosie away from her.

Mildred knew she was going to lose her last link with Rolf. On top of her other troubles, this seemed the end.

Chapter Twenty

Saturday came and Cathy still had a lot of packing to do. Danny went to a sale and at mid-morning, Cathy decided to return home and get it done. She expected to find Mildred at work in her sewing room, but she was up in the flat sitting in Otto's chair and staring into space.

'Mummy's home,' Rosie squealed as soon as she saw her, and began jumping up and down.

'I've come to pack. I really need to get down to it.'

'Pack my toys first,' the little girl demanded.

'Right.' Cathy took off her coat. 'Let's get started.'

She was surprised to find Mildred following them into the bedroom Rosie shared with her. Cathy was afraid it would upset her more to see her fold Rosie's little petticoats and dresses, so she decided to start instead on her own and Danny's clothes.

'You can pack your own toys,' she told Rosie. 'Here's a big box to put them in.'

After setting the child to work she found Mildred perched against her bed, apparently at a loose end. 'Nanna will help you, Rosie,' Cathy said, and headed to her own bedroom.

When she turned round, she found Mildred had followed silently behind her. She could see her steeling herself to say something she thought important. Cathy shivered, dreading what was coming.

'I've been thinking, Cathy – I could come and live with you. I might just as well.' Her words were coming out in a rush. 'I'll be more than happy with the single room. You'll have a double bedroom for Rosie and your new baby. I won't be any trouble, I promise. In fact, I'll be able to help. With you having another baby, you'll need another pair of hands.'

Cathy was astounded; it was the last thing she expected. 'I thought it was all agreed,' she stammered, 'that you'd stay here.'

'I'll be able to help you with Rosie. I don't want to leave her.'

'It's better if you stay here, Mildred. You have your dressmaking . . .'

'I'm not going to give that up. I'll come back here every morning.' Mildred's dark eyes glittered with fervour.

In the past, Cathy knew she'd allowed Mildred to persuade her to do things she didn't want to. She couldn't do that again.

'This has been your home for years. All your memories are here, you have friends next door. It never occurred to me you'd want to leave. I don't think you'd be happy anywhere else.'

'You're saying no? That I can't come?' Mildred's eyes were wild. 'Please . . .'

Cathy was upset that she had to refuse, but she couldn't let her come. She had to think of what Danny wanted now and what was best for Rosie and herself.

'This is your home, Mildred, you'd be far more comfortable here. You can come up and see Rosie as often as you like.'

'So it's no?'

'It hasn't worked out, us living together. You know that. You haven't been happy.'

Mildred's face twisted with venom. 'You bitch! You ungrateful little bitch,' she spat. 'After all I've done for you.'

Mildred rushed out of Cathy's room slamming the door behind her. The girl was hateful, wouldn't give an inch, and Danny was even worse. They'd taken all she could give without one word of thanks, and now they'd squeezed her dry they were going to abandon her.

Sunday came, and they told her the decorators had finished in their flat. They'd always had Sunday dinner together, and Mildred usually cooked a good meal for them, but Danny said, 'We've a lot to do to our new home. I'm keen to go over there and put the furniture back. We'll get on with it and make do with a sandwich today.'

They had no thought for her. Mildred didn't want to be left here on her own all day. She worried herself sick if she had nothing to do.

'D'you want me to come and give you a hand?' she offered.

'You said you'd make new curtains for us – why don't you start on those?' Danny had a very uppity manner sometimes. 'Have you done with that old curtain of my mother's?'

'Not yet. I haven't had time.'

She hadn't had the energy either. She hadn't been able to sleep for worry. But the police wouldn't be round on a Sunday, she'd be safe today.

'Why don't we measure it now? That's all you need it for, isn't it? Then we'll hang the old ones and you can take your time making the new. We don't want you to feel pressurised.'

Mildred was indignant. 'How long d'you think it takes me to make two pairs of plain curtains? I've had other orders to see to, that's all.

248

They've had to take their turn. I'll do them today, even though it's Sunday.'

'Tell you what, Mildred.' Danny was smiling at her. 'You run our curtains up and we'll come and fetch you this afternoon to see our place. We'll put up the curtains if they're ready, and go for a run in the car after that. Let's say, around half three. We'll all have had enough by then.'

Mildred found the morning peaceful though she had to school herself to keep her mind off that fire. She'd always found straightforward sewing therapeutic. She had finished making the curtains and even had time to iron them before Danny came to fetch her in the car.

She'd been satisfied with her own home until she saw what Cathy was moving to. The flat above McLelland's Antiques was very spacious and it looked smart, light and clean. There would have been plenty of room for her. Mildred swallowed her disappointment and insisted on hanging the curtains. She was pleased with her workmanship.

Cathy was delighted. 'They're lovely! You've done a marvellous job.'

Mildred took her money when payment was offered. Why not? She'd given her and Danny more than enough. Not that they hadn't paid for their lodgings, but that was only fair.

She thought Danny was trying to make amends. He probably felt guilty about trying to put distance between her and her own grandchild. Mildred knew she was right when he stopped his car outside a café in West Kirby and treated them all to a tea of ham and chips followed by cream cakes. She enjoyed that and the walk along the front holding on to Rosie's hand, even though the wind was cold and blustery.

But Mildred felt low when they all went back to Market Street, knowing it would be the last night she'd be sharing her room with Rosie. She was finding the nights harder to get through than the days, even though she had all those hours when she didn't have to worry about finding a police officer coming into her shop.

Cathy and Danny were still packing when Mildred went to bed. She pulled the blankets up round her ears and tried to keep her mind blank. If she let her guard down for an instant she'd be back on the step of Dick O'Mara's shop, with the flames licking up inside. Now that she knew the fire had killed him she wished she hadn't lit it. She should have thought more about the consequences of what she was doing. The fire might bring her more trouble than she'd bargained for. She should have thought of some other way of getting even with him. She could hear the flames roaring through her head every time she thought of it.

She ached with love for Rosie and lifted her head to look at her. In the dim light she could just make out the small mound and her mop of curls. She was breathing lightly and evenly; nothing ever woke her up.

Mildred felt weary and longed for sleep, yet at the same time she feared it. She was sure she'd get another visit from the police and must prepare herself for it. She tried to rehearse what she must say when questioned, and particularly what she must *not* say.

She'd never felt this frightened before and her mind was going round in circles.

Cathy shut their bedroom door quietly but firmly and started getting ready for bed. 'Our last night here,' she whispered to Danny, glad they'd soon be gone.

'Mildred's been a bit better today,' he mouthed.

'I'm not so sure. I think it's all still there simmering away inside her.'

'She's been in a terrible state since we told her about Jackson taking that stolen table of hers to the police.'

Cathy had seen a tremor in Mildred's fingers, and her nerves had seemed raw. 'I think it's partly our fault for tackling her the way we did.'

'I thought I ought to warn her the police might come round here to question her.'

'Yes, but she was already upset that we'd be moving to Exmouth Street. She took it very hard. Was it the stolen table or the fact that we're leaving that's bothering her?'

'Both, I'd say.'

Cathy's sigh was troubled. 'The night we told her, it was impossible to console Mildred.' She'd wept till her eyes were red and puffy. Even at bedtime tears glistened behind her swollen lids. 'I promised I'd continue to come round to help her on Thursday afternoons.'

'I was there.' Danny pulled a face. 'Mildred was sniffing into her handkerchief and very ungrateful. She said, "You'll only come because Harriet does".'

Cathy groaned; there'd been enough truth in that to sting.

Danny had been quick to say, 'You must come and have your Sunday dinner with us. Regularly, I mean. And pop up to see Rosie whenever you want.'

They'd gone to bed early that night, all subdued, all glad to part company. Cathy had been plagued with awful suspicions ever since.

'I think it's the police. She's scared stiff they'll come round to talk to her again.' Cathy pulled on her nightgown and got into bed. 'Do you think she's more involved in this than we thought?'

Danny turned out the gas and got in beside her. He moved closer and put his arm round her. Cathy spoke softly into his ear. 'Do you think she had anything to do with that fire?'

She felt him tense. 'What makes you think that?'

'She couldn't get up the next morning – she said she was ill.'

'Perhaps she was ill,' he said doubtfully.

'She hangs her coat out on the landing. I thought I smelled smoke on it that morning.'

'Everything smelled of smoke. O'Mara's place isn't far away. You're imagining it.'

'You said something woke you that night. You got up to look out of the window.'

'It was the noise outside.'

'I got the impression you'd heard Mildred moving about.' Cathy snuggled closer to him. 'She had a fresh burn on her finger that morning too. I've had these awful doubts ever since.' She sighed. 'Am I suspicious by nature? It's horrible to be like this, always thinking the worst of people. I was just the same with Old Benbow when I first met him.'

'But not with Jackson.'

'I knew him well.'

'Not well enough, Cathy. And you were wrong about Benbow anyway. You'll be wrong about Mildred.'

She felt his lips touch hers. 'Go to sleep, love. We've got a busy day tomorrow.' She knew she was already drifting off.

She didn't know how long she'd slept, but Cathy was jerked back to wakefulness by a sudden piercing scream. It was very dark. Sodden with sleep she clutched at Danny when it came again.

'It's Mildred,' he whispered. 'She's shouting something.'

Cathy slid out of bed; the night air was cold against her bare shoulders.

'I didn't do it!' Mildred was screaming. 'It wasn't me!'

Cathy felt her way towards the bed in the next room. She sat on it and put an arm round the darker mound. 'Mildred, wake up. You're having a nightmare.'

She couldn't see her but she felt her shudder, felt the terror cold and heavy that tormented her. It made Cathy shiver. Mildred was awake now, alert and panting, like a fox ready to run for its hole.

Cathy took a deep steadying breath. If Mildred was having nightmares it seemed she must know more about the fire at Dick O'Mara's than she was letting on. Another thought made her come out in a cold sweat. Could she have done it?

Her voice was shaking but she had to ask. 'Mildred, did you have anything to do with that fire? Did you go out that night to start it?'

'Of course not!' The night vibrated with Mildred's vehemence. Then more calmly, she asked, 'Whatever makes you think that?'

Cathy's mouth was dry; her tongue felt twice its normal size. She couldn't form the words to tell her. Didn't dare. If she'd thought first, she wouldn't have said anything. She was almost overcome with fear, in case Mildred might do something else. Was it safe to leave Rosie in this room?

'No,' Mildred said more confidently. 'I didn't do it but I'm not sorry somebody else did.'

Cathy jerked to her feet. 'You're all right then?'

'Yes, yes I'm fine. Sorry I disturbed you. What did I say? In my sleep, I mean?'

'You were just shouting . . . Nothing that I could make out.' Cathy shot back to her own bed and into Danny's arms.

'You're shaking,' he whispered, holding her tight. 'And you're cold.'

'I'm sure she did it.' Her teeth chattered with terror. 'She lit that fire. She killed O'Mara.'

Danny's arms tightened round her. 'Did she say so?'

'No, she denied it, but I'm almost certain she did. She's having nightmares about it.'

'That's hardly proof, Cathy. After all, she knew him better than we did. If you knew somebody who'd been killed like that, wouldn't it give you nightmares?'

Cathy felt agitated. 'I told you I was suspicious, and why. I just have that feeling . . .'

She heard Danny's slow intake of breath. 'Perhaps you should tell the police? Let them know.'

'No! No, Danny!'

'Shush!'

'I couldn't do that. Not to Mildred.'

'But if you're so convinced . . .'

'No, she'd see that as betrayal. What if I'm wrong? She'd never forgive me.' Cathy struggled out of Danny's arms and tried to think. 'If I'm right, Mildred could be charged with arson and also with murder.'

Danny said softly, 'If she's done it once, she might do it again. You wouldn't want that.'

'No, she won't. She's going out of the secondhand furniture business. It can't happen again. She was taking revenge on O'Mara because he put stolen property into her shop.'

Danny was asleep long before she managed it. It was hard to believe

Mildred might have murdered O'Mara, but Cathy was glad this would be the last night Rosie would share her bedroom. She'd never trust her to look after Rosie again.

Then she told herself she was being silly. Mildred would never harm Rosie, she loved her dearly.

Mildred felt she didn't know where to turn. To have Cathy ask her outright if she'd started that fire had thrown her completely off balance. She'd had that nightmare several times and it frightened her that she'd been shouting aloud. She'd shouted enough to make Cathy suspicious, and not knowing exactly what that was had left her hanging in mid-air. But Cathy was more than suspicious: she'd guessed the truth. Mildred knew she'd conveyed to her the agony of that awful dream in which she'd seen and smelled and heard O'Mara call for help as he'd burned on a funeral pyre of his stolen goods.

At least it wouldn't matter if she talked in her sleep again. They wouldn't be here after tonight.

In the morning, before going to work, Danny collapsed Rosie's bed and took it down to the shop. He and Cathy stacked the pieces with the heavy baggage which they'd carried down last night. With the empty space in her bedroom, and the baggage piling up in her shop, everything seemed very different to Mildred, almost alien.

Cathy was boiling eggs for breakfast.

'Don't do one for me,' Mildred told her. She knew she couldn't swallow even a mouthful. They, of course, had hearty appetites and finished off all her bread. She was glad to see them drive off. When she went to open up the shop, Mildred saw Polly Weaver washing her own shopfront down, and went out to pass the time of day with her.

'Did you hear there was another fire last night?' Polly said. 'And another man burned in his bed?'

'No!' Mildred's first thought was that it might be a good thing for her if a serial arsonist was suspected.

'It was in Claughton this time. D'you know Tollemache Road?'

Mildred was eager to hear the details Polly was giving out but she could see Jackson coming, and what she intended to say to him was better said out of Polly's hearing. She was a bit of a gossip.

'Come round after your tea tonight,' Mildred told her, 'and let's have a good old chinwag. I'll be on my own, for the first time. Cathy's deserting me.'

She shot into her shop and closed the door before Jackson had pulled the cart into the kerb. The lad came running in to let her know they were here. Jackson followed more slowly, swaggering towards the pile of baggage he was to take away.

His attitude irritated her. 'Have you brought that two guineas you owe me?' she asked sharply.

'No, and I'm not going to.'

'You owe it.'

'I want more than that from you in recompense,' he said spitefully. 'You've got me into a load of trouble.'

'What sort of trouble? You been charged with something then?'

'No, but no thanks to you,' Jackson snapped. 'I was the innocent victim, wasn't I? You knew that table was stolen and you didn't tell me.'

Mildred was glad the boy had taken a couple of cases out to the pavement and didn't hear that.

'No, my trouble's come from Benbow.'

She wished hers did. She wasn't afraid of anything Old Benbow might say. 'You've dropped me in it by taking that table to the police, haven't you?'

'If I have, it's your own stupid fault.'

She didn't want to argue, couldn't this morning, she wasn't herself. Slowly the floor of her shop was being cleared until it looked as bare as the rooms above. She heard Jackson say to the lad, as they lifted Rosie's mattress between them, 'She's a real witch, that one. You'll stay clear of her if you've any sense.'

That made her fume. She slammed the shop door shut behind them knowing her nerves were raw. She needed an hour or so at her sewing machine – that always relaxed her. But the cart had hardly had time to pull out of Market Street when she saw the policeman through the shop window. The blood rushed to her face and she closed her eyes, willing him to move past the shop door.

The bell clanged as he came in. It was a different policeman this time, bigger and broader and somehow more threatening. The crisis she'd been expecting was on her, and she was in no fit state to manage it.

She told herself she must not mention Dick O'Mara or the fire on his premises. That must not come out. Her heart felt tight and she was shaking but she made herself say, 'Good morning,' and sound civil.

'Mrs Mildred Godfrey? I'm Constable Thomas Ingram.' He was looking round her shop as he took a notebook and pencil from his pocket.

'A Mr Jackson Jackson brought a small table into the station.' He consulted his notebook. 'An early Victorian papier-mâché occasional table, the top painted with a Highland scene. It's been identified as stolen property. He says he's known to you. Did you sell him such a table?'

'Yes,' she admitted. 'Not that he's paid me for it.' She told herself she shouldn't add anything to what she was asked. Shouldn't volunteer a thing. She needed her wits about her.

'How did you come by it?'

'I bought it in good faith. I had to stock my shop.'

'Who from?'

'A man. He brought it in and asked if I wanted to buy it.'

'You know him? His name and address?'

'No. I'd never seen him before.'

His gaze swung to her face; he was staring her out. 'Didn't you ask? Didn't he give you a receipt for your money?'

'No. He was just an ordinary person. Out of work, he said, and he was trying to raise a few pounds on his possessions to tide him over.' She'd done it again, added more than she needed to. She had to keep a grip on her nerves.

'If you buy from a stranger, you should always ask for identification. You didn't get it from a Mr Richard O'Mara?'

He'd mentioned that name first, but it made her heart bounce against her ribcage. 'Not that table.'

'But you do buy from him?'

'Yes, I have in the past.'

'Is that how you usually buy your stock?'

'Yes . . . No . . .'

Mildred took a step nearer the counter so she could support her weight against it. This wouldn't do, she mustn't go to pieces.

She took a deep steadying breath. 'People buy for me at sales and house clearances, that sort of thing. They bring stuff here sometimes.'

'Can I see your accounts?'

Reluctantly, Mildred reached below the counter for her book. 'I've never handled stolen goods, never thought I was likely to. I only realised that table was stolen when the constable brought the list into my shop. I panicked and denied having it. I'm very sorry. Then I sold it to Jackson to get rid of it.'

'I see.' Again those steely eyes were boring into hers. 'I'd like to keep your account book for a day or two. Take it to the station, to be examined. Do you have anything to support these figures? Invoices? Receipts?'

'I have copies of the bills I make out for customers.' She found the little book with carbon paper sticking out.

'But you didn't issue a bill for the table when you sold it to Mr Jackson?'

'No, he didn't pay me, or I would have done. I'm sorry I got him into trouble. I didn't tell him it was stolen.'

'I'd like you to come to the station, Mrs Godfrey, if you don't mind.'

She felt fluttery with panic. 'What for?'

'We need to find out if we're talking about the same table.' Mildred didn't think there was much doubt about that.

'I'd like you to identify it.'

'I have to mind my shop,' she said quickly. 'It's my livelihood.' There were no customers about; it didn't seem vital.

'It won't take long,' he said soothingly. 'Before we go, I'd like to look round your premises and see the rest of your stock.'

'You're looking at it,' she snapped. 'I'm going out of the furniture business after this. That's all I have left,' she waved towards the chest of drawers. She was pretty sure the only trouble with that was its size. It was too big for a modern room, it had a couple of knobs missing and was generally a bit battered.

'Feel free to look round,' she told him. She stayed two steps behind as he poked round her sewing room and even the back yard and her outside wash-house. She knew there was nothing else he could find. He was heading for the door.

'Shall we go then? Do you want to get a coat?'

'Now?'

'If you wouldn't mind.'

Mildred was breaking out in a cold sweat. She was desperate to be on her own if only for a few minutes.

'I'm not walking through the streets with you!' She was indignant. 'What will the neighbours think? I've got my reputation to think of.'

'As you wish, madam. You know Brandon Street? You can find your own way to the station?'

'Yes. I close for dinner at half past twelve. It would be more convenient for me to come then.'

'Right, we'll expect you by a quarter to one.'

Mildred went to the back room and flopped down in front of her sewing-machine, resting her forehead against the cold metal. She had a thumping headache and could feel herself shaking. It was the shock.

After ten minutes, she locked the shop door, and turned the notice round to read Closed. Then she pulled herself upstairs and put the kettle on to make some tea. While it was coming to the boil she swallowed two aspirins and splashed cold water on her face.

She knew she should eat something to give herself some energy, but she felt a little sick. She'd meant to finish the scouse left over from yesterday for her dinner, but couldn't face that.

She opened her store cupboard and saw a tin of plums. She'd been saving it for a special occasion, counting fruit a treat, but they'd slide down. She hacked open the tin and ate half the contents directly from it. Then she took a cup of tea to her bedroom and lay down on her bed.

She thought she might sleep after her disturbed night, but it was not to be. It was time to leave before she felt ready, but she was a little calmer. She took her coat from the peg on the landing, but remembered it was the one she'd worn that night. What if . . .?

She put it back and fetched her best coat and hat from her wardrobe.

She'd hoped the fresh air would do her good too, but dread was a physical ball in her throat. She'd had time to think through what she'd told Constable Ingram. She was ready to accept that she might be charged with receiving, but so far he hadn't mentioned either the fire or Dick O'Mara's death. If she could get out of the police station without that happening, she would feel things were going her way.

The police station was a forbidding place; it was dark inside. Mildred was asked to wait. Waiting was scary; she tried to keep her mind blank. She felt cold, like a block of ice inside, and her head was whirling again. Please, please, she prayed silently, don't let them start questioning me about that fire now. She didn't feel well enough to cope with it.

Constable Ingram appeared before very long and led her off to view the table. She confirmed it was the one she'd sold to Jackson. He told her she'd have to make a statement, and that he'd write it out for her. He led her through her answers again, comparing them to the notes he'd made in her shop. There were more questions about her business connections. She was on the edge of her seat the whole time, but again there was no mention of the fire or Dick O'Mara's death.

Mildred had another even longer wait before her statement was ready to be signed. She was shown to a row of chairs in the hallway and sat, keeping her head down and her eyes closed. The other people sitting there looked like criminals.

Her stomach began to rumble and she felt hungry; the wall clock told her it was almost three before she was led back to an interview room. The constable there read her statement through to her slowly and asked if she agreed it was what she'd said. She signed it, expecting to be allowed to leave, but no, she was instructed to wait again.

She made herself ask, 'What happens now?'

257

'The facts of the case will be assessed, and a decision made whether to charge you or not. This is your first offence?'

'You've asked me that already. I told you, I've never had any contact with the police before.'

She was left alone to wait in the small room this time. She felt jittery and couldn't sit still. She paced up and down. The door had been shut, it seemed like a prison cell. Dare she open the door? She wanted to go home, was desperate to get out of here. Her head was reeling.

Finally, she couldn't say how much later, she heard heavy footsteps coming down the passage, and the door was flung open. Two police officers came this time. One started reading something out to her, but she could hardly take in what was being said. It took her a moment or two to realise she was being charged with receiving.

'Your case will be heard here, in Brandon Street.'

'When?'

'In a few weeks. You'll be informed of the date and time later.'

Mildred stuffed the documents she'd been given into her handbag and followed the policeman out. He still hadn't said anything about Dick O'Mara or the fire that had killed him.

Mildred walked home slowly, aching with exhaustion and burning with indignation about the way the police had treated her. None of this was her fault: it was Dick O'Mara who had got her into this trouble.

At the back of her mind was the feeling she should be glad about something. She was certainly thankful it was over for the time being. She warmed up the scouse and bolted it down. Then she went to lie on her bed and fell into an uneasy sleep.

It was dark when her doorbell rang. Mildred had just got up and put the kettle on. She found Polly Weaver on her doorstep, and until she mentioned it, Mildred had forgotten she'd invited her round this evening.

They had been in the habit of having cups of tea at the back of each other's premises. On many an afternoon, Polly would leave her husband to look after their hardware shop, and if Mildred was busy she would even go upstairs and make tea for them. She took over now, filling the tea pot.

'I'm really at sixes and sevens tonight,' Mildred said, though her mind felt clearer after her sleep. 'What with Cathy moving out and leaving me on my own.'

That was hurtful, it made her draw closer to her old friend Polly. She went on to tell her about her other grievances – how she'd been taken in by a man who'd brought a little table he'd stolen into her shop and begged her to give him a few pounds for it.

'The policeman came in here and demanded I go to the station with him. Very officious, he was. Now I'm in trouble over it.'

Polly was sympathetic.

'I have to be so careful,' Mildred moaned. 'I'm afraid this will be the end for me.'

'I wondered where you'd gone. It's not like you to shut up shop. You should have kept that little girl Jessie on.'

'Jessie couldn't help with my dressmaking. She wasn't much use at all, really.'

'Oh, by the way,' Polly recalled suddenly, 'one of your friends came in our shop asking for you. The one who comes to help you.'

'Harriet Bott? Cathy's friend?'

'Yes, that's her.'

'Oh dear!' Mildred was sorry she'd been out and had missed her. 'I'm making a couple of dresses for her daughter-in-law. She was coming in for a fitting today.'

'Yes, the girl was with her.'

It hurt that she hadn't been able to get close to Harriet. Cathy attracted her attention and they had no thought for anyone else. She felt a pang of jealousy. 'A strange woman, Mrs Bott.'

'I thought you liked her?'

'I did, to start with.' Mildred had to find some reason. 'She's a bit mixed up – in her mind, you know. Something happened to her years ago and she hasn't been like the rest of us ever since.'

'That's right,' Polly said. 'I remember it well. It was a nine days' wonder all over town.'

'I don't!' Mildred was taken aback. 'Why didn't you say?'

'I thought you knew. Anyway, George said it was best forgotten after all these years.'

'Tell me,' Mildred persuaded. 'What exactly *did* happen at Cooper's Yard?'

Chapter Twenty-One

Cathy really enjoyed the few days it took to fix up the flat in Exmouth Street. She chose six dining chairs in the Hepplewhite style from the shop and Danny brought up a grandfather clock he admired. By Wednesday afternoon, they had everything in its place; even the ornaments were set out. However, now Cathy was in the last weeks of her pregnancy she didn't have the energy she used to have.

Danny was relaxed and happy and spoke of a feeling of release that at last they had a home of their own.

'I no longer have to keep a watch on my tongue or worry because Mildred's in one of her moods.'

'I wonder how she's getting on by herself,' Cathy said. 'Whether she's managing.'

'She's probably glad to see the back of me, whatever she feels about losing you and Rosie,' Danny laughed. 'But you're going to take it easy from now on. I want you to have a very different time with this baby.'

He told Peggy he wanted her to be more help to Cathy up in the flat. 'You can take it your days of helping in the shop are over. There'll be two children to look after soon.'

'That suits me,' Peggy said. 'I'm happy to be a fulltime nursemaid. From now on I'll make Rosie's bed and keep her room tidy.'

She also bathed the child and washed and ironed her clothes, and would make something for her to eat if need be. Peggy was the sort who wasn't above bringing up a bucket of coal to make up the fire, or doing the washing up. She helped Cathy look out the baby clothes and bedding that Rosie had used and washed them in preparation for the new baby.

Although Rosie wasn't due to start school for another few months, Cathy took her to see the headmistress of the Woodlands School, which was the nearest to them, to make sure she'd have a place there in September.

On the first Thursday in their new home, Cathy said at dinnertime, 'I'd better go down to Mildred's this afternoon, see how she is and give her a hand with her sewing.'

Danny was going to a sale. 'Are you sure? I thought she was giving you the willies.'

'She was, but I told her I'd go. I can't just move out and never go near her again. I ought to see how she is.'

'If she scares you, love . . .'

'Botty will be there too.'

'Tell Mildred you won't be able to go for much longer, it'll be too much for you. I'll give you a lift down on my way over to Liverpool.'

'No, Danny, you'll get me there too early. Botty said she'd be late. I'll walk down with Rosie.'

'Rosie too?'

'It's what Mildred wants. Besides, Peggy has to have some time off and she's always had Thursday afternoons.'

'All the same . . .'

'She'd never harm Rosie.'

Cathy felt anxious as she walked down, wondering how things had gone for Mildred. She'd seemed a bundle of nerves and almost at the end of her tether, during the last few days they'd spent in her house. She and Danny had found her very difficult.

Now with such a change in her own life, it seemed to Cathy that all that had happened a long time ago. As she neared the shop, she knew there was something different about it, but it took her a moment to realise that the name Second Time Around had been painted out.

The shop was open but it seemed bare. As the clanging of the bell died down, she could see very little for sale in it. Cathy went to the sewing room but there was no dressmaking on the go and nobody about.

'Where's Nanna?' Rosie asked.

Cathy felt a shaft of worry. Was Mildred all right? She said, 'She must be upstairs.'

But Mildred had heard them and was out on the landing before she and Rosie reached it. It reassured Cathy to see her throw her arms round the child and twirl her round with more energy than she'd shown for a long time.

'How are you, love? Have you missed your Nanna then? What's the matter with your knee?'

'I fell over and hurt it.'

'Oh dear, no Nanna to look after you now.' Mildred looked as though she needed someone to look after *her*. Her face was grey; she looked ill. 'I have missed my little Rosie.'

Nowadays she wore her dark hair pulled back into a neat tight bun, but today much of it had broken loose and was hanging in lank and greasy clumps about her shoulders. Her dress showed food stains down the front, which wasn't like Mildred. It was only when she turned to her that Cathy noticed how wild and feverish her eyes looked.

'Come on in,' Mildred laughed, and the sound was shrill, uncontrolled and mirthless.

Cathy followed her into the living room, worried about the change in her. There was ironing everywhere; some in neatly folded piles, some in bundles waiting for attention. There was a smell of freshly washed linen and she could see a flatiron heating in the fire. Mildred's sewing was here, freshly pressed and festooned round the room on hangers.

Mildred closed the adjoining kitchen door almost to, sat down in Otto's chair and pulled Rosie on her knee. Cathy sat down too. She'd have liked to find Botty already here, and was about to ask if she was still expecting her, when Mildred said, 'It's such a long time since I've seen my little Rosie, but you've been busy, Cathy, I suppose. How's your new home?'

'Lovely. We've got it as we want it now.' She had a moment of misgiving; she mustn't seem too glad to have escaped from under Mildred's roof. Rosie struggled down and went to play with her bricks. Mildred stood up as though to follow. 'You must come up and see it,' Cathy said.

'I saw it last Sunday.'

'We still had a lot to do then. Now it's finished. Come for your dinner this coming Sunday.'

'Yes, I will, thank you. I'm glad you're pleased with it, but you have to be after turning Danny's mother out to get it.' Cathy felt Mildred's resentment and animosity like a fence of barbed wire. 'How's poor Ettie getting on?'

Cathy said stiffly, 'They have a cottage in the yard that's been empty for a while. They aren't living with the rest of the family, you know. She says she loves it, and she's been made to feel very welcome.'

Mildred's face twisted with spite. 'Well, she won't be happy for long,' she hissed, 'not with *that* family. They've got quite a history and they're keeping it very quiet.'

'What d'you mean? Everybody likes the Botts.'

Mildred was keeping her voice low. 'I don't think they do, not those who know . . .'

'Know what? What is there to know?'

'Harriet Bott's your friend, but she's kept it from you, hasn't she?'

Cathy hated these pinpricks about her friend. 'Kept what, Mildred?'

263

'It was all over town when it happened. A real scandal. You know that business used to belong to Herbert Cooper?'

'She's made no secret of that. Botty was their housekeeper.'

'Well, they gave out she was his housekeeper, but it wasn't just housework she was doing. She was sleeping with him.'

'No! I can't believe that of her.' Cathy wanted to laugh. Harriet Bott was rather demure; it wasn't the sort of thing she'd do.

Mildred was aggressive. 'She took up with him all right, and he looked after her children as though they were his own. How else would she come by his home and his business if she wasn't his mistress?'

'No Mildred, you're making a mistake. She wouldn't do such a thing, not Botty.' Mildred had done that herself, so why did she feel it was so wrong for other women?

'Reckon she did. It's true enough,' Mildred went on, her voice only a little above a whisper. 'Wait till I tell you the whole story.

'Luella Cooper got a bit above being the wife of a carter, even one with a good business. She ran off with some toff of a fellow who was visiting family up here, and abandoned poor Herbert.'

Cathy was shocked into silence; she could hardly get her breath. Mildred's manner was vindictive. Hadn't poor Otto been abandoned like that, too?

'Mrs Cooper thought she'd gone up in the world – her new gentleman friend was providing her with champagne and roses. They were staying in the best hotels, but within months she found he had no savings and no financial sense. There were times when they were living hand to mouth. It's said she even went hungry. After a year or two, he fancied someone else. So Luella Cooper came home meaning to make things up with her husband but found he'd moved another woman into his bed. She flew into a rage and knifed both of them.'

Cathy felt sick. Botty did have that ugly scar down the side of her face. Nobody knew how she'd come by it. 'An accident,' she'd said once when Cathy had asked her.

'What happened to Mr Cooper?'

'He died of his wounds.'

'Oh my goodness!'

'But he'd rewritten his Will, leaving his house and business to his fancy woman. That's how the Botts came by it.' Mildred's hands were on her hips, her face full of envy. 'It was handed to them on a plate. They didn't have to work for it.'

Some noise behind her made Cathy turn round. Harriet Bott was standing stock-still in the kitchen doorway clutching a flat iron. She looked as though she'd been there for some time. A flush of anger was spreading up her cheeks.

'You can finish your own ironing, Mildred,' she said, slamming the iron down on the hearth, 'and don't expect me back next week. I won't be coming to help you again.' Her face was drawn and shocked, and she pushed past Cathy as though she hadn't seen her.

'Wait a minute!' Cathy hurtled downstairs after her. She caught her up as Harriet went to the back room to get her coat.

'I can't wait, not now.' She was marching past her again to get out into the street. Cathy followed and caught at her arm, pulling her to a halt in the shadows of the Market Hall.

'Botty, I want you to know I think of you as a friend.'

'I thought *she* was my friend!'

'Whatever Mildred says in a moment's outburst doesn't alter how I feel about you. I've known you for years. You were always kind to me, even when I was the new tweeny and you were the powerful housekeeper. You're a caring person to everybody, and nothing can change that. I'll always be glad to count you a friend.'

'Thank you.'

She would have turned and gone if Cathy hadn't been hanging on to her arm. Her face had crumpled, and the scar stood out. 'It was more than twenty years ago and it wasn't like Mildred told it,' she said. 'People only half-remember, and because I inherited the business, they assume I was Herbert's mistress.'

'I wouldn't assume that for one moment,' Cathy assured her.

'It never goes away.' Harriet pulled out her handkerchief and dabbed at her face. 'Wherever I go, whatever I do, there's always somebody who thinks they remember.'

'I'll walk you home,' Cathy said. 'As Mildred sees it, she was in a similar position to you, living with a man whose wife had abandoned him.'

'Cathy, I was living in a cottage on Herbert Cooper's premises, as his housekeeper. That's all I ever was to him.'

'But you ended up with a thriving business and—'

'The business is what stops us moving right away, where nobody would know us. It's both a blessing and a bane. It's the one trade the boys can cope with; they were brought up to it, they enjoy the work.'

Cathy said, 'As Mildred sees it, she's been left with nothing, no family and no business. She's jealous of what you have.'

'She hasn't had the publicity either. The Bott name has been infamous, in its time.'

'And you're finding people remember and gossip about you? Get things wrong?'

'That can be hurtful, but it's not just that. Painful memories . . .'

'I'm sorry.'

'I can't talk about it now.' Botty blew her nose. 'It brings it all back and makes me feel raw. Makes me remember what I lost – what we *all* lost. Perhaps one day, when I'm feeling strong, I'll tell you the full story.'

For Mildred to see Cathy running after Harriet to comfort her, to take her side, made her really cross.

'Where's your mother gone now?' she demanded of Rosie. 'She's more interested in Mrs Bott than she is in me.'

She took the hot iron from the fire and spat on it savagely. Her spittle ran off in a fizz. Rosie clapped.

'Can I do that, Nanna?'

'No, love, it's hot, you could burn yourself.'

Mildred polished the bottom of the iron with the cloth she kept for the purpose and the smell of singeing cotton stung her nostrils.

In the kitchen she banged and pressed on the crisp cotton lace, venting her ill-humour on that.

Rosie tugged on her skirt. 'I want my mamma. Where's she gone?' she asked plaintively.

'She's no thought for us at all, rushing off after Mrs Bott like that. She should be here doing this for me.'

Mildred ironed out every tiny crease, intent on perfection. Suddenly, she missed Rosie, and felt her first misgivings. She went to the living room to find the door to the landing was open. She flung the iron on the hearth and ran down to the shop. The shop door was open too; she shot out into the street.

Polly Weaver had Rosie by the hand and was bringing her back.

'Thank goodness! Thank you, Polly.' Mildred felt weak with relief and mopped away an anxious tear. 'She ran out after her mother.'

'I saw her go past our shop. Can't turn your back on them for an instant at this age, can you?'

'I want my mamma.' That went through Mildred. Round brown eyes lifted to her. 'Where's she gone, Nanna? I want Peggy to play with me.'

Mildred took in a swift angry breath. So she wanted Peggy, did she? Even Rosie was turning against her! Nobody wanted her, but she was glad to have Rosie safely with her before Cathy came back. If she knew she'd let her wander off, Cathy would think she was incapable of looking after her.

But she wasn't her usual self this week. With all her problems and disappointments, she was at her wit's end and no one had the time of day for her. She needed support but she wasn't getting it.

Cathy came running back upstairs, looking vexed. She threw herself on a chair and pulled Rosie on her knee. 'Whatever made you say those things about Botty?' she demanded.

'I didn't intend to upset her.'

'I think you did, Mildred. You knew she was in the kitchen. You must have known she'd overhear you. That was very unkind.'

Mildred said sharply, 'If people overhear things about themselves, they can't expect it always to be praise.'

'I thought you liked her.'

'*You* like her. She was whining on, full of her own problems today.'

She saw Cathy's arms tighten round her daughter. 'What about?'

'One of her grandsons is ill. It's probably just a head cold but you'd have thought he was at death's door.'

'She's good to you, Mildred. Always here doing things for you.'

'She only comes because you're here. It's you she comes to see. She was quite put out because you were late.'

'She said *she* was going to be late – that she was going over to Liverpool with Iris and her grandsons.'

'There you are, you see? I'm right. You're only here to talk to each other, that's all.'

'It's not all. She sews and irons for you. Does what she can to help you.'

Mildred hadn't got over Harriet's manner when she'd stormed out of her kitchen brandishing the flatiron. 'She said she won't come in future.'

'I don't blame her. You pretend to be friendly but you use her, and now for some reason you've turned against her. Wherever did you hear that story about her?'

'What does that matter now? I did hear it.'

'I wouldn't come again if I were her.'

'Cathy! Don't *you* turn against me.' Mildred felt near to tears.

'I don't intend to. I'm grateful for all you've done for me in the past. But Danny's mother has married into the Bott family. You and Harriet falling out, it'll make things awkward.'

'It won't, Cathy. I won't let it. If she doesn't come here, when are we likely to meet?'

She saw Cathy stand up and reach for Rosie's coat. 'You aren't going straight away?' Mildred felt everybody was deserting her. 'You say you come to help me but you've done nothing yet.'

'Botty's done most of your ironing. You and I, we don't seem able to do anything but argue these days. I'm not in the mood to sew now.'

'Well, thank you very much!' Mildred's temper flared. 'I have to work whether I'm in the mood or not.'

'We'll see you on Sunday about one o'clock, yes?'

Mildred didn't answer. Receding footsteps on the stairs meant everybody had turned against her. Even Rosie was pleased to go, and neither had offered a goodbye kiss.

Mildred was fuming. She had so much to tell Cathy and she hadn't been given the chance to open her mouth. All this trouble with the police, it might have soothed her to talk it through. As things were, she felt she was falling apart, but she'd work it off, she'd have to.

She slotted one of her flatirons into the grate and while it heated, started taking the garments she'd made for her clients downstairs to the sewing room. It took several trips.

The only ironing remaining was the bedding off Cathy's bed that she'd washed through before leaving on Monday. Normally Mildred only ironed the tops of sheets that she turned down over the blankets, but today it soothed her to press out every crease. These sheets would not be needed again. She'd put them away in a drawer. The finality of that caught in her throat.

She folded them neatly and took them to the empty bedroom. The bed had been stripped. The striped ticking of the pillows was visible for once, the mattress covered with a skimpy washed-out flannelette sheet. This was Rolf's marriage bed; he'd bought it for himself and Cathy. Rosie had been conceived in it.

But Cathy had taken it over and brought her lover here in Rolf's place. That had been a bitter pill to swallow, Mildred could feel her rage building. Cathy had conceived another child here, and now wanted nothing to remind her of Rolf and his family.

She'd actually told her off for being unkind to Harriet Bott. For goodness sake! It rankled that Cathy had gone and left her here on her own. She blamed Danny – he'd probably talked her into moving out. She should have stood firm.

Mildred had expected better from Cathy after all the kindness and generosity she'd shown her. To have Rosie prised from her, to be left alone to stew in her own juice, it was out-and-out rejection. That stung.

The self-control she'd worked so hard to maintain snapped. In an explosion of fury Mildred leaped at the pillows, trying to tear them apart. She pummelled and punched but they were soft and yielding like

Cathy herself. It was impossible to hurt her or damage them. That infuriated her further.

But there was always a way. She ran to the kitchen to snatch up her carving knife.

In a frenzy of frustration she laid into the mattress, jabbing the knife in up to the hilt, tearing and cutting at the cover, until sweat was pouring off her. She raised her arm again and again, bringing it down with all the force in her body.

'*I'll make them pay for what they're doing to me*,' Mildred swore. She'd like to boil them in oil, or shoot them. She remembered then what she'd done to Dick O'Mara, razed his shop to the ground and burned him in his bed. That was one way she could deal with Cathy and Danny.

But then she thought of Rosie's mop of curls showing above her pink eiderdown. She couldn't! She'd never do anything that would harm her little granddaughter.

Grey flock was spewing out of the mattress, and the old sheet was in shreds. She'd have to think of something else; there was always a way if you wanted it badly enough. Then she attacked the pillows until she couldn't see across the room for flying feathers.

She had manic energy and carried on jabbing and cutting until she was exhausted and could no longer raise her arm. Hurling the knife into a corner she threw herself on what was left of the mattress in a storm of tears.

Cathy found living in Exmouth Street a delight. Breakfast was now a peaceful and leisurely meal.

Danny had slipped down to take the bolt off the shop door and turn the sign round to Open, so his mother and Peggy could come in when they arrived. Customers were few, this early in the morning, and the shop bell would alert him to their arrival.

'It's so much easier to live over our own business,' Danny said, taking the top off Rosie's breakfast egg for her.

Cathy knew he found Mildred's absence the greatest benefit. No longer did they have to contend with her moods or beware in case they said something to upset her. Rosie was quick to pick up on things, and they still had to be careful not to say anything against Mildred in front of her, but that was all.

Cathy had told him how Mildred had turned against Botty. 'She turns against everybody who tries to help her.'

'We couldn't stay there,' Danny said. 'She was making our life a misery. Now we've got this flat organised and we're on our own, I want you to relax and take things easy. You surely must be feeling more tired now?'

'No,' said Cathy. She was within a month or so of the birth of her second child. 'I feel fine.'

'I don't want you to work in the shop any more,' he told her. 'You'll have more than enough to do getting our meals and shopping for groceries.'

The shop doorbell clanged. Danny's mother called out and they heard her footsteps running up.

'Good morning.' Cathy was reaching for the extra cup she'd brought to the table for Ettie, who looked upset.

'Terrible news this morning,' she told them. 'Billy, Iris's little boy, is very poorly. The doctor says he's got diphtheria and they've taken him to the fever hospital.'

Cathy was shocked. 'Poor Iris, she must be worried stiff.'

'She is. They all are. There's a lot of it about at the moment.'

Danny asked, 'Is Georgie all right?'

'So far. His father's taken him on the van with him this morning to get him out in the fresh air. Iris was told not to send him to school. They think he might get it and infect the rest of his class.'

Cathy could feel herself going rigid. Iris had come up to see the flat and had invited them all down for their evening meal.

'Ettie, we were all down at Cooper's Yard the other night. The boys were playing with Rosie.'

Danny's eyes met hers, full of concern. 'That was Tuesday.'

'Yes, I know. Iris said she thought Billy was a bit off-colour then,' Cathy remembered.

Danny put in, 'But he was playing quite happily with those trains.'

Ettie said, 'He went to school the next morning, but when he came home for his dinner, he said he didn't feel well, so Iris didn't send him back in the afternoon. But he didn't seem that bad, didn't even say he had a sore throat. She didn't send for the doctor until Thursday.'

'Diphtheria, that's awful.'

'I'm sorry. Is Rosie all right?' They were all looking at her.

'Yes,' Cathy said. 'You feel fine, don't you, love? She's eaten her breakfast.'

Rosie nodded and got down from her chair. She'd heard Peggy arrive and went out to the stairs to meet her.

'You mustn't worry,' Ettie said.

'No, she's hardly ever ill,' Danny agreed. 'She's not likely to catch it.'

Cathy couldn't help being a little anxious. She telephoned Iris to ask how Billy was.

'The hospital says rather poorly – he's had that membrane thing across his throat. He has to lie flat in bed without a pillow and they don't want me to go in to see him.'

'Oh Iris!'

'Billy's having antitoxin now. I'm hoping he'll be better soon, but I'm worried about Georgie. He doesn't seem well. It's nothing I can put my finger on, but then there wasn't with Billy. I've asked the doctor to come.'

'I hardly know what to say . . .'

'I wish I hadn't invited you all down on Tuesday. I'm sorry, Cathy.' The woman's voice broke and she put down the phone.

Cathy found herself watching Rosie like a hawk. When dinnertime came she couldn't eat all her food. Usually, Peggy took her out for a walk after that, but today she looked pale and dispirited.

'Come and lie down on our new couch,' Cathy suggested, plumping up the cushions for her. 'Peggy will fetch your eiderdown so you can snuggle under it. Would you like her to read you a story?'

Rosie nodded.

Cathy wished Danny was here, but he'd gone to a sale in Liverpool. She was undecided about whether to ask the doctor to call straight away. She went down to the shop to have a word with Ettie.

'Rosie doesn't seem that ill – she's not complaining of a sore throat or anything,' she told her. 'If I didn't know she'd been in contact with Billy, I wouldn't be that concerned, but I'm afraid she's ailing, that it might be diphtheria.'

Five minutes later, Peggy tiptoed down to say Rosie had fallen asleep.

Cathy saw that as a bad sign. 'She gave up her afternoon sleep more than a year ago.'

Ettie crept upstairs to look at her. Cathy followed and laid her hand gently on the child's forehead. 'She doesn't seem to have much of a temperature.'

'Ask the doctor to come, Cathy,' Ettie advised. 'Illness frightens the life out of me.'

Cathy shuddered. She was reminded that Danny's father and siblings had died of TB.

'It'll put your mind at rest, even if it's just a cold. The doctor told Iris to keep a close eye on Georgie. That if he caught it too, the sooner he started on the antitoxin the better.'

Cathy blessed the day Danny had had the telephone put in and went to use it.

Two hours later, the doctor was climbing the stairs. Rosie had woken and was now sitting on the hearth rug hugging her teddy bear. Cathy lifted her back on the couch so he could examine her. He took her temperature and her pulse.

'Her pulse is rapid and she has a slight temperature. Well, little girl, let me look in your throat. Does it hurt?'

She shook her head then said, 'A bit.'

He felt her neck and sighing heavily, listened to her chest. 'She hasn't vomited?'

'No.'

Looking very serious, he said, 'I'm afraid I can see membranes starting to grow on her tonsils.'

'Is it diphtheria?' Cathy felt a wave of horror wash through her.

'I think so. We can only say it's definitely diphtheria when we have bacteriological confirmation. But that takes time and we need to start her on antitoxin as soon as possible. It's hospital for you, young lady, I'm afraid.'

'Don't want to go 'opital,' Rosie croaked.

Cathy swallowed hard. 'Couldn't I look after her here?'

'No.' The doctor was decisive. 'No, you live over a shop, with people coming and going all the time. You have no choice in this, Mrs McLelland. She must go to the fever hospital and go alone in the ambulance. Now she's ill, Rosie will act as a carrier of the disease to others, and she needs urgent treatment if she is to make a good recovery.'

Cathy drew in a long shuddering breath. 'What sort of treatment?'

'As well as the antitoxin she must have absolute rest. A careful watch will be kept on her heart because the toxins can damage that. Also a watch for signs of paralysis, because that, too, can happen.'

'Paralysis?' Cathy was alarmed.

'It usually isn't permanent, but she might need massage to help it clear. So you see, the fever hospital is the best place for her.'

He patted Cathy's arm. 'Besides, there's you to think of. Adults can catch this too, though it's more often children. I'll arrange for you to have some antitoxin too, Mrs McLelland. We can't risk you catching it when you're so close to your time. We have to think of the coming baby too.'

Cathy nodded.

'As far as Rosie is concerned, the disease is still in the early stages; the sooner she starts on antitoxin the better chance she'll have. You did well to call me straight away. I'll send for an ambulance for her.'

Cathy stirred. 'We have a telephone out on the landing.'

When he went to use it, she put her arms round Rosie. 'I want to stay with you, Mamma,' she wept.

'Darling, I'm sorry. You have to go to hospital where they'll make you better.'

The doctor came back. 'It won't be long. Put a few things together for her, but bear in mind everything will have to be stoved before it comes out again. So don't put in anything of value.'

When Cathy went downstairs to see him out, she was glad to see Danny's car pulling into the kerb. The doctor paused to tell him about Rosie having to go to hospital.

Cathy hurried back to sit with her and hold her hand until the ambulance came. Danny came up a few moments later to hold her other hand. But Ettie was running up five minutes later to say the ambulance was at the door.

Rosie was gripping her hand with the strength of a vice as Cathy went to see her off. As Rosie was stretchered inside the ambulance, she could hear her calling for her mamma and sobbing pitifully.

With Danny's arm round her waist, Cathy went back upstairs to her flat feeling despondent and drained. Ettie followed, looking shocked.

'Shall I make a cup of tea?'

'Yes, please, Mam,' Danny said. 'And will you ring Cooper's Yard to let them know what's happened?'

'I'll do it,' Cathy said. When she got through, she could hear Iris weeping at the other end of the line.

'I'm so sorry, I'm sure you must blame us.'

'No, it's nobody's fault,' she told her.

Iris said, 'Harriet wants a word with you – hang on.'

Harriet's voice, calm and steady, said, 'Shall I come up and keep you company, Cathy?'

'Yes, I wish you would.' She felt relieved. 'Danny's got to go out again and Ettie has to look after the shop.'

It seemed to Cathy, as she put the receiver down with trembling hands, that her life had been turned upside down. Already she felt lost without her beloved Rosie.

Chapter Twenty-Two

By Saturday morning, Mildred was finding it a real struggle to get through her work. She made herself go down to her sewing-machine but was achieving only half her usual output. Customers came to be fitted and others brought dress-lengths for her to make up, but she felt she was looking down on herself talking to these people, as though she was not in her own body.

She certainly didn't know what had got into her on Thursday. She'd felt ashamed when she saw the mess she'd made in Cathy's bedroom and had turned the mattress over so its ruined state wouldn't be so obvious. She'd swept up the feathers too, or as many of them as she could. They'd proved elusive, fluttering away from her brush.

Mildred was running up a flower-print dress when she heard her shop bell clang. She went out to the shop to find a young girl, with a thick brown plait hanging down her back, holding out an envelope to her.

'Mrs McLelland asked me to give this to you.'

'Do I know you?' Mildred asked as she ripped open the envelope. The girl looked vaguely familiar.

'I'm Peggy Ellis. I look after Rosie.'

'Of course.' Mildred looked her up and down. She wasn't much more than a child herself. Whatever made Cathy think such a young girl would take proper care of Rosie? 'You haven't brought her with you?'

'She's in the fever hospital, sent there yesterday.' The girl bit her lip. 'It tells you in the letter.'

'Goodness gracious! Let me read it.' That *proved* the child wasn't being looked after properly. 'What's the matter with her?'

But by then Mildred had read enough of the letter to know it was diphtheria. Children could die of that! Poor darling Rosie must be very poorly.

'Where have you been taking her?' she asked accusingly. 'Rosie should never have been allowed to go gadding about town, to places where she could catch these dreadful fevers. She'd have been much safer here with me.'

'They think she caught it from her relatives at Cooper's Yard. The two boys from there are sick with it too.'

'The Botts!' Mildred exploded. 'But they aren't Rosie's relatives.'

The girl stared at her silently.

'Who took her there? Her mother?'

'Yes, they're a family connection.'

'They've no business taking my granddaughter there,' Mildred stormed. 'That place is a hotbed of infection.' Hadn't Harriet Bott been whining on about it on Thursday? 'Cathy should have known better than to take her there. *Both* boys, you said?'

'Yes. Georgie has been taken to the fever hospital too.'

Mildred read more of Cathy's note.

I know I asked you up for your dinner on Sunday, but I hope you don't mind if I put you off. Sunday afternoon, two till four, is the only time visitors are allowed in. Then it's only parents and only one at a time. Rosie's isolated in a little glass cubicle and we aren't allowed inside that. We have to look at her through the glass.

We'll be going with Iris and Jim. Both their little boys are in.

It's a very worrying time. I can't think of anything but Rosie. We'll ask you up for your dinner some other time.

Mildred couldn't suppress a grunt of disgust. It wouldn't have hurt Cathy to give her a dinner on Sunday. They'd be eating themselves, wouldn't they? How many times had she fed them?

She would have liked a trip out to the fever hospital with them. The nurses would probably have let her in to see Rosie. She was her grandmother, after all, and had looked after her all her short life. Anyway, it would have been an outing for her and she'd have felt nearer to her little darling.

'Poor Rosie, she must be really ill.' To Mildred it felt like one more disaster in her own life. 'Tell Cathy I'm very sorry.' She wiped away a tear. 'Very upset. Tell her I want to know how Rosie gets on. Ask her to keep me posted.'

When the girl had gone, Mildred went back to her sewing-machine and rested her feet on the treadle while she reflected.

The child had never had a day's illness in her life before. This was just one more instance of Cathy's high-handedness causing mayhem. She blamed Danny, too; he had put her up to all these changes. How she loathed them both. Mildred vowed that if it was the last thing she did, she was going to make them suffer too.

She couldn't work today, just couldn't. All this trouble was making her head reel again.

Suddenly she straightened up. This could be a heaven-sent chance. She could burn down the antique shop Danny thought so much of, and at the same time damage Cathy's fancy flat. She could ruin all Danny's expensive antiques too. Ruin everything for them. Rosie wasn't at home, so she couldn't be hurt – only Danny and Cathy. Danny deserved all he got, but Cathy? Yes, she did too; she'd turned against her.

The more Mildred thought of the idea the better she liked it. If Cathy and Danny died, she'd be Rosie's next-of-kin. Rosie would be all hers. She would no longer have to concern herself about what Cathy wanted.

Now Mildred had made the decision, she felt full of bounding energy. She couldn't improve on what she'd done to Dick O'Mara's premises. It had worked for her then, it would again. She'd need soft dry rags. As a dressmaker she had plenty of them; she picked out three of the most suitable. Newspapers now, no shortage of them either. She went to the cupboard where she kept her bottle of cleaning fluid. It was well-nigh empty. She'd need more of that.

She went down Market Street to the shop where she'd bought it years before; it had lasted her for ages. Here she discovered that it was no longer sold in pint bottles. Dry-cleaning fluid now came in tiny ones holding only an ounce or so, with a sponge on top to rub straight onto the stain. She'd need a lot of them and the sponge would make it difficult to get out.

But why bother? She could buy petrol more cheaply – that should work even better. There was a garage on New Chester Road where Danny had stopped for petrol when he'd taken them for a run in his car.

She'd need a bottle. No, a garage would think it strange if she took a bottle to a pump and asked for a pint of petrol. If questions were asked afterwards, she didn't want to be remembered. A tin would be better. Outside in the wash-house she found just what she was looking for. Fortunately, Otto had never thrown anything away. She sniffed at it, wondering what it had been used for. Paraffin, perhaps? It would do.

She put on her coat and locked up her shop. It was a pleasant day, but the garage was further away than she'd thought. The lad on the pump sold her half a gallon, though she wouldn't need anything like that amount. She was tired when she got back home but she put together the other things she'd need, her torch and some matches.

The tin was too bulky to carry all that way through the streets; it was heavy too, and might draw attention to her. She decided to refill the bottle she'd used before. She did it out in the wash-house in case she spilled a little. The lack of a funnel meant she spilled quite a lot of it all over her hands and down her coat.

She washed her hands thoroughly but they still reeked of petrol. So did her coat; she left it there instead of taking it indoors.

Three in the morning would be the best time to set out. There'd be nobody much about in the streets to see her do it. Danny and Cathy would be asleep and wouldn't wake up in time to get out.

Mildred raved on to herself. They deserved it, they wouldn't listen to her. She could be dead in this flat and not found for a month, that's how much they cared about her.

She went to bed very early and set her alarm clock for a quarter to three. She heard it go off and opened her eyes. To her consternation, there was so much light in her room she thought it was morning and her normal time to rise. On lifting the curtain, she found it was a clear bright night with a full moon and plenty of stars. She could see clearly across the deserted Market Square. Mildred felt her first misgivings. This wasn't what she wanted, but she couldn't wait for the moon to wane, because Rosie might be home again.

Dressing quickly, she crept outside to the wash-house. As soon as she opened the door, the smell of petrol was strong enough to catch in her throat. She propped the door open, trying not to cough, and reached for her Wellingtons. Last time, her footsteps had sounded frighteningly loud in her ears; they wouldn't tonight. She pulled on her coat. It smelled of petrol too, but it would smell of smoke by the time she got back.

As she let herself out of her back yard, the night was silent and there was nobody about, but Mildred knew she'd be easily seen, should someone happen to be awake and look out. She glanced up at the Weavers' bedroom window but the whole place was in darkness.

She felt more nervous than she had last time – she could feel herself quaking inside – but she also felt more driven, more sure she was doing the right thing.

It was quite a walk up to Exmouth Street, but she knew the way well. She kept to the back streets where she'd be less likely to meet a policeman on his beat.

Once, a heavy lorry chugged in the distance and she rushed to hide herself in the shadows of a nearby back entry, but it drove along the next street and she didn't even see it. Her heart throbbed, seeming to make almost as much noise as the lorry engine. She hadn't moved when she heard voices. Two half-drunk lads were walking along the street, presumably going home after a night on the tiles.

The bright moonlight was giving her the jitters. She hesitated, undecided whether to go on. But that meant Cathy would get off scot-free: she'd have a wonderful life with her new husband and they'd go on humiliating her. If she was to have Rosie to herself, she had to do it. Rosie was her flesh and blood, part of her Rolf: it was only right.

Mildred had reached Exmouth Street. Danny's shop was one of ten in a block. The silvery moonlight was bright enough to pick out every detail of the mahogany dining-table in his shop window.

She knew there was a back entry behind the row of shops and went to have a look. It was darker here and there'd be less chance of being seen. Danny's back yard was inside a six-foot brick wall. She tried the solid gate but it was bolted and she couldn't get near to the building.

A black cat came out of the shadows and made her jump, but there was no light in Cathy's bedroom window and no sign of human life. There was nothing for it: the job would have to be done in the open. Mildred went back to the front step and set to work. She'd never looked closely at Danny's shop door before; it was smart and tight-fitting, with a letter flap at waist-height.

She found she could only slide pages of newspaper under the door if they were flat, and then only one or two at a time. She sprinkled petrol on them but even that made them too lumpy, so she wouldn't get the same effect she had at O'Mara's. It was a slow process and she became careless, sloshing petrol all over the step.

It was easier to crumple up several pages of newsprint, douse them well and push them through the letter box. Her petrol-soaked rags followed; she left part of one to act as a wick through the letter flap.

What was that? All of a sudden she could hear the throb of another engine, louder as it turned the corner. Mildred leaped back against the door in alarm, knocking over her bottle of petrol. She pressed herself against the door, terrified she'd be seen in the bright moonlight and the headlights, and it would be obvious what she was doing, but the lorry chugged on past without stopping.

She was ready but her head was reeling from the shock and she could hardly get her breath. She took out her box of matches. 'Be careful,' she told herself, and took one last look round. Right, there was nobody about, so she rasped the match against the box and achieved a tiny flame.

She held it against the petrol-soaked rag hanging from the letter flap. Moments later there was a flash which blinded her with its brilliance, followed seconds later by an almighty bang, the force of which hurled her backwards and slammed her down onto the pavement. Her body crumpled in utter pain and terror.

She screamed and screamed. There was black choking smoke swirling all round her and she could see yellow flames engulfing her, roaring up her coat, feel their searing heat, smell her own hair singeing.

Cathy was having a disturbed night. She'd lain in Danny's arms for ages talking about Rosie, worrying about her. Rosie must be feeling really sick, and on top of that, she'd been snatched away from her mother, her home and everything she knew. She must be feeling terrible, and Cathy longed to be with her to comfort her.

Danny was fast asleep, but she'd slept only fitfully. Silvery moonlight was shafting between the curtains, and the alarm clock was ticking busily. She thought she could hear other vague sounds from the shop and raised her head from the pillow to listen. She couldn't think what it might be, probably nothing; she wasn't used to the night sounds of this shop yet. Cathy awkwardly curled herself up on her side and tried to go back to sleep.

The explosion as the shop window blew out jerked her instantly to full wakefulness. She shot out of bed and flew across the landing to the stairs. The door at the bottom had been left open, giving her a glimpse inside the shop. Thick black smoke was swirling into the staircase. Through it, the shop was lit by incandescent light and leaping yellow flames.

Shock whacked into her gut, making her grab for the bannisters. The smoke was choking her, but she knew what she had to do. Running down the last few stairs she slammed the door hard shut and rushed back to the landing. She grabbed for the telephone, screaming, 'Danny, wake up! It's fire! The shop's on fire!'

She was coughing and panic-stricken and hardly able to get the words out. 'Help,' she shouted at the operator. 'Our shop's on fire. Send the Fire Brigade quick, it's urgent.'

Black smoke was making her choke, but the operator's voice was asking her to stay calm and give her address.

Danny was up and charging past her. 'We've got a fire extinguisher. I'll put it out.'

She grabbed at him and swung him round. 'Don't go down there. You won't get out that way.'

The telephone operator was still asking her questions; she did her best to answer them. Danny was clinging to her.

She pulled him back to their bedroom and shut the door. The window was open a few inches at the bottom. She staggered over to it and took great gulps of cool fresh air. Danny opened it as wide as it would go. 'How did this start?'

'Don't know.' The roar of the fire seemed as loud as a train. She was still choking and coughing on the black smoke.

'I'll try to climb down the drainpipe.'

'No, the Fire Brigade will come. Wait till they get here.'

'Cathy, will you be able to get out through this window?'

She was eight months' pregnant. She looked down at the yard below and shuddered. 'I'll have to, the shop's an inferno.'

He was standing behind her with both his arms wrapped round her. His body pressed against hers, a protective shield between her and the fire. Lights were coming on in the houses in Back Exmouth Street.

'They won't know we're here.' Cathy's teeth were chattering.

'You're cold. Put some clothes on, your best coat. It's in the wardrobe.'

He got it out and bundled her into it. Cathy felt for her slippers. 'I told them we were trapped upstairs.'

'Well done, but they'll come to the front. If I go to the living room I'll be able to see—'

'*No*, Danny! Stay here with me and keep the door closed. It's our best chance. Did you hear that?'

'Yes.' The whine of the fire engine and its clanging bell was coming closer. 'At last.'

'Thank goodness,' Cathy wept.

Moments later they could see figures running up the back entry. Danny opened his mouth and yelled as he never had before.

'They've seen us,' Cathy gulped. 'Thank God.'

But there was no missing their indecision. 'The back entry's too narrow for the fire engine to back up it.' Danny's voice was agonised. 'And there are two heavy bolts on our back gate.'

The firemen tried to batter it open but it wouldn't give. At last Cathy saw ladders being brought. A fireman came up over the wall, dropped into the yard and slid the bolts back. The ladders were rushed closer and propped under their window.

One of the firemen shouted, 'How many are there of you?'

'Just us two,' Danny replied.

'There's nobody else in the building?'

'No, but my wife's eight months' pregnant. I don't know whether she'll be able to manage the ladder.'

Cathy thought it looked exceedingly flimsy. To climb out and on to it hardly seemed possible, but Danny was more in control now they'd made contact. She herself was shaking with cold and terror.

'Don't worry.' A helmeted figure was climbing up, to sit astride the windowsill. Another more burly figure was on the ladder. His shoulders came up in front of Cathy.

'All right, lass, come out here on the sill. Don't worry, I've got you. You won't fall.'

Cathy didn't share his faith, but with some help from Danny she did as she was told.

'A fireman's lift for you.' She was being pushed over the other man's shoulder. 'Hang on, you'll be all right.'

Cathy closed her eyes; she felt anything but all right. In fact she'd never felt less secure in her whole life, but there was nothing she could do for herself. She had to rely on this fireman. Bent double over his shoulder she felt him descending into the yard, slowly, step by step. At last strong arms were lifting her off.

'You've been right brave,' she was told. A blanket was wrapped round her, she was put to lie down on a stretcher and carried out to a waiting ambulance that had been parked in Exmouth Street.

The whole street was now lit up like day. There was great activity round the fire engine, with helmeted figures pumping and others spraying water from hosepipes. The fire in the shop was not yet out, but the men seemed to have it under control. A small crowd of spectators was gathering.

'Danny?' she asked the ambulance attendant.

'He's all right, he'll be coming with you.' Danny came padding up to the ambulance in his bare feet, still in his pyjamas. A blanket was wrapped round his shoulders.

'We made it,' she smiled, feeling weak with relief. 'We both got out unharmed.'

'Thanks to you,' he said, feeling for her hand. 'You came to very quickly. Kept your wits about you, too. I didn't realise the place was on fire, not at first.'

'I was awake before it started. I thought I heard something before that bang when the window shattered.'

'Was there a bang?'

'It was earsplitting, sounded like one of those big guns you hear about in France, firing straight at us.'

She'd been awake, worrying about Rosie, but now she was glad that her daughter hadn't been at home. Rosie would have been terrified of the fire.

'Why would anyone attack our shop?' Danny asked, baffled. 'Who, in God's name, would do a thing like that?'

Cathy clung on to Danny's hand as the ambulance sped towards the Borough Hospital. They were taken to the Casualty Department, where

Danny was checked over by the duty doctor and discharged. The doctor told Cathy she would be admitted to a ward. 'Just to be on the safe side. You've inhaled quite a lot of smoke.'

She could smell it on her hands, in her hair and on her nightie. Danny waited beside her trolley.

'It's disaster all round. First Rosie's taken bad, now it's you. And all that damage to the shop.'

Cathy could see he was desperately worried. When she was moved up to a ward, he came with her. She heard the nurse tell him that if she went into labour she'd be sent by ambulance to Grange Mount Maternity Hospital.

'If she's still here, there's visiting this afternoon between the hours of two and four. You can come in and see her then.'

Cathy was reminded that she and Danny had intended to visit Rosie at that time. Things had gone very badly for them over the last few days.

She was glad when the nurse ran a bath for her. She was given a clean nightdress and put in a clean bed. She felt better and a bit of a fraud, but the nurse hadn't let her wash her hair and it still smelled of smoke.

She felt absolutely exhausted after her wakeful night but she couldn't sleep with the life of the ward going on round her. Breakfast was being served; she wanted nothing but tea. Her mind was going round and round with worry, switching between Rosie and the damage the fire had done to their shop. Her new home with all its fresh paintwork had surely been ruined.

Cathy wondered how they'd have fared if Danny had not had the telephone fitted, but what bothered her more was how the fire had started.

The morning seemed long. She was given a good Sunday lunch, but had difficulty eating it. Afterwards, the other patients began to get ready for their visitors. She could feel their anticipation mounting but didn't think Danny could be in two places at once.

She was right. Promptly at two, the ward doors were opened and the visitors swarmed in. It was an anxious Botty who came to her bedside. She kissed her and laid a bunch of flowers on her bed.

'What a terrible thing to happen. Are you all right, Cathy?'

'I'm fine really. I wish they'd let me go home.'

'You mustn't worry. Danny's gone to see how Rosie is. He said he'll be here before Visiting finishes. That's one advantage of having a car.'

'How are the boys? Have you heard?'

'We're worried about Billy. He's said to be very poorly. Jim and Iris have gone to the hospital with Danny. We'll know more when they get back.'

'I'm worried about the shop too. Is all the stock burned or is some salvageable?'

'Most of it has gone.'

'And my beautiful flat – has that survived?'

Botty was shaking her head in despair. 'I'm afraid the living-room floor gave way and fell in. The firemen evacuated all the buildings nearby, but they seem all right. Danny's staying with us for the time being and you'll have to, too.'

'It's as bad as that?'

'Yes. The shop floor burned out, so did the stairs. It was the fact that the door at the bottom was closed that held the flames back long enough for you to get out.'

Cathy shuddered. 'I slammed it shut. Before I phoned.'

'What a good job you thought of it.'

'I wasn't thinking at all. I just wanted to shut off that smoke. It was like a black swirling tide and I felt it was taking me out to sea with it.'

Cathy felt overcome by the disaster and was wiping away a tear when she saw Danny hurrying down the ward to her. He slipped onto a chair on the other side of her bed.

'Cathy love, how are you?'

'I'm fine. Well, fine physically. Tell me about Rosie. How is she?'

'The ward sister said she's doing well. She was started on the antitoxin without any delay, so the toxins and membranes didn't have time to develop. It's being given through a drip in her arm. I saw her but only through the glass of her cubicle. She was fast asleep.'

'So she didn't see you?' Cathy's lip began to quiver.

'No. Sister said they're giving her sedatives, because they want to keep her as still and rested as possible. Perhaps it's just as well, love. She'd have wanted to know where you were.'

'How did she look?' Cathy's voice was tight with fear.

'Pale, but pretty with her curls spread out round her face. No pillow, she won't be allowed one for at least a week. They think she'll be all right, Cathy. That's all I can tell you.'

'She must be frightened; it must seem a very strange place to her. If she'd seen you, she might have been reassured. That we haven't abandoned her, I mean.'

Danny shook his head. 'Sister said parents are reassured when they see their children, but that Rosie would be upset when I went away and left her. Really, she thinks it better for Rosie to be asleep and not see me. She says she's not unhappy.'

'She must be,' Cathy said. 'I'm sure she's missing us.'

'Rosie has to be there, love. They know how to look after her.'

'I'm frightened for her,' Cathy admitted. 'I wish she was well enough to come home.'

'Did you see my grandchildren?' Harriet asked fearfully. 'Do you know how they're doing?'

'I didn't see them, but I took Iris and Jim in my car. They were going to catch the bus home. Iris had been in and had come out so Jim could see them. It's strictly one at a time. She said Georgie's doing well, but Billy isn't so lucky, poor little soul. His membranes were well developed before he started treatment.'

'It all blew up from nowhere and happened so quickly,' Harriet sighed. 'You were going to the police station this morning – what did they say about your shop?'

'They're waiting for a report from the Fire Brigade, but they believe the building is unsafe. That it will probably have to be demolished.'

'Oh my goodness! Our shop and our home!' Cathy was appalled. There seemed no end to the bad news. 'Is anything salvageable?'

'Perhaps some of our bedroom furniture. At least it was all well insured,' Danny sighed. 'I keep telling myself that, so it shouldn't be a total loss. I can set up somewhere else.' He looked down at his wife. 'I'm glad Botty is here, because there's one other frightful piece of news.'

'What's that?' Cathy demanded, bracing herself.

'It seems they found a badly burned body close to my shop.'

Cathy was clutching at the neck of her nightdress, twisting it tight. 'Do they know who it was?'

'No.'

'Surely it can't be Mildred?' Cathy had been scared of what she might do, but to deliberately burn them in their beds was the act of a madwoman.

'I've been round to her place, but she isn't there. Mrs Weaver hasn't seen her since the fire.'

'Oh my God!' Cathy breathed. She'd had a dreadful suspicion that Mildred had set fire to Dick O'Mara's shop, but given that he'd died in the fire, surely she wouldn't have risked doing that to her and Danny?

She felt totally overcome that Mildred could have been so filled with hate as to set fire to their shop. She couldn't get it out of her mind. It was horrific. She'd been right to be scared of her.

Cathy spent another restless night in hospital and was seen by a doctor during the following morning. It seemed her chest hadn't been badly damaged by the smoke and her baby wasn't going to be born just yet, so she could go home. Before midday, Danny came to collect her.

'How's Rosie?' she asked immediately. 'Have you heard any more?'

'Yes, I rang again this morning. She had a comfortable night, they said, and continues to improve.'

'Thank goodness for that.'

Danny had brought her some of Iris's clothes. 'It's the best I could do, I'm sorry.'

Cathy got dressed in them. Iris was much broader than she was and they covered her bump easily. Danny wanted to take her straight to Cooper's Yard but she insisted on going to see their shop in Exmouth Street on the way.

She found the whole shopfront a blackened ruin. There wasn't a window intact. The shops on either side hadn't entirely escaped but they were open for business. The demolition men were already on site and were lowering pieces of furniture to the ground.

The Botts' cart was parked out in front. Jackson was helping one of the lads to load Rosie's little bed onto it. Cathy hardly recognised it; everything had been blackened by the smoke.

'It'll clean off,' Danny consoled her.

Cathy wound down the car window; the smell of fire was still strong.

'They'll salvage what they can. It'll be only the bedroom furniture, I'm afraid. What we had in the living room fell through the floor to the shop and was burned, but we'll have most of our clothes. Those shut into drawers and wardrobes could well be all right.'

She said, 'I can see my chest of drawers. I'll go and check what my clothes are like now.'

'No, love.' Danny put his hand on her arm to stop her going. 'I want you to take things easy. Jackson will bring it all to Cooper's Yard. They've sold two of their horses now they've changed to motor vans and Frank says we can use the old stable to clean up our furniture. You'll be able to look through everything at leisure.'

Cathy shook her head. 'I'm so sorry, Danny. All the work you put into building up your business and it's all gone. You've lost almost everything – your shop and our home.'

'I haven't lost you or our unborn baby. And young Rosie's going to be all right too, thank God.'

Tears were pricking Cathy's eyes. The next moment she felt Danny's arms go round her. 'It could have been worse, love.'

'I know, much worse,' she choked.

'And there's the warehouse,' he reminded her. 'As luck would have it, there's a fair amount of stock there.'

'I can't get over that it was probably Mildred who did it.'

'You said you were afraid of what she might do.'

'I never thought she'd want to kill me. After what happened to Dick O'Mara she must have intended that.'

He was frowning. 'I should have taken your worries more seriously.'

'And I should have guessed we'd be at risk once Rosie was taken to hospital. She'd never have done anything that might hurt Rosie. Poor Mildred, she was so mixed up, never happy about anything I tried to do for her. And I did try.'

'We both did, Cathy.'

Full of concern, Botty came out to the car as soon as it pulled into Cooper's Yard.

'I'm so glad you're safe. What a terrible shock to find your home on fire. Come on, Cathy, let's get you inside.'

'I'm all right,' Cathy smiled. 'I'm just about over the shock.'

Harriet said, 'Dinner's almost ready. I'll show you where you'll be sleeping while you're here.' She led them up the wide staircase to the first floor and flung open a door.

Cathy looked round the large comfortable bedroom. 'Botty, this is your room. You shouldn't have moved out for us.' She held back on the threshold. 'We could manage in something less grand.'

'No, you couldn't. Your baby's probably going to be born here, and you'll need space for Rosie when she comes out.'

'You've already made up this single bed for her.'

'Yes, I wanted to have things ready.'

'But even so, to give up your own bed . . .'

'Harriet,' Danny said. 'You gave me a room last night. I expected Cathy to share that with me.'

'I was shocked about the fire and not thinking straight when you came. That was Frank's old room but with only a three-quarter bed, neither of you would have much comfort there. The thing is, we have empty rooms but they haven't been used for so long they're in a poor state.'

'Mam said . . .'

'Yes, Ettie and Frank have done their spare room up over in the cottage. I had to fight them to have you here. I thought it would be better for Cathy – with me and Iris always around.'

'You're very kind.'

'You know I like to have family and friends round me. Ettie and Frank are coming over for dinner. Poor Ettie's very upset about the fire.'

'She's probably looking for something to do, now she can't go to the shop.'

As the family gathered round the table for dinner, Iris dished up stew and dumplings.

'I'm so grateful for the loan of your clothes,' Cathy told her. 'Thank you.'

Iris managed to laugh, although the strain of her boys' illness was etched deeply into her rounded face. 'I can't say that dress flatters you. You'd have room for twins inside it. Even in your condition, it's still too big.'

'We'll soon get your own things here, Cathy,' Botty said, and the talk turned to the fire.

'I can't believe Mildred could be so vindictive as to set your shop on fire,' Frank said. 'Do you really think that body is hers?'

Cathy shuddered. 'I'm horribly afraid it could be. She hasn't been seen since, and the police say it's a woman.'

'Why don't they ask somebody to identify her?'

She bit her lip. 'Too badly burned,' her voice croaked, 'to be easily recognisable. They say they're assessing, you know – the evidence.'

Frank said, 'She wasn't in her right mind.'

Cathy said slowly, 'She wanted Rosie so much, I think she was prepared to do anything. Do you know, she tried to persuade me to leave Rosie in Market Street with her?'

Iris was astounded. 'Not many mothers would agree to that.'

Harriet shook her head sadly. 'Mildred thought we were all a bit strange, but she was the strange one. She must have been mentally deranged to do what she did.'

'She was crazy.' Jackson helped himself to more cabbage. 'Look at the trouble she got herself in, by trying to pass that table off on me.'

There was silence except for the scratch of cutlery on plates. Cathy didn't point out that Jackson had done the same to Benbow.

He said, 'If she'd told me it was stolen I'd have known where I stood.'

'I think she was emotionally disturbed,' Cathy said gently. 'Everything was getting on top of her.'

'Her friend next door told me she'd been charged with receiving,' Danny said, 'and that she was desperately worried.'

'That's no excuse to set fire to your shop,' Ettie said sternly. 'She almost burned you in your bed.'

'It frightens me, but I think that's what she intended,' Cathy whispered. 'I'm almost certain she'd done it before. I think she burned Dick O'Mara's shop.'

'Cathy!' Botty said. 'Surely not?'

Danny dropped his knife on his plate. He looked agonised. 'The police are coming here to talk to us tomorrow. You must tell them of your suspicions.'

'I will.' Cathy pulled a face. 'You suggested I do it before, but I couldn't bring myself to make more trouble for Mildred.'

Ettie said sadly, 'You might have saved yourself and Danny a whole heap of trouble if you had.'

Cathy covered her face with her hands. 'Yes, I might.'

Chapter Twenty-Three

Danny was going out again that afternoon. Cathy knew he was busy and wanted to go with him to help.

'You must rest,' he said.

'I've been resting in hospital. I feel all right. I want to do something.'

'Think of this as waiting time,' he insisted. 'If it was left to you, you'd go on working until five minutes before your baby was born.'

Once Danny had gone, Cathy persuaded Botty to take her over to the old stable so she could find out if their clothes had survived the fire.

'They're all right!' Cathy was exultant when she opened the drawers. 'At least I have all my clothes, and so has Danny.' Botty helped her carry armfuls of them back to her room. They smelled of smoke, some more than others.

'We could hang them on the line,' Botty suggested. 'Leave them out in the fresh air and sun for an hour or two.'

'I'm so glad all the baby clothes have survived.' Cathy hugged the bundle to her. 'I wouldn't want to start putting another layette together now.'

Iris picked them over and offered to rinse through those that had dirty marks on them. She, too, found it hard to sit still, so agitated was she about her sons. Any job was welcome.

'No, Iris, you have enough to do. Peggy will be here tomorrow, she'll be happy to do them then. Danny had given her a few days off, but he thinks she'll run round me now and make me rest.'

Botty said, 'The birth won't be what you planned, Cathy, but it wasn't last time and you managed, didn't you?'

'With your help,' she smiled.

When Danny returned that evening, he told her that news of the fire and its cause was all over town. He'd called on his insurance company to get claims forms, and they'd told him to fill them up and present them, but as the police and Fire Brigade were investigating the case, his claim couldn't be met until they'd assessed their reports. He said he'd half-expected this but he was very put out.

'We need to make a list of all the things we've lost. That's something you can help me with.'

'But that will take ages – and what if they won't pay?'

Danny covered his face with his hands. 'It doesn't bear thinking about.'

'That means all the hard work of building the business up will be gone?'

'Most of my capital will. We lost a lot in that fire.'

'Don't think about it,' Cathy said. 'It might be all right.'

'If I don't think about that, my mind's on you, Rosie or Mildred,' Danny fretted. 'I ought to go to her shop and make sure everything's securely locked.'

'Didn't you go once already?'

'Yes, but when she wasn't there, it threw me. I hardly knew what I was doing. I'll pop round now.'

'You aren't going there without me,' Cathy said firmly.

'Come on then.'

They found the door locked and everything just as Mildred had left it. Cathy wandered round. There were several garments in her sewing room, some finished, some half-made.

'I ought to see that the finished ones are handed over to the customers who ordered them,' Cathy said. 'She'll have names and addresses for them in her book.'

'Leave that for now.'

'I don't think she'll be coming back.'

'Probably not, but leave it for now. The police asked me for a key. We'd better wait until they say we can move things. They're coming to interview us tomorrow. There'll be an inquest.'

'When?'

'I don't know yet.'

They went upstairs. 'I suppose we could come back and live here,' Danny sighed. 'It seems no time at all since we left.'

'Do you want to?' Cathy was looking round the living room.

'It's one answer. Even if there's no insurance money, we'd have a home of our own and a shop.'

Cathy turned over the possibility in her mind and shuddered.

He said, 'Mildred's probably left her business to you. You'd inherit the lease. We'd just take it over.'

'Yes, I suppose so.'

'It's probably the safest thing to do. The best thing, if we don't get the insurance money. We should look to see if she's left a Will.'

'What if she hasn't? She didn't expect to die yet.'

'She's got no other relatives, Cathy. We could live here for a short time; if nothing else, it would tide us over the next few months.'

Cathy shivered. 'I can almost feel Mildred's presence – as though she's here with us. It's quite spooky.'

He asked, 'You don't want to live here again?'

'No. Do you?'

'No.' Danny ran his fingers through his straight hair. 'But it's probably what we'll have to do if—'

'Don't think about that. You're too ambitious for Market Street.'

Danny sighed. 'There's a thousand things we should do. Pay her rent up to date and let the agent know what's happened.'

'Really, we need to close her business. If things go right for us, I could ask Mr Chesters, the estate agent, to sell on the rest of her lease.'

'There's no hurry for that. You're supposed to rest, love. I'll see to it. I want to call on Mr Chesters anyway. I'd like to get another shop.'

'If all goes well you will.'

'But it's urgent, Cathy. Until I get another shop, and open it for business, we have no income.'

Cathy sat down on Otto's armchair. 'Do you think the lease on that shop in Grange Road will have been taken? Have you noticed anyone moving in?'

'No. It would be marvellous if it was still available.'

'If it is . . .?'

'I hardly dare hope. But it would be a risk to sign a lease without knowing whether I'll get the insurance. I'll go tomorrow morning and see if Chesters has that or anything else on his books. No harm in going that far.'

'Let's call in now on the way back,' Cathy urged. 'He was open late that night he told you about the shop. He might be open now.'

'It wouldn't hurt,' Danny said cautiously. 'But you must stay in the car. You only came out of hospital this morning. You're doing far too much.'

Before he'd brought the car to a stop outside, Cathy said, 'It *is* still open.' She was tense with anticipation as she watched Danny go inside.

A few minutes later he came rushing back to yank open the car door for her. 'The lease on that shop is still available!' He was excited. 'Come inside – I've told him we'll take it. I've got to sign for it and pay a month's rent in advance.'

Cathy was suddenly scared. 'Should I be encouraging you to do this? It's a risk.'

'Yes, it is – but he says there's someone else interested. I know it would be wiser to settle for Market Street, but if I want this one, and I do, we've got to make up our minds now.'

'Let's do it,' Cathy breathed.

'It's bigger than the shop in Exmouth Street.' Danny couldn't stop. 'I can't remember much about the house part, though I did see it. I feel a whole lot better now I've found a shop I really want and somewhere for us to live.'

'You won't be sorry,' Mr Chesters assured them. 'I thought it would suit you the moment I saw it. Just the place to sell antiques.'

An hour later, with the paperwork completed, Danny rattled the keys. 'Come on, Cathy. Let's go and have a look at our new shop.'

She said as they went back to the car, 'This is a change. A little while ago, you were trying to stop me doing anything.'

'This will do you nothing but good,' he laughed.

'I know. I like Grange Road – we'll be close to all the big expensive shops.' These had closed for the night when Danny parked in Grange Road.

When they went inside the shop Cathy beamed at him. 'It's grander as well as bigger than the old one.' She climbed the stairs to the rooms above. 'These are bigger too.'

'In need of redecoration.' Danny looked round, picking at the wallpaper. 'I'll have to get the painters and decorators in. We'll be starting all over again.'

'But we can make it really lovely,' Cathy said. 'I'm thrilled with this.'

'You'd better start thinking about what we'll need. It'll be a whole lot more than we did for Exmouth Street – curtains for every window, not to mention mattresses and bedding.'

When they returned to Cooper's Yard, Ettie was there. She said, 'I'll run some curtains up for you on my machine. I made them for our cottage. Now for heaven's sake, get in and sit down, the pair of you, while I put the kettle on for some cocoa. Iris has made a stack of rock cakes – we'll have one of those too.'

A police officer came the next morning and Danny took him into the formal dining room where the three of them wouldn't be disturbed. They sat round the big mahogany table. The visitor was a large man in late middle age with a pedantic manner.

'Now then,' he said, opening some papers on the table. 'Fire Officers were called to your Exmouth Street premises at . . . let me see . . . three-forty in the morning of Saturday, the fifteenth of March.

We have received their report which states that in their opinion, this was a case of arson.

'They called an ambulance to attend to a badly burned person who had apparently been blown to the opposite side of the street. There were no signs of life and the body was subsequently taken to the police morgue. As I said, it was badly burned and therefore not easy to identify.

'However, Mrs Mildred Godfrey has been reported missing since the night of the fire. We have a description of her, and we believe the body to be hers.

'I understand, Mrs McLelland, that you are related to her, and that you lived together until recently?'

Cathy gripped the table. 'Yes, she was my first husband's mother.'

Danny added, 'He was killed in France in 1916.'

The policeman asked Cathy a lot of questions about Mildred's state of mind over her last days, which she did her best to answer fully. He went on to ask how well they got on and why she and Danny had moved out.

'This is the second arson attack in the district. There was another, let me see . . .' He riffled through the pages of his notebook for the date. 'Yes, a Mr O'Mara's shop in Market Street. I understand he was known to Mrs Godfrey? The method used there closely resembles that used in your shop, and we believe it could have been done by the same person.'

Cathy shivered. There were more questions about Mildred's business, and about the occasional table with the painted scene on top.

She found the whole process horrible. She knew she had to be honest, but felt she was betraying Mildred. By the time the policeman got up to go, Cathy was totally drained.

For Cathy, the days that followed passed painfully slowly. Every morning she telephoned the hospital to see how Rosie was faring. The news continued to be good. Rosie and Georgie were both making good progress, and even Billy was said to be over the worst.

She had long discussions with Iris about the children and their illness, and the two women tried to comfort each other. On Sunday afternoons, the only time when visiting was allowed, Danny drove them all to the fever hospital, where they could see the youngsters through the glass. It didn't settle Cathy's mind though, because they were not allowed inside Rosie's cubicle and had to wave to her through the glass. She longed to be able to hold her daughter in her arms and talk to her properly.

'I don't think it does the children much good either,' Iris commiserated. 'We're so near and yet so far. I think they find it as frustrating as we do.'

A nurse reminded them, 'We have to keep them isolated to prevent the spread of the disease.'

Cathy knew Danny was very worried about whether the company would meet his claim. 'We'll be in real trouble if they don't,' he fretted.

They spent many hours trying to list all the things they'd lost in the fire, then went on to list all the things they'd need for their new premises, and what they'd be likely to cost. It seemed a prodigious amount.

'We've got to carry on preparing the Grange Road shop,' Danny said. He wanted some of the fixtures and fitting removed and when that was done, he arranged for the painters and decorators to start work. Once again, he and Cathy chose the wallpaper and paint.

Cathy woke up on 13 April 1921 feeling oddly disorientated. Ettie had offered to go to the market with her to choose more material to make curtains, but it was the date on which Cathy had been told to expect her baby, and during breakfast she thought she could feel a slight contraction. Botty persuaded her to lie on the living-room couch and rest instead of going out.

'I'll keep you company,' she said, getting out her knitting. She was making a matinée jacket for the new baby. They had the room to themselves. Iris was baking in the kitchen, the men were at work.

Botty said, 'I do admire you and Danny. You have the most traumatic experiences but you manage to pick yourselves up and keep going.'

'We have to, Botty.'

'I never did. I let my troubles overwhelm me. They've haunted me for years. Stopped me doing things I should have done.'

Cathy's attention was captured. It sounded as though Botty wanted to talk about her past.

She went on, 'In a way, seeing how strong you and Danny are has straightened me out. I should never have been so weak.'

'You're not weak! Perhaps your troubles were greater?'

'I'm not sure whether that makes a difference, Cathy. Anyway, I'm quite ashamed I haven't told you all about it yet.'

Cathy smiled. 'You'd never do anything to be ashamed about. Never in a month of Sundays.' Botty was kind and gentle, even devout.

Botty looked up from her knitting. 'Rather, it's what I haven't done, what I haven't told you.'

'And what's that?'

After a short pause, she said, 'I knew your mother, Cathy.'

'*What*? You *knew* her?' Cathy was amazed, shocked even. 'But why didn't you tell me?' She'd often talked to Botty about the Orphanage, how she'd dreamed endlessly about having a mother.

'I should have done. Now you see why I'm ashamed.' She was hanging her head over her knitting.

'Go on,' Cathy urged, trying to curb her impatience.

'You've heard some of the story.' Botty's voice was agonised. 'Mildred was going on about it that day I was ironing in her kitchen, but she got it all wrong.'

Cathy pulled herself slowly into a sitting position, her discomforts forgotten. 'Tell me about my mother.'

'Her name was Alice Tanner; she came here to live with Herbert Cooper.'

'As his mistress?'

'If you want to call her that. He couldn't marry her, as he already had a wife, Luella, even though she had deserted him. For two years, Alice was his wife in everything but name.'

'Where is she now?' Cathy saw Botty flinch.

'I'm afraid she was killed. Oh Cathy, I feel so guilty about what I've done to you.'

'Guilty? For heaven's sake, Botty, nobody could have done more.'

'But I've deliberately kept my mouth shut, though I knew what it would mean to you.' Harriet covered her face with her hands and rocked herself back and fore.

'I made up my mind not to say anything. I thought least said soonest mended, but it doesn't work like that. It's been on my conscience for years. I can't bear the burden of silence any longer. I have to confess.'

Cathy was riveted now. 'Go on.'

'You half-know the story already. Although I kept quiet, others didn't and incidents leaked out. I came here as Herbert Cooper's housekeeper, a widow with two young sons to support. He had a prosperous business, there was a cook called Margery. We got on well together and managed the household between us.

'Mr Cooper was a kind man. He allowed me to have the cottage in the yard and to bring Jimmy and Peter with me. They were ten and six when we came.'

'Peter? What happened to him?'

Botty let out a pent-up breath and held up her hand. 'You'll understand about Peter in a minute. It broke my heart that he . . .' Harriet's voice cracked and a tear trickled down her face.

Cathy wished she hadn't interrupted. It took Botty a moment or two to regain her composure and go on.

'As I understood it, Mr Cooper was married with a much younger wife. Alice was in her twenties, while he was twenty years older. I always addressed her as "Mrs Cooper", but between Margery and the lads who worked in the yard, I soon learned it was a courtesy title. Mr Cooper was popular with his staff, they both were, and were always given the utmost respect.

'But it didn't stop the lads taking a great interest in their boss's circumstances. Their gossip had it that his wife Luella had left him some years earlier. She'd gone off to London with another man, leaving Mr Cooper on his own. It had taken him two years to install Alice in her place.'

'Tell me about her,' Cathy urged again.

'They said she'd come to work here as his clerk and they'd fallen in love. When I knew her, she was still keeping his accounts, taking bookings for his vans, drawing up timetables for the work, that sort of thing.'

'Was she happy?' Cathy asked.

'Yes, very happy, I'm sure. They seemed devoted to each other. I'd been working here for over two years and was content with my place. My boys went to school but loved to play about the yard when they were at home. In the school holidays the men took them out on the vans, glad of a boy to hold the horse. They helped with the loading and unloading and groomed and fed the horses.'

'What about Frank? He's your nephew, isn't he? How did he come here?'

'Yes, he's my brother's child. Ted was a soldier. He was killed in the Boer War – I met my husband through him. Frank's mother was ill for a long time,' Botty sighed. 'She had cancer. I did what I could to help. Mostly that was looking after Frank – he spent a lot of his time here. Gladys died young; he was thirteen at the time and very upset, of course.

'He was about to leave school so I asked Mr Cooper if he'd give him a job and if he could live with me so I could keep an eye on him. We were all sorry for him then, but Frank settled down and was always a willing worker. My own boys had set their minds on working in the yard too. I felt enormously lucky to have my family settled and content.

'The Coopers considered Sunday to be a day of rest. Margery, the cook, took it as her day off. The family got up late and liked to have a brunch about eleven. One Sunday, I was getting it ready in the kitchen when I heard the front door open and bang shut.

'I was alarmed and went to see who it was. A fierce-looking woman I didn't know was coming up the hall. "What d'you want?" I asked her. "This is a private house, you've no business to come in here."

'I was scared. She was striding round throwing doors open as though she owned the place, and she'd apparently let herself in with a key. "Who are you?" I asked.

'She retorted, "Who are *you*, more like?"

' "I'm the housekeeper here. I think you'd better go," I told her.

'She found the living room deserted and was pushing me back into the kitchen. "Where's Herbert?" she demanded.

'At that moment Alice came downstairs. She was pregnant by then. Pregnant with you and almost as near her time as you are now.' Botty paused and took a deep, shuddering breath.

'She was smiling. "Morning, Harriet," she sang out. "Who's this, a friend of yours?"

'I said, "Mrs Cooper, this woman has forced her way in. I can't get her to leave."

'At that, the intruder swung round to glare at Alice, her face twisting with outrage.

' "What d'you mean, *Mrs Cooper*?" There was raw hate in her eyes. "*I'm* Mrs Cooper. Mrs Luella Cooper."

'She snatched up the carving knife I'd been using to cut rinds off the bacon and flourished it at Alice.

'I was shaking in total dread by then. Dear God, I knew exactly what I'd done. I'd let Luella Cooper know her husband had taken another woman in her place. A much younger and prettier woman, who was heavy with his child.

'Alice screamed and ran for the stairs, but was hampered by her pregnancy. The real Mrs Cooper, although older, was more fleet of foot. She was shouting and swearing and caught her halfway up the stairs. She dragged her to her knees and started stabbing her with the knife. Alice was screaming in terror, but that seemed to make her stab even more viciously.'

Cathy clutched at Botty's hand. Her stomach was churning with horror, hearing of her mother's life and death like this, all in the space of a few minutes.

'I was panic-stricken,' Botty went on, her voice choked. 'I couldn't believe what I was seeing. I rushed up and tried to protect Alice, and got this for my pains.' Her fingers traced the length of her scar. Her face was agonised.

'Peter, my little boy, ran up and started to flail at her with his fists. He was trying to protect me, to stand between her and me. She stabbed at him, of course. He bled to death.'

Cathy felt herself come out in goose pimples. Her mouth was dry and she couldn't swallow.

Eventually Harriet went on, her voice soft and level. 'Mr Cooper heard the noise and came to help, but the woman turned on him. She slashed at him with the knife and ripped his right arm open, so he couldn't do much to defend himself. He tried to retreat but she was on him, still stabbing. She'd gone completely berserk.

'I sat on the stairs with one arm round Peter and the other round Alice. They were both covered with blood and moaning with pain.'

'Oh my God!' Cathy breathed.

'Peter died in my arms, there on the stairs. He'd just had his eighth birthday. I found it so hard to live in this house after that.'

Botty wiped the tears from her eyes. 'Well, to cut a long story short Alice was taken to hospital in labour. You were born some twelve hours later. Your poor mother died of her injuries an hour after giving birth.'

Cathy felt tears burning her eyes. 'Botty, that's terrible,' she whispered. 'And my father? He was killed too?'

'Not immediately. They patched him up in hospital and he came home again. I looked after him but with Alice's death, he seemed to give up hope. He hovered for months, but never fully recovered from his wounds. Poor Herbert. He couldn't look after himself, never mind a newborn babe.'

'What about Frank and Jimmy? They weren't hurt?'

'It was the one Sunday they were not at home. They were always about the place. We used to eat all our meals together in the kitchen. But it was high summer and Frank had taken Jimmy camping. They'd cycled to Anglesey with a tent for a holiday.

'The awful thing is, Peter had wanted to go with them, but I told him he was too young. I thought he'd be safer at home with me. Of course, if Frank and Jimmy had been here, two strapping great lads as they were, they would have been able to overpower Luella before she did so much harm. They came home a few days later. While I nursed Herbert, they kept his business going.'

Cathy asked, 'He left it to you, with this house?'

'He left me a third share. Frank was his foreman by then – he and Jimmy inherited a share each. They grew up working in it – it's the one business they can manage. It gave them the chance of a lifetime.'

Botty was silent for a long while. Cathy waited, willing her to go on. Eventually she had to ask; 'What made the first Mrs Cooper come back home?'

Botty gave a deep sigh. 'Her whole story came out at the trial. It caused a scandal. The man she went off with was not all she'd believed him to be. She'd thought him wealthy but he was far from that. He was a conman and a minor criminal. Luella had a hand-to-mouth existence with him, living on what he could cheat and steal from the pockets of others.

'Her health had not been good during that time, she was in and out of hospital with ear infections and was growing increasingly deaf. As a result she became moody, depressed some of the time and almost hysterical at others.'

'Unstable?'

'Yes. Her mother, it turned out, had had a history of mental illness. When her lover abandoned her for another, she had no means of support so came back to see Herbert, meaning to make things up with him and return to what she saw as her rightful place. But then she found your mother installed here, and I think the sight of Alice so obviously pregnant sent Luella Cooper over the top. She went berserk.'

Cathy was clutching her throat. 'How awful! What happened to her?'

'She was hanged for killing your mother. Well, for triple murder really. Your father had died before her trial and she was charged with murdering him as well as my son.'

Cathy shuddered. 'It must have been dreadful for you.'

'And for the boys. I lived at home with them for a while – they were quite young at the time – but in the end I had to leave.'

Cathy could finish Botty's story now. 'I wondered sometimes why you were working at Halesworth when you had this house and business.'

'I had to get away. I couldn't get over that attack or the needless deaths, particularly that of my little Peter. I'd thought Luella was going to kill me too. After the court case, I couldn't stay here in Cooper's Yard. Halesworth Hall isn't all that far away, but I was able to disappear for a decade and a half. I thought everybody would have forgotten by the time the major died.'

'But they hadn't?'

Botty was distressed. 'Everybody knows Cooper's Yard and links our name with it. The story will never be forgotten, it's too salacious, but after all this time people get the details wrong. Because I inherited the business, it's assumed I was more to Herbert than his housekeeper. Everybody forgets Alice and forgets you. I can't endure their snide smiles; the whispers behind my back, the knowing eyes following me. I've tried to ignore them but I can't.'

'Botty, it was a terrible thing to happen. Poor little Peter. And both my parents killed like that.'

'And you just a tiny baby. Truly, I couldn't get over it. All these years it's been on my mind that you have a right to know. I knew how driven you were, how much you longed to know about your origins. I wanted to tell you, but somehow I couldn't. To start with, I didn't think it would help a child to know facts like these.' Botty's dark eyes were entreating her.

'When I was grown up,' Cathy suggested gently, 'it would have set my mind at rest. It will now.' The silence dragged on too long. She cast around for some way to make Botty go on, and asked, 'Did my parents not have other family?'

'Yes, but your mother's family disowned her when she came to live with a married man.'

'I suppose people were very strict about that in those days,' Cathy said sadly.

'Still are. I found the address of your maternal grandfather and wrote to tell him about you. He didn't reply. I wrote a second letter in case the first had got lost in the post, but still received no reply.'

'He didn't want to help.' Cathy knew she had to face facts. This was how she'd come to end up in the Orphanage.

'He should have done – an innocent baby and his own grandchild. Herbert Cooper had a brother who'd died young and left a wife. I wrote to her, but she wanted nothing to do with what she called . . .' Botty broke off uneasily.

'The wages of sin?'

'Something like that. I've wanted to tell you all this so often, but I was ashamed of what I did.'

'Botty, you went to help my mother when she was stabbed. What more could you have done?'

'I don't mean then. Later on, I could have done a great deal. I feel guilty whenever I think about what I did to you.'

'But you've always been kind to me!'

'No, I haven't. Herbert Cooper was your father. He was ill and grieving for Alice. Years earlier, he'd made a Will leaving everything to Luella and was determined to change that.

'A week before he died, he asked me to fetch a solicitor to his bedside, which I did. I knew it was to rewrite his Will, but I honestly didn't realise he was making me and my family his beneficiaries. I counted it none of my business to know who he willed it to.'

Harriet's gentle dark eyes looked up to meet Cathy's. 'By rights, this house and business should be yours. He knew you existed because I told him myself, but he never saw you. He certainly forgot you when he drew up a new Will. He was in a lot of pain; perhaps his mind wasn't as clear as it had been. I didn't think to remind him, but I should have done.

'When I found out, I was grateful that he'd remembered my boys. Owning a share in this business has given Frank and Jimmy a very much better life. I didn't want to take that from them. I wanted your inheritance for my own family – that's what I'm ashamed of. I've never been able to enjoy what I was given.'

'You must, Botty, it's your right. What could a newborn baby do for him? You looked after him, your boys kept his business going. Without them, there would be no business now.'

'I keep thinking, we were on hand at the right moment, but if things had not gone so badly wrong for Herbert Cooper, all this could have been yours. Should have been yours.' Harriet sighed and went on, 'I will, of course, make my share over to you now. But will you ever forgive me?'

'Botty! I don't want your share. I have Danny now – he'll soon set up again and I'll have a share in his business. That's more than I'll ever need. I'm sure you nursed my father well, although you'd lost your own little boy and had had your face slashed. If I lost Rosie, I wouldn't want to live.' Cathy shivered as she thought of her daughter lying sick and among strangers in the fever hospital. 'Herbert probably wanted to reward you and your family for your friendship and support.'

'I was afraid you'd take against me.' Cathy could see more tears in Botty's eyes. 'It stopped me even mentioning it to anybody and certainly not to you. Cathy, I stood by and let them put you into an orphanage. I wasn't thinking straight at the time. I've wondered many times how I can make it up to you. My conscience was heavy and still is.'

'It needn't be. I wasn't unhappy there.' Cathy paused; this was helping her see her past in a different perspective. 'Was it you? Did you remember my birthday every year? Send me presents?'

'Yes,' Botty admitted.

'They told me my mother was dead but I didn't really believe them. I thought they might be coming from her.'

'Oh Cathy! They were a sop for my conscience. I wanted to send you little treats. I should have thought about the effect they'd have on you.'

'I loved them and they gave me status amongst the other girls there. I had what we all wanted, somebody in the outside world who cared about me. I truly believed that one day, if not my mother, then some relative would come for me and take me away. I was always waiting . . .'

'You said you weren't unhappy there?'

'I wasn't, but I wanted a mother. Somebody who'd love me. All of us lacked that. All of us yearned for it and I never stopped. That's what Mildred meant to me. I wanted to be part of a family, Rolf's family. I wanted his parents to care for me as if I was their own.'

'That doesn't make me feel any better. I mothered Frank, and I could have brought you here and mothered you, if I hadn't been so obsessed with guilt about owning what should have been yours.'

'You mothered me when I arrived at Halesworth, but I was too blind to see it. Botty, you were the nearest thing to a mother I could have had. If only I'd realised that at the time, I wouldn't have tried so hard to attach myself to Mildred. I didn't need Mildred – I had you long before I had her. D'you know, Botty, I can't believe you actually knew my mother.' Cathy felt so moved by what she'd been told. She was having difficulty keeping her tears under control. 'What was she like?'

'A sweet girl. She risked everything for love.'

'Am I like her to look at?'

'She had curls like yours *and* you have her colouring. I can show you a photograph.'

'Oh! Can I see it now?'

'It's in a box at the back of my wardrobe – *your* wardrobe at the moment.'

'I want to see it.' Cathy pulled herself off the sofa and made for the stairs. Botty followed. 'You don't know what it would mean to me, to see a picture of her.'

'There are several. You can have them all.'

A few moments later, Cathy held the faded photograph of her mother in her hand. Gentle eyes smiled up at her. Cathy studied every plane of her face – the happy smile, the curving lips, the thick mass of curls. She was like her, especially about the eyes.

The tears came in a rush then; she couldn't stop them. Botty gathered her into her arms. 'I'm so sorry,' she whispered. 'Quite a confession, isn't it?'

Cathy could feel Botty's own tears against her forehead. 'I know now; who my parents were and why they couldn't look after me. That's what I've always wanted.'

And then a pain gripped her, and for a long, gasping moment, she could say nothing more at all.

Chapter Twenty-Four

Cathy had been feeling vague pains all the time Botty had been pouring out what she called 'her confession'. Now she was sure her second child was about to be born. Her mind was whirling with what she'd been told. Botty had given her answers to questions that had tormented her all her life. She understood all too well why the other woman hadn't told her sooner, but it would have been a comfort at the time she was leaving the Orphanage to know Botty had specifically asked for her to be sent to Halesworth Hall.

Cathy felt very different at this birth from how she'd felt at Rosie's. She was never alone – Peggy was there to attend to her every wish. Her extended family was all round her. Botty sent word to Danny at the same time she sent for the midwife. They both arrived soon afterwards. Danny sat by her bed encouraging her through the first stage of her labour. With the midwife in charge, she felt she was in competent hands and the birth was an orderly progression of the normal. Lenora May, weighing seven pounds two ounces, was born at three-twenty that afternoon.

Cathy felt she'd had an easy time of it, and the most emotional memory was of Danny holding his daughter for the first time. Little Lenora was wrapped in a bath towel and hadn't yet been washed, but the look of adoration in his eyes would stay with Cathy for ever.

As soon as she'd had a rest, the family were in and out. Botty asked, 'Are you going to call her Lenora, or just Nora?'

'We aren't going to shorten it,' Danny assured her. 'We both like the name Lenora.'

'It's a bit of a mouthful for such a tiny scrap.'

Iris wanted to hold the new baby. 'I'd love to have a daughter,' she told Cathy wistfully. 'Ooh, won't young Rosie be excited! And isn't she like Danny?'

Cathy wasn't sure. To her eyes, Lenora had the wrinkled red face of the newborn.

Ettie was in tears when she held the baby. 'My first grandchild. This is a big moment for me. There were times when I thought I'd lose all my children before they could have children of their own.'

Jackson came and pressed silver coins into the baby's palms. 'It's said to bring luck. You know what, Cathy? I'm envious. I'd love to have a daughter of my own, but it hasn't been my lot in life to be a parent.'

'You were like a father to me when I first went to Halesworth,' she told him. 'You can be grandfather to this one.' She saw him smile with satisfaction.

A few days later, Old Benbow arrived with a big bunch of tulips and iris for Cathy. 'From my garden,' he told her. 'And this is a gift for Lenora.' He put a small parcel wrapped in tissue paper on Cathy's bed.

'The flowers are lovely,' she smiled. 'Am I allowed to see what you've brought for Lenora?'

'Of course, open it up.'

The package contained a silver rattle with a teething piece of coral.

'It's eighteenth century,' he said. 'I bought it in a sale the other day.'

'It's beautiful, Benbow, thank you, but far too expensive for a baby to bite on – she could spoil it. I'll get her a hard rubber one. She'll appreciate this when she's grown up.'

'Antiques are all I know,' he said. 'How is Rosie?'

'Out of danger and feeling much better, thank goodness. I ring up every day, but they don't tell me much beyond that.'

'So she'll be coming home soon?'

'Well, I'm hoping in a couple of weeks. She has to provide three consecutive negative throat swabs first. That's to prove she's no longer infectious and can come out of isolation. They take them at weekly intervals now she's convalescent. She's provided one so far.'

'It looks hopeful. What about the little Bott boys?'

'Georgie's at the same stage as Rosie, he's doing fine. Billy's feeling better but no negative swabs as yet.'

'They're all over the worst, Cathy.'

'Yes, we no longer have to worry about the outcome. Iris pretends she's enjoying a rest from them, but I know she misses them badly. Even Botty says the house is too quiet without them.'

Cathy smiled. Their troubles had drawn her family and friends closer.

Every evening when Danny came home, he had something to tell her about their new premises. Today he came home earlier than usual to say the decorators had finished and his mother had taken Peggy there to clean the place up

Cathy sighed. 'I wish I could do something. I know I'm supposed to lie-in for three weeks and I've only done one, but I've had enough of lying here all day with nothing to do but nurse Lenora. I'm bursting with energy, and I want to see our new home.'

Danny always seemed to understand her needs. 'Come on then while the babe's asleep. I'll ask Harriet to listen out for her while you get ready. I'll run you up in the car.'

To Cathy it seemed a long time since she'd been out and about. Grange Road was still busy, although the shops would be closing soon. There were more cars about than there used to be. She was able to pick out their new shop from a distance; the signwriter was just finishing off. It read McLelland's Antiques. Danny had wanted it to be an exact copy of their old one. The whole shopfront had been repainted; the wet-paint signs hadn't yet been removed. It positively sparkled in the spring sunshine.

Inside, the smell of new paint was strong but it all looked fresh and clean. The shop seemed an absolute cavern; it was so much larger than their old one.

'Lovely and spacious, isn't it?' Danny said. 'I'll have to arrange things differently.'

There was only one door at the back of the shop, which led into a passage. 'There's a cloakroom here for staff and a storeroom. Not that we'll be able to store much furniture in it.'

'If you put shelves up,' she suggested, 'you could store household bric-a-brac, ornaments – that sort of thing here.'

'I thought perhaps I'd make it into an office. Look, we have our own front door here,' Danny chortled. 'Our visitors can come straight up instead of having to go through the shop.'

'That's a big improvement. At least then we'll know whether they're visitors or customers,' Cathy said.

'Come on upstairs and see where you'll be living.' A boxed-in staircase went up the wall. The stairs were not too steep. Cathy looked round eagerly. 'Much bigger rooms, aren't they? Much lighter.'

'Mam has been to hang the curtains she made for our bedroom. That's about ready.'

Cathy opened the door. 'It is ready,' she laughed. 'Only needs the bed making up. It's lovely! When can we move in?'

'The Botts' van will fetch most of the furniture from the warehouse tomorrow. Once it's in the shop, you can choose what you want to bring up here. But we need a new carpet before we can do that.'

'We'll be in before Rosie comes out?'

'Yes, within the next few days, I hope. Her bedroom's almost ready. It's across the passage, there.'

Cathy went to look at it. Rosie's little chest of drawers and bedstead had been cleaned up, but the bed needed a new mattress as well as bedding.

'I wish I could get out and buy what we need,' she said, 'instead of being cooped up indoors.'

'You have to rest, my love. You're not out of your lying-in time, and already you're getting dressed every day.'

'Well, they're very sociable at Cooper's Yard and if I'm dressed I can join in. It's no fun being shut away in a room by myself and being told to rest, especially since you're out so much.'

'I'm rushing round all the sales I can – so is Benbow. Our pressing need is for stock. I've got to build it up before we can open the new shop.'

'I know,' Cathy smiled. 'I do understand and you've managed miracles in the time.'

Before driving her back to Cooper's Yard, Danny took her to choose carpet and lino and arranged for the shop to lay it for them. 'It'll save us time.'

Harriet and Iris took Cathy on a tour of all the empty rooms at Cooper's Yard looking for items that she and Danny could use. They even searched through chests and boxes in the attic.

Ettie was scouring the market and the shops for the essentials on Cathy's list. Often she bought things on sight, sometimes she took Cathy back to get her approval first, but slowly they were amassing what she needed.

The day came when Danny agreed that everything was ready for them to move in. Cathy packed her clothes and Lenora's equipment and Jackson ferried them up on the cart.

Moving in wasn't easy with a newborn to care for too, but she had Peggy to help her and the girl willingly turned her hand to everything. A few days later, they heard the wonderful news that Rosie was well enough to come home.

It was late afternoon when the ambulance brought her to the new shop. Cathy hugged and kissed her little girl at the door, overjoyed to have her back. She couldn't let her go. It seemed an age since she'd held her close like this. She'd only been able to mouth words to her and wave from the other side of the glass. Rosie looked pale and wan and hadn't yet regained her usual bounce.

'We'll soon have you fighting fit again,' Danny told her as he carried her upstairs to their flat. 'We've got a new home and a new shop. Isn't it exciting?'

Rosie nodded her brown curls. Cathy took her by the hand and led her from room to room to see it all.

'This is your new bedroom. Do you like it?' Rosie was nodding, not yet entirely at her ease. Cathy led her into the room she shared with Danny.

'And here we have a special surprise for you. I promised you a new baby sister, didn't I? She's waiting to meet you.' The baby was just waking and beginning to cry.

'This is Lenora,' she said, lifting her from her cradle. 'Your new baby sister.'

Rosie clapped her hands. 'Want to hold Nora!' She held out her arms.

'Lenora,' Cathy corrected, settling Rosie on to a firm armchair before laying the baby in her arms.

Rosie smiled down at her. 'My new sister Nora,' she lisped.

'I knew we'd have trouble calling her Lenora,' Danny grinned. 'Rosie's right, it's too formal for everyday.'

The inquest into Mildred's death was held the following day. Cathy had been told she'd be called as a witness and had been dreading it. Danny took her. He'd been to an inquest before, and she clung to his arm feeling emotional and fraught. 'What am I going to tell them?'

'It'll be questions you have to answer. Just tell the truth as clearly and fully as you can.'

When they arrived, he whispered, 'I didn't expect there to be a jury.'

The Coroner opened the proceedings by outlining the case. He read part of the autopsy report which explained that death had occurred as a result of an explosion and that relatives had not been asked to identify the body because it was so badly burned as to be unrecognisable. But what evidence they had, pointed to it being that of Mildred Imelda Godfrey of Market Street.

Then the police officer who had come to Cooper's Yard to interview them gave evidence, much of it familiar to Cathy. A man got up to question him.

'Who's that?' Cathy whispered.

'Mr Parbold. He represents our insurance company.'

Cathy was tense with anxiety. 'That means . . .?'

'Yes – he'll decide whether to meet our claim or not on how he assesses this.'

Then Cathy was called to the stand. She'd never doubted that it was Mildred who was responsible, but could not bear to think of her end. The questions came, including some from Mr Parbold, and she did her best to answer them fully.

She felt weak at the knees as she walked back to her seat next to Danny. 'You did well,' he whispered. But then it was his turn to face the questioning. By the time he was returning to her side, the Coroner was already summing up.

He said, 'So far as we can ascertain, Mrs Godrey was in Exmouth Street in the early hours of the morning for the purpose of setting fire to shop premises in which Mr McLelland carried on business.

'We must draw the conclusion that in all probability she had not foreseen the consequences of her act. She lost control of the blaze she lit, there was an explosion which threw her across the road and engulfed her in flames.'

They had to wait for the jury to deliberate. Cathy was cold and shaking, so Danny took her out to a nearby café to get a hot drink. They returned in time to hear the verdict delivered as Accidental Death.

Cathy was in sombre mood as Danny drove them home. 'We'll never know why she did it,' she sighed. 'I could never understand her.'

'Mildred kept her dark side to herself. I'll make the funeral arrangements, shall I?'

'Please. I've just got to put all this behind me and think of the future.'

'That's right, love, though we should try to settle her affairs.'

'And we still have to tell Rosie. She was very close to her Nanna. I'm afraid she'll be upset.'

'We'll do it together,' Danny said.

As soon as they reached home, Rosie ran to meet Cathy with Peggy not far behind, carrying Lenora in her arms.

'Give us a few minutes,' Cathy said to Peggy, who went off to cuddle the baby and change her napkin.

They took Rosie to their own bedroom. Cathy put her arms round her daughter and said, 'I'm afraid we have some bad news about your Nanna.'

'When are we going down to see her?'

'Darling, poor Nanna had a nasty accident while you were in hospital. She's gone to Heaven.'

Cathy had explained about death some time ago when a neighbour had died.

'That's where old people go when they're too tired to carry on living, isn't it?'

'Yes, that's it.'

'We can't see Nanna?' Rosie's face screwed up with concentration. 'Ever again?'

'No,' Danny said gently.

'Can she see me? From Heaven?'

'Yes, I'm sure she can.' Cathy felt Rosie was accepting it. 'She'll be watching over you.'

'Nanna always did watch over you,' Danny assured her.

'Poor Nanna,' Rosie said. 'I hope she likes it there,' and then she struggled out of Cathy's arms to go and look for Peggy and Lenora. Cathy clung to Danny with relief.

The next day, Danny said, 'I want to call in and see Mr Parbold. I won't be able to settle to anything until I know whether they're going to meet my claim. Do you want to come with me?'

Cathy felt she'd need time to pull herself together if Danny's claim wasn't approved. For him, it would be like starting the business again from scratch.

'Do come,' he urged. 'I might need your support.'

So Cathy went with him, feeling great trepidation. Once shown into Mr Parbold's office, however, her spirits lifted. He was smiling, and didn't look as though he was bracing himself to give them bad news. 'We've assessed your claim and decided to meet it in full,' he told them immediately.

Cathy could see from Danny's face that he could hardly believe it. As soon as they were back in their car, he hugged her and said, 'Our luck held this time. What a relief!'

She felt as though a load had lifted from their shoulders.

'All that remains to be done now is to put Mildred's affairs in order,' he said.

'I'll go down to Market Street later on and see if I can find a Will.'

After dinner, having fed Lenora and tucked Rosie up for her afternoon nap, Cathy went to her old home and made a thorough search through Mildred's papers. She came across a life insurance policy first, but soon found that Mildred had left a handwritten Will, leaving everything she owned to her grandchild, Rosie.

'At least we know where we stand on that,' Danny said, when she took the documents back to Cooper's Yard. 'We'll bank what money we can get in Rosie's name and keep it until she's grown up. It's her inheritance from Rolf's family. I think I'll take this Will to the solicitor to see if it's legal. Then we'll have to apply for probate.'

It took longer than Danny had expected to collect enough stock to be able to open his new shop.

'I have to have good quality pieces,' he said, 'and the right mix for sitting rooms and bedrooms. I'm going to make this a good-class antique shop, of the standard to rival the best in Liverpool.'

When he was almost ready, he got the Botts to distribute leaflets all over town to advertise the opening. Cathy knew he was very pleased with his new shop.

The day the doors were finally opened, Benbow came in to help. He and Ettie were kept busy showing the furniture to customers. They sold more in one day than Danny had ever done before. He was excited and running up and down the stairs by the minute.

Cathy had asked all their friends and family round for a celebratory meal when the shop closed that evening. Botty and Peggy did most of the preparation, setting the food out on the living-room table.

They came in twos and threes. Frank drove Iris and Jim up with Georgie who had also come home.

Iris seemed very happy. She said, 'We think Billy may be home next week. We're keeping our fingers crossed that he'll get his three clear throat swabs.'

Old Benbow was out of breath when he returned with a big cardboard box. Danny opened the door to him.

'Something for the shop?' he asked.

'No, a present for Rosie. Carry it upstairs for me, will you?'

Cathy and Rosie were at the living-room door. After just a week at home the little girl had more colour in her cheeks and was much more her old self.

'I've got a new sister,' she told Benbow as he came in. 'Her name's Nora.'

'Lenora,' he corrected. 'I've brought you a present, Rosie.'

'What is it?'

Benbow cut the string and lifted out a big doll's house. Rosie shrieked with delight and couldn't stand still.

'It's magnificent,' Cathy gasped. 'It's fully furnished and there's even little dolls inside. Is it an antique?'

'It's late Victorian.'

'Nice!' Rosie was jumping up and down. 'Nice doll's house for me!'

'What d'you say, Rosie?'

'Thank you, thank you, Mr Benbow.'

'What about a kiss then, young lady?'

Rosie lifted her cheek to him. 'Thank you.'

'I don't have to tell you she loves it. But isn't it too good for a child to play with?'

'Cathy, I wouldn't make that mistake twice,' he smiled, 'even though

I'm not used to children. The Victorians made things to suit their purpose. This was meant to be played with – it's robust. I'd let her loose with it if I were you.'

'You're very generous,' she told him. 'Thank you. Danny, you'd better put it in Rosie's bedroom. You be careful not to break anything in it,' she cautioned her daughter. Georgie followed Rosie and the doll's house.

'I've never had a family of my own,' Benbow said, stroking his grey beard. 'Regret it now I'm in my dotage.'

'You'll be seeing plenty of mine,' Cathy told him. 'You'll have to make do with us.'

'I'll be glad to – you've a lovely little family. I'll be in and out of your shop every day, won't I?'

'We can't do it without you!' Cathy told him. With a full heart, she looked round at them all – at Ettie and Frank, Iris and Jim, Jackson and Botty. Their family and their friends. Then her eyes met Danny's across the laden table. For them, the future looked golden.